I0740983

WINTER SQUAD

JOHN CAMPBELL REES

The Timeless Press

South Wales

ISBN-13: 978-0-9576444-0-3

ISBN-10: 0-957-64440-3

This book is a work of fiction. All characters mentioned are fictitious and any resemblence to persons living or dead is purely coincidental.

First published in the United Kingdom in 2013 by
The TIMELESS Press, 12, Stuart Street, Treherbert,
Rhondda, CF42 5PR.

For my Family.

CONTENTS

PART ONE
THE SPRITE

CHAPTER ONE

THE LAST DAY OF SUMMER

A solitary apple tree stood at the bottom of the garden. An ancient and magnificent specimen, ten foot tall from floor to the highest twig.

However, nothing is as it seems. We live in an universe infinite not just in size, but infinite in possibility. Anything that can happen, does happen within alternate realities throughout the endless Cosmos. Some of these realities share so many similarities they almost touch. At weak points in the fabric of these realities, where events in one seep through the boundaries and have an effect on the other, a special type of creature lives one life in multiple universes. We call these creatures apple trees.

Our world has a parallel in another reality called Arbouron, the World of Trees. Every inch of a tree here on Earth is equal to a mile for the same tree on Arbouron which towers above the landscape. One of these mighty citadels in a solitary apple tree. An ancient and magnificent specimen, one hundred and twenty miles from floor to its highest twig. Five large branches arch out from a crown, and then fork into many sub-branches and twigs. It is identical in shape to the apple tree standing sideways in time on Earth, in a Welsh garden. However, everything here is on a much grander scale. In the Spring, when new leaves unfurl here on Earth, massive solar powered machines are deployed on Arbouron. An infestation of aphids here on Earth would be manifested as an attack by armoured war-machines on Arbouron.

Apple trees usually grow in orchards and are naturally very social creatures. Whilst its isolation had no visible effect on the apple tree here on Earth, on Arbouron things were quite different. The life-fource of the Tree had no orchard-mates to talk to. Also in its youth it was isolated from the Arboreal communication network. It developed a novel way of fighting the boredom and loneliness. Within its body it produced an army of humanoid servants and soldiers to maintain and defend itself. All trees on Arbouron do this, but the Apple Tree created a complex ecosystem and society for its soldiers, giving each one an unprecedented degree of individuality. He provided sources of food, heat and light with a level of technology bound only by his imagination. He spent happy days watching how the society grow. He guided the soldiers, pointing and prodding them in certain directions.

Years passed an the apple tree became old enough to communicate with the other trees on Arbouron. Like a teenager he soon forgot the toys of his childhood, arelely checking on the society he had created, a society that him as a distant good to be feared and worshipped as the Spirit of the Tree.

‘**Y**ou! Sprite!’ barked Captain Samnundsya. ‘Sprite NM331/29! Are you daydreaming again?’

At a desk in a long corridor, sat a leaf opperating sprite had not been concentrating on its job. It jumped to attention and saluted.the Captain. The hatred was mutual, but as a sprite it had to obey the Captain's every command.

‘Don't you know how important today is? I cannot afford to have a pathetic non-entity like you day-dreaming impossible dreams about becoming an officer.’

‘The Spirit of the Tree, all praise it, created you to be a sprite and a sprite you will remain until you recycle. Now get back to work!’

‘I'm sorry, Ma'am, I'll get right back to it.’ NM331/29 instantly knew that it had just made things so much worse. Sprites normally talked about themselves in the third person, and being neither male nor female use "it" to describe themselves. So NM331/29 should have said "it is sorry, the sprite will get right back to work." so that it would blend into the background. This was not the first time in recent weeks it had been caught using the first person, a crime Captain Samnundsya did not hesitate to punish.

‘What did you say sprite?’ She took the swagger stick out from under her arm. ‘Did I just hear you trying to impersonate an officer by displaying individuality? You know what the punishment for that is?’

‘Yes, Ma'am, the sprite is sorry.’

The expected lash from the swagger stick did not come, Nevamar was surprised, Captain Samnundsya never missed a chance to punish and humiliate a sprite.

‘It's a good job for you that I'm far too busy, with the preparations for the evacuation to deal with you now. Wonderful, wonderful Autumn and Winter, when my exile is temporarily lifted and I can return to civilisation down in the Roots, whilst you and your fellow non-entities snooze away.’

With that, the Captain was gone, but something had snapped within NM331/29.

'You are Nevamar now,' whispered a voice inside its head.

'That's right,' it said to itself, 'my name is Nevamar and I will be an officer before this year is out.'

E very year, when the Canopy shed its leaves, and shuts down for Winter, the entire population relocated to the Roots. The officers have Winter homes and jobs there. The sprites are surplus to requirements. On arrival at the Roots, all sprites are tested for potential Officer Training. Most fail this test and spend their Autumn and Winter in suspended animation.

Sprites that pass the test become Officer Cadets. During the sixteen weeks of training Cadets undergo massive transformations. Whilst one sprite is identical to the next, officers are individuals. They choose an unique name to go with their rank and serial number. They have identifiable faces. Cadets grow at different rates so their final height and body type varies from officer to officer. The most important change is developing a gender. However amongst all the words for things masculine and feminine, the Spirit of the Tree had neglected to add the words "Man" and "Woman" to his officer's vocabluary, so they created their own words to fill the gap. The once neuter sprites becomes either masculine anthers or feminine styles.

Nevamar now desperately wanted to be an officer. This meant it was ready for promotion. However, Captain Samnundsya was from the Roots. Unlike the rest of the Tree, only sprites created to be an officer could advance down there. Nevamar knew because it was an ordinary working sprite, its ambition was offensive to the Captain.

If the old Branch Captain had not recycled the previous Summer, then Nevamar would have been an Officer Cadet the prevaious Autumn and would now be living the life of a junior officer.

The previous Branch Captain had been a kindly old soul who had been a sprite from the Canopy herself. Captain Roctwoosya had encouraged ambitious sprites to become officers. She had celebrated whenever one of her sprites made the grade. The new Branch Captain hated all sprites, especially the ones she called "Uppity".

N evamar could hear the other sprites grumbling. After a few minutes it could take it no more.

'What?' it asked no-one in particular.

'It always causes trouble for this twig,' piped up the sprite at the leaf two seats away from Nevamar.

'It should just get on with its job and not answer back,' added another.

'But it is the most efficient sprite on the twig, its leaf has produced more Nutrient than any other leaf all year.'

This was JE375/28, the sprite who operated the leaf on the opposite side of the twig to Nevamar. It was on a par with Nevamar, ready for a new life.

'It thinks it's better than the other sprites in this twig because it was originally created to operate an apple,' said one sprite.

'The Branch Captain's right,' said another sprite. 'It is uppity.'

'Its apple never ripened. Jettisoned as unsatisfactory,' said the first sprite. 'If the sprite was really that efficient this would never have happened.'

'It must have been a coward, too afraid to make the journey into the Outer Void,' said a third sprite from further along the twig.'

'That is not NM331/29's fault, there are many sprites in the branch who were created for failed apples. NM331/29 was more than ready to make the supreme sacrifice.' JE375/28 once again jumped to Nevamar's defence.

'Thank you JE375/28, you are my friend,' said NM331/29. Oh dear, another cardinal sin, sprites were not supposed to have friends. 'But to be perfectly honest with the rest of you lot,' Nevamar continued with the revolutionary fire burning in its belly, 'I don't give a stuff what the rest of you think.'

The other sprites were horrified. A sprite was blatantly using individuality.

'If it continues being so insubordinate it will surely be recycled, and the Captain might choose to recycle the entire twig. We will all be punished for its sins.'

Nevamar could see the others would remain sprites all their lives, only the lucky ones moved on. Then it realised it was not luck, it was a natural progression. It was ready, JE375/29 was ready, as were half a dozen others on the branch. Ready they may be, but if Branch Captain Samnundsya Zilfarayts 101/20 had her way they would remain as sprites. Nevamar had to take its destiny into its own hands. It had been no accident that no sprite in the branch had been promoted since Captain Samnundsya's arrival. Something had to be done about that.

'That's right dear, go on get used to being a sprite for the rest of your life. But why should you get used to it? This is not the Roots, it is the Canopy and here all sprites should be tested for potential Officer Training before being suspended. Those who succeed will spend the Autumn and Winter awake, training for a new life. We won't get that, just like last Autumn we will be cheated of our chance. We will be shuffled straight to storage by that snob and her cronies. We will have a brief icy chill and it will be Spring again. We will spend our entire lives working, eating and sleeping, with six months of the year stolen from us, and eventually we will become worn out and be recycled.' Nevamar felt as if it was on fire. Where was this all coming from? It knew it had to do something to escape.

'And I for one,' said Nevamar to its shocked colleagues, 'am not going to just lie down and accept it.' A plan had formulated in Nevamar's brain and it was going to follow it through.

CHAPTER TWO
THE GREAT ESCAPE

ATHER EARTH AND MOTHER SUN MUST HAVE BEEN SMILING on Nevamar because Ensign Serynazsya 178/20 had been put in charge of the shut down of this section of the branch branch. The Ensign was far more forgiving than the other officers, so Nevamar's plan was far more likely to succeed.

Ensign Serynazsya 178/20 had been activated just over a year earlier. This was her first posting after Officer Training. Ensign Serynazsya wanted to be a nurse more than anything else in the Tree. There had been no vacancies in any of the Tree's hospitals, so she had been assigned this job, a Duty Tour, a six month contract, up here in the Canopy, so far away from her home in the Roots that she was dreadfully homesick. Despite being Serynazsya's legal guardian as well as Commanding Officer, Captain Samnundsya had done nothing to help her further her ambition. Instead of finding a vacancy in a hospital school of nursing for Serynazsya to transfer to, she had arranged for the girl to attend a branch management school during the Winter, forcing Serynazsya into a Duty Tour spent learning how to do more efficiently the job she hated. Then another tour up here, paying the branch back the tuition fees.

Branch Captain Samnundsya had lots of other ways to make Serynazsya's life a misery. Every day the Captain would say something hurtful to her about her appearance. Roots born styles were all supposed to be blonde, beautiful and elegant. Poor Serynazsya was only blonde. The Captain constantly belittled her in front of her contemporaries. She would be glad to be back home in the Roots for six months, away from that harridan.

'At last, here she comes back from the trough,' Captain Samnundsya sneered as the Ensign returned from her lunch.

'Sorry I am late, Captain.'

'Well, this is the last bunch. Who knows, you might manage to go through a whole day without a screw-up.'

Ensign Serynazsya knew better than to complain that the Branch Captain was being unfair. It would only result in more vitriol. Only a couple of hours and Serynazsya would be on the way home. If only one sprite would stop being so very slow. Strange NM331/29 was usually the most efficient sprite she had ever seen.

'Do hurry up NM331/29, you are holding us all up,' said the Ensign. NM331/29, or Nevamar as it now called itself, did not need to be so thorough with its shut-down procedures. It was hoping Ensign Serynazsya would leave with her sprites and not notice she was one short.

'The sprite is sorry Ensign, but the workstation is being slow.'

Serynazsya had no idea the Sprite NM331/29 had become capable of lying and it just wanted the Ensign to go.

'Well, I suppose there is nothing that can be done about that. Hopefully you can catch up with the rest of the troop when you have finished.'

The Ensign had not given a direct order so the sprite had no intention of catching up. This act of defiance would have far reaching effects on both their lives.

In our World the Tree was just a plant made of solid, living wood. The tree had been old thirty years earlier, when Mr Spenser had bought the house and garden. Generations of the previous owner's family had cared for the tree, being rewarded with delicious red apples. Some said it was at least 120 years old. It was actually closer to 200 years old and would, barring accidents, be around for at least that long again.

Mr Spenser found the tree a great source of satisfaction. Something stable in a changing world. He had forbidden his sons to play football in the garden or to do anything that might damage the tree, so now he forbade his grandsons from playing within the vicinity of the tree. He did his best to make sure that the tree was healthy, pruning it regularly, although this was becoming more difficult as the years went by. It had been a very poor year for the Tree, very little blossom in the Spring with even less fruit from it in the Summer. He realised that it now needed professional attention.

His son was parking his car outside the house. What wonderful timing, thought Mr Spenser. His son Brian was a History lecturer at the local university which had a Botany Department that specialised in orchard trees, perhaps they could give it the once over.

'Grandad, grandad!' the three boys made their usual effusive greetings, and then ran into the kitchen to see what treats their grandmother had for them.

'Hello Brian,' Mr Spenser said to his son as he locked his car.

'Hi Dad. The tree is looking a bit sorry for itself this year, isn't it?'

'I don't know why I haven't thought of this before. The Botany Department at your University deals with apple trees and other orchard plants, doesn't it?'

'Yes, it does.' Brian had been thinking the same himself. 'I've never seen an apple tree like it. I'm pretty sure David Fraser and his team haven't either. They will love the challenge of treating that old beauty.'

'So you will have a word?'

Mr Spenser was immensely cheered.

'First thing on Monday morning, Dad.'

'Thanks,' Mr Spenser said as they both entered the house.

In the beginning, said the Holy Book of the Tree, there was the Earth, steadfast and dependable, like a good father he always provided for his children.

In the heavens was the Sun, loving and giving, like a good mother she shone her love and light, warming the entire World as a mother warms the hearts of her children.

Like all good parents Earth and Sun did not smother their children, but they were always there giving them room to grow. Mother Sun spread her love and spent time with all her children. The dark of night falls when Mother Sun is far away. When she is close at hand it is day and all is light. Sometimes she had such a long way to go to see her other children, that the hours of daylight are far shorter and Winter falls on the World. Sometimes her other children are close at hand, so the hours of daylight are long and Summer fills the World.

Father Earth and Mother Sun brought forth the Apple. From the Apple came the Seed, from the Seed came forth the roots and shoot that became the Sapling.

Despite the love of its mother and father, in those early days, the Sapling was under attack from all sides. In the Apple and the Seed there had been only sprites. At first this had been the case in the Sapling, but as it grew, the sprites alone were not up to the task of defending their home. The Sapling therefore took the sprites that had been in the apple and made them grow stronger bodies and creative minds. They became the anthers who could organise the defence of the Sapling.

Mother Sun had smiled upon the Sapling and it grew strong, with more than enough anthers to defend the Tree. From that day onward, only the brightest and the best of the new sprites would become anthers and join the officer Class, replacing those anthers who had come to the end of their lives.

In those early days, all anthers were simply taller, stronger and cleverer versions of the sprites. As the Sapling grew and each region became more specialised the officer Class changed. The hair and eye colour of an anther instantly showed where it had lived and worked as a sprite. The Sapling declared that each officer should be an individual, have an unique name as well as number with an unique face to go with that name.

Then came the terrible day. The Roots of the Sapling were separated from the Stem and there was much lamentation in what remained. The survivors could see no future because without the Roots there could be no water. With no water, there could be no growth. With no growth there could be no life. Father Earth and Mother Sun however, smiled upon the survivors, for a new root-stock, which had survived the loss of its stalk, was grafted to what remained of the Sapling. Both halves needed each other and the graft became permanent.

The Roots grew and spread, embracing Father Earth. The Stalk became the Trunk growing tall and straight. The Trinity was complete when the Canopy grew lush and strong from the top of the Trunk, reaching out to embrace Mother Sun. And so the new composite Sapling gave forth its first fruit. Thus was born the Tree of Life.

Each original plant had a different processes for turning sprites into officers. This created two mutually compatible sexes in the new composite Tree. Initially the new female officers were called root-style anthers, which quickly became root-styles to avoid confusion and then simply styles.

It was easy to tell the genders apart. Styles were smooth and soft whilst anthers were rugged and rough. Styles had no hair upon their chins, but long flowing hair on their heads whilst anthers grew beards and became bald with age. Styles were curved and had a pair of rounded breasts whilst anthers had broad shoulders and the organs of masculinity between their legs. Styles had high voices whilst anthers had deep voices.

When a sprite became an Officer Cadet nobody, not even the Cadet, knew which gender they would become until the process had finished. Once differentiation occurred, any doubt the former sprite might have had was instantly washed away. They were what they were, always had been and always would be.

'Wake up, Sprite NM331/29,' said Branch Captain Roctwoosya. Nevamar had fallen asleep in its hiding place and found by the Branch Captain. It was not Captain Samnundsya, somehow it was her predecessor.

'Tell me Sprite NM331/29, if you were to become an officer, which would you rather be, anther or style?'

'The sprite does not have the choice, Ma'am,' Nevamar replied. 'It would be whatever the Tree wants it to be.'

'That is a sensible answer, you are a sensible sprite, but it is not the answer I want.'

'If it is a sensible sprite, then it would like to be a sensible anther.'

'You would not want to be a style like me?'

'No, Ma'am.' NM331/29 had gone bright red, even sprites could blush.

'Don't worry, just say what you think.'

'Its just that styles are weird, they wear the strangest things on and off duty. Shoes with high heels. Things called skirts that hang from the place where their curved bodies narrow at the middle, exposing the bottom of their legs,' said NM331/29, stopping to take a breath.

'Go on sprite, this is amusing.'

'Older styles like yourself wear skirts that end around their knees. Younger ones wear skirts that barely cover the tops of their legs, even on duty.'

Captain Roctwoosya was laughing, 'you always did keep me entertained NM331/29.'

'How are such silly garments even allowed,' Nevamar wondered out loud. 'If the sprite becomes an officer it would never wear anything so stupid.'

'What else is weird about us styles then sprite?'

'Painting your faces when you are not on duty. That's silly.'

'What you are doing now is also silly, isn't it NM331/29?'

'It has to be done, Ma'am' said Nevamar. 'I have to wait until the coast is clear. I have to make sure that I miss my assigned shuttle down to the Roots.'

'Tell me sprite, why is this?'

'That shuttle has a crew of Root-born officers aboard. Instead of being dropped off at the Central Hub for testing, all the sprites aboard will be taken straight to the storage facility. No test, no chance of better things.'

'This was not always the case, was it?' asked the Captain.

'No, Ma'am, when I first went to Winter storage, you took all your sprites to be tested. Some sprouted hair and new faces and went to do Officer Training, but not me, I kept failing by the narrowest of margins. I had fully expected to pass on the fourth attempt. Captain Samnundsya saw to it this attempt never happened. I refuse to be cheated again.'

'So sleeping in the cupboard you are supposed to be hiding in, instead of running to the Shuttle Station isn't very sensible, is it?'

'No, Ma'am, I will go now. At the station the crew of a different shuttle will make room for me. After all, what's one more sprite in a hull full of them? I will go to a testing centre in the Central Hub. This time I will pass with flying colours. All I have to do is arrive at the Shuttle Station after my official shuttle has sailed.'

'Talking to your dead Branch Captain is also not very sensible.'

'No, Ma'am,' replied Nevamar, who at that point woke up and realised its meeting with Captain Roctwoosya had all been a dream.

S prites did not dream. Nevamar was starting to wonder what dream meant. No, it told itself, that is a waste of good thinking time. Thinking time that should be used on getting to the Shuttle Station in the Crown as quickly as possible.

Completely awake now, Nevamar peaked out from the cupboard. Sure enough, the branch was deserted, the last officer had left an hour earlier. Nevamar glanced at the clock on the wall. It was late now, it would have to run to make up for lost time.

CHAPTER THREE
DISASTER AND DISGRACE

T he Summer season in both realities had been blighted. *In our World, in a reality way beyond the imagination of the inhabitants of the Tree, it was one of glorious late Summer, early Autumn, afternoons that makes the thought of the coming colder seasons almost bearable. The air was warmer than it had been for weeks and the sky was a* shade of the bluest blue. The boys had been back in school for a week now and during that time the weather had been dry, sometimes as sunny as today. This really upset the boys, because their Summer holidays had been a complete washout. They knew they were not allowed to play football in their

Grandfather's garden, but they just couldn't help themselves, not on a day like today. This is how the ball ended up in the top branch of the rare and ancient apple tree.

'Jordan, you idiot!'

'I'm sorry Ben, it was an accident.'

The older boy was far from forgiving. 'How are we supposed to get our ball back. We can't tell Gramps, he'll go spare.'

'Perhaps we could just leave it,' said Jordan, who was close to tears.

'And he will spot it as soon as he comes back from the shops, we'll be for it from Dad and Gramps.'

'Why don't we give the tree a shake, there aren't any apples and it's not as if we would be hurting it,' said Arthur, the middle boy who was always the most practical.

The boys knew nothing of the tree's longevity and cared even less for its rarity. There were only two other examples of this variety of apple tree in the UK, both nearly two centuries old and still producing fruit. They shook the tree to try and free their ball. They would not normally dream of doing this, as it would have dislodged apples as well as their ball. This year there had been very little blossom and no fruit. Blithely unaware of the havoc this world's action was having on another world, they shook it again, and the ball finally fell, but the damage had been done. One of the smaller side branches snapped as the ball fell free in a shower of brown and orange Autumn leaves. The boys recovered their ball and ran off, branch in tow, certain that their grandfather would never know what had happened to a branch that was so high up in the canopy of the venerable old plant.

In an adjacent reality, in the Arbouron version of the Tree, pandemonium had broken out. Everyone who lived in the Canopy was used to the upper branches of the Tree moving. The Outer Void was full of strange winds that made them dance when they blew, but generations had passed since the Trunk had swayed in the wind. It had been a long time since anyone had ever experienced the whole Tree shaking like this.

Then the shaking came again, worse than before, the sprite knew that the trolleybus system, that connected every part of the Canopy, would have ground to a halt. It would take ages to restart after a Code Alpha situation like this. The section of the branch Nevamar was now passing through had a cargo shoot that it could safely slide down, to make up the lost time. The journey would be terrifying, but it was that or spend hours running down stairs, ramps and corridors. It emerged shakily from the shoot in a Maintenance Regiment office opposite a trolleybus stop. The green light on the shelter meant that a capsule was waiting. Excellent, it was a trolley which would travel non-stop down to the Shuttle Station. No, best let it pass, the one of the passenger benches was occupied by none other than Ensign Serynazsya, no doubt waiting for the capsule to become operational again. She the last person Nevamar wanted to see.

After the capsule departed, Nevamar spotted something lying on the floor of the platform. It was Ensign Serynazsya IndesnCard. Losing that would make Serynazsya's life so much harder and Nevamar's so much easier. Nevamar could now plug it into any workstation to alter the ticket attached to its much simpler IndesnCard, using a PIN code it was not supposed to know. It could now legitimately travel on any shuttle, no need for lies and acting. All it had to do now was make its way to the Shuttle Station and get down to the Roots and a new life.

The public address system in the office was still operating in receive-only mode at full volume, so Nevamar heard the incoming message with crystal clarity.

'Will somebody please get their bums into gear and increase the water pressure to this branch.'

It was the voice of an older style. It reminded Nevamar of her old Branch Captain. All sprites are hard-wired to obey the voice of an officer. So instead of catching the next station-bound trolleybus, it activated the interface of the nearest work station. An officer's override would be needed to alter any pressure settings, but Nevamar had Ensign Serynazsya's IndesnCard, which had just the right clearance level to issue that override. Oh, what a resourceful sprite it was.

'I'm activating the coupling brackets and filtering the flow,' said a much younger voice, probably a Cadet. Nevamar could have told the Cadet that this was the worse thing that could be done in this situation. It had been studying maintenance for two years whilst the old Branch Captain had been alive.

'No, don't, you need to increase the flow into the branch, not reduce it,' said Nevamar. Sadly no-one heard Nevamar, it was not plugged into that communication channel. Not that anyone would have listened to a sprite's advice anyway. Still, the sprite was programmed to try and help.

There was a series of loud bangs and crashes.

'Captain Sannarlsya, what should I do now?' begged the younger voice.

'Try to open the pin-cot valve and build-up some pressure,' replied Captain Sannarlsya.

'But I can't, the system has failed in this section. The gap in the wall, to get to the manual override, is too small I can't fit in any more. I'm too tall now.'

Nevamar could fit into any crawl space because the gap would be sprite-sized. There would be a secondary control panel that it could remotely operate the inaccessible valve from. It found the clips and released the hatch in the wall, then squeezed into the dark interior. There it was, the secondary control panel, still online ready for Nevamar to use. Far away the valve turned to the open position. There was still no increase in pressure. It was time for Plan B.

'Unless we can get the pressure back up in this section there will be a chain reaction and the whole trunk might split.' said the Captain.

'I'm on it Captain, a team will be there in five minutes with emergency pin-cot amplifiers,' said a new voice. 'That should solve the pressure problem.'

'No good Brigadier Myghcomant. My readings show that the valve needs to be opened immediately by an explosive charge to discharge from the prime ventricle,' said the Style.

A Brigadier? High ranking officers rarely came to the extremity of the Canopy Nevamar worked in. So the name Brigadier Myghcomant meant nothing to it.

'Not an option Captain,' said the Brigadier, 'you would be lost if that were to happen, you and young Cadet Kalvromant.'

'Brigadier, I think it is too late for me and my Cadet. For the good of the Tree, you must do it.'

Returning to the workstation, Nevamar had heard the exchange and could see what the Captain was trying to do, but it knew there was a better way. It dashed through the control codes, not making a single typing error. Far away in the branch the rarely used lever automatically swung into the open position. Now the pressure would treble without the need for an explosive charge.

'Where the hell did that come from?' The Brigadier was honestly surprised as the pressure began to rise back to normal. 'Report! Who is up there?'

Every instinct Nevamar possessed was screaming at it that it had to report to the superior officer, but it knew it didn't have time. It had to get to the Shuttle Station before the last shuttle left for the Roots. This was not the behaviour of a well behaved sprite. If the old NM331/29 could see itself, it would be horrified.

Then the whole Tree shook again. Something large banged against the outer Trunk. One of the recently re-inflated tubes ruptured, and pressure dropped to zero in the branch where the officer and Cadet were working. Nevamar stopped in its tracks. The whole Trunk could rupture and everything in that entire section of the Canopy would be irreparably damaged whether the branch was jettisoned or not. It returned to the service duct. The main ventricle pin-cot for that side of the Tree was nearly twice its height, and maybe three times its weight, but there was no option. Nevamar started pushing. Fortunately the lever began to turn and painfully slowly the spray of liquid from the burst tube slowed to a trickle, but it was too late for the branch and the officers within. The sprite heard the far away echo of distant bulkheads crashing shut then the explosive crack of the branch beyond being jettisoned. With the voice of the officer tragically silenced, there was nothing to keep Nevamar at its station and it was on its way back to the Shuttle Station.

The Spirit of the Tree quickly realised that allowing sprites to develop into officers was a double edged sword. They were fully sentient intelligent creatures who could cause no end of damage if that intelligence was not channelled. In wartime, the channelling was done by the officer Corps. It gave the defenders a chain of command and made their job more efficient.

The Spirit of the Tree also knew his officers could not simply be knocked on and off like the sprites when not needed. During peace time the officers would get bored and a bored officer was a dangerous one. So the Spirit of the Tree found them peacetime jobs, within his world, that sprites were incapable of doing. The military nature of the officers spilled over into their peace-time careers. Professions were arranged into regiments and ranks became pay-grades. For instance all cooks belonged to the Catering Regiment, all hairdressers and all barbers belonged to the Haircare Regiment. The practicality of the rank structure and not having to worry about what to wear to work appealed to the Tree people, as it made the transition from waiter to warrior that much easier.

The highest ranking officer is the Tree Marshall. During peace time he or she is the head of the High Council. When the Tree is under attack and Marshal Law declared, the High Council is suspended and the Tree Marshall becomes supreme commander whose word is law. Every Tree Marshall hopes they never have to know the loneliness of ultimate command.

R eligion in the Tree was organised as strictly as the Officer's Corps. The Church devoted to the worship of the Tree, splits into the House of Laity, to which most officers belong, and the House of Clergy, for those who can hear the Spirit of the Tree speaking and spread that divine word to the masses. An Offeriad is a priest of the Spirit of the Tree. It is they who officiate at Pair-Bondings and Recycling services as well as the weekly Sunday Temple Parades. With no parishes to support them, offeriad must have a secondary trade to pay the bills.

The truly devoted became fully professed members of either the Grand Order of the Anther or the Sacred Sisterhood of the Style. Tree Monks and Tree Nuns are rarely seen outside their Monastery or Convent, calling their lives of prayer and contemplation the Tree Within.

For many years after a flood in the Roots the Sisterhood's most sacred book was missing. All that remained was a very poor copy. All styles were taught if they heard the voice of the Tree, they had a True Calling and must instantly abandon their old lives beyond the cloister, regardless of willingness or suitability. Then a decade ago, everything changed again. Unwilling sisters were allowed to leave the order. They gave no explanation when they returned to their old lives. Once again, only willing styles vanish into the Tree Within forever.

The Captain and Cadet must have been with the Winter Squad. That meant that the rest of the Winter Squad was already in the Canopy. Nevamar did not want to meet any of them; they would delay its vital journey to the Roots.

It didn't have time to glory at the magnificent chamber it had entered, the Crown, where Trunk became Canopy. Nevamar hurried on its way to the Shuttle Station, safe in the knowledge that it still had plenty of time to get aboard the last shuttle of the year down to the Roots.

All parts of the Tree were supplied with life giving water and had their waste taken away by a network of pipes and channels that ran the length of the Tree, from the very tip of the longest root to the highest leaf on the most remote twig.

Most of this network was found in the walls of the Tree. However, movement of cargo and passengers also occurred in this network, along a series of arterial waterways called the Grand Central Channel. Whilst they were certainly the most impressive looking part of the network, they were also the most inefficient. As a result, shuttles were slow. A so-called Express Shuttle took nine hours to make a one way trip. Most shuttles stopped at every junction way-station so it took three days to make the journey. During the Winter, with the Canopy effectively abandoned, the sections of the channels, that travelled through the ten miles of solid wood from the top of the Trunk to the Crown were closed. Most of the passenger shuttles went into dry dock and the cargo shuttles ran a greatly reduced service.

The Shuttle Station was on the banks of the largest body of open water in the Tree. This lake was created at the head of the Grand Central Channels. During the Summer officers on their down-time would come here to swim and enjoy the warm relaxed atmosphere of the Crown. Nevamar had no time for any of the other buildings in the Crown.

The sound of the klaxon was a complete surprise. The last shuttle had stalled its hatches and was about to depart. Nevamar increased its pace, but it was too late. By the time it reached the Shuttle Station the last shuttle was gliding majestically from the dock to the middle of the lake where it opened its ballast tanks and slowly sank towards the down channel and its slow decent to the Roots.

How could this have happened, Nevamar knew that the last shuttle was not due to depart for ages. It walked up to a display board, halting the board's shut-down procedure for long enough to see that an emergency order had been issued instructing all the remaining shuttles to depart immediately.

Nevamar slumped down on the spot and began to cry. It was now a Sprite Without Function. It now had only one duty, to offer itself up for recycling, to stop the drain it would make on the precious resources of the Tree.

Nevamar got up and started walking towards the recycling shoot. The sprite was so full of its own misery that it failed to notice the two officers and nearly walked into them. One of the officers was beautiful golden haired and pale skinned style. Nevamar could see that her beauty, which even by Roots standards was stunning, was clouded by an incredible sadness. The other officer, a more mature anther, was obviously trying to comfort the style. Both seemed to be facing up to a terrible tragedy.

'Sprite, report!' The male officer barked. Nevamar looked up at the long outer lapel of the green wrap-around uniform jacket. It was decorated with three golden apple leaf rank pips. This was the Brigadier that Nevamar had heard on the intercom earlier, he was wearing the insignia of the Winter Squad. It really did not want to see this officer now, when its disgrace was so high. It had been insubordinate and not gone to storage with the rest of its branch, it had tried to buck the system, and had failed, it must now be punished.

'I said, report!' repeated the Brigadier, 'I've just lost one senior officer, who was also a good friend, and a promising young Cadet, I am not really in the mood for silly games.'

'Sir. NM331/29. Sir'. The sprite saluted and handed the Brigadier its IndesnCard. 'The sprite has to report that it is a Sprite Without Function and is reporting for recycling.'

'Why, sprite? Why are you without function?'

'I. I mean it, it means the sprite has to report that the sprite missed its shuttle down to the Roots for winter storage.'

'So, how did you miss your shuttle?'

'The sprite deliberately missed its assigned shuttle, I hoped, err, that is the sprite hoped to get on a later shuttle so that it would be tested for Officer Training,' said Nevamar. The Brigadier was intrigued by this reply.

'All sprites receive testing before they are put into storage, you must know that?'

For some reason, although this officer was so far above it in the pecking order, he put Nevamar at ease. 'Sir, my Branch Captain does not believe in promoting sprites, if I, I mean if the sprite had been aboard the assigned shuttle, then I, er, it would have missed its test again this year.'

'The plot thickens; tell me sprite, what was the name of your Branch Captain?'

'Captain Samnundsya 101/20 Zilfrayts, Sir,' replied Nevamar.

'So that's what happened to her.'

There was a flash of recognition on the face of the officer accompanying the Brigadier.

'Elucidate then Lieutenant Sharlensya, now this is getting interesting.'

'Yes, Sir, the officer the sprite is referring to was a classmate of mine at a Pure-Stock Elite Academy. The rumour was that she was somehow connected to Brigadier Sandampsya's coup attempt a few years ago. She disappeared after that. It looked as if her politics earned her a posting up here as a punishment.'

The Pure-stocks were all the product of two ancient sprite-pods that pre-dating the Graft. Pure-stock officers are all tall, blonde, blue eyed and beautiful on the outside. Sadly far too many were ugly on the inside, thinking themselves to be a cut above everyone else.

'Ah, Roots politics. Enlightening, but sadly not as interesting as I had hoped.' Whilst this exchange took place Nevamar had shuffled itself further away from the officers.

'Where do you think you are going sprite?'

'I'm not going anywhere, Sir.'

'Oh, I wouldn't say that, my comlink has just identified your IndesnCode. I can see why you would want to get yourself tested. You only just missed two years ago. I see another narrow fail last year and a convincing fail this year. Which is odd, as the test is dated 1B10, in three days time. Somebody is rubbish at faking records. I will have to flag this and authorise a proper test. I hate seeing potential officer material squandered.

The Brigadier turned his glare full on Nevamar. 'It looks to me that in the recent tragic incident, it was your quick thinking that saved the Tree from any further damage. Well done Sprite NM331/29, very well done.'

'Lieutenant Sharlensya, with the tragedy that has just befallen your dear mother, I was afraid that we would be under staffed this Winter'. He looked sadly at Nevamar, 'we will never replace your mother dear, but it looks as if we have found ourselves a replacement Cadet, Also Captain Treslelant tells me that there is an Ensign trapped up here because she lost her IndesnCard and could not get on any of the shuttles. Both you and Treslelant will be legally responsible for her for this tour.'

'Sir, what if this Ensign is completely hopeless and this little one doesn't pass the test?'

'Trust in the Spirit of the Tree, Lieutenant Sharlensya, it will provide,' said the Brigadier. 'Also think about it, this sprite showed original thinking during the crisis and came up with original ideas That is not the way a normal sprite would have acted. Listen to the way it talks, does it sound like a normal sprite?'

The Brigadier turned to face Nevamar, who had been watching with interest.

'In my book

Sprite NM331/29 here has passed a Field Cadet Selection Test with flying colours and is more than ready to be promoted to the rank of Cadet, with all the responsibilities and privileges that rank holds. I have no doubt when Major Keltonnant performs the formal test, it will pass.' The Brigadier winked at the sprite, 'but if I were you, I would keep out of that Ensign's way for the next few weeks, and it would be best if you gave me her IndesnCard, the one you used so cleverly. I'll make sure it gets back to her. After all you don't want her making your life hell until next Spring, do you?'

Nevamar looked bemused. Was that Brigadier really saying it was about to become an Officer Cadet? That it had achieved its goal? That it was no longer a sprite without function. Soon it would no longer be a sprite at all.

'Don't thank me yet. We have a difficult few months ahead of us, short of rations and with some difficult tasks to fulfil before the Tree can live again. There will be times when you will wish you were down there sleeping through the Dark Time with your colleagues.'

The Brigadier turned to address the other officer. 'Lieutenant Sharlensya 115/30, I'm still giving you the rest of the day off, I wish I could give more considering your loss, but on the other hand work will help you get over your grief. However, before you go off duty, take NM331/29 to Major Keltonnant for testing. I have no doubt it will pass and soon be one of your pupils. As its mentor, you will have to sort out its billet and help it choose a name.'

CHAPTER FOUR
ACTIVATION

As if to prove the military nature of their society, the Canopy residents always left the place looking like a battlefield after the fighting. Somebody had to tidy it up ready for the population's return the following Spring. There was also the maintenance work that was impossible when the leaves were producing Syrup to their full capacity.

A team of dedicated volunteers elected to stay up in the Canopy all through the Dark Half of the Year. Their official title was the First Battalion (Autumn and Winter Repairs) of the Maintenance Regiment. They were commonly known as the Winter Squad. Members referred to themselves as Squaddies. Theirs was not an easy task. They never had a large enough budget for what they needed. Every Spring their commander, Brigadier Myghcomant 200/01, would hand in an estimate for the following Autumn and Winter based on the previous year's experience. He would then spend the whole of the Spring and Summer arguing with committees and accountants. On average the Squad would receive three quarters of what was needed. The whole of the Maintenance Regiment was dangerously underfunded, but to the Brigadier's continued annoyance, the demands of the Roots always took precedence. He could not understand why maintaining the Canopy had such a low priority. Possibly because few on the High Council, the Tree's government, ever went there even though they could not live without the Syrup it produced.

In order to balance their books, the Squad agreed to take four recently sprouted Cadets with them to the Canopy for Officer Training subsidised by the High Council. The Cadets followed the official curriculum and passed out as Ensigns during the Tour of Duty, whilst filling the gap created by the absence of sprites.

Departure might be chaotic but the return to the Canopy on the other hand was a well planned operation. When the first team of leaf and flower builders from the Second Battalion (Leaf and Flower Construction) of the Maintenance Regiment, arrived a week or so into the New Year, the Canopy was always immaculately clean and refreshed. Once the leaf builders had finished in a section, the leaf operating sprites and the officers of the Branch Management Regiment would return to the Canopy. Over the course of the first two weeks of Spring, the top of the tree would return to life, as the Winter Squad returned to their base in the Roots to plan for next Autumn and Winter.

Nevamar's head was spinning, as it had just realised the significance of who the two officers it had been speaking to was. They could only be members of the legendary Winter Squad, who had an almost mythical reputation amongst the sprites who spent their Autumn and Winter in cold storage. It was said that the hunger, the cold and the loneliness had driven the members of the Winter Squad completely mad. That at the start of Spring, they cooked and ate the first batch of sprites to be sent from the Roots. During the Spring and Summer, so the sprite legend said, the Winter Squad was kept under sedation in padded cells. Nevamar had always thought that this was a ridiculous story. Spending Autumn and Winter cut off, with only the rations they had brought with them, must be very challenging. However, Nevamar knew as the safety and future of everything in the Tree depended on these dedicated officers, the High Council would hardly entrust the future of the Tree to a group of lunatics. Anyway, the young Lieutenant and the Brigadier it had been talking to looked perfectly sane and well balanced. The only frantic member of the Winter Squad Nevamar had encountered was the poor Cadet who had been trapped in the broken branch, and he had good reason to be frantic.

Each branch has a circular cross section. For the people of the Tree, it was the central core of the branch where life took place. Motor vehicles, either driven or automated, fly through circular central tunnels called roadways. In near horizontal branches the base of the roadways have paved paths which pedestrians and cyclists use. In near vertical branch sections, these paths spiral up the inner walls of the roadway. Around the roadways, the branch is divided into decks.

Junctions between branches were usually wider than the branches on their own. Sometimes these junctions had quite a large flat area where the roadways joined. These junctions were prime real-estate. Attractive gardens could be planted on the flat surface of the junction, surrounding entrance porches leading to pleasant residential units below or above.

More light fell onto the surfaces of the Tree every day than could ever be used by it's inhabitants. The bark absorbed as much of this energy as possible, sending some to the Day-Lighters, the large light fittings which recreated daylight within the Canopy, Trunk and Roots of the Tree. The rest went to Power Houses in the Trunk which stored the sunlight and then released it as electricity for all industrial or domestic processes within the Tree.

'Wow!' said Nevamar.

With no overpowering need to hurry, Nevamar could appreciate the glory of the Crown. The great translucent vaulted dome at the base of the Canopy was created by the trunk splitting into five branches.

'Surely you have been to the Crown before?' asked Lieutenant Sharlensya.

'I, it means the sprite has always been too busy to appreciate it, Ma'am.'

'You can stop all that third person nonsense now. If the Brigadier is correct you are about to become a proper person.'

'Ma'am, you're not going to punish me for displaying individuality?'

'In the Tree's name why should I? You are ready to sprout. Developing a Sense of Self is an obvious sign of that readiness,' said Lieutenant Sharlensya.

'Captain Samnundsya said it was being "Uppity", and a sprite should know its place.'

'That figures,' said the Lieutenant and they continued their journey in silence.

At the centre of the Crown was the lake created by the mouths of the Great Central Channels. This was surrounded wide golden beach. On the southern side of the lake, on a bay, stood the Crown Officers' Residential Complex or CORC. It stretched all the way from its elegant façade of the Central Mess Hall on the lake shore, into one of the largest of the Branches. Within its precincts were hundreds of buildings, shops, trade schools and houses for the summer residents. Those who lived in communities in the branches during the Summer, would regularly visit CORC and use its facilities.

Next door to the Central Mess Hall was the Command and Control Centre the administrative heart of the Canopy. Next to that was the Grand Order of the Anther Hospital. On the western headland of the bay, surrounded by glorious green lawns was the Temple, a circle of pillars made from white marble, the oldest religious site in the Tree, venerated by both styles and anthers. On the side of the bay was the Shuttle Station that Nevamar had been in such a hurry to get to. That just left the Central Data Transfer Centre which did not quite fit in. All the other buildings had classical pillars and colonnades, this building with mirrored glass and metal walls made a definite architectural statement.

The inhabitants of the Tree would not see the irony of growing plants within a plant because they would not believe that they were in a plant. They where living in a sealed environment created by a marvellous living machine, from which all life sprang. They knew there were other trees in the outer void, for where else did the pollen come from, but these other trees were also not just plants, they were also sealed environment, supporting life within life. The Crown had been beautifully landscaped into a magnificent park that was a joy to behold.

Nevamar had spent all its life tightly packed in with its fellow sprites, and was quite overwhelmed by the large rooms and comfortable spaces when it arrived in the Central Mess Hall. It could tell the mood was far more sombre than usual. The Lieutenant greeted her colleagues quietly. All of them expressed their condolences and tried to ease the burden of her grief at the loss of her mother. Well intentioned, but counter-productive. There was only one person that Lieutenant Sharlensya wanted to talk to, and she had just been ordered to deliver Nevamar to him.

With just forty two people living and working up in the Canopy during the Winter, the hospital was mothballed like the rest of the Crown. Major Keltonnant, the Medical Officer, set up his small Medical Centre in the rooms he used every year. It was as comfortable for him as an old pair of slippers. Here was the equipment to test if Nevamar was indeed ready to become an officer.

'Right then sprite, let's see if the Brigadier was right about you,' said the Lieutenant. She knocked on the door.

'Enter.'

'Major Keltonnant, Sir.'

'Yes,' said the Major without turning from the box he was emptying. The older officer was a very distinguished looking anther who at twenty eight, was middle aged, or as he preferred to call it "The Prime of Life". He was almost bald, and what little hair remained was peppered white, as was the neatly clipped goatee beard and moustache, which made him look far older than he really was. He had qualified as a doctor twenty years earlier and had been the Winter Squad's Medical officer for nineteen of those years. He was also Lieutenant Sharlensya's uncle, he was touched by that morning's accident, when he lost his sister so tragically.

Great green apples, what was Sharlensya doing here now he thought. Major Keltonant was having difficulty controlling his own grief, yet she was coping with hers so well. Obviously she was her mother's daughter in that respect. It had been his sister Sannarlsya, who had arranged for him to get this job all those years ago, to help him get over a broken relationship. For the first time in all those years, his Medical Centre was officially closed.

'The Brigadier wants this sprite tested for Officer Training, Sir'

'In the Tree's name where did this little one come from?' asked the Major. Shock and curiousity were temporarily replacing grief and anger. All sprites should be safely packed away in cold storage down in the Roots. However, given the way the Canopy was abandoned, he was surprised that there were not more little lost souls up here.

'It was caught in the cross-fire from the accident,' said Sharlensya as she handed her uncle Nevamar's IndesnCard. The mask was slipping. Keltonnant could see tears welling up in his niece's eyes and hear the grief in her voice.

'I should be more grateful to it. It tried to save her, tried so hard...' For a few brief moments the mask slipped. 'Oh Uncle Kelly, what are we going to do without mam.' Then the cool professional reserve made a pretty good job at reasserting itself. '...but. But a secondary problem occurred which nobody could have foreseen. This sprite was there again, apparently it was responsible for shutting off the damaged pipework and preventing the break getting any worse.' Protocol and formality be damned, this was his niece, the daughter of his beloved sister, they shared the same loss. He hugged the style, and then looked at the confused sprite standing next to his niece. Back to work, it is what Sannarlsya would have wanted.

'So, let's see if this youngster has got the right stuff then? Hop up onto this couch.' Nevamar instinctively obeyed.

'Yes, its looking good, Beta Suppressant levels low, Almanic levels high, and yes, increased brain activity. All the signals suggest a positive response to activation.' The Major turned from his monitor and addressed the sprite directly. 'Right then NM331/29, relax, I am about to send the test pulse.'

Nevamar tried to obey the order, but as soon as it felt the pulse, relaxation was the last thing on its mind. All sorts of new ideas were racing through its mind. Colours seemed so much more vibrant, smells far more pungent. Everything seemed so much better.

'This test carried out on sprites, just before they get stored, looks for First Stage Differentiation. Unless this has occurred, then the activation will not work,' said the Major. Great wads of data were appearing on the Major's workstation monitor. All of it pointing in one direction, that Nevamar was ripe, maybe even over ripe, for change. 'I can't for the life of me see why this little one hasn't been given the chance to sprout?'

'Maybe because the branch it was working in was managed by a Pure-stock crazy-bitch from hell.' You could hear the anger in the Lieutenant's voice. 'Mother Sun, I hate that sort of person.'

'You know something Sharlee, I really think you should go on an anger management course about your issues with Pure-stocks,' said the Major.

'Seriously?' asked his niece.

'Yes, seriously. You might end up doing something you regret. I know you have good reason to dislike the zealots, but they are not all like that. Hating all Pure-stock with a passion makes you as bad as the zealots.'

'I suppose so. Right, about this sprite.'

'Oh yes, the Brigadier was right, its ready. So, let's get on with it.'

Nevamar could hardly contain its excitement. The test had never had this effect on it. Not even close.

'You might feel a little giddy for a few moments,' said the Major, who was busy getting the equipment ready for the activation. He looked more like a crazy alchemist than a doctor. He turned back to his display, typed in a few words on his keyboard and then placed a small acorn shaped capsule into a goblet. Alchemy or magic, the changes that were about to be made to the sprite were breathtaking.

'Now then sprite, don't take your eyes off the contents of this goblet.' Orders were orders, it would stare at that capsule until it recycled. But this was the last order that Nevamar would ever blindly follow without thinking.

Something made the liquid in the goblet fizz and bubble like crazy. The acorn cracked down the middle, and Nevamar saw a small squid-like creature emerged. The Tree had originally created creatures like this to turn sprites into anthers, calling it a Key. These creatures continued to do their age old job, but now half the sprites contained the coding to become anthers and half the coding to become styles. Not that this mattered to the Key, it was driven by instinct. Like lightening, it leaped on to Nevamar, wrapping its tentacles around the sprite's arm and sinking its fangs deep into its flesh. However, this was no deadly venom, this was an elixir of life. The chemicals pumped into Nevamar had a mind-bending as well as body altering effect. The Cadet was so enraptured by what it saw that it had not realised that the Major and the Lieutenant had left the room. Only the new Cadet saw a fantastic light show and heard the heavenly choir. The only person in the room was Cadet Nevamar, a sprite no more. The pattern of that body had been rewritten at a cellular level and was beginning to change, tearing itself apart and rebuilding itself from the rubble, using plans given to it by the Key.

For Nevamar, the test signal had been a mere foretaste of what it was now feeling. That light show had been the most beautiful thing it had seen in its life, and it wanted to see it again.

Within the Tree the concept of babies and toddlers is alien. Officers are created from sprites and an officer's life begins from the moment the differentiation process is activated and they became individuals. On the first day of their new life they would look like ten year old children on our world. In three months rapid development occurred, with five years worth of growth and physical development taking place in a single season. For the inhabitants of the Tree the next great milestone was on their fifth Registration Day when a young officer became an adult with all the legal rights and responsibilities that entailed.

'Again,' Nevamar demanded, like a toddler on a carousel, as the officers returned to the room.

'No Cadet, you don't need to see it again, once is enough, in fact more than once is positively harmful,' said the Major as he returned to his monitor.

'That's strange, the sprite pattern has been overridden by the Primary Differentiation and individual features are emerging even as we speak, but there is no sign of Secondary Differentiation the development of gender,' said the Major. 'Oh well, sometimes it can take a couple of days. In rare cases it may take weeks for this differentiation to happen. The auxins in this little one are fluctuating like crazy. Just like that other Canopy sprite who activated a couple of days ago.'

'Cadet Pezimeg, is one of mine this tour.'

'That's the one, although I think you'll find the name is Pemiseg. It had fluctuating auxins and could also go either way. If they are both still indeterminate this time next week, it might be a new factor developing up here.' The Major made a note to check both Cadets in seven days time. 'I doubt if either are neuter, far too healthy for that.' The Major then turned back to Nevamar. 'So Cadet, welcome to the officer Corps. Your whole system has been through a major shake-up in the past few minutes. I am ordering you to rest in that cubicle over there for the next few hours.'

He then turned to the Lieutenant, his face softening as all formalities were dropped. It was like a trigger as the Lieutenant finally collapsed into deep racking sobs.

'There there Sharlee dear.' He put an arm around her shoulder. 'My sister, your mother was a remarkable style, but you know that, you and I will miss her terribly. You and I will also remember the good times we had together. She would want that.' The two officers hugged, supporting each other in their grief. It was obvious to Nevamar that the Major was also in tears. Mother, mam, uncle and sister, what did all these words mean, was that the connection between these two officers and the Captain who died in the accident? It desperately wanted to know, but was too tired and dizzy to ask.

From a draw the Major removed an ampoule of medicine from its packaging and inserted it into a hypo-spray.

'You are also a remarkable style, the way you have kept together under the circumstances, when others would have gone to pieces, does you credit. Now the time for holding together has passed. You need to let go. You also need some sleep, or you will destroy yourself.' He injected the contents of the hypo-spray into his niece's arm. 'This will help you sleep. Its not much, but it is better than you keeping yourself awake with your grief.'

Again Nevamar wanted to know more, but the effect of the sedative it had been given was getting stronger, whilst the two officers continued their conversation.

The strange thing was that Nevamar did not want to rest. Far to many interesting things were happening. However, it had been ordered rest to by an officer. Orders were to be obeyed without question, but it was questioning. Up until a few minutes earlier, even the notion of not wanting to obey an order would have horrified Nevamar. And those officers kept on calling it Cadet instead of sprite.

'Oh great green apples!' the Major had just remembered something. He poured a brown liquid into a pint glass. 'Drink this. You need the energy.'

Nevamar took a mouthful of the liquid, it was horribly sweet and metallic at the same time. It drunk the rest of the liquid down in a few mouthfuls.

'Uncle, you have just given it a whole pint of pure refined Syrup, that is about eighteen thousand calories.' Even in grief, that raised a smile from her.

'And it is going to need it. It might sleep for the next few hours, but inside its body will be far from restful, it will need as much energy as it can get. Every one of those calories is going to be burnt by the morning.'

'Your the medic.'

'Right then Sharlee, I know you have been given the rest of the day off, you need to rest. You can pick up your charge tomorrow, when you are both fully rested. The paperwork can wait.'

Finally the sedative it had been given won the battle with Nevamar's metabolism and it dropped into a deep sleep.

CHAPTER FIVE
CHOOSE A MEMORABLE NAME

Nevamar found itself sleeping on a proper bed for the first for the first time in its life. This was so much better than a hammock. It felt so good that when the time came it had been reluctant to wake. Even for the Lieutenant, who it seemed had brought it here only a few minutes earlier.

'Wakey wakey sleepy head! You've been asleep for a whole day,' said the Lieutenant, who was looking smart in a neatly pressed dress uniform. Except it was a shade of dark orange that was unlike anything Nevamar had ever seen before.

'There is a Memorial Service for my mother,' the voice emotion seemed to overwhelm the Lieutenant, 'and Cadet

Kalvromant being held at the parade ground in an hour. You need to be dressed and ready for that.'

'But I have no equipment,' said Nevamar, whose sprite jump-suit was all ragged where seams had split and its sleeves now ended at the elbow and the trousers above its ankles, 'and my standard uniform seems to have shrunk overnight, Ma'am.'

'Your old uniform hasn't shrunk Cadet, you have started growing. I would say you are already three fractions taller than you were yesterday. One of the joys you have to look forward to is sudden unpredictable growth spurts. It will mean that you have to alter all your kit, so it fits you properly. Then when you have got the size right, the shape will change, depending on when you become a style. Thank the Tree for enprintable fabric.

That comment had gone right over Nevamar's head. It watched in amazement as the jump-suit's legs grew, and it was not quite as tight, however, the sleeves were now a thing ofthe past.

'Oh, and do stop stroking your hair, its not going to go away you know.'

'Hair?' All thoughts of clothing vanished, like the jump-suit's sleeves.

'Yes Cadet, your hair. Hadn't you noticed it.'

'No, Ma'am. I had assumed I was still bald.'

'It's all spiky now, but it is a very pretty coppery red colour, it will grow quickly for the next few days.'

'Will I need to have it cut, Ma'am?'

'On a regular basis, but not yet. At the moment it is only quarter ofa fraction long.'

Nevamar swung itself out of bed. Suddenly it wanted to see itself in a full length mirror, but Lieutenant Sharlensya marched it out of the Central Mess Hall and deeper into the small town that was the Crown Officers' Residential Complex.

'Ma'am?'

'Yes Cadet.'

'Why was the Major so surprised to see me. I can't be the only sprite stil in the canopy?'

'Right, you were indeed the only sprite left in the Canopy.' She smiled that dazzling smile again.

'Although not any more. You haven't been a sprite for the past twenty four hours.'

Nevamar's head was spinning. No sprites, but who would do all the donkey work?

'Your next question is going to be why not? Well , it's all to do with budgets. No sprites, only subsidised Cadets.'

'It looks as if we have been assigned the same set of rooms in J Block we always get. Your accommodation will be on the same corridor as mine and your fellow Cadets. I am to be your mentor during training.'

'Other Cadets, Ma'am?' So much to take in. What was enprintable fabric. And the fact that it was already three fractions taller than yesterday was just weird. All its life Nevamar had been three units and five fractions tall, the same as every other sprite in the tree.

'Yes Cadet, there are four ofyou.'

After a few minutes a new question had popped into Nevamar's head.

'Permission to speak?'

'Granted.'

'Ma'am how many people are in the Winter Squad?'

'The Winter Squad consists of Forty Two personnel normally. The twenty officers from the Maintenance Regiment, fourteen specialists from other Regiments seconded to the Squad, four Ensigns in the final year of their apprenticeships and four Cadets. You have brought the numbers back up to four Cadets. Only one pair-bond with a child this year. Treslelant and Tarprycsya and their daughter Ferngarsya. She is a third year Day-Lighter Engineer now, it only seems like yesterday that she was one of my first Cadets. There are only nineteen regulars now,' she said with a slight sniff.

'You have brought us an extra Ensign. But don't tell Ensign Serynazsya that.'

The jollity was a little too forced. Nevamar could see that the stream of unnecessary additional information was the Lieutenant's way of fighting back the tears.

'When my old Branch Captain recycled, I was so upset. The other sprites did not seem to notice she wasn't there any more, but I did.' They stopped walking, 'now I think how proud she would be of me today. One day you will feel the same.'

'Thank you little one,' Lieutenant Sharlensya said. Then the strangest thing happened. Instead of punishing it for speaking out of turn, the Lieutenant picked Nevamar up and hugged it. This broke the ice, and they started chatting with none of the formality that protocol demanded.

'Right, home sweet home dear. One of the advantages of the Canopy being deserted is that you get a room to yourself from day one. If you were down in one of the academies in the Roots now, even the Pure-stock ones, you would be sharing a room with three other Cadets.'

'I'm used to sharing. I think I prefer it,' said Nevamar.

'That will soon change dear. You will get used to your privacy,' said the Lieutenant, who was almost laughing.

'So have you given some thought to your name little one?'

The Lieutenant smiled her lovely smile. 'Well, the basic rule is that all formal names are ten characters long. They have three elements. The first element starts with the first letter of your current IndesnCode and is four letters long. The second element starts with the second letter of the IndesnCode and is three letters long. This is your root-name. The third element is the suffix for gender. For anthers it is A-N-T, for styles it is S-Y-A and I don't know why it is usually pronounced "shah". Have you got that.'

'Why not S-T-Y?' asked Nevamar.

'Because it is not pretty enough dear,' Lieutenant Sharlensya smiled. 'Right, I was SL115/30, I chose Shar and Len and because I am a style, gained the S-Y-A sufix, making me Sharlensya 115/30. Do you understand?'

'I think so,' said Nevamar.

'Good. Any thoughts?' asked Lieutenant Sharlensya.

'Do you like Nevamar?' replied the youngster.

'Yes I do, Nevamarsya is so pretty.'

'Or Nevamarant if I'm an anther.'

'Indeed, or Nevamarant, but for the moment, just the root-name matters. You have until start of shift on Monesday morning to decide, when your name will be officially registered.'

'Is Ensign Serynazsya real y mad at me?'

'I see your sense of humour hasn't kicked in yet, little one,' she smiled. 'No Nevamar, the Ensign blames herself for being here. After all, we are all responsible for our own IndesnCard, nobody else. She lost hers, its her own fault she couldn't get a ticket for a shuttle. And anyway, nobody can tell one sprite from another, and you're Nevamar now, not a sprite. There is no way she could recognise you. If by any chance she did I would take a very dim view of her or any other officer in the Squad, who started picking on one of my Cadets.'

'Thank you, Ma'am,' said Nevamar.

'Right, your old sprite IndesnCard won't work any more so you will not be able to lock your door this weekend, not that we ever need to in the Winter Squad. You wil get a permanent officer's IndesnCard when you are registered.

'You have twenty minutes to get changed and report back to me at the stairwell. A dress uniform has been supplied. It will be a bit baggy at first, but the enprintable fabric will alter to fit smartly. So Cadet you are dismissed.'

The former sprite saluted and opened the door of the room and stepped into another shock.

From the moment it emerged from a sprite-pod, there was no such thing as private space for a sprite. They lived their lives crammed tightly together in dormitories where they slept in hammocks. This room seemed so huge and so empty. That it was exclusively Nevamar's seemed so strange. 'Nevamar's Room.' it said to itself. Yes that did have a pleasant ring to it. A room to itself, and a name to go with it. It looked around this amazing room again, still not quite believing it would not have to share. In the corner was what looked like a very comfortable bed. To its leftwas a cupboard and a chest of draws. The cupboard had a full length mirror on one of the doors. At the foot of the bed was something Nevamar thought was called a dressing table, with another mirror on it.

Nevamar's own personal work station sat on a desk, a brand new wristlink and comlink sat next to it. These devices would keep Nevamar plugged into the Tree's data-network. All officers were issued with basic units when they first sprouted. As soon as they could afford it, most upgraded to better models. For now, it was a sign that Nevamar was going up in the world.

Most miraculously of all an en suite shower-room, a toilet a wash basin and fluffy towels. Nevamar knew that of icers had a better life than sprites, but this basic room was a level of luxury it had never dreamt of.

Nevamar shivered slightly even though the room was warm. It knew that deep down in the Roots its former colleagues were far from warm. They would already be locked in the icy grip of the Storage Facility, metabolism slowed to a crawl and mental activity virtually non-existent. They had been consigned to this long sleep without having a chance to try for the better things Nevamar was now experiencing. That thought made the freshly minted Cadet very angry. JE375/28 and a few other sprites on the twig were on a par with Nevamar. Repeat that through the branch and the Spirit of the Tree itself only knew how much potential was being wasted. All because of some silly idea of social superiority held by her former Branch Captain.

Nevamar was sure that what Captain Samnundsya and her cronies were doing was both illegal and immoral but it had no idea what to do about the situation. So many big thoughts and new ideas it did not understand running through its head. So many irritating gaps as well. Half ideas looking for their other halves. Nevamar could hardly wait for training and its education to start. The joys of finding all those missing half ideas.

All that was in the future, Nevamar's first concern was getting ready for the Memorial Service. It slid open the cupboard door and found it contained only a formal Dress Uniform which had lots of braiding and shiny buttons that Nevamar was certain of icers did not normally wear. It quickly changed out of its old sprite uniform, which it dropped into the laundry shoot. Sadly the new uniform did not fit at all. For starters the waistband on the trousers was far too large. Nevamar tried to find a way to tighten it, but to no avail.

Then it had a brainwave, perhaps the belt on the jacket would help hold the trousers up. It crossed the left hand side of the jacket across its middle and buttoned it to the inside of the right hand side, which it then wrapped over its middle and attached it to the row of four buttons visible on that side, and it had the "Y" shaped lapels. Then it fastened the belt the best it could. The damn thing was far too baggy and didn't help with the trousers in the slightest.

'It's made from enprintable fabric, let the mirror scan you thoroughly and it wil be adjusted to fit youproperly,' said a voice that shocked Nevamar who visibly jumped. Just like Nevamar, the newcomer had no rank designation on its lapel, so it had to be one of Nevamar's fellow Cadets.

'Oh sorry, I didn't mean to startle you, I'm Cadet Natalicsya 199/20 by the way. You must be the sprout. Have you chosen a name yet?'

The newcomer was at least half a height unit taller than Nevamar and was obviously a stage or two further along the dif erentiation process.

'Cadet Nevamar 331/29, pleased to meet you. What were you saying about the mirror scanning me?'

'Great green apples, you are new, aren't you. How long ago did you sprout?' asked the newcomer as she gently pushed Nevamar closer to the mirror. After a few seconds the dress uniform began to visibly change, fitting far better.

'About twenty four hours ago. It was fun. What's a sprout?' asked Nevamar.

'Newly sprouted Cadet, less than three days old.'

'Are you a sprout too?' asked Nevamar.

'No, I sprouted a week ago,' said Natalicsya. So, despite appearances not that far ahead of me, Nevamar thought, which pleased it a great deal. It would have pleased it even more if Nevamar had known the other Cadet had only found out yesterday how the enprinters worked.

'Real newcomer, not even seen my face yet,' said Nevamar. It really did have its own face. Well obviously it had always had eyes, nose and mouth et cetera, but it now had an unique face all of its own, nothing like the bland uniformity of a sprite's face. Its nose was quite narrow and long, but not unpleasantly so. Ears looked average, and did not stick out at all. Eyes, round and still quite large and deep emerald green. Mouth, pleasant, top teeth about right. The only problem was its chin seemed to have shrunken inwards and back, a slight overbite, but nothing to worry about. As the Lieutenant had said, it had coppery red hair with burnt orange highlights. Already Nevamar's IndesnCode was invisible beneath it. The rest of its body was still as straight and uninspiring as a sprite, lacking either the bulk of an anther or the gentle curves of a style. Give it time, hadn't the Major said it could take up to eight weeks.

The first long appraisal of what it looked like was interrupted by noises coming from within the cupboard.

'That will be the rest of your kit arriving,' said Natalicsya. 'All your work clothes, a weeks worth of clean undies and two leisure outfits are given to you when you first pass the test and become a Cadet. Anything else, like replacements and additions to your kit or extra leisure outfits for when you are of duty, you have to pay for yourself from your wages.'

'Wages?' asked Nevamar.

'Great green apples, you really did only sprout yesterday. You have got a lot to learn. Wages are what you get paid for the work you do. You're not a sprite any more, you have to earn your keep.'

Nevamar was coming to the conclusion that Natalicsya was a bit lacking in the tact department.

'These leisure outfits, what do they look like?' it asked.

'A bit dull, long on practicality and short on glamour. Definitely unisex.'

'Good, have you seen some of the things styles wear when they're off duty'.

'Yes, divine aren't they.' replied Natalicsya dreamily. Nevamar took another look at its new colleague.Dressed like a young style. wearing its golden hair in a very feminine fashion and Natalicsya's voice was a higher pitch, and not the squeaky higher pitch of a sprite, she definitely had a girl's voice. No doubt she was already fully female.

'Any idea which flavour you are going to end up as? I so wanted to be a member of the Sacred Sisterhood of the Style. Looks like that's the case.'

'Really, your going to be a Tree Nun.' How had she known that?

'No silly, a lay member. All styles belong to the Sisterhood, all anthers to the Order. They are called lay members. Only the really devout go and devote their lives to the Sisterhood or the Order.'

'Well, in that case I am hoping to be inducted into the Grand Order of the Anther. You are welcome to all that girly stuff.'

'I think you're going to be disappointed. There is something very stylish about you.'

An alarm on Natalicsya's wrist comlink sounded, before Nevamar had a chance to say anything. A similar looking device began to chime on Nevamar's workstation desk.

'That's us, we have to head of to this memorial. Hey, don't forget your comlink,' said Natalicsya. Both Cadets began giggling girlishly. Then remembering where they were going, stifling their laughter as they headed for the door.

T he memorial ceremony was a very sombre affair. The forty three strong Winter Squad barely filled a corner of the central parade ground. Hymns were sung, stories of the life of the recently deceased Captain Sannarlsya were told, and nice things were said about young Cadet Kalvromant. Nearly everyone wore the most formal of dress uniform with orange armbands, to show their respect.

Everyone except for Lieutenant Sharlensya, Major Keltonnant and two others Nevamar did not recognise, who as principle mourners wore ultra formal dress uniforms in the deepest of burnt orange. Nevamar still did not know what a family was, so was still at a loss of what the connection between these two officers and the dead Captain was.

'He was the late Captain's brother,' one of the Ensigns informed Nevamar, 'Lieutenant Sharlensya was her daughter. She is supposed to be real y nice, but you will find that out over the next few months. Its such a shame that this happened.'

More questions than answers. What on earth was a brother, did it have something to do with the Order, and why was being the daughter of the dead style dreadful?

'I know, you want to ask me what all that means, don't you? I will explain it later.'

A silence fell over the parade ground. With the Canopy all but deserted, when a mournful bell began ringing after the silence, it seemed to Nevamar that it filled the whole Tree.'

'Parade, dismissed!'

The ceremony was over, the various members of the Winter Squad would change into their working clothes and return to the jobs they had been doing that day.

Nevamar realised that it was Ensign Serynazsya it had been talking to, and despite what the Lieutenant had said, Nevamar decided it would be wise to keep its distance from that Ensign. Even if that did mean going to the library to look up all these strange new concepts all by itself.

CHAPTER SIX
ENSIGN SERYNAZSYA
178/20

Nevamar's ambitions sent ripples throughout the Tree. Ensign Serynazsya had no way of knowing the long term benefits she would receive from the last day of Summer. As far as she was concerned, her life at the moment was becoming more horrible by the minute.

The sprites had not been a problem, well most of the sprites. They had been ordered to sit down and stay quiet, and they had obeyed that order. Of course they had, they were sprites. Except that little rat of a sprite NM331/29 who had failed to turn up at the Shuttle Station for embarkation onto the shuttle down to the Roots. The Branch Captain was furious.

'You go back up and find it, and drag it down here by the time this shuttle is ready to leave,' ordered Captain Samnundsya.

'Yes, Ma'am, I will do that, Ma'am'.

'And I don't want to see your piggy little face until you have that runt. If you don't, I am going to deduct the replacement cost from your wages.'

'Yes, Ma'am.' Serynazsya saluted and left the room.

Why did she always have to make nasty comments about her appearance? Serynazsya couldn't help it that she had a large flat nose. It was not by choice that she was not the ideal of Pure-stock roots-born physical loveliness like many of the pure-stock she had met in her short life. At least she had a pleasant personality, but that counted for nothing with Captain Samnundsya.

Serynazsya had enough credits for an express trolley-cab to jet her all the way back up to the branch. The whole place was shut down and quiet. No sign of the missing sprite. No doubt, NM331/29 had managed to get down to the Crown all by itself, and was stowed in the hold of the shuttle already.

Much to her annoyance, the trolley-cab stopped for refuelling on the return trip. Health and safety rules forced Serynazsya to get out of the cab during the refuelling so she sat herself down on an uncomfortable bench at a tedious trolleybus station. The vehicle was almost ready to depart when the whole tree began to shake violently. The trolley-cab was delayed for an additional forty minutes. Her comfortable margin was shrinking by the second, so when she finally got back to the Shuttle Station, she was not at all surprised to find the shuttle her ticket was for sealing its hatches.

'What do you mean, you won't let me on board?' Ensign Serynazsya asked the burly deckhand who was barring her way.

'You haven't shown me your IndesnCard, so I can't check your ticket. You could be anyone,' replied the deckhand.

'But I am not, I am Ensign Serynazsya 178/20. Look there's my signature,' said Serynazsya as she pointed at the deckhand's paperwork. 'Two hours ago I boarded thirty nine sprites, and look this morning three batches of forty. You must recognise me,' she said as she slammed her finger down on the previous page.

'Nope, do you realise how many people we see in a day. That could be anyone's signature?' replied the deckhand.

'Look, here's my Indesn... Oh great green apples, where has that gone.' She scrambled through pockets, looked in her bag, checked her purse. No sign of her card.

'See what I mean, yer trying to pull a fast one.' Uncharitably, Serynazsya thought that the anther was as stupid as he was ugly.

'Trying to get on a better quality shuttle to the Roots than the one you are booked on. I didn't sprout yesterday, you know.'

Yes you were Serynazsya thought, you must have been. Or you really are that stupid. All shuttles are the same.

'No, honestly, I'm booked on this shuttle and I have lost my IndesnCard, I must've dropped it when the Tree shook.'

'Well, when you find it, the shuttle you are booked on will let you embark and you will be on your way.'

'This is the shuttle I am booked on. Go and check with my Branch Captain. She is in cabin 333D.'

'No. I have to seal this boat up, we are departing now.' He pressed a few buttons and the ramp began retracting. A klaxon sounded, and Ensign Serynazsya noticed that all the other shuttles were doing the same. Oh great, what was she going to do now?

'They have all had orders to depart immediately,' said a voice behind her. The old anther was smirking. How dare he. 'Couldn't help over hearing your chat. Looks like you are stuck up here for the Autumn and Winter with us Squaddies.'

He was wearing an Ensign's single silver leaf. That can't be right. He was a wiry anther with a shock of grey hair which meant he must be approaching his mid thirties, old enough to be her grandfather. There was no way she was the same rank as him.

'Yes, that's right girl, I've been busted down so many times, I stopped trying to get back up again. Tabbernant's the name. I'm the cook with the Winter Squad. Come with me, I had better let the Brass know about you.

Before the Spirit of the Tree Graft the tried to create female officers. At the same time the Root-stock tried to create male officers. All attempts failed, leaving as its legacy a minority of effeminate anthers and butch styles. After the Graft, each of the orginal plants had provided what the other needed, two genders which spread evenly through the Tree.

The Spirit of the Tree found he could further improve his soldiers by giveng them an additional dose of auxins and stem cells when they were eighteen months old. The method that previously activated styles in the Root-stock was recycled. It used creatures called Locks, which are similar to Keys but far more intricate. They can only grow to maturity if they find a host style. For nine weeks the host's body swells to accommodate the guest in her uterine chamber. Once the fully grown look emerges, it absorbs two pints of the chosen youngster's blood and replaces it with the vital cocktail. It then makes its way back to the waterways of the Tree, to produce the next generation of Keys and Locks.

During the nine weeks of the "pregnancy" the host style also receives a dose of the auxin cocktail the youngster will receive. As each Lock is unique, this creates an unbreakable bond between adult female and youngster, becoming mother and child.

When the twenty eight styles from the Root-stock who had survived the Graft became mothers, the Twenty Eight Families were created. The original styles became the Matriarchs of those families and met with the twenty eight surviving anther's from the Sapling to form the first High Council. Ever since the oldest female relative of a dead Matriarch inherits her title.

Where there really Cadets up here? Ensign Serynazsya looked at the three youngsters sitting in the main reception of the officers Mess. All looked slightly over awed by their surroundings. So small, with ill-fitting uniforms that appeared three sizes too large. Obviously nobody had told these recently sprouted kids how to use the fabric enprinters.

'Hi kids, what are you doing here?'

'We have just started Officer Training,' the one speaking sounded so proud, bless it. 'I'm Cadet Pemiseg 197/51.' It had thick curly brown hair and was already wearing a pair of glasses. It was unusual for a Cadet to develop sight defects when they first sprouted. Usually it took a few weeks for lifelong problems to appear.

'Has no-one told you how the enprinters work?'

'No, Ma'am. How do they work?' the three asked in unison.

'Gather round, I will explain it to you. The clothes you are wearing are made from something called enprintable fabric. The cloth is made from millions and millions of little bubbles that are held together by electromagnetic forces.'

'Cool!' Pemiseg was obviously a bit of a tech-head.

'When a current is passed through the fabric, a current so small you can't even feel it, the bubbles revert to their default size and shape. If you pass another current through it, this one pulsing to a pre-set pattern, the bubbles will form into a new size and shape, so you can change what you are wearing instantly.'

'Ensign Ralkzotsya's clothes used to change when she was looking at herself in the mirror. She used to wear such pretty dresses on her days off,' said one of the Cadets, who had tried to fold and pin its uniform into a better fit.

'That's right, you have to be standing in front of the mirrored surface of a Fabric Enprinter. Data is transferred to and from the cloth by a laser and controlled by the image in the reflection.'

Serynazsya looked at the Cadet who had talked about dresses, obviously it was going to be a style, already it had long hair tied into a ponytail. 'What's your name, by the way, or haven't you chosen one yet?'

'I'm Cadet Natalicsya 199/80. I'm from the Roots, like yourself, Ma'am.'

'Natalicsya, that's such a pretty name. Although you are a little young to be so certain about your gender?'

'Thank you, Ma'am, but I'm a week older than those two, Ma'am. I know I'm a style.'

'Oh, right. However, I'm only an Ensign, you don't call me Ma'am. That is for older style officers. Subalterns and up.' Ensign Serynazsya felt a million years old when she was incorrectly called Ma'am by these little ones.

She got them all to stand in front of the mirror of a public enprinter so that their uniforms fitted them properly. They still looked wrong on kids that small, but Ensign Serynazsya knew from experience, they would not stay that small for long.

'Please Ensign Serynazsya. How do I get this to change into a skirt?' asked Natalicsya

'You just swipe your IndesnCard against the enprinter, select the outfit from your wardrobe software, and let the machine do all the rest.' There was a voluble buzz as Natalicsya's clothing changed and started looking even more like a style than it had previously.

'What if you need a coat, and you haven't got one with you?' the little one asked. 'I'm Cadet Althall, by the way.'

'You have to be wearing the same amount of fabric in your current outfit as the one you want to change into. You can borrow enough enprintable fabric to make the coat, but you have to return it at the end of the day.

'And if you are wearing something hot and heavy, then want to change into something lighter?' asked Althall.

'Then you dump it into a laundry shoot. Your ration of fabric will be returned to your quarters. Any excess will be returned to whoever you borrowed it from. When you get home at night, you drop the clothes you are wearing into the basket by your wardrobe and the clothes get recycled. Your wardrobe software keeps the patterns of all the clothes you own and your fabric ration. The following morning you get clean brand new clothes made to the pattern you need for the day.' Great green apples this was tiring. Ensign Serynazsya knew she would never be a teacher.

'And when I have enough money to buy new clothes, do I actually buy more enprintable fabric or just the pattern to make them?'

'That is a very good question Cadet Natalicsya. When you get to visit clothes shops, you see two prices quoted. One is for pattern and fabric, the other is for pattern only.'

At that point, much to Ensign Serynazsya's relief, Captain Treslelant came to take the Cadets off her hands.

'You handled that very well Ensign. I have come to take these kids back to their accommodation. My daughter Fernee, sorry Ensign Ferngarsya will take you to see the Brigadier.'

'Yes dad, er sorry, yes, Sir' said the plump apprentice, who made an attempt at a salute. 'See you later dad.'

In her new quarters later that evening, Serynazsya could not believe that everyone was being so nice to her, even though she had been so dreadfully inefficient. A million miles away from the way Captain Samnundsya treated her. Even the Brigadier who should have been angry about the inconvenience she must be causing him and the Winter Squad had been pleasant.

It was just that she would be spending another six months away from the bright lights and big city atmosphere of the Roots. No matter how nice the people were, it was still another six months in this hick back-water. She would kill that little runt NM331/29 if ever she saw it again.

Builders, decorators, plumbers and assorted trades. Three sets of overalls had been supplied when her replacement clothing had arrived. I am going to be spending all Autumn and Winter covered in dust and paint she thought. Serynazsya hated getting dirty, or being unhygienically grubby, complete with dirty fingernails. She looked at herself for a few minutes. At least her new Dress Uniform would be pin and paper perfect tomorrow at the memorial service.

PART TWO
THE CADET
(JUNIOR GRADE)

CHAPTER SEVEN
CADET NEVAMAR 331/29

In the third week of the tenth month, or 1-C-10, would celebrated with cards, presents and registration day parties by Nevamar. Today it was simply Cadet Nevamar 331/29's first working day as an Officer Cadet.

'So that concludes this morning's roll-call, and it is so nice to see you all so bright eyed and bushy tailed,' said the Brigadier. It was 0730 in the over lit windowless and dreary Conference Room #5 and the Brigadier's humour flew over the heads of most of the Winter Squad. Those who had the weekend off were already missing their beds. Those who had been working all night on a burst pipe, in branch BH24, were barely awake.

Ensign Serynazsya was already sleeping in her seat. All except Nevamar, who was looking forward to a morning at work and an afternoon in the classroom.

'Well, one of you at least. Oh to be freshly sprouted.'

Nevamar knew the Brigadier was looking at it, so jumped to attention and saluted.

'At ease Cadet, you will soon be as reluctant to return to work as the rest of us.'

'Sir? Yes, Sir,' it replied.

'So, now you are no longer a sprite, what name have you chosen for yourself.' The Brigadier had his comlink tablet in hand, awaiting Nevamar's decision.

'Nevamar, Sir.'

'Spell the first element?'

'N. E. V. A.'

'And the second.'

'M. A. R.'

'Good, thank you Cadet Nevamar 331/29. It appears that there is not, nor has there ever been, an Officer with that Root-name. So whether you be style or anther, Nevamar it is.'

There was a racket as the Squad all stood up.

'Winter Squad. Attention. Winter Squad, by the left. Dismissed.' Everybody saluted then filed out of Conference Room 5 and headed to Bernie's for breakfast.

As sure as night follows day, faults hidden throughout the Spring and Summer, raised their ugly or raised their ugly heads as soon as the Winter Squad begins its work. They interrupted the smooth transition from one season to another. These additional tasks were the jobs that had given Brigadier Myghcomant his grey hair. Not because they were difficult, but because they swallowed the limited resources of the Squad.

Not that budget debates and funding applications bothered Nevamar and its fellow Cadets. They just had to do the jobs their superiors told them to do. Somethings had not changed.

'Right Class. This morning you will be carrying out an unpleasant job up in branch CB38,' said Lieutenant Sharlensya as she briefed her class after morning roll call. 'The food waste disposal unit at CB38 2NA has been malfunctioning all Summer, we have to get it clean before the plumbers can get it fixed.'

The four youngsters groaned.

'It's no use complaining about it class, this is exactly the sort of job you will be doing in the mornings for the next few weeks, and in the afternoons, you will be back here having your school lessons.'

There was another groan from all the class except Nevamar. Oh joy it thought, proper lessons instead of the odd stolen minutes when Captain Samnundsya was not about.

'**M**athematics this afternoon,' said Althall. 'But I can already count to hundred and do adding and taking away. What more do I need?'

'There is more to Maths than just counting Althall.' The shocked Cadet had no idea that the Lieutenant was standing behind him, having changed into similar protective gear as the Cadets.'

'There is Geometry, Algebra, Trigonometry and all sorts of wonderful arithmetical arts to master. You could spend your whole lifetime studying it.'

'Yes, Ma'am.'

'Good, now lets work shall we, otherwise you might never know.'

It was a pleasant surprise to see their mentor pitching in with them throughout the morning. Lieutenant Sharlensya would go wherever her class went. Technically supervising, practically being an extra pair of hands.

Over the weekend Nevamar had got to know its new colleagues and was sure it had a handle on its three classmates. It was not what they said but how they acted that filled in the bigger picture. So despite the fact they were all wearing masks, gloves and protective clothing, that should have made it impossible to tell them apart, Nevamar was certain it knew who was who.

'So where are you from Natalicsya?' asked Althall during the mid morning break, with a steaming hot mug of Instaht in his hand. 'You look like your from the Roots but you are officially registered as being from the Trunk.'

'I'm from the Roots originally.'

'Were you grown specifically for Officer Training?' asked Nevamar.

'No, I emerged from a working sprite that used to clean tables in restaurants, all over the Roots.'

'But ordinary Root sprites don't get tested,' said the confused Althall.

'I was not in the Roots when I sprouted. I was in the Trunk,' said Natalicsya, but Althall looked as confused as ever. 'This year I was working as an aide to a waitress on board The Gleaming Prospect, that's one of the shuttles in dry dock for the winter,' Natalicsya continued her explanation, and she started smiling. 'Ensign Ralkzotsya, the waitress, was a great boss. She used to wear a pretty uniform with white collar and cuffs and a frilly cap and apron in work, it looked so cool. She had some lovely dresses off duty as well.'

'What has that got to do with the price of protein? asked Pemiseg. It was still showing no signs of being anther or style and its behaviour fluctuated between the genders.

'Just adding some detail. Anyway, instead of the expected reassignment at the end of Summer, I got tested, and I sprouted.'

'Even in the Trunk, the Root officers make sure no ordinary Root sprites get tested,' said Althall.

'That is right. However, the First Mate who normally does the tests was on sick leave, so the Captain administered them. He included all the sprites aboard, even the three ordinary Roots sprites. Which is why there was the delay in me starting my Officer Training. In the end, only the Winter Squad would have me.'

'Because you are an officer from the Roots who should not be an officer,' said Pemiseg. 'You didn't come from their precious officers only sprite-pod. Somebody reckoned that you are not good enough to go into one of their snotty nosed academies down there, so you ended up being shunted further and further up the Tree. Now you are as far up as you can go.'

'Was I talking to you?' said Natalicsya. They just did not get on. Natalicsya saw the other Cadet as being to clever by half, and Pemiseg thought Natalicsya was far too interested in her appearance.

'No, but I thought I would say it anyway. Just adding some detail.' They exchanged poisonous smiles as they pulled their respirator masks back on.

Nevamar ate its lunch quickly and alone. It was so excited, the thought of going to school made it feel happy inside.

It had been surprised to learn that school time had a different styleof uniform. In a standard officer Corps uniform, the four Cadets had felt so grown-up. In their school uniforms they felt like sprites again.

'Don't you ever knock?' complained Nevamar.

'Well, what do you think?' asked Natalicsya, who had made it known how much she hated the school uniform. She had managed to stick to the letter of the uniform's definition, but had played fast and loose with the spirit.

'I can't see the Lieutenant letting you wear that!' said Nevamar.

'Nothing wrong with this, the rules did say I could wear a skirt.' Natalicsya replied.

'Yes, but I don't see you wearing one.'

'Oh. Ha. Ha!'

'All right, one that extends down a bit more than that, it is far too short,' said Nevamar.

'Still denying your destiny I see.' Quickly changing the subject Natalicsya tapped a few buttons on the side of Nevamar's wardrobe and the trousers Nevamar was wearing reformed itself into a prim pleated skirt.

'Stop that, I am not going to be a style. How many times do I have to say it.'

'Keep telling yourself that love, until you wake up one morning with breasts and long hair. I'm off to have lunch'

'Well it shouldn't take you too long. You starve yourself.'

With that her friend was gone and Nevamar was left looking at herself in the mirror. Actually I don't look too bad as a girl. She felt a cold shiver instantly forgeting the thought and then reset its uniform back to one for a boy.

There was no dedicated Cadet Academy up in the Canopy. Instead Lieutenant Sharlensya had requisitioned a small meetings room just off the foyer of the Central Mess Hall to be her classroom. The large oval table and twelve chairs surrounding it, that usually sat in the middle of the room, had been replaced by four desks for the Cadets facing a larger desk that Lieutenant Sharlensya was sitting at. The flip-chart easel was still there, but the interactive white board on the wall, that was seldom used during the Summer, took pride of place. Here I go again, she thought, another group of Cadets will gain a basic education from me, learning the skills that will allow them to use the Career Training System. Along the back wall stood a row of well worn workstations that the Cadets would eventually graduate to when they became Ensigns.

'Enter,' said Lieutenant Sharlensya. Her thoughts interrupted by a knock on the door. She glanced at the clock on the wall, then back to the door, not surprised to see young Nevamar who had arrived five minutes early. 'My, you're enthusiastic?' said the Lieutenant.

'Yes, Ma'am, very enthusiastic, my Branch Captain did her best to discourage learning, I'm making up for lost time.'

'Well, that doesn't surprise me.'

'Permission to ask a question, Ma'am.'

'You want to know what's so damn special about being Pure-stock, don't you?'

With that, the rest of the class barged into the room.

'Next time, you will line up outside the classroom,' said an annoyed Lieutenant Sharlensya, 'and wait until you have permission to enter. Do I make myself clear.'

'Yes, Ma'am' they chorused.

What was that girl wearing, the Lieutenant's disapproving eyes registered what Cadet Natalicsya was passing off as her uniform.

'And Cadet Natalicsya 199/20, that skirt is outside the Dress Code for the day. It is far too short for anyone your age, change it at once.'

'But, Ma'am, you're still wearing the uniform U3,' Natalicsya chipped in.

'Less of the lip Cadet,' said the Lieutenant.

Nevamar could feel the older style's embarrassment and its friend's defiance, almost like smell and a bit like taste. It was odd either way.

'Over here, young lady,' the Lieutenant ordered Natalicsya to stand next to her in front of a long mirror attatched to the wall by her desk. 'I will be using this to maintain the Dress Code, which will be school uniform until you get your commission,' she said as her own and the girl's clothes, rearranged themselves into something more formal by the emprinter. 'After that, and when the day's Dress Code permits, then you can wear what I was wearing. Not now. Do I make myself clear.'

'Yes, Ma'am,' replied Natalicsya.

'Class stand by your desks,' the Lieutenant ordered.

The rest of the class jumped up immediately, and Natalicsya returned to her desk.

'And its not as if Natalicsya had legs worth looking at,' added Pemiseg, a very masculine comment from the undifferentiated youngster, which earned it a poke. 'Ow!' it responded in a very feminine manner.

'That will do class. Stand by your desks!' Once she was sure she had her class' attention she took the register.

'Welcome to the Class of Autumn 183. You may be seated.'

There was a scraping of chairs as the four youngsters sat down.

'Right, before we begin exploring the Arithmetical Arts, very brief History lesson.' Keep it short, keep it simple, Lieutenant Sharlensya thought to herself. Father Earth I hate winging it. Why did she agree to this.

'After the Graft, the Tree grew a new set of sprite-pods, as so many had been lost. These new sprite-pods naturally contained material from both parts of the newly formed composite entity. It helped to unite the population whilst preserving what was best of both originals.

'However, two sprite pods, one from the Sapling, one from the Root-stock survived. Forty years after the Graft, the Roots' Management Group decided that only sprites especially produced from selected sprite-pods would become officers. Other parts of the Tree continued to promote the brightest and the best, but the Roots did not want to rely on anything so random. They chose to use these two ancient sprite-pods as two of their four officer-only pods. Some of the styles who emerge from Sprite-pod S and anthers who emerge from Sprite-pod D think this makes them somehow special. It does not, but nothing can crush that illusion of Pure-stock superiority.'

There was a hand up. Great green apples, I hope it is the only question, Lieutenant Sharlensya thought.

'Cadet Nevamar.'

'Ma'am, doesn't that mean that all Pure-stock styles should be identical?'

'That is the funny thing, there must have been some sort of contamination, as anyone who emerges from Sprite-pod S or Sprite-pod D is as individual as anyone who emerges from any of the other sprite-pods. So you see, they are not even truly "Pure-stock".'

Nobody else had a question. Good, they seem satisfied, time to move on. Lieutenant Sharlensya believed in well prepared lessons. The well prepared lesson today was Mathematics.

'We will be studying History in more detail later. Right now onto the Arithmetical Arts.'

The day ended quietly with Nevamar reading a book in Room E-10-S, the small and comfortably furnished lounge for the exclusive use of Cadets and Ensigns. It had a selection of books, music and games. There was a knock on the door. On seeing Lieutenant Sharlensya walk through the entrance, Nevamar instantly sprung to attention.

'As you were Nevamar, we are both off duty now, and its too late in the evening to be bothering with formalities anyway.' As Nevamar sat back down on the sofa, Sharlensya sat in a comfy chair near to it. 'I thought I saw a light on in here.'

'I like this place, Ma'am. Its special,' said Nevamar.

'So you stuck with Nevamar then?'

'Yes, Ma'am.'

'As I said, it's late, and you know my name is Sharlensya.'

'But it doesn't sound right, Ma'am, er Sharlensya. I've always only ever responded Ma'am or Sir. I've never had to pay attention to an officer's name.'

'I know dear,' said Sharlensya.

Nevamar felt the surprise in the mentor as it realised the level of familiarity she adopted.

'And that is something you will never hear me calling you when we are on duty,' said Sharlensya.

'No, Ma'am, downtime is something I've never experienced before.'

'Yes, it's still a new concept for you, one you will soon get used to. Remember dear, during downtime, if neither you nor anyone you are talking to are still in uniform then the use of rank is inappropriate. Its names only. Why do you think we bother dreaming them up in the first place?'

'But even in downtime, just using a name seems so disrespectful to anyone who is older than me.'

'Which is why you use the full Formal Name.'

'Formal Name mam... er, Sharlensya?'

'Yes my dear, the full formal name that they are registered as. Your Formal Name is currently your Root-name Nevamar. Upon differentiation it will become Nevamarsya.'

'Or Nevamarant.'

'Indeed. However, you will also gain an Informal Name. My friends and family call me Sharlee in informal situations, old Bernie insists on calling me Shaz. I would take great exception to you, or anyone else, calling me Sharlee or even Shaz without my permission.'

That made sense, but it would still take getting used to. Nevamar suddenly felt tongue tied.

'Yes, erm, Sharlensya, I stuck with my first choice. My only choice really, nothing else seemed to fit.'

There, done it twice now, the next time would be even easier thought Nevamar.

'You know that your old designation code, NM331, will eventually be reassigned to a new sprite.'

'Yes, maybe as soon as next year. It will be an odd experience to meet NM331/30.' Nevamar shuddered. 'I hope it doesn't get the sort of Commanding Officer I had, and that if it is good enough, it won't have to jump through hoops, as I did, to become an officer.'

'Look Nevamar, I know you have an issue with your former Branch Captain, but don't worry, your not alone. I had a miserable time as a sprite as well.'

'You were a sprite, I thought Pure-stocks were activated straight away. Differentiation from day one.'

'No, even we have to wait a year before we can be activated. During that year we get the sort of education that you are enjoying now. But I was different, I was not a perfectly formed sprite, despite the fact that my mind had become fully activated, my body didn't start sprouting and there was no apparent differentiation. The officers down there in the nursery didn't bother to check for problems, they just assumed I was a dud, that I would only ever be a sprite, and worse of all, so did I. At the start of my second year, I was dumped out of the pampered nursery and into the real world as a working sprite. So I saw with an officer's eyes in a sprite's body how badly treated sprites could be. I found myself working for Major Keltonnant, packing his stuff ready for a tour of duty up here. He could see I was not a normal sprite, so I was tested again and my problem intrigued him. He was working on the research into officer Differentiation that is now required reading in Medical School. Finding a cure for my problem fitted his research so well, he brought me up to the Canopy that Winter. This was back before the last budget cut, when the Squad could afford to bring sprites with us. Finally in the last week of that tour, we found out what had been preventing me from sprouting and I became what you see today. Thank the Tree for my Uncle Kelly.

'Well, on my return to the Roots, being a Pure-stock Cadet, I was sucked back into the Pure-stock system. I found myself attending one of their elite academies, but I had seen life in the Tree from a different perspective. I could not swallow the garbage they tried to drum into me. They tried to break me, making my life miserable. So I rebelled and ran away. The Major's sister found me wandering the streets and took me in. She saw how unhappy I was, so arranged for me to be transferred to a different academy. Then she adopted me, became my mother. I owe her a debt I can never repay. As her child, I was expected to travel up to the Canopy with her during her tours of duty with the Winter Squad. After training as a mentor, I joined the Squad when they started training Cadets. I have been here every Winter since then.'

'You've never told anyone this, have you. Only Major Keltonnant and I know.' Nevamar could see that Sharlensya was visibly shaken by this sudden unexpected openness, and was close to tears. Instinctively it got up and hugged the older style, who was still deep in grief for her mother. Lieutenant Sharlensya would never normally have allowed this much familiarity with one of her Cadets. Once Nevamar sat back down in its chair, instead of chastising it, Sharlensya continued her story, a life long bond having been forged between them.

'Yes, you and the Major are now the only members of the Winter Squad who know my story. The silly bitches down in the Roots know, because I was able to level a complaint against them once I was commissioned. The Enquirers investigated and the Nursery officers were found guilty of negligence and demoted. They were never allowed to have influence over the young ever again. Don't know what they are doing now, don't particularly care much either. Small revenge, but better than none at all. The important thing is that once you gain your commission, you will be able to issue a complaint, just as I did. Anyone can see what Captain Samnundsya was doing was wrong. The Enquirers will have to investigate. It will go before a Court Marshall. Given her record, old Samnundsya will be bounced back down the rank structure. She will probably end up like Bernie, an Ensign until she retires. With a bit of luck your old branch will have a decent Captain running it after that.'

So, thought Nevamar, once I get my commission, things will improve not just for me, but for everyone I used to work with. They, and their successors, will not have to put up with the rubbish I did. It was something to work towards. Nevamar had found itself a goal.

'Sharlensya, thank you.'

'Good night, dear.' The older style was heading for the door. 'Remember dear, another busy day tomorrow, don't stay up too late.'

'Goodnight mam,' Nevamar didn't know where that had come from and hoped the Lieutenant had not heard it. Or if she had, she hoped that it had sounded enough like "Ma'am" not to cause too much embarrassment. Nevamar fervently hoped that when it was adopted into one of the families, and had a "Mother" assigned to it, that that "Mother" would be someone like Lieutenant Sharlensya.

CHAPTER EIGHT

PHOTOGRAPHIC MEMORY

Captain Sannarlsya Fangkart 106/73 owned a small apartment in CORC, unlike her daughter and brother who made do with accommodation rented for them by the Maintenance Regiment. She had been in the process of taking this apartment out of mothballs when she responded to an apparently routine call-out, which turned out to be farfrom routine, and ultimately led to her death.

Nobody had been to the apartment for three weeks, and Major Keltonnant found everything exactly as it had been that tragic day. He had come to sort through his sister's things, a job more exhausting than he had ever imagined. He sat himself down in one of Sannarlsya's favourite armchairs, which had a photograph album lying on a table by its side. His sister had loved photography and this album contained his sister's favourite photographs, chronicling her life with the artistry of shutter and lens.

Two of the pages were stuck together. Keltonnant knew exactly why this was but something drove him to separate them. Sure enough, there it was, a photograph of a considerably younger Keltonnant, recently qualified and recently promoted. He had more hair in this image than he could remember, and still clean shaven, the beard had come later. He was laughing and so was the attractive young style in the photo with him. Luscious long black curls cascading over her shoulders, wearing a beautiful blue and purple dress. They made a handsome couple, it looked as if they were having the best day of their lives. Sadly Keltonnant knew this photograph had been taken on the worse day of his life. The day he lost his beloved Kanonypsya.

The weather then had been perfect for the last week of the Summer. Mother Sun was still high enough in the sky to make it pleasantly warm. The circulation of air in the Crown produced pleasant breezes from the Lake at the top of the Central Channels. Off duty anthers and styles, in brightly coloured swimming costumes, were having a happy time on its beach, enjoying the last few hours of daylight. Keltonnant had reason to celebrate. He had recently qualified as a doctor and received a promotion to Commander. He was also deeply in love. The object of his desire was Kanonypsya 049/05 Rust, a Paramedic Captain and a wonderful style. As their relationship had blossomed from friendship to love, they had given each other romantic names only they used. He called her Konny, she called him Kelts.

Walking along the promenade she looked stunning in an evening dress that showed off all her curves beautifully. They were heading to the best restaurant in the Crown.

Tonight he would ask her to pair-bond with him. Keltonnant had a ring box in his tunic pocket. The ring would seal the deal.

'Let's go that way darling, its prettier,' she said. They had left the main path to follow a smaller path enclosed in a tunnel of climbing rose bushes.

'If you like.' Keltonnant had spotted a procession of eight Tree Nuns. Four of them betrayed no emotions whilst the other four all looked desperately unhapppy. 'Oh dear, how many girls are going to have their lives ruined today?' he asked.

'Kelts, it is called answering the Supreme Calling. We have no choice. If the voice says go, you go, or they will come and fetch you.'

He could see that the previously happy styles on the beach were crying as one of them, young Annaprisya wasn't it, pulled a plain green dress the Tree Nuns had given her, over her bright blue and purple bikini. She had stopped crying and was snivelling loudly as she took her place in the procession. Two of the Tree Nuns placed a hooded cape around her. The enprintable fabric rapidly reset itself to wimple and veil. Whether she liked or not, Annaprysya was now one of the Tree Nuns.

'Come on my love, chop chop, we'll miss our booking,' said Kanonypsya.

If you are so concerned, why the detour, no make that detours dear, he thought. You have had us chopping and changing like crazy.

Despite another random change in direction, the Tree Nuns were heading towards them. Keltonnant wondered why they had stopped there blocking their route? No I don't have to ask, do I. They have come to take my beloved Konny. It would explain the distracted way she had been acting for the past few days.

'Kanonypsya of the family Rust,' said the most senior of the Tree nuns.

'No, not today, not ever,' said Kanonypsya under her breath.

'You have been called to enter the House of Clergy. A call you cannot refuse to answer.'

'There must be some mistake, Me, a Tree Nun?' said Kanonypsya with mock surprise. 'I don't think so.'

'The Spirit of the Tree does not make mistakes.'

'Are you certain. This is not the way it used to be?'

'It is the way the Spirit of the Tree wants it to be now.' The senior Tree Nun had an answer for everything.

'My voice is too poor for the Choir.'

'There are many tasks that one of the Spirit of the Tree's chosen Handmaidens can carry out serving the Tree.'

'I don't want to be a bloody Tree Nun. I serve the Tree as a paramedic and I love my job. Add to that my beloved Kelts, he is going to propose to me. I will be happy with him. Stuff your House of Clergy.'

'You have no choice in the matter. You have been hearing the inner voice for a month, but you have chosen to ignore it. You must have known your name was on my list of the recalcitrant and I, the Mistress of Novices, was looking for you. Now you must accompany me to our Convent, where you will begin your new life.'

'You bitter twisted old witch,' Keltonnant could not control his anger. 'You know that you are despised by every style in the Tree, even your fellow Tree Nuns, why don't you make do with the styles who want to join your Convent. The Order only takes dedicated anthers who want to be Tree Monks. Why go around destroying the lives of those who don't have that dedication?' Keltonnant had never been so angry.

'Do not be angry with our Sisterhood, anther. We are following our Holy Book, just as your Anther Order follows its sacred text. Be angry with this recalcitrant one for giving you false hope. She knew we would be coming for her sooner rather than later.'

'The Spirit of the Tree gives us free will when it raises us from sprites.' Kanonypsya spat that out with venom. 'You should respect that free will. I do not want to enter the convent, I have never wanted to be a Sister, my chosen life is out here in the real World!'

'If you honestly thought that, why do you wear blue and purple, the traditional colours of the aspirant to the Sisterhood?'

As with all clothing in the tree Kanonypsya's beautiful blue and purple evening dress was made from enprintable fabric. The mirrored pommel on the end of the staff the old Tree Nun was carrying, contained a fabric enprinter which triggered a change in Kanonypsya's outward appearance. Like Annaprisya on the beach earlier, she was now wearing a long green dress a great deal plainer and a lot less flattering than her previous outfit.

'Kelts, I'm sorry, I'm so very sorry.' was the last thing he heard her say, as beaten and bowed, she too took her place in the procession. One Tree Nun wiped away the make-up whilst another gave her a plain white hooded cape, that reset to complete the transformation. If it were not for her face, now ringed by a wimple, he would not have known it was Kanonypsya. She was indistinguishable from the other members of the styles' religious order.

'Your life is in the House of Clergy. When you have learnt the lessons we will teach you, you will repent your arrogance and gladly take the vows you have been denying you must take.' The Mistress of Novices turned to the crowd that had gathered. 'Let this be a lesson to all you young styles out there. If your inner voice calls you, you must answer immediately. Set down whatever you are doing, you have to fulfil a greater duty.'

Joining in with the song of the Tree Nuns, Kanonypsya's voice blended into the harmony. The singing, that resonated with the Song of the Tree itself, powered the Sisterhood's ability to travel anywhere in the Tree. The song carried the procession back to its Convent, fading away like mist in the morning, leaving only the last echo of their song. He knew he would never see her again. Suddenly the pleasant evening was bitterly cold.

For Major Keltonnant that day twenty years earlier had been a a turning point. When his sister had told him the Winter Squad's doctor was retiring, he had applied for the post. He devoted his life to medicine, whether in general practice in the Roots or in isolation in the Canopy.

He slammed the album shut. Why had he insisted on separating those pages, he knew that this would be the result. Perhaps he should destroy the picture. No, it was not his to destroy, it was part of his sister's estate, and would eventually become Sharlensya's property. However, before he could do anything, he heard the sound of people entering the apartment. Sure enough, his niece and young Nevamar were now standing in front of him.

'Afternoon Uncle,' his niece said, 'young Nevamar here has come to help us pack.'

'Afternoon Sharlee, Nevamar, good of you to finally turn up,' said Keltonnant rather grumpily.

'Well, we didn't want to disturb your nap,' Sharlensya said with a voice dripping with mock concern. 'You older people need your rest.'

Sharlensya could see she had said the wrong thing, her uncle looked so sad.

'I think I should leave, this is obviously a private family moment,' said Nevamar as it backed towards the door.

Keltonnant marvelled that one so young could be so tactful, and that Nevamar always knew the right thing to say and when to say it.

'Thank you Nevamar, but don't go too far, we will still need your help.'

'I'm sorry Uncle. This can't be easy for you.'

'Nor for you dear, nor for you. This was after all your childhood home in the Canopy. You must have many happy memories of this place.'

'Yes Uncle. I do.'

'Then I won't spoil that.' He smiled. 'Right, to business,' and the awkward moment passed. 'I will leave this album with you. It might be very educational.'

'No doubt, Mam loved her cameras. But as you said, we have so much to do now.' She walked into the adjoining room where Nevamar was sitting reading a book. 'Right dear, we are ready now.'

'OK Sharlensya, where do we start.'

CHAPTER NINE
A LAND OF
MILK AND HONEY

'You are officially five weeks old Cadet Nevamar, not five years old,' said Ensign Serynazsya.

'But what about the time I was a sprite, that was part of my life?' It annoyed Nevamar, how anyone could disregard their time as a sprite.

'Do the avians regard the time they spent in an egg as part of their lives?' Ensign Serynazsya had asked Nevamar.

'How should I know, they're just creatures,' replied Nevamar.

'Believe me they don't, and neither should you.'

'I was never an egg.'

'When you were a sprite you were in an egg.'

'It was a funny shaped egg then.'

'Look Nevamar, you're a person now,' Ensign Serynazsya continued, 'you will forget your past. It doesn't matter because you are growing into your real life.'

'If I do that, I forget JE375/28 and all the others who should be here now with me. Oh why can't I remember them?'

'Precisely because they're still sprites you're not. You are an officer now. Forget your past and worry about your future.'

Serynazsya was still making threats against Sprite NM331/29, but Nevamar had stopped trying to avoid the girl. It was becoming too suspicious and eventually Serynazsya would demand an explanation. Nevamar feared it had just given the game away, so watched with relief as the Ensign finished hoovering the waiting room and went to clean another part of the Medical Centre. It knew now the girl only remembered the IndesnCodes of one sprite in the old branch, NM331/29.

N evamar was now a full height unit taller than it had been a month earlier. Its red hair was a mass of uncontrollable curls that it could not drag a comb through. It was regularly cut according to the regulations for an anther.

To Nevamar's dismay the way it wore its hair was the only thing masculine about its new body. Everything else was completely neuter.

Althallant had completely differentiated in week two of training. Pemisegant, who until a few days ago had been as gender-less as Nevamar, was now very definitely an anther. This was much to the surprise of everyone, not least of all the newly minted Pemisegant. Everyone was so certain he was a she, he had started wearing style clothes all the time. In the middle of class his voice had broken, and he had run back to his quarters and locked himself in. A polite veil had been drawn over that day. A day later, Lieutenant Sharlensya had stumbled over his name as usual whilst calling the register, stopping as soon as she realised her mistake. He had liked the sound of Pezzi so much he had chosen it as his Familiar Name.

If they lived in our reality, then the four Cadets would be mistaken for a group of thirteen year old school pupils. Obviously no longer children, but at the same time definitely not adults either.

So instead of being in class on this Duosday afternoon, Nevamar found itself in the office of the Squad's Medical officer.

'Stop worrying about it, Cadet,' advised Major Keltonnant, 'that part of growing up is just delayed for you. It is unusual for differentiation to happen completely overnight. Your friend Cadet Pemisegant might look completely masculine now, but he will have a couple of weeks before all the internal changes are complete.

'You will wake up one morning and realise your body has started changing, and a few days later you have totally accepted you are a style.'

'But I don't want to be a style, Sir. Why does everyone keep saying that?' Nevamar had protested. 'They were all wrong about Pezzi.'

'You will be whatever the Tree wants you to be.' The medic looked at Nevamar over the rims of his glasses. 'However, after that incident, lets play it safe.'

The Major took a sample of Nevamar's blood and analysed it. The results were as inconclusive as they had been since day zero.

'Couldn't you help the process along, give me a dose of the right auxin?' Nevamar asked, out of desperation.

'No I could not, because if it proved to be a dose of the wrong auxin, it could have all sorts of dire consequences for your long-term health.'

'But you know more about the differentiation process than anyone else in the Tree. You wrote the book on it.'

'Flattery will get you nowhere Cadet. How did you know about that book, it is a highly specialised textbook.'

'I have been reading up on the subject. Read the summary of your book on the wiki page. The book itself was far too complicated'

'Well ten out of ten for effort. But that wiki page leaves a lot to be desired. I keep meaning to edit it myself, correct some of the mistakes on it. Also, it looks like you and young Pemisegant might warrant a new chapter in a new edition of the book.' The Major laughed, 'but I shall need some more samples and run some additional tests, to find out what is happening in there.'

'I'm desperate to be one thing or the other, like my friends. An anther by choice, but a style if that is what the Spirit of the Tree wants me to be. Being neither is starting to embarrass me.' Nevamar rubbed its arm, still sore where the samples had been taken.

The Major saw the crestfallen look on Nevamar's face.

'There is no need to feel embarrassed Cadet, as I have said before, you are too healthy to be neuter. Stop worrying about it and enjoy life. Things could be worse. You could still be a sprite in a deep freeze now, just remember that.'

On that ominous point, Nevamar took the late-note for Lieutenant Sharlensya's class from the Major and headed to school.

'I hope you have a good reason for being so late Cadet Nevamar?'

'Yes, Ma'am. I was at the Medical Centre,' replied Nevamar, handing the mentor the late-note.

'Right. See me after school Cadet. Now carry on with the work we started yesterday.'

'Yes, Ma'am.'

Nevamar walked to its desk feeling desperately miserable. To make matters worse, the lesson was in handwriting as there were still tasks that required pen and paper. The other Cadets had taken to handwriting like a duck to water, Nevamar found it more difficult than words could say. It could not write at anything like a proficient speed. So when the bell sounded for the end of class, Nevamar was still struggling to complete the exercise the others had finished half an hour earlier.

'I really don't understand it dear, you pick up the things other Cadets find difficult so quickly, and yet simple things like handwriting really stump you.'

'I am really sorry, Ma'am. My hands just will not do what my head wants them to do.'

'Although you have no problems with typing little one?'

'No mam, just writing.' The single handed chording keyboard everyone used in the Tree required less hand movement.

'Not to worry Nevamar dear. Its obvious you have some problem with writing. We will just have to find ways of helping you get around using pen and paper. When I was a Cadet, I knew a young anther who had terrible trouble with writing, but he was the cleverest person in the class.'

'I thought you went to one of the female Pure-stock Academies mam?'

'Until I transferred from there to a much better one dear.' She smiled at Nevamar before returning to her original point. 'They eventually got him special pens with thick rubber grips, I will have to see if I can get something like that for you. And of course, more time to finish your work.'

'Thank you mam.'

'That's all right my little one. Finish that tomorrow.'

Nevamar was almost leaving the room when she heard the Lieutenant call her back.

'You know my dear, if I had a brain, I would be dangerous. I meant to talk to you about your worries with differentiation.'

'No point worrying, as Major Keltonnant says, when it happens, it will happen. And nobody knows more about it than him.'

'Indeed, just look at Pemisegant. He is so glad he finally became an anther.'

'But he so wanted to be a girl, Ma'am. Now he hates being reminded about it.'

'He was so embarrassed when it happened, wearing a girl's uniform then suddenly speaking with a boy's voice.' The memory brought a smile to Sharlensya's face.

'Sooner or later then mam'

'That's right dear. So, are you hungry, I am? Race you to Bernie's.'

The fourth week of the tour of duty saw the first level of rationing introduced. Perishable seasonal foods that could not be frozen or duplicated by the food synthesizers disappeared off the menu. Not that the store cupboards were ever generously stocked. They knew from bitter experience that the accountants in the Roots with their tables and statistics, would query what the Winter Squad knew it would need. At the end of the day, the suppliers did what the accountants told them, never quite giving the Winter Squad all it would need.

It had all made sense yesterday at lunchtime, when Pezzi had explained what he was planning to the Cadets, before their afternoon class started.

'Every year, at the start of the Spring,' he explained, 'our first job as leaf operators used to be cleaning out the distribution tubes from our new leaves to the phloem. The Leaf Builders didn't do it because it was not part of their job.'

'No matter how much about my life as a sprite I might forget, I will remember that as the worse job of the year,' Nevamar added. 'Sticky green snot that had to be flushed from every valve and tube in the connector before the leaf would start working at 100%.'

'But it can't be any worse than some of the gross things we have had to clean over the past few weeks, can it?' said

Natalicsya who had never been really dirty in her life until this Autumn.

'It is indeed Lisha, nothing quite like it,' said Pemisegant pulling a notebook from his school bag. 'And I think I know where it comes from, and how we can turn it to our advantage.'

'If I never see that muck again, it will be too soon,'passion bleeding from Nevamar's every syllable.

'But I need you to come with me tomorrow Nevamar.' said Pemisegant.

'Come with you where, and in precious weekend downtime?' asked Nevamar.

'You'll be there, I can explain why. Look at this diagram everyone.' The notebook had been opened to a very dog-eared page. 'At the end of each Summer, we used to disconnect the old leaf from the system, set up a series of explosive charges in its stem, and seal the system off from the rest of the Tree. I used to think that as soon as we left for storage, the charges would be detonated. Turns out this is not the case. Sometimes it takes weeks for all the leaves to fall. My theory is the old leaves are still producing a minimal amount of Syrup right up to detonation. Those seals are not completely effective, so this residual Syrup leaks into the valves and tubes on the tree side of the seal. Along comes the frost and it all goes to pot. The Syrup ferments and turns to the poisonous gunk that we had to steam clean six months or so later.' explained Pemisegant.

'I don't see how this could be of any advantage to us Pezzi.'

'Well Alth my friend, if we can get the system to clean the valves and tubes now, transferring the fluid produced to a Concentrator Tank, I estimate that it will produce enough Syrup to last us until the end of Winter.'

Nevamar looked at Pemisegant's figures. 'That can't be right. With that much Syrup, there would be no need for rations, and no going hungry when the supplies run low, because there will be Toffee for the food fabricators.'

'If you can call that synthesised stuff food Nevamar, said Althallant, Nothing synthesised by food fabricators ever tasted as good as the real thing. Coming from the hydroponic farms of the Trunk, Althallant regarded anything from the synthesizers as inedible muck. 'There is no difference between that and the building materials we use every day.'

'Be that as it may, nobody in their right mind would waste that much Syrup.'

'They would, if they didn't know it was there,' said Pemisegant, looking very smug. 'Which is why I'm heading off tomorrow to visit a branch and test my theory. You game Nevamar?'

'Again, why me in particular?' asked Nevamar.

'Because like me you were a leaf operator, and you know one end of a stalk node from the other.'

'Have you told the Lieutenant what you are planning to do?' Ever cautious, Natalicsya wanted to know that they were not doing anything that would get them into trouble.

'No Lisha, if I had, I would have to clear my idea with Captain Grilbarant from R&D. He would refuse to let me try. He only gets sent up here with the Winter Squad so that R&D can get on with actual research into old problems and develop new solutions.'

'I thought that is what Research and Development is supposed to do?' asked Nevamar.

'You see Nevamar, that old fool is a throwback to when the Regiment was called Methodology Discipline. When the Regiment's purpose was to stifle new developments not encourage them.'

'That's crazy.' Even a traditionalist like Althallant can see things need to move forward.

'I totally agree Alth, but that used to be the case. Anyone found not using traditional methods would be punished,' replied Pemisegant.

'But things have changed,' said Althallant.

'Indeed they have, mostly for the better as well. I'm going to change things some more.'

So against its better judgement, Nevamar found itself out in a branch with its friend, doing something it had hoped it would never have to do again, stare down the business end of a leaf joint. It had expected to find it already coated with a fine layer of the green gunk that made the start of each Spring so unpleasant. To its surprise, there was a small amount of syrup in the node instead.

'Yep, as I thought, full of weak but usable syrup. Now its just a question of getting at it.' Pemisegant was really excited, it looked as if his theory was about to be proven.

'Is it still soluble?'

'It is. We'll give the whole branch a blast from the steam cleaners, it hasn't started to ferment yet.'

'Are you sure? Haven't they been shut down for Winter as well?'

'I have just accessed their control module, they only need priming.' Pemisegant got up from the workstation he had been using and walked over to Nevamar. 'I'm positive now that it is the frost that does it. Turns useful Syrup to poisonous gunk.'

'Pezzi, it will start getting dark in twenty minutes, it will be dark in thirty, by the time we have primed the system. There is no frost forecast, can't we come back tomorrow.'

During the Winter, all the street lighting beyond the Crown is switched off. No amount of jiggery-pokery would get it switched back on again. It was even beyond the power of the officer of the Watch down in Command and Control.

'No worries, I brought torches. If it takes longer than twenty minutes then we use them. But it won't take that long, we will be all done in ten. There will be no stumbling around in the dark.'

'OK, we can stay here for a maximum of thirty minutes, then we start making our way back.'

'Oh do stop being so girlie and afraid of the dark. If you are going to be such a wuss, I will do this on my own.'

If there were marks out or ten for Pemisegant's frightening lack of tact, that would have scored the full ten. Nevamar hated being called girlie.

'Suits me fine, do it yourself. I will sit here and do my homework,' said Nevamar. 'No point wasting the whole afternoon. That will take ten minutes, then I'm off home. If you don't come with me then, you can stumble back to the Crown on your own.'

'Good, I can get more done without you nagging me.' he replied.

'Pig!'

'See you later then.'

Natalicsya had said for weeks now that Nevamar was a style. After today's performance Pemisegant was starting to agree with her. Thinking about it now he realised something decidedly feminine had started to emerge around the edges. Yes thought Pemisegant, every so often when Nevamar was not concentrating, the mask slipped, just like a few minutes ago. Could everyone see it except Nevamar?

Pemisegant had fully accepted he was an anther. Although, no matter how hard he tried, he could never be as macho as the three other boys, Althallant and the two Ensigns, Cemnentant and Dukecamant. He just looked like a wimp in comparison.

If he had the prettiest young style in the Crown as his girlfriend, then that would be one up on the macho brigade. He knew that Nevamar's face was just too pretty already to be an anther's face. Its body too curvaceous as well, no amount of baggy clothing could hide that. Final differentiation couldn't be that far away and she would be Nevamarsya, the most beautiful young style in the Crown. No forget the Crown, the most beautiful young style in the whole of the Tree of

Life and his girlfriend to boot. After all Nevamar was his best friend, they shared so many common interests. When she became a style it was inevitable that he would be her boyfriend. Damn, who put that open drainage duct there.

Nevamar sat down and took out of its backpack. The topic was so engrossing that it totally failed to notice that a half hour had passed since Pemisegant had said anything. It only stopped reading because it was now too dark to see the page.

It got up and walked for a few minutes in the direction Pemizigant had taken.

'Pezzi, where are you?'

'Nevamar, help. I'm stuck.'

Oh great green apples, what had the silly little boy gone and done now. 'Stuck where?'

'In a drainage duct. I fell in whilst I was looking at a flow meter.' He was too embarrassed to tell his friend why he had really fallen into the duct. 'The comlink isn't working.'

'You weren't to know that,' said Nevamar, trying to reduce the level of panic in its friend's voice.

'I did Nevamar. That's why I chose this branch. Our tests would not have set off any monitors in C&C because there was no network.'

'Oh Pezzi dear, that was very silly. Although don't worry, I will go and get help.' Off Nevamar ran, down what it thought was the roadway down to the Crown. The torch made a tiny pool of light that was just about bright enough for it to follow. But after a few minutes, as the surrounding gloom grew thicker, the torch light began to fade. Typical of Pemisegant, bringing torches that were not properly charged. Hopefully, it would be back in civilisation before it ran out. No, why did I think that? The torch began to flicker ominously and each time it lit, it was a little dimmer than the time before. Only a few more minutes before the battery would be flat. Hopefully

Nevamar would be back where the Comm Network wa working before that happened.

Chapter 14
A Hole in the Ground

In the drainage duct, Pemisegant felt a wave of vibrations and knew that the duct was about to flush. *Why is this process still running at this time of year?* Because its running the programme you have just set up, stupid, he thought to himself. He was sucked from the duct and into the draining tube and started sliding. He knew if nothing stopped him, he would keep on sliding until he reached the main storage tanks. *Oh great* he thought, *I am going to drown in the fuel the Squad relies upon for the Winter.* Fortunately his slide was stopped by a filter at Concentrator Tank CF42.

'Oh I'm a stupid, stupid creature,' said Nevamar to no one in particular. It hated being on it own in unfamiliar places and terrified of the dark. 'All I need to do is stop panicking and then things will not seem so bad.' The sound of its own voice was normally comforting but today, it was just adding to the panic. 'Shut Up!'

'Who said that?' There was a voice in the gloom. 'Is that you Cadet Nevamar 331/29. They have been looking for you and your mate down in the Crown. You have been gone for far too long.'

'Ensign Tabbernant, is that you?'

'One and the same.' Ensign Tabbernant would reach retirement age of thirty five at the end of this Tour of Duty. He would be a Pensioner and outside the rank system.

Until then Brigadier Myghcomant was the only person who would tolerate Tabbernant in his command. So he cooked for the Squad during the Winter and was the Brigadier's batman in the Roots during the Summer. Ensign Tabbernant loved the Winter Squad, it had been the best posting he had ever had, and in some ways he was sorry that this would be his last tour of duty with them.

'We're not in trouble are we? Yet?' Then in deference to his age and protocol, Nevamar snapped to attention and saluted.

'At ease kid. There's no need to be so formal now,' the old anther smiled. The last duty of the day for the Cadets was helping Tabbernant to clean his kitchen, but he was always so formal then, this was not the Ensign Tabbernant that Nevamar was used to.

'No, not in trouble, but young Shaz is just worried about you. She's a good kid you know always concerned about her little ones.'

'Thank you for coming out here looking for us.'

'I'm not looking for you per se, I'm out here moonlighting, just to keep my hand in. I'm repairing the dodgy comlink relay that has meant that you two have been invisible to C&C in the Crown.'

'Ensign Tabbernant, its Pezzi, he fell and got himself stuck down a drainage duct twenty or so minutes ago.' Nevamar was close to tears.

'Oh great green apples, with no link to C&C the system runs on back-up. That duct would have cycled by now and he will be down in whatever pipe the duct was connected to. What sort of duct was it?' asked Tabbernant.

'A leaf syrup duct.'

'OK, that puts a whole new layer onto the situation. Yes, you are definitely in trouble.' All the while the old anther had been carrying out his repair, and at that moment the comlink squawked to life.

'Have you found my missing Cadets, Ensign Tabbernant?' asked Tabbernant?'asked Lieutenant Sharlensya, sat at her workstation in the Crown. 'Yes and no, Ma'am, I have the girl here with me now, but the young lad has got himself into a spot of bother.' Tabbernant was more worried than he was letting on she thought. He never called anyone, Ma'am or Sir, even when on duty.

'Can you fill me in?'

'Now that the sensors here are working again, get C and C to scan the leaf drainage system for life signs, Ma'am.'

'Great Mother Sun! How did he get in there?' the astonished Lieutenant asked as a schematic appeared in a window on her screen.

'Slipped and fell apparently. Children, don't you just love them.'

'I'm sorry Lieutenant, it was an accident,' said Nevamar. The camera moved to show the youngster. 'He wanted to see what a leaf station looked like in Winter, why they were so dirty by the start of Spring. How they got that way. He had this crazy theory about Syrup and the muck. We quarrelled and he just wandered off.' Nevamar began to cry. 'I'm sorry mam.'

'Don't worry my lovely, it could have happened to anyone.' There had been something in the tone of Nevamar's voice which struck a note and triggered a softening in her tone. She had made it a rule never to have favourites, to treat every Cadet she mentored the same, but there was something about this little one. So desperate to learn, so generous, so funny, so infuriating at times. Now so desperate for a mother's love. For a few seconds the formal Lieutenant and Cadet relationship went out the window as she comforted the child like her mother had once comforted her.

'We'll get him out my dear.'

'It's all gone horribly wrong mammy,' sobbed Nevamar.

'You know, you should have told us where you were going and why dear.'

'I know mammy, but Pezzi didn't want to tell Captain Grilbarant.'

'Oh, well we will deal with that later, don't you worry dearest.'

'So what happens next, Ma'am?' asked Tabbernant. The image of the old anther now filled the screen and the moment passed.

'Right, Ensign Tabbernant, a rescue team is on its way. ETA five minutes. Can you and Cadet Nevamar rendezvous with them at the junction of branch CF42 and CF42-5.'

'Copy that, Ma'am. On our way.'

T here we go Nevamar thought back to the formal and professional. Nevamar could not forget the last conversation. Lieutenant Sharlensya had been exactly how she imagined she would be if she really were her mother. She called her "dear" and "my lovely" in a way that could not be faked. When the time came was she going to be the style who adopted her? Be her mother? Then the other side of her brain cut in telling Nevamar not to be so stupid. Someone like Lieutenant Sharlensya was from the Roots, and a Pure-stock. Even if she was thinking of becoming a mother she would not be interested in adopting a piece of Canopy riff-raff like Nevamar. She would adopt some bright blonde girl whose name started with an "S". It was all academic now anyway. Neither individual was in a position where one could adopt the other. Adoption candidates had to be at least eighteen months old. Their bodies need something only their mother-to-be could give them. The Lieutenant would have to give up nine weeks and go through all sorts of physical discomfort for the biological part of the adoption process. That sort of thing would not happen during this tour of duty, and who knew where Nevamar would be after it finished.

'Right, tell young Pemisegant to stay in Concentrator Tank CF42 and wait for the rescue team.'

'That's not an option, Ma'am,' Pemisegant's tired voice came weakly over the comlink.'

'Oh great green apples, why not?' asked the Lieutenant.

'Because that...' the connection between the young anther and the comlink network faded.

'Because that is the Concentrator Tank we have primed to receive two hundred and fifty gallons of scalding hot Syrup solution. We were hoping to get at least five gallons of usable stuff out of that.'

'Exactly what have you youngsters been up to?' Brigadier Myghcomant, from his eerie in Command and Control added his voice to the conversation.

Nevamar briefly explained what they had been doing that afternoon, and why no senior officers knew about it.

'Great Father Earth, do you think I would have let anyone stand in the way of anything that would increase our rations this winter.' It was always hard to tell if the Brigadier was angry or not.

Colonel Rumsfelant and half a dozen Squad members had arrived in the branch. 'We heard what this youngster here said, and I suspect that we are going to have to cut directly through the floor plate and yank the silly boy out from that tank. I estimate it will take twenty minutes.'

'That's good, Sir, the system is primed to go off in twenty-five minutes.'

'No pressure then,' said the Colonel. In his role as the Squad's Offeiriad Pastor, began praying silently whilst his team started digging up the floor, making slow progress. Nevamar did whatever it could to help, but felt that it was getting in the way. It saw Ensign Tabbernant grinning, was the old anther mad. How could anyone feel like grinning at a time like this.

'You know, this is exactly the sort or crazy scheme that used to get me into trouble when I was young. Always inventing things, always getting punished by the Methodology Discipline Regiment.'

'Why were they so set against new developments, what harm could looking at new ideas do anyway?'

'It was all to do with the religious attitudes of the day.' Tabbernant pointed to the Day-lighter, now cold and switched off for the night, that hung from the ceiling. 'Who invented the Day-lighter up there? Who invented the enprintable fabric we wear? Who built all the major structures in the Tree? Answer, the Tree did, they were already in existence when the first sprite emerged from the seed. Also the Tree created the great factory farms of the Trunk.'

'So why would that cause the downer on change?'

'Because change was seen as blasphemous. The Tree had provided, who were we to try and improve upon the wisdom of the Tree.'

It sounded to Nevamar as if old Ensign Tabbernant was

raking up some bitter memories.

'It all changed when the Tree got too big for the old ways. Methods that worked fine when the Tree was half its current size became less and less effective. About fifteen years ago we had to find new ways of doing things or die. Thus was born the Research and Development Regiment.'

'Why didn't you join the new Research and Development Regiment when is was established?'

'Because I had so many demerits on my record, they would not even consider my applications. If they had bothered to look to see why I had received the early ones then things might have been different. Unfortunately my reputation as a trouble maker preceded me. So all they saw were my later, well deserved ones.'

There was a cheer as the final layer, separating Pemisegant from his rescuers, was breached. 'I reckon that once we pull that young man out of the pickies, I could have some interesting conversations with him. You as well Girlie.'

Why does everyone insist I am going to be a style, even this old anther. Another voice, one deep within its mind whispered, 'Because you are.' Just for once Nevamar did not try to disagree.

'You do realise that you two are going to take some flack for not going through channels.' There was another cheer as Pemisegant was pulled to the surface. He looked so frightened. And why was he looking at Nevamar in that odd way. What was he looking at.

'I do. Things have gone horribly wrong.'

'Oh I wouldn't say that. Three hundred and five gallons of Syrup solution has just flowed into that tank.' The old anther showed Nevamar a display on his comlink. 'When that works its way through to the storage tank, that will be six gallons of Grade "A" Toffee. I think proving your point will greatly reduce the amount of demerits you get. It might even equate to a credit if the Brigadier is feeling generous.' Nevamar didn't hear a word of that. It was crying, and rushed up and hugged Pemisegant.

The lamp of his rescuer's helmet nearly blinded Pemisigant. The young anther felt strong arms pull him out of the tank.

As soon as he was clear there was a clang as the section of the tank roof was put in place and it was sealed shut.

'OK people, close her up tight enough to stop any leaks,' Colonel Rumsfelant ordered. 'Don't over do it though. We will be back here next week decommissioning the whole thing.'

That's right, Pemisegant thought, the new central processing plant, right in the lowest decks of the Crown, would be on-line from next Summer onward.

'You lad are both very foolish and very lucky.' The Colonel looked as if he was about to explode. 'If this stupid stunt had not produced usable Syrup, you would be doing the rest of your Officer Training in the Guard House. As it is, I just have to hand you and your little girlfriend over to your mentor.'

Pemisegant had never seen a face change from anger to joy so quickly.

'I want to see all your notes and plans at 0830 tomorrow morning, when we can discus how to scale this up a few notches. OK then sonny, the rest room is over there, go tidy yourself up.'

What was the matter with Nevamar, was it a trick of the light, or was she glowing. His normally neuter friend looked so different, its copper red hair all soft and beautiful. He could see why Colonel Rumsfelant had called Nevamar his girlfriend. She looked so very female. Added to that Nevamar was crying. Pemisegant wondered if he was dreaming as a big soppy kiss was planted on his grubby face, and his friend hugged him.

'Don't you ever worry me like that again Pezzi my dear.' Then it kissed him for a second time.

'Do that again,' requested Pemisegant, but at that moment something strange happened. Nevamar shivered and then just walked away.

The rescuers were too busy replacing the floor plates to notice what had just happened. But Pemisegant knew he was right, Natalicsya was right, everyone except Nevamar itself knew it was right. It would soon be a she. The only question was when and not if. This made Pemisegant extremely happy.

Lieutenant Sharlensya hurried the young anther to the Medical Centre. No harm had been done, so he was discharged. That evening the two youngsters received a lecture about responsibility, health and safety and good manners from an annoyed Lieutenant Sharlensya and were sent to bed without supper.

'That never happened, understand,' Nevamar hissed into Pemisegant's ear a few minutes later.

'What, when you started acting like a proper style at last.'

'I was over come by the situation. If you tell anyone what I did, I will deny it. Do you understand.'

'Yes Nevamarsya.'

'Don't call me that. I am going to be an anther.'

'No you're not.'

Pemisegant's only reply was a slamming door.

It was late and Sharlensya had gone down to the refrectory for refectory for a cup of tea and a chat with old Tabbernant.

'You getting broody, young Shaz?' Old Tabbernant had spotted something.

'I don't think so.'

'Well you could have fooled me,' said the old anther as he pulled a seat next to Sharlensya and like a magician produced her favourite cake. 'I knew you would want to talk to me about it. Old Kelly is a bit too close.'

'Talk about what?'

'How lonely you are feeling without your mum.'

'How did you know?'

'The way you spoke to young Nevamar this afternoon. You sounded just like your mum, Father Earth give her rest, when she would talk to you when you were upset, and like her mum when she was a child, and her mum before that.' Tabbernant had always been a good, if unlikely, friend of both her mother and uncle. She had known him all her life.

'I know, we call them Officer Cadets, expect them to follow rank and protocol, but at the end of the day, they are still kids.'

'I sensed more than that Sharlensya. There's an emotional bond developing between you two. Just remember, parenthood is damned hard work. That is why I have worked so hard to avoid it.'

'I know. I know it is a life changing step.'

'You will be good at it. But like I said, think very carefully before you take the first step. It won't just be your life you can screw up.'

'I know. That is why the Adoption Accreditation System exists. Nobody can adopt unless they have the accreditation.'

'You just happen to have accreditation?'

'I do. Mum made me apply last year. I passed the assessement. If I wanted to I could adopt up to three children in the next ten years.'

'Well good for you. I know you will be a good mother when you chose to take that step.' He smiled. 'Feeling better?'

'Yes thank you Uncle Bernie.' Mother Sun, she had not called him that for years.

Sharlensya went back to her quarters and sat looking at old photographs for hours. Yes the time for moving on to the next stage of her life was fast approaching.

In the hush of night she was sure she could hear someone crying herself to sleep. The sound was coming from Ensign

Serynazsya's quarters. Now there was a mixed up kid for you. Whilst she was mostly employed as mentor for the Cadets, her responsibilities were elastic enough to include being in loco parentis for the unaccompanied juveniles in the Squad. The four year old Cemnentant, Dukecamant and Hanazofsya could look after themselves. Ensign Serynazsya's presence in the Crown was a headache. Technically she was not old enough to be here unaccompanied, but circumstances had lead that way. From now on Sharlensya thought to herself, I am going to have to spend more time with that girl. It sounds as if she needs all the help she can get.

F ortunately, Brigadier Myghcomant was feeling generous a day later, when both Cadets were marched into his office.

'At ease Squad,' ordered the Brigadier. Nevamar was still not sure if they were about to receive a dressing down or a commendation from him.

'You see youngsters, there are reasons why you have to submit any bright ideas you might have for evaluation. You caused a great deal of unnecessary expense and a great deal of unnecessary worry with your unauthorised shenanigans.' A shamefaced Pemisegant nodded in agreement with the Brigadier. 'We also need to do things safely. Life is too precious to waste on proving a point. Do you agree Cadet Pemisegant?'

'Yes, Sir.'

'Good,' he slid open a draw on his desk and handed the Lieutenant a pair of envelopes. 'You know what to do with these?'

'Yes, Sir, thank you, Sir.' said the Lieutenant.

'Lieutenant Sharlensya, it looks as if you have your hands fuller than usual this year, with this lot.'

'Yes, Sir, they are a lively bunch,' she replied.

'You have given them a suitable punishment Lieutenant?'

'Yes, Sir, they are already halfway through that Brigadier.'

'Good, so you two,' the Brigadier turned towards the two Cadets. 'Squad, attentinon!'

All three snapped out of their parade rest, wondering what their commander was going to say.'

'I have decided to be lenient on you two young fools this time. I do not want to have to repeat this lecture in future. Do I make myself clear.'

'Yes, Sir.' Nevamar and Pemisegant replied.

'I am not going to add to any punishment your mentor prescribed and I will not detain you from it any longer. Dismissed'.

The three saluted, turned and left the Brigadier's eerie. During the march back to their quarters, Nevamar was itching to know what was in the envelope, but decided it would be better to wait until it was told.

'You have given them a suitable punishment Lieutenant?'

'Yes, Sir, they are already halfway through that Brigadier.'

'Good, so you two,' the Brigadier turned towards the two Cadets. 'Squad, attentinon!'

All three snapped out of their parade rest, wondering what their commander was going to say.'

'I have decided to be lenient on you two young fools this time. I do not want to have to repeat this lecture in future. Do I make myself clear.'

'Yes, Sir.' Nevamar and Pemisegant replied.

'I am not going to add to any punishment your mentor has prescribed and I will not detain you from it any longer. Dismissed'.

The three saluted, turned and left the Brigadier's eerie. During the march back to their quarters, Nevamar was itching to know what was in the envelope, but decided it would be better to wait until it was told.

'I have decided to be lenient on you two young fools this time. I do not want to have to repeat this lecture in future. Do I make myself clear.'

'Yes, Sir.' Nevamar and Pemisegant replied.

'I am not going to add to any punishment your mentor has prescribed and I will not detain you from it any longer. Dismissed'.

The three saluted, turned and left the Brigadier's eerie. During the march back to their quarters, Nevamar was itching to know what was in the envelope, but decided it would be better to wait until it was told.

C leaning potatoes, a punishment detail every facet of the Universe, had been assigned to the two young miscreants. Whilst it was true this was not the way they would normally choose to spend their Saxearthday afternoon off, they could no longer see this as a punishment. In a few short days since the incident, old Bernie had become far friendlier. This duty allowed Nevamar and Pemisegant time to talk to the most interesting person they knew.

'What exactly is the point of styles wearing such short skirts Bernie?' asked Nevamar. 'I mean, they don't cover anything, they just flap around their bottoms, looking decorative. Skirts that short must be powerfully cold.'

'As an anther, I can't say that I have ever experienced what it is like to wear a miniskirt. Each morning, I thank the Spirit of the Tree, that I don't have to go through the palaver, that styles go through to get dressed. On the other hand, I am extremely glad that the attractive young styles do go through that palaver and chose to wear miniskirts for whatever reason. It makes life more entertaining.'

'But why?'

'OK then, lets take for example your precious Lieutenant Sharlensya,' the old man was going to be waxing lyrical on one of his favourite topics, Nevamar could tell. 'Young Shaz is a bit of a sex-bomb.'

Nevamar did not think it would get used to old Tabbernant calling Lieutenant Sharlensya "Young Shaz". OK he was the oldest person Nevamar knew, so he must see everyone as being young, but "Shaz" just did not sound right. Nevamar held its mentor in a reverent state of infallible awe. This was not a view held by some of the male members of the Winter Squad. Some of her downtime outfits were typical of the silly things that styles got into their heads to wear. Which brought them neatly back to the question in hand.

'There is no doubting that Shaz is gorgeous. All Pure-stock are beautiful, but she just takes it to another level. She knows it, and come downtime, when she doesn't have to wear the butt-ugly green uniforms that the High Council insist upon, then she likes to show this off.'

'What's a sex-bomb?' Poor naïve Nevamar caused her two anther colleagues to dissolve into a fit of laughter.

'An extremely attractive person you would like to have sex with.' explained Bernie. This lead to the inevitable.

'But what's sex?'

'Pezzi my boy, please don't laugh so vigorously when you have a sharp knife in your hand.' He looked sternly at the young anther and then continued. 'To us tree people, it is just a form of entertainment. Our bodies seem to be based on a pattern that uses sex for reproduction, like in cats, but for some reason, those parts are not fully functional. Well they don't need to be, we all come direct from the Tree, we don't need any other way of reproducing.'

'Oh its entertaining each other. That is why some of the anthers look at Lieutenant Sharlensya in such a strange way when she wears something that leaves her legs naked,' said Nevamar as the penny dropped.

'Have you kids had sex education lessons yet?'

'Nah, not yet, its on the timetable though,' said Nevamar. Pemisegant seemed to find this hilariously funny, Nevamar was at a loss to understand why.

'Don't worry Girlie,' Tabbernant said conspiratorially, when you have finished growing, and your skirts are as short as all the other young styles, you will understand perfectly.

'I don't think so, I'm going to be an anther.'

'If you say so girlie.'

'I am!' said an exasperated Nevamar.

'Give it up Nevamar, the only person who still thinks that is you,' chipped in Pemisegant.

'Oh don't you start again.'

'A little less chat, a lot more peeling, if you please Cadets, or we will be having this meal next Sunday, not this.'

The rest of the afternoon was spent with Tabbernant giving the two fascinated Cadets the full birds and bees lecture, as they prepared the vegetables for the following day's communal Sunday dinner. Whilst it did not want to appear to be a prude, Nevamar was horrified. That people did that for pleasure was mind boggling. That styles let anthers do all that to them was further proof that they were crazy and it definitely wanted to be an anther.

T he weather beyond the Tree was taking a turn for the worse and beyond the warm and wet atmosphere of the Crown the temperature fell dramatically at night. In a few weeks it would be cold enough to freeze the contents of any unprotected pipes in the Canopy. This gave the Winter Squad a narrow window of opportunity to recover good quality Syrup from the branches before the frost came and broke down any unrecovered Syrup into an unusable slurry that would ferment over the rest of the Winter. With this extra source of Syrup for the food fabricators there would be no rationing this year.

However, what made Nevamar happiest was that it would help make the lives of its former colleagues a little better. At the start of Spring many leaf operating sprites would not have an unpleasant job awaiting them on their return to the Canopy. A small but appreciable victory.

CHAPTER ELEVEN
ALL GOING SWIMMINGLY

Trenitsday mornings were devoted to military training. Drill Instruction with the Ensigns under the eye of Lieutenant Crysgoxant, followed by target shooting with Colonel Gwilwalsya.

For Nevamar the pain continued as the afternoon would be devoted to something sporty which it found just as physically demanding. This Trenitsday morning had been unusually warm for the time of year, almost like a Summer's day. So Lieutenant Sharlensya had decreed that, that afternoon they would be having a swimming lesson in the naturally warm waters of the central lake. Not that anyone needed swimming lessons, Tree people could swim instinctively. This was a smokescreen, her kids deserved a treat and the hardest part of Officer Training was on the horizon.

Nevamar was not looking forward to this lesson. Cold and wet with pysgods, the Tree's version of fish, swimming beneath it. No thank you very much.

'You have to learn to swim Girlie,' said the old anther, helping to keep up the pretence. As usual, old Ensign Tabbernant was having his lunch at the same time as Nevamar and Pemisegant, keeping a close eye on what was going on in his kitchen.

'You never know when you might need that skill, it could save your life,' continued the old anther.

'But it will be cold in that lake, why can't we use the heated swimming pool in the Mess Hall,' asked Nevamar.

'Because that would require getting the equipment in the pool working again, filling it and dosing the water with chlorine and finally turning the heater on. Do you realise how much fuel would be needed to warm the pool up?' asked Tabbernant.

'And the lake will be warmer than you think. Warm currents still come up from the Roots, even if no shuttles travel on them. And don't forget the warm overflow from all those hydroponic farms in the Trunk.', Pemisegant chipped in.

Nevamar knew that Pemisegant was quite looking forward to the lesson. It was one of the few things he knew he would be able to beat the more athletic Althallant at.

'Look, it will be fun. If Pezzi there is looking forward to the lesson I know you will Girlie.'

'Will you please stop calling me that, I am going to be an anther.'

'Why did you chose such a girlie name then? Eh, Girlie?'

'I did not, anyway, root-names are neutral until they get a suffix.'

'I'm afraid the old fool has a point.'

'Thank you Shaz, I love you too.'

The two Cadets jumped to their feet and saluted their Mentor.

'As you were kids.'

Nevamar and Pemisegant slumped back onto their seats. I wish the Lieutenant would stop creeping up on us, thought Nevamar. Tabbernant is far too busy picking up bad habits from us Cadets to teach us any in return.

Lieutenant Sharlensya ignored that last comment. 'Of the four officers who currently have Neva as the first element of their name, only one is an anther. Historically, the element Neva is associated with styles.'

'I wish I had known that a few weeks ago.' Two wishes in two minutes, be careful not to make it three in three, the third always comes true.

'I did warn you to take care when choosing your name.'

'You did, Ma'am, but something in here insisted on Nevamar.' It tapped its skull. The voice had just been too strong to resist. 'There is no real problem, Ma'am, I still like my name. I'm used to it now and I would not want to change it.'

'No-one ever really knows why they choose the name they do.' Tabbernant had a strange far away look in his eyes.

It just comes to you on a breeze. It just blows in there. Usually the first choice sticks.'

For the first time, a niggling doubt appeared in Nevamar's mind. What if I am wrong, sometimes I wish I was a style after all. It shuddered, three in three. No, don't go there, silly superstition. But deep down in her psyche the bottle was opening as the genie pushed against the stopper. Once it was out it would not go back into the bottle again.

O utside, in the unseasonably warm Autumn afternoon, the hut besides the lake, that had for generations acted as changing rooms for off duty officers wanting to spend their downtime on the beach, should have been replaced years ago. Its plumbing leaked, the showers were never very warm and there was precious little privacy in the cubicles. There were never enough funds at the end of the Winter, for the Squad to replace it, and nobody would pay for its replacement during the Summer.

Nevamar pulled on the baggy swimming trunks and looked at itself in the mirror. As usual it had chosen the anther's changing room but the gender-less reflection was unchanged for weeks.

'You'll have to take that t-shirt off you know. If you insist on covering up, you might as well have a styles swimsuit on.'

Nevamar decided to ignore that comment.

'It will hinder your swimming. Like those trunks you and Pezzi are wearing.' he continued.

'Nothing is going to hinder your swimming with those Alth.' said Pemisegant.

Althallant was wearing the skimpiest of swimming trunks imaginable. There was no hiding his masculinity in them. 'I hesitate even to call them trunks, there is not enough material in them to justify the name.'

'Yep, that's the point Pezzi, they are racing trunks, all the top swimmers wear them.

'Yes, to impress all the styles watching the races.'

N atalicsya and the Lieutenant were already waiting. For once, Nevamar thought the styles were wearing something more sensible than the anthers. They were both wearing knee length baggy dresses and beneath that was a long pair of thin trousers. On their heads they had voluminous frilly hats.

The four youngsters lined up along the jetty.

'Right, are we all ready to learn to swim?' asked the Lieutenant.

'Permission to speak,' said Althallant.

'Granted.'

'You two aren't really going to be wearing those during the lesson, are you, Ma'am?' asked Althallant.

'Of course Cadet. Modesty must be preserved.'

She said it with such a straight face, the boys honestly believed that the lesson would continue with the styles wearing their old fashioned costumes.

'Take a float from the pile and climb down that ladder, into the water.'

Natalicsya lead the group along the small jetty, daintily entering the lake. Her voluminous outfit swirling as she did so. When Nevamar and the two young anthers joined her in the water, they heard the sound of laughter. It was Tabbernant giggling like a child, he was taking an afternoon off to try and catch some pysgod. This practical joke had been his idea. Once the mood had been broken, both the styles also began laughing.

'Oh the look on your faces was priceless.' Natalicsya had climbed back out of the water, using her towel to make sure that she was as dry as possible before resetting her costume. Although the enprintable fabric only needed a tiny current to change it from one structure to another, she was not about to take any silly risks. There was still a slight tingle as the old fashioned green and white outfit reset itself into something more modern, and definitely more form fitting.

To Nevamar's utter surprise, its reaction to the new swimming costumes was not the usual incredulity at the stupidity of style's clothing, but how good it would be wearing one just like that. The urge to change almost won out when Nevamar felt something cold brush its leg. Yuck, a pysgod, and all thoughts of changing suddenly flew from its head.

Nevamar was not the only one thinking how good she would look in one of those swim suits. Once the inevitable happens Pemisegant thought, she is going to look a knock-out. Oh Nevamarsya why are you being so stupid, you know what must happen. If he had known exactly what Nevamar was thinking at that second, it would have brightened his day beyond measure.

After a few minutes, the youngsters instinctive ability to swim kicked in and the formal lesson ended. They were now swimming just for the joy of it. Pemisegant loved the fact that his wiry frame, so puny compared to muscular Althallant, gave him an amazing turn of speed in the water.

He spotted the buoy, it was a short distance from the edge of the jetty. Just the right height to climb up and surrounded by water deep enough to jump into. It just had to be done, and he was going to be the first to do it.

This was the best sports lesson ever, without a shadow of a doubt. If it could be called a lesson. Everyone seemed to have forgotten they were supposed to still be on duty.

The Lieutenant was relaxing in a deckchair, absorbing the rays of Mother Sun in what appeared to Nevamar to be only her underwear.

Nevamar loved the way the water gave it far more freedom of movement than it had on dry land. Nobody would ever call its swimming graceful, but it didn't need to be graceful.

Nevamar could see that Pemisegant had swum to a small buoy and was climbing it. Dull so and so, that was taking things too far, the Lieutenant would not be happy.

'Cadet Pemisegant, get down from there at once and back to this jetty.'

Right on cue thought Nevamar, and it knew exactly what Pemisegant was going to do next. Yes, he jumped from the highest point on the buoy, and then swam back to the jetty. 'That was a very irresponsible thing to do Pemisegant. I thought better of you than that,' the Lieutenant told the boy as he climbed out of the water.

'Don't worry, it is not as dangerous as it looks.'

'Less of the lip Cadet,' a more formal edge returned to her voice. Pemisegant jumped to attention, which looked ridiculous in the shorts he was wearing.

'You have only just learnt to swim, you will have to wait for lessons in diving. The art of safely and gracefully entering the water, I will demonstrate.'

Lieutenant Sharlensya tapped a code into her portable enprinter, changing back from bikini and blouse to a one peice costume. She walked to the end of the jetty, where the lake was at least twenty units deep, and elegantly dived into the water, with barely a ripple.

Ensign Tabbernant was sitting on the end of the jetty, dangling a baited line into the water.

'Caught anything Bernie?' asked the dripping wet Lieutenant as she climbed out of the water, giving the old anther an eyeful on route.

'Nah, they just aren't biting, are they,' he said as he pulled an empty catch net out of the water. 'Those kids splashing around are scaring them off.'

'Not that you were ever really after catching your supper, you were only really interested is catching a peek of me in a wet swimming costume, weren't you, you old perv?'

'I am a letch, not a perv. There is an important difference, thank you very much. I am still a normal anther, I can still appreciate an attractive fully grown style, even if I am considerably older than her. It brings back happy memories of when I was twenty years younger. That is being lecherous, which makes me a Letch.

'OK, I'm sorry. You old letch you.'

A wide grin sat on his face. 'What's that young idiot up to?'

Pemisegant had walked up to the end of the jetty and tried

to emulate the Lieutenant. Failing hopelessly, he tripped and hit the water like a sack of spuds. He must also have hit his head on the legs of the jetty, as when he surfaced, he was not moving. Quick as a flash, the old anther had jumped into the water, and was pulling the unconscious youngster out.

'Some things you never forget,' he said as he started giving the kiss of life. The Lieutenant pumping on the boys chest. 'You given these kids any first aid lessons yet?'

'No, not yet.'

'Can't see your uncle being best pleased about that.'

'Why, he will be giving the lessons himself, after boot camp. Shouldn't you be saving your breath for more important things?'

Pemisegant started breathing again, coughing and spluttering.

'You know Pezzi, for a clever young anther, you can be really stupid some time,' said the old anther, smiling as he admonished the youngster.

'Cadet Pemisegant, you should consider yourself on a charge of reckless endangerment,' said Lieutenant Sharlensya, who on the other hand was not nearly as forgiving. 'That is twice in one lesson you have done something needlessly stupid.' The Lieutenant was really more angry with herself than with the young anther. She should have realised that Pemisegant would want to emulate her dive. 'However, as you will be spending a night in the medical centre, just to be on the safe side, which means you will be subject to Ensign Serynazsya's cooking, I will let the matter pass.'

T he Grand Central Channels, and the hydroponic farms they fed creature that all officers rely upon as part of the complex biology of the Tree of Life. In their juvenile form they're creatures, that swim free in the waters of the lake and channels.

Once every twenty eight days a style would release a nutrient filled cyst and become receptive. If an unprotected style went for a swim on that day, there was a chance a juvenile lock would enter her body. The lock would fuse with the cyst and implant itself in the wall of the style's uterine chamber, where it would then grow and mature for nine weeks, before being ejected by the host style's body.

Lieutenant Sharlensya should have been quite safe, like all styles old enough, she had been fitted with a contraceptive implant, another symbiotic creature, created by the Tree, to regulate the population of officers. Had she known her implant had died and today she was fertile Sharlensya would never have dived into the water. As it was, nature had followed its course. By the time she woke up for work the following day, one of the juvenile locks was ensconced within a cyst and had implanted itself within her uterine chamber. She was pregnant.

'Eat it, its good for you,' ordered Ensign Serynazsya.
Of all the things she could have cooked for the only patient in the Medical Centre that night, she had chosen pysgod protein. The steak looked as if she had boiled all the goodness out of it, and the parsley sauce was almost as lumpy as the mashed potato.

'I don't like pysgod.'

'Liar, whenever Bernie cooks battered pysgod and chips, you are there asking for seconds.' Serynazsya was determined the patient would eat something.

'Yeah, the difference is that Bernie had cooked it.' said the boy.

'Eat, that's an order.' said the exasperated girl.

'You're only an Ensign, you can't order me about.' replied Pemisegant.

'Just eat it. I did.'

'As if that's any recommendation.'

'And you were such a nice young sprout Pezzi. You have turned into a proper horror.'

Lieutenant Sharlensya had been right, Pemisigant thought, this was a terrible punishment.

Even though Serynazsya was only the Domestic Assistant in the Medical Centre, she did not care. It was working in a medical environment, it was a step in the right direction. This had originally been Ensign Dukecamant's assignment. It took a week for Major Keltonnant to finally lose his temper and demand a replacement.

Everyone knew how desperately Ensign Serynazsya wanted to be a nurse. Swapping assignments had been wonderful. Trying not to get under the feet of the medical staff, she was learning what she could whilst she was there. Once young Pemisegant finished his meal and the galley was spotless, her official job was complete. Ensign Serynazsya sat down and began reading her textbook. Not the Branch Management textbook she was supposed to be reading, but the General Nursing Textbook Lieutenant Voynvalsya had lent her.

On the hour, Lieutenant Voynvalsya would return from her break. Anything Serynazsya did not understand in her reading matter would be explained by the nurse in a calm and patient manner. Lieutenant Voynvarant also encouraged Serynazsya's ambition but not as actively as his twin sister.

The only fly in the ointment for Serynazsya was the silly schoolgirl crush she was developing on Lieutenant Voynvalsya. The nurse was a style damn it, this was not supposed to be happening. She should be crushing on the Lieutenant's good looking brother, not the incredibly sophisticated, gorgeously sexy and kissable sister. Stop it Rynzee, she's a style like you. Just stop it. Perhaps she was just envious of her uniform. Yes, that was it. The starched apron, the cap sitting jauntily on the top of her head, the wide belt, the black stockings that looked so sexy that Serynazsya wanted to peel them off Voynvalsya's legs as they undressed each other. No! Stop it! This was not what a well brought up Pure-stock style was supposed to be thinking about. She glanced up at the clock on the wall, was it that time already. Here she was, the object of Serynazsya's desire.

'Serah, I have had a letter from my boyfriend, it has a message for you,' said the older style.

'Warning me off is he? I know. I know, you are not interested in styles, I should try to find someone my own age, even if it is another girl. Etcetera, etcetera, etcetera,' said Serynazsya dejectedly.

'What are you talking about?' asked the nurse.

'I love you, but you will never love me back, will you?'

'Serah dear, I had no idea. I'm flattered, but this has come as a bolt from the blue.' Voynvalsya's expression had changed from excitement to bewilderment.

'Oh great green apples, what have I said, what have I done.' She was so beautiful thought Serynazsya, and now she hates me. Serynazsya couldn't cope any more, she ran, crying as she went. Why is my life so awful. Why did all the good things she was given turn to snot. It must be something poisonous in her. It's all that sprite's fault. She had been able to keep her inner ugliness under control, now it had come to the surface and ruined everything. If only I hadn't been trapped up here in the Canopy by NM331/29, she thought as she ran from the building, passing Nevamar, who was coming to visit Pemisegant. Even hoping NM331/29 had died of starvation weeks ago, alone out there in its branch was of no comfort to Serynazsya.

Once Mother Sun had dipped below the horizon, the weather inside and outside the Tree had reverted back to its seasonal norm. Dripping wet mist shrouded the lake shore.

Sharlensya had been called back on duty by her concerned uncle. Lieutenant Voynvarant had already started looking for Serynazsya whilst his sister remained at her post. Sharlensya had tried all the usual suicide spots, and thankfully found nothing. All that remained was the mist shrouded jetty.

'What are you doing out here Ensign Serynazsya?' It was a silly question, Lieutenant Sharlensya knew exactly what the distraught young style was planning on doing.

'Leave me alone,' said Serynazsya with an air of desperation in her voice. 'I need to do this. I need to end the ugliness.'

'Lieutenant Voynvalsya is worried about you. The way you ran off.'

'No she isn't, nobody is.' The girl was sobbing.

'She is, we are all worried about you.'

'Yeah, right.'

'Two negatives make a positive, but two positives don't make a negative. We are all worried about you.'

'They are not, and neither are you. You are a mentor, you are paid to show concern, its your job.'

'That is not true, and you know that Serynazsya. You have proven to be a very useful addition to the Winter Squad, we would all miss you if you did anything silly.'

'But I'm ugly. Powerfully ugly. Captain Samnundsya was right, the ugliness without is a reflection of the ugliness within. I disgust people, I do, that is why they all hate me.'

Captain Samnundsya, that explains a lot thought Lieutenant Sharlensya. She was the silly bitch who had given her dear little Nevamar such a hard time as a sprite. Her low opinion of that style was being reinforced by the minute.

'Nobody hates you Serynazsya and you are not ugly. Look, come back inside. Get yourself warmed up, and tell me all your problems. You really do need to tell somebody. It's not good trying to bottle them all up inside.'

'You will laugh, I am so stupid, so very stupid.'

That was the last comprehensible thing the young style said that day. She had rolled herself up into a ball and was crying inconsolably. Sharlensya really did not want to sedate the girl, but knew there was no other way to get her to the Medical Centre.

Pemisegant was roused from his slumbers, quickly discharged back to his quarters. The Major gave him a stern warning not to tell anyone what he had seen during the night.

M ajor Keltonnant had called the case conference. As Medical Officer he would be responsible for Serynazsya's treatment, but her problems went far beyond medicine. So he sat listening to all opinions before even starting to devise a treatment. He was surprised so many people had turned up at such short notice. Something had to be done for the poor young girl still sleeping in the room next door. Everyone felt they had let her down badly and now had to make amends.

'I had no idea that she had been that close to cracking up,' said Lieutenant Voynvalsya in an embarrassed whisper. 'I didn't know she had been developing a minor crush on me, but adolescents go through that sort of thing.'

'I have been checking up on her records. She seemed such a bright and helpful youngster, but it is obvious now that she has very low self-esteem,' said Lieutenant Sharlensya, as she handed everyone a copy of the print-out. 'Her mentor in the Pure-stock Academy mentioned in her Graduation Report what a happy and caring youngster she was, and how it was a shame that she was unable to follow her chosen career stream.

'Just to think, I was going to give her some good news before she went off the rails so spectacularly.' said Lieutenant Voynvalsya.

'Really, in what way.' asked the Major.

'Commander Veltpigant, a tutor at the Nursing School at the Sacred Sisterhood Hospital, informed me that if I agreed to let Serynazsya be my apprentice, then her merits from this tour with the Squad would get her a place in their school automatically in the Summer.'

'And you are willing to do that?'

'Certainly Major, all I needed was your agreement, as we are both working in your establishment. Given the circumstances, it would now be better if my brother took my place. He is a better teacher anyway.'

'You have no objections from me Lieutenant Voynvalsya, but does your brother agree.'

'Of course I agree. I'm quite looking forward to it in fact,' said Lieutenant Voynvarant.

'All this will have to wait until the young lady is made well again, she will not be able to do anything too strenuous. Ensign Serynazsya has gone to pieces, and until she is put back together, then her dream will have to remain just that,' said the Major.

'Something really has to be done about that Branch Captain, she can't go around ruining lives like this,' said Lieutenant Voynvalsya rather absentmindedly.

'Unfortunately, whilst she appears to be a monster to the sprites she controls, there is no evidence that she is directly responsible for Serynazsya's condition,' said Lieutenant Sharlensya.

'Even if she isn't responsible for the girl's condition, she has caught my eye.' Inspector Galeroysya, who had been silently making notes in the corner replied. 'I have been building quite a dossier on that worthless creature. I had a very constructive chat with Cadet Nevamar last night. Her treatment of sprites is shocking, but that's just a bud about to open. Once I have built up a case, Lieutenant Voynvalsya, I will throw the book at Captain Samnundsya. If that does not cheer that poor kid up, I don't know what will.'

'The sad fact is her problems lie even deeper than that,' Lieutenant Sharlensya continued. 'I should be out with my pupils now. Instead Captain Treslelant is supervising them and Colonel Gwilwalsya will be teaching them this week. I will be spending my time straightening out Ensign Serynazsya's deeper problems. I fear it may be too little, too late.'

On that gloomy note, the case conference broke up.

CHAPTER TWELVE
WHAT'S NEW PUSSYCAT?

'What in the Tree's name was that?' Pemisegant asked 'Maybe its a ghost, replied Althallant, using an antigrav belt to float just above Pemisegant's head.

'Oh don't be silly, only sprites believe in ghosts.'

'So the question remains, what was it?' asked Natalicsya as she gracefully took off in her belt.

There was no doubt about it, there was something down that corridor. The branch was supposed to be deserted, abandoned during the Winter months.

The Cadets had been sent out as trainee illumination engineers, inspecting broken day-lighter fittings. The job docket the Winter Squad received would say something unhelpfully brief like, "Day-lighter fitting P7E not working in Branch SA17-8EE". So the Cadets were evaluating each reported fault and creating a more accurate list of jobs. When they finished at one day-lighter, an automated utilivan would take them to the next badly reported problem.

When the defective day-lighter was working, it was impossible to look at directly. Day-lighters brought the light of Mother Sun from the outermost bark of the Tree down into the heart of the branches, Trunk and Roots, projecting the image of a perfect blue sky. Now all the Canopy's daylighters were on standby and only the gloomy standby lighting was available.

Natalicsya and Althallant were both high above checking the broken equipment with scanners, hunting out what was wrong with the malfunctioning equipment. Nevamar and Pemisegant were logged into workstations busily updating the job dockets with the data that their friends supplied.

'I don't see why they should have all the fun?' Pemisegant was envious of his two colleagues.

'Lieutenant Sharlenya told you there was no way you would be allowed to use the anti-gravity belts. Not after the incidents during the swimming lesson two days ago.' Nevamar told him.

'That's not fair, I didn't slip on purpose.'

'She said "I can't trust you not to do something foolish." Also you are still in disgrace after being hauled out of the drainage system.' Nevamar quoted the Lieutenant word for word.

'So are you, but she didn't say you couldn't use the anti-gravity belt.'

'First, you were silly to ask. It only reminded the Lieutenant of how reckless you can be. Second, I really don't trust the anti-gravity belts. Flying up to the day-lighters with nothing to support me but a current flowing through rings of super-conductive alloy in a belt, doesn't appeal at all. Especially not in the twilight gloom that the malfunctioning day-lighters create.'

'So you're telling me you are quite happy at that workstation?' asked Pemisegant.

'Yes.' replied Nevamar.

'I don't believe you.'

'Whatever.'

The Cadets should not have been left on their own on such a dangerous assignment. However, for a second day other duties called their mentor away. Pemisegant knew it was because of Ensign Serynazsya, who had gone from being a carer to being cared for so quickly. He had given his word as an officer to keep the Ensign's troubles secret, so his classmates remained in the dark.

After briefing, Lieutenant Sharlensya handed the Cadets over to Captain Treslelant. He had dropped the Cadets off here, and gone to do another job in this part of the Canopy. Lieutenant Sharlensya would be livid if she found out. If they were careful, she never would and they could continue to enjoy this level of respect. Which meant Pemisegant was definitely not going to be allowed to wear an anti-gravity belt. His friends did not trust him either.

'There's a cat down there,' said Natalicsya, who had spotted the creature from her vantage point up by the broken day-lighter.

'Are you sure, all the registered pets would have been taken down to the Roots by their owners at the end of Summer.'

'Positive Pezzi, I can see it from up here,' she said in a tone both, informing and taunting at the same time.

'Perhaps its a stray.'

'Nobody lives on this section of this branch, its just pipes and conduits beyond the roadway, so no strays or missing pets would have been reported around here.' added Nevamar.

'Mystery cat. Cool!' Pemisegant loved a good mystery.

'Thank you detective Nevamar.' said Natalicsya.

'My pleasure Lisha. Is it still there?' Nevamar had always loved cats. Her old Branch Captain had owned one. To the delight of the sprites, the cat used to inspect the twig in its haughty feline way. Nevamar had often wondered what had happened to the cat when the kind old style had recycled.

'Yes, it appears to have got itself stuck, that is why it is making that horrible racket.'

'Obviously doesn't know the area, probably been wandering for weeks.' said Nevamar.

Skillfully Natalicsya floated down the sub-branch to where the poor creature was trapped. She carefully lifted the cat from the pipe it was trapped on and landed next to Nevamar and Pemisegant.

'Looks like she used to belong to someone, she's got a collar.'

'How do you know its not a Tom?'

'Don't be silly Pezzi, would you put a collar like that on a Tom?'

'Good point, well made,' Pemisegant conceded. 'But she is ginger, do you know how unusual that is. Usually only male cats are ginger. Genetics.'

Natalicsya hadn't known or cared. She just thought the cat was wonderful.

The cat had obviously been spooked by the flight down and did not appreciate the presence of all these strangers. In a few fluid moves, she was free from Natalicsya's grasp, and was away.

'Naughty kitty, she must have caught her claws in my tunic on the way down. I'll have to repair that now.'

Everyone was amazed. Normally if something damaged what Natalicsya was wearing, she would sulk for hours. Today she just accepted it.

'Well Amber is so cute, and its not as if the tunic has been ruined.'

'Amber?'

'Yes Nevamar, that is what I have called the little beauty.'

'You do know we are not allowed pets Lisha.' said Pemisegant.

'So, it's not my pet, it's a stray, nothing to do with me.'

'You just called it Amber.'

'Still nothing to do with me, I just thought the name suited it.'

Natalicsya had pulled something short and stubby from her pocket. It had a dental mirror attached to a telescopic aerial. She pointed it at the tear and with a buzz it repaired it.

'Wow, where did you get that?' Nevamar was duly impressed.

'From Pezzi, he does have some uses.'

'It was a little something I dreamt up a couple of weeks ago. Mostly to re-attach buttons to shirts.'

Pemisegant looked extremely pleased with himself. 'I knew that Lisha here would thoroughly field test it for me.'

'It's so compact. I didn't know anyone made portable emprinters that small.'

'Nobody does. Bernie got me to patent the idea. He says it could be worth a fortune.' The young anther was obviously proud of this gadget.

'Oh yes, I believe you.' said Nevamar.

However, as much as he was enjoying the praise for his new invention, it was wasting time.

'Am I the only fool doing any work around here?' asked Althallant from on high.

'OK, sorry Alth. Back to work everyone, what was the serial number of that part?'

'How should I know Pezzi,' Natalicsya said. She could see the envious look in Pemisegant's face every time she took off or landed. So just to wind him up she floated a few fractions above his head. 'I'd better go up and check.'

Nevamar and Pemisegant were on Punishment Duty whilst Althalant was off playing some silly ball game or other, so Natalicsya was left on her own and she was bored. She decided to find that cute cat again and give it some tit-bits. This was how the young style found herself getting an object lesson in how large the Canopy really was. Natalicsya had pedalled for two hour and fifty minute to branch SA17-85. The utilivan the previous day had taken a quarter of the time. Then it had taken another half an hour to find any trace of the cat again.

'Aw baby, come to your Aunty Lisha,' she had cooed at the cat, but every time Natalicsya got within a few units of Amber, the cat would scoot off. 'You're trying too hard, Lisha old girl.'

Why was she talking to herself. Because she was mad, why else had she come on such a wild goose chase. Or should that be wild cat chase. No, Amber was definitely domesticated, none of the feral cats up here would have let a human get within half a mile of them.

Poor little Amber did not look at all well. It was staggering as it walked and had stopped trying to run away. It just sat there mewing pathetically. It did not even eat the little tit-bits Natalicsya had brought with her. She picked the cat up and put it to lie more comfortably on her lap.

'Poor, poor Amber, you are a sick little kitty,' she said, as she stroked the creature. The cat tried to purr, but it was a very weak effort. When that stopped, Natalicsya knew there was something seriously wrong. She scooped the now unconscious cat up, put it in the basket at the front of her bike, and rode hell for leather.

Cadet Natalicsya, you do know I am not a vet. I do not treat creatures.'

'No, Sir. But you were the only person I could think of Sir. Major Keltonnant was trying to relax, so he was sitting in a lounge close to his quarters. As the only doctor in the Canopy, he never really felt off duty, so was always in uniform. The window of the lounge overlooked the Garden that Natalicsya had just raced through on her bicycle. In the gathering gloom the garden looked ghostly and dark.

'And neither am I much of a logician,' he said, 'if this Number Set puzzle is to be believed.' He gave up on the Tree's version of a Sudoku and walked over to the girl and sick cat. 'At ease Cadet. Let's have a look at it shall we?'

The Major quickly assessed the cat and diagnosed extreme malnutrition and estimated that it was having four to six kittens.

'You do realise that you are not allowed to keep pets.'

'Yes, Sir, I never intended for it to become a pet, I was just concerned for its well-being.'

'Well, you are responsible for it now Cadet. And soon you won't just be responsible for its well being, there are its kittens to consider.'

The Major could see that the girl was visibly upset, the situation was getting worse and worse. Maybe he had overdone the gruffness. Time to turn on the charm.

L ike all the trees of Arbouron, the home of Nevamar and her friends, towers above the surface. The thin atmosphere that surrounds Trunk and Canopy is inhospitable to all but a handful of gigantic creatures and even they are dwarfed by the scale of the Tree. Smaller creatures live in a habitable zone extending a few miles upwards to the tips of the grasses and downwards into the labyrinth of tunnels and caverns around their roots. Some of these creatures are a permanent threat to the Tree, and the officers of the Defence Regiment are constantly on their guard against them. Others are welcomed visitors. In its youth, when the

Tree had been unable to create what it needed, it had allowed some of the creatures from outside to take up residence and adapted them to fit its needs.

Cats are a prime example of visitors who have become part of the Tree's rich ecosystem. When the Tree had accidentally produced mice, the ancestors of the modern cat had been enticed into the Roots. Their abilities as nocturnal hunters made them ideal for controlling the mouse population so they were allowed to stay. The people of the Tree found these aloof and proud creatures fascinating and soon they were the pet of choice within the Tree.

Because cats were alien to the Tree, having two genders was a necessity and not a happy accident. Cats would mate and the females would give birth to from five to ten kittens, which she would raise alone, until they were self-sufficient.

A few hours after helping Natalicsya with the cat, Major Keltonant Keltonnant sat in the living room. Amber was responding to treatment and he was absentmindedly stroking her.

'You're a soft touch Uncle Kelly,' said Sharlensya, who had called in to the flat above the Medical Centre for a chat. 'But I have to admit she is a gorgeous cat, no wonder Lisha went so gaga about her.'

'Soon there will be more, when she has her kittens.' Her Uncle was smiling. That was always a bad sign. 'The problem is, I can't keep them here. Far to unhygienic.'

'Don't look at me, my quarters are in the same corridor as the kids, the one with a ban on pets.'

'Don't worry, I already have someone to look after them. Bernie owes me a favour or two.'

'But Bernie loathes all things feline.'

'Apparently he wants to keep the location of his latest scheme mouse free. Cats will do the job nicely,' said her Uncle.

'Those kids spend far to much time with that old reprobate, I am afraid he is teaching them bad habits.'

'You really should cut Bernie some slack Sharlee. He is not that bad.'

'Really, you are the last person I would have imagined who would tolerate that ne'er do well.'

'He was a good friend to me, when I was a clueless Ensign.' A far away look came into his eyes. 'He persuaded your grandmother to adopt one last child. If he had not introduced your mother to me, we would not be family members.'

'I never knew that,' said Sharlensya, who was genuinely surprised.

'I really should tell you some of our family history.'

'Maybe tomorrow night, school day tomorrow, its not just the kids who should be in bed early.'

'But you haven't got classes tomorrow, you are still busy putting young Serynazsya back together again.

'I feel I've let her down badly. She was an unaccompanied child, one far to young to be here on her own. The victim of freak circumstances. I should have paid her more attention. Instead of concentrating on my little lot.'

'To be honest dear, that is your main job.' Her Uncle was being perfectly honest, the mentoring of the older kids was a secondary responsibility.

'Yes, but that poor girl has been thoroughly worked over by her former Branch Captain,' she said with growing anger in her voice. 'That style is evil, and I think you are right about anger management, because I don't know what I would do if I ever came face to face with her.'

Her Uncle was nodding in agreement. 'I think you would have to join the queue.'

'Serynazsya finally opened up this afternoon, thanks to young Nevamar. It brought her a get well card from its class, whilst I was getting a mug of Instaht.'

'That was a remarkably foolish thing for young Nevamar to do, considering her background,' said her Uncle.

'I know, but Nevamar didn't say anything, just sat there holding that poor young girls hand as she let it all pour out. I am so glad I had left my voxcorder running. What I can gather from that remarkable stream of emotion is not only was Captain Samnundsya a bully, she was doing a damn good job of turning most of the young officers under her into bullies as well.'

'I'm afraid I know the type all to well Sharlee.'

'It's worse than that Uncle. Poor Serynazsya refused to be moulded into the Captain's image of what a Pure-stock officer should be. She said she had been kind and tolerant towards the sprites, treating them with a degree of respect for the work they did. Her Captain saw this as a sign of weakness, an abhorrent weakness at that. It is as if that evil old witch did her damnedest to destroy Serynazsya. Using the poor girl's dreams of becoming a nurse and her desperately wanting to be part of a family as weapons against her.'

'It's not surprising that Serynazsya is so emotionally scarred,' said Keltonnant.

'Remind you of anyone, Uncle.'

'Vaguely dear, you are similar in some respects.'

Keltonnant's mind ran back eleven years or so, to when the young Sharlensya had run away from the bullying of the Pure-stock Academy. His sister found the young style hiding in her home in the Roots. Sharlensya was lucky, Sannarlsya had found a way to help and eventually adopted the girl. Now all these years later Sharlensya was dealing with a youngster who had not fared so well.

'All because she wanted to care and be cared for.' Keltonnant said regretfully. 'If she were part of Family Fangkart, her problems would be our problems, and that witch would rue the day she crossed our path.'

'Say that again Uncle.'

'What, about it being a family problem when she joins one.'

'Uncle Kelly, you are a genius.'

Suddenly it all clicked into place. The loneliness after losing her mother. The love and support she had received from her family over the years. The need to repay that love in some way. What Tabbernant had called her broodiness. Sharlensya knew how to cure the loneliness of one poor damaged girl who just wanted to be loved.

'Uncle, who is doing the the night shift downstairs?'

'Voysha. She is on nights all this week,' said Keltonnant, confused by this sudden turn of events.

'Excellent, she is the style I want to see.'

L ieutenant Voynvalsya was in the galley at the back of the Medical Centre, making a cup of cha when, Sharlensya and her bemused Uncle came down from the apartment upstairs.

'Evening Sharlee, how are things? There is tea in the pot if you fancy a cuppa?'

'Not at the moment Voysha, I am on a mission.' She sat down next to her cousin, with her uncle at the top of the table.

'After speaking to her today, I have come to the conclusion that young Serynazsya's problems, her feeling of low self-esteem and self-worth all stems from the fact that she thinks she is all alone in the World. I intend to remedy that.'

'Are you serious Sharlee?' Voynvalsya had realised what was coming next.

'Perfectly serious Voysha, losing my mother has been a shock, but it was the family that helped me get over it. The family has always been there for me. The only practical way I can pay the family back is by giving the love they have showered on me to someone who deserves a mother's love showered on her.'

'You plan on adopting this child?' Asked her uncle.

'I do.'

'Have you asked her?' Here cousin wanted to know.

'Not yet Voysha. She is obviously in need of someone who will rebuilt her shattered ego. As my daughter, she will get my one hundred percent support.'

'This is a serious commitment Sharlee, not one to be taken just because you feel sorry for the child. Your whole life will change.'

'Oh Voysha, I thought you knew me better than that. This may seem like a spur of the moment decision.'

'So what about young Nevamarsya?' asked her Uncle.

'What about her?'

'Oh don't try to deny it, but you mother that one. Its a wonder it hasn't triggered off jealousy in her classmates.'

'And there was I hoping nobody had noticed,' Sharlensya said.

'Oh come off it Sharlee,' added her cousin. 'It's been obvious for weeks you're broody and have formed a maternal attachment with that little one. She is going to be dreadfully disappointed you have adopted someone else.'

'When she finally differentiates as a style, which cannot be that far off, she still has a year to wait before anyone can adopt her. When she needs it, I will be there for her. However, the priority now is Serynazsya.'

'I don't understand, why do you want to speak to Voysha here?' asked Keltonnant.

'As Lieutenant Voynvalsya is responsible for housekeeping in this establishment, she is Ensign Serynazsya's direct superior.'

'No need to ask. Of course I will grant permission when you formally apply to adopt Serynazsya, Sharlee dear.' said her cousin.

'Sharlee, your mother would be so proud of you.'

'I know Uncle Kelly. She would be over the moon at the prospect of being a grandmother.'

'Why are you doing all this for me? I am just not worth it.' Nobody had realised that Serynazsya was not sleeping.

'But you are dear. Life has dealt you a dreadful hand, that dreadful style has made you think you're a monster. You're not, she's the monster. You are an angel, and I would be proud to have you as my daughter.'

'You would be my mummy? Really? Oh yes please.' And she burst into tears again. Another dose of sedative quickly returned Serynazsya to blissfully happy dreams of belonging at last.

PART THREE
THE CADET
(SENIOR GRADE)

CHAPTER THIRTEEN
BOOT CAMP

Bluntly speaking Nevamar was rubbish at all things military, which in a society of soldiers was not good news. officers had been created to defend the Tree in times of peril, all hoped they would never be called upon to put themselves in harms way. As the Autumn had progressed progressed, the amount of military training in the curriculum had increased. It had originally taken up Trenitsday mornings. For the past two weeks it had swallowed up the whole of that day and all of Fursday as well.

'I never thought I would miss Trenitsday afternoon sports lessons so much,' said Nevamar to Tabbernant, as they ate their lunch.

'You still have Hell Month to come,' said the old anther. 'Your first Boot Camp.'

Nevamar's heart sank at the thought of a month of never-ending Trenitsdays.

'Thanks Bernies.'

I certainly know how to cheer you up, Girlie.'

'A whole month, 24/7, I don't think I will survive.'

Tabbernant was laughing wickedly. Sometimes the old anther really wound Nevamar up.

'It's only a training exercise, no one trying to kill you.'

'I suppose so,' said Nevamar grudgingly.

'You'll be a Senior Grade Cadet. All plain sailing to passing out, safe in the knowledge that Military Training will only be on Trinitsday afternoons for a whole year.'

'Hopefully I will finally be an anther when I get back. Then you will have to stop calling me Girlie.'

Every officer had to be able to prove that they maintained a constant state of military alertness. For adults it usually meant spending a week a year with the Defence Regiment. For children, it meant a period of intensive military training, for no less than 28 days every year. Ensigns who joined the Defence Regiment full time, after completing Officer Training, would complete this commitment within their first year, for every other Cadet and Ensign in the Tree it was an annual bind.

Brian Spenser had, as promised had a chat with one of his colleagues at the University, and on a cold late October morning, he paid his father a visit with Dr. Fraser, an expert on apple-trees.

'Good morning Dr. Fraser, nice to meet you.'

The man who got out of Brian's car looked to Mr. Spenser as if he had not missed a meal in his life, and he instantly disliked him. Give him chance he thought, don't judge on first impressions.

Sadly, as they walked to the tree, first impressions proved to be completely accurate. This Dr. David Fraser was an unpleasant fellow. Still, if he could do something to help save his precious apple-tree, then all sins would be forgiven.

'Good Lord. Malus Ortusedenii,' said Dr Fraser.

'Is that good or bad.'

'My dear Mr. Spenser, it is very good. Malus Ortusedenii is believed to be the first varieties of domesticated apples bred from the Malus Sieversii. It was named after the Garden of Eden.'

'I knew it was old, but not that old.' said Mr. Spenser.

'Ah, it has been grafted with a modern root stock, well modern for the 1830's.'

'1830's? That is old.' Brian Spenser was trying to get his head around that fact. Goodness, and still producing fruit.

'Plus or minus five years.'

'Its a shame it is dying then,' chipped in Mr. Spenser.

'I don't think so, just in need of some specialist care and attention.'

Dr Fraser spent the rest of the day studying the tree. On the following morning he returned with his four man team with trucks full of equipment. They were very thorough in their examination. They told Mr Spenser that they had only ever seen a tree like this in the UK once before, and that it had been as ancient and marvellous as this one. The owner of the other example was a recluse who refused to let anyone within a mile of his home and precious tree.

'The good news Mr. Spenser is that this tree is definitely not dying. It just needs a bit more of a pruning than it normally gets.' Dr. Fraser told the tree's worried owner.

'Well, I'm not as young as I used to be. I suppose I have become less vigilant with the secateurs.'

'And when we have finished, this venerable plant will out live all of us.'

'That is good to know Dr. Fraser.'

Dr. Fraser said nothing of the cuttings that he would take back to the laboratory at the University. The following year hundreds of new saplings, of this variety, would appear in orchards up and down the UK, preserving the variety and earning him a tidy little nest-egg.

The worse part of the Winter Squad's tour of duty had just passed. For the past week everything had been topsy-turvey. Each year, something would remove dead, dying and unwanted branches from the Canopy. Not in a sustained malignant onslaught, but in a neat orderly fashion. The Squad had to tidy up and make good the damage. This year seemed to be worse than normal. The attacks had come during a concentrated seventy two hour period, removing roughly thirty percent of the volume of the Canopy. Everyone had been on full alert.

This extra work had meant that classes had been suspended for the week. After the first good night's sleep in days, this was the first time that the four Cadets and their mentor had met in their classroom on a Saxearthday morning. This weekend class was not at all popular. However after ruining their day, Lieutenant Sharlensya was about to ruin her pupil's next four weeks.

'Right then class, I have an announcement,' said the Lieutenant at the start of the lesson. She picked a document off her desk and showed it to the class.

'As it now appears that the Pruning has passed for another year, the senior officers of the Squad have given me permission to take you and five of the Ensigns who are training with us this year to a Boot Camp during weeks eight, nine, ten and eleven of this term.'

The Cadets exchanged worried glances. They had heard about boot camps from the Ensigns. None of them were looking forward to their first Hell Month.

'Right, I have been reviewing your Progress Reports,' continued the Lieutenant, 'and this exercise cannot have come a minute to soon.' She picked up a thick file from her desk. 'Complaints about insubordination that are in this file are at an unacceptably high level.' The file was dropped back onto the desk with a loud bang.

'So now that I have your attention, Cadet Pemisegant, tell the class what would happen if you told a sprite to shoot Cadet Althallant in the head with a rivet gun?'

'It would kill him, Ma'am, and the sprite would go off satisfied by a job well done.' Pemisegant, who had been whispering something to Althalant and not really paying attention, was taken off guard by the sudden change in topic.

'So Cadet,' she turned to Altallant. 'What would happen if I told you to shoot Cadet Pezimegant in the head with a rivet gun?'

'I wouldn't do it. I would go and fetch Major Keltonnant, or one of his staff, and they would sedate you for your safety and that of the Squad.'

'And that rather gruesome example proves my point.'

Lieutenant Sharlensya had picked up a swagger stick which was now sitting under her arm. Nevamar had a book of memories about what such a stick could do that needed to be catalogued in the library of its past. It shuddered slightly.

'When you were sprites, you obeyed without question, no matter how foolish, dangerous or illegal the order was. Now you have gained the ability to think as you are carrying out commands and to evaluate orders when you receive them. This in its place is a good thing, but at the moment, you have gone to the opposite extreme and are questioning everything. Neither extreme is acceptable in an officer.

'In the years to come, you will be in command of numerous sprites, if you progress up the rank structure, you will be in command of other officers. The prime requisite of being able to lead is being able to follow. At the moment you have gained the ability to lead, but you are in danger of losing the ability to follow. These exercises will help you get that back.

'Our rank structure comes from the earliest days of the Tree, when officers and sprites actually had to fight invading menaces on a day-to-day basis. So for the next month we will be devoted to military discipline. Instead of two days a week, you will receive military training every day, putting what you have learnt in your classes to the test.

Hell Month on top of the Pruning. That was just being nasty. The Cadets studied the list, all essentials, no luxuries. The first question had been why do we need to take so much? This had been answered when they saw where they were camping. Out in the farthest reaches of the Canopy. At this time of year there would be no fabric enprinters and Bernie would be down in the Crown. Everything they needed they would have to take with them. So far away from convenient luxuries, the youngsters would have to learn self reliance. Last but not least, it looked like they would be marching to the Boot Camp

'I am distributing a list of the equipment you will require to pack into your backpacks. It is not to be deviated from. We depart at 0600 tomorrow morning, the rest of today will be spent in preparation. Since 0900 this morning and until further notice, all downtime has been cancelled. Class dismissed.'

'No downtime, and I was going to the concert tonight,' said Natalicsya in a low moan.

'You go to a concert, wonders will never cease.'

'Can it Pezzi, why do you always have to wind me up?'

'Well, somebody has to.'

When he saw how close to tears Natalicsya was, he became more conciliatory. 'But do you really think I want to go on a camping trip up in the wild extremities of the Canopy? I spent far too much time up there as a sprite. I had hoped I had finally managed to get away from the outer extremities, living and working down here in the Crown, when I became an officer,' moaned Pemisegant. 'Now we will have weeks of square bashing, long distance runs and all sorts of pointless physical activity in that old dump? No thank you.'

'Oh great green apples,' cried Natalicsya. 'They have done it already,' she said, bursting into tears. 'recycled all my lovely dresses, that includes the dress I was going to wear tonight. It was so pretty.' Natalicsya had quickly run out of spare enprintable fabric for her downtime clothing allowance, so she had begun using her spare uniforms as a source of material, which under normal circumstances would not have been a problem.

'Don't worry, Lisha, now you have the patterns in your wardrobe, it will be easy enough to recreate them,' said Nevamar. Natalisya's obsession with clothes amused Nevamar. Although where its friend was getting the money to pay for all these outfits was a bit of a worry.

'But that is the point, I don't have their patterns in my wardrobe software. They were all unique designs. I hadn't decided if I wanted to keep them or not. All that hard work wasted,' said Natalicsya, each word punctuated with a sob.

'You make all your downtime clothes?' asked Nevamar, who was now starting to see its friends obsession from a completely new angle. Not a dangerously expensive addiction, but as the work of a genius.

'Of course, how do you think I can afford to be such a clothes horse on our tiny salary.'

'Did she say all the Ensigns?' Althallant barged into the conversation, it had been about clothes, and girls clothes at that. For him, his question was far more important, even if the Cadets all knew the answer already, none were willing to say it.

'Well, all except Bernie, he doesn't need to prove his military competence like the other Ensigns, he is retiring in a few months,' Pemisegant pointed out helpfully. 'Also Dukecamant doesn't have to come, but probably will just to show off,' continued Pemisegant.

'He'll be there. After screwing up his assignment so badly, he has to,' said Nevamarsya.

'Hasn't Hanazofsya done her five boot camps?' asked Natalicsya.

'I think so. She is five soon, like Ducky, isn't she?' asked Pezzi.

'I think so, and given the amount of plumbing work the Pruning has caused, the pressure will be on for her to stay and work with the Squad,' said Nevamar.

'Lucky so and so.'

'Yeah, she doesn't have to spend a month with Misery Guts' continued Althallant.

'You shouldn't call her that, its not nice,' said Nevamar, 'maybe a month with us will help her lighten up a bit.'

None of the senior officers would say why Ensign Serynazsya had been so ill. She had been hospitalised for a week. Nevamar had known Serynazsya for longer than her friends. She was the only officer Captain Samnundsya had brought with her from the Roots, who Nevamar had fond memories of. This was possibly because the Captain had disliked Serynazsya as much as she had disliked all the sprites. Lieutenant Sharlensya was treating Serynazsya like she was made from the most delicate protein glass. Nevamar found itself more than a little jealous of this. What was wrong with the young style that made the Lieutenant so protective of her. It was not just Lieutenant Sharlensya, it was all her relatives as well. It was as if Family Fangkart had closed ranks around one of their own. But Serynazsya wasn't one of them, she was still an unadopted child. Great Green Apples! That was it. The

Lieutenant was planning on adopting Serynazsya. No that was not fair. In Nevamar's dreams it was going to be her first child. Nevamar thought she had done the Ensign a favour getting her as far away from Captain Samnundsya's malignant influence. Now it could see that it had introduced an usurper into its life. Serynazsya was Pure-stock, just like Lieutenant Sharlensya. She tried to say it meant nothing, but Nevamar could see that this simply was not the case. Just as Nevamar had feared, Sharlensya had chosen a blonde girl whose name started with "S" over a redhead Canopy hick like Nevamar. From now on, Ensign "Misery Guts" Serynazsya 178/20 was its Number One implacable enemy.

Trees grow upwards towards the light. Eventually the trunk splits into many branches, so that the search for light can expand over a greater and greater surface area. To the religiously inclined the Canopy spreads to embrace Mother Sun just as the Roots spread to embrace Father Earth. For the practically inclined, it meant that the Tree had many ramps and slopes and a great deal of stairs. The force behind the annual Pruning had also forced the Tree into its current shape. All the major branches were as close to horizontal as possible. Sub-branches might shoot upwards but were soon also forced to become gently sloping themselves. This greatly increased the habitable and productive areas of the Tree.

The Canopy also had the Trolleybus System. Bubble like carriages travelled through each branch. It was one of the most complicated pieces of machinery the Tree had grown within itself. It seemed almost alive as it had to know where each of its carriages was and move them without crashes or congestion. It was maintained by highly trained sprites and their dedicated officers during the Spring and Summer, for the rest of the year, it was the responsibility of the Winter Squad. They only used a fraction of its potential, as they knew it needed to rest during the Winter as much as the rest of the Canopy. This is why Lieutenant Sharlensya was marching her little troop of Ensigns and Cadets from the base of the Canopy, all the way up to one of its most isolated branches. That march would take three days and after just a few hours, the youngsters were ready for a break.

The Troop was far to full of their collective misery to notice their surroundings. Sore feet and aching limbs dampened the appeal of the beautifully landscaped park, around the small pavilion they were resting in. The Lieutenant had vanished into another room, looking as green as her uniform and she was in a foul temper.

'Are all the ramps so steep in the Canopy?' Natalicsya had never been this far from the Crown, even when hunting for Amber, Bernie's cat. She was not enjoying the experience.

'You wait until we get to the stairs. I imagine lifts are going to be forbidden as well.' Ensign Serynazsya was being her usually morose self.

'I am not that much of a sadist Ensign, where we need to take a lift, we will,' said the Lieutenant.

The Ensigns and Cadets came messily to attention.

'That was pathetic troop. I expected better from you Ensigns. I can see I have a lot of work cut out for me. At ease troop.'

Lieutenant Sharlensya wandered back to the pavilion, where her restorative cup of tea had cooled to just the right temperature. Her uninvited guest was making its presence felt for the first time. This was making Lieutenant Sharlensya very short tempered.

'You know, I used to really like her,' said Natalicsya.

'You're not supposed to like her Lisha, you are supposed to obey her,' said Althallant, who was the only person really enjoying himself. Even with Ensign Misery-Guts in the party.

'I'll watch the door, if she comes back in, I will order you all to come to attention,' Serynazsya suggested. She had been entranced by the beautiful plants in the garden. This whole section of the branch had grass instead of concrete floors and had been landscaped. The Spirit of the Tree liked its people to be surrounded by a pleasant environment, which was lovingly tended by the Tree Monks during the Summer.

'I'll come with you,' said Ensign Hanazofsya, who to everyone's amazement had volunteered for an extra Boot Camp.

'Don't bother,' said Natalicsya, 'she'll find any excuse to be miserable on her own.'

'Oh give her a break Cadet.' said Ensign Hanazofsya.

'You don't fancy her, do you, Ensign?' asked Natalicsya.

'Oh please. This is not the time for childishness.' said Pemisegant.

'Well, if she doesn't, you must,' replied Natalicsya. 'Pezzi fancies misery-guts. Pezzi fancies misery-guts. Pezzi fancies misery-guts.'

'Squad, attention!' called Ensign Serynazsya.

'Cadet Natalicsya 199/20, don't let me ever hear you referring to Ensign Serynazsya 871/59 as misery-guts ever again. Do I make myself clear?'

'Yes, Ma'am.'

'That goes for everyone. Name-calling is for sprites. Do I make my self clear?'

'Yes, Ma'am' chorused the troop.

'Right, pack up your things, we move out in five minutes.'

CHAPTER FOURTEEN
HOME SWEET HOME

The troop had arrived at its destination and Nevamar recognised home territory immediately. Everyone was shattered, so being made to vacuum clean and polish the barracks had seemed sadistic.

The branch was as empty now as it had been that fateful day when Sprite NM331/29, had run alone down from its twig, hoping to catch an express trolleybus to the Crown, then a shuttle to a new life. Well, that plan had gone pear-shaped, but Nevamar had still managed to find a new life.

'Looks like we will be sleeping back in my old billet again. Still, at least Captain Samnundsya is down in the Roots, so I don't have to see her smiling face each day. I think that if she could see me now, she would be spluttering into her cocoa.'

'You! You were that sprite, the one who gave me so much trouble on the last day of Summer. If it wasn't for you messing about, I would have been down in the Roots now!'

'Pardon Ensign, I don't understand.' Nevamar was horrified, it had not realised it was saying everything that crossed its mind. Now Ensign Serynazsya knew the truth.

'Oh don't try to act all innocent. You sabotaged my whole Autumn, maybe even my whole life. Nevamar, with a name like that your IndesnCode must have started NM' She looked evilly at Nevamar, I'm right, aren't I? What is your full designation.'

'Oh all right, I am Cadet Nevamar 331/29, and I was Sprite NM331/29. But its your own fault you lost your IndesnCard and ended up stuck in the Canopy.' So much for keeping her secret from the Ensign for the duration of Hell Month. Blew it on the first day.

'And you would still be doing Hell Month,' Nevamar continued, 'its compulsory for someone your age. But you would be in the tips of the Roots and not up here at the tip of the Canopy.'

'Don't think you have heard the last of this. You will be sorry you ever crossed me.' And she flounced out of the barracks.

'Drama Queen.'

'So, What's her problem?' asked Natalicsya.

'She has just worked out who, or rather what I was. Blames me for all her problems. Its sad really. You styles are so melodramatic.'

'You styles?' said Natalicsya incredulously, 'Nevamarsya, when are you going to realise you are a style and accept it. I'm sure this stubbornness is what is stopping your differentiation.'

'To be perfectly honest, I 'd take anything at the moment. I'm still neither one thing nor the other. It's getting on my nerves.'

'Good, moving forwards,' said Natalicsya.

'Though I would still prefer to be an anther. Which is why I am here in the anther's dorm, yours is next door.'

'Two steps forwards and one step back.'

'I can't believe the Lieutenant chose my old billet for our base. Of all the branches in all the Tree, she had to make us walk into this one,' said Nevamar.

'Did you really sleep in one of those diddly little hammocks Nevamar? They are so cute.'

'Cute they may be Lisha, comfortable they were not. I am so glad we have brought sleeping bags.'

Yes it had slept in the hammocks, but it was so much taller now. At a height of four units eight point five fractions, Nevamar was too tall to even think of sleeping in one of those diddly little hammocks. It would probably break one if it tried sitting on it.

'Ugh, sleeping on the floor. What a horrible thought. Even as a sprite I never did that. I had a nice comfortable shelf in the dorm to sleep on,' said Natalicsya.

'Troop attention! Commanding Officer in the room,' bellowed one of the Ensigns.

'Right troop, as you were. I want you to get a good night's sleep. For tonight we sleep where we drop, from tomorrow, this will be the anther's dorm and next door the style's dorm. They will be strictly segregated. We start the exercises at 0630 hours sharp tomorrow morning with two hours of drill practice. Then we will prepare breakfast at 0830. 0900 kit inspection, 0930 more drill until Noon. Then lunch and the afternoon briefing. Lights out in ten minutes.'

The Cadets and Ensigns looked at each other in amazement. Lights out in ten minutes, it was only 2105. What was the Lieutenant on about. Not a single one of them was still awake at 2130, the day had been more exhausting than they realised.

Being undifferentiated meant that Nevamar had been able to chose which dormitory it would sleep in. As it knew it was destined to be an anther, it chose the boys dorm.

'Father Earth adolescent anthers can be really gross at times,' Nevamar said as soon as it had woken up.

'That's a bit full on, isn't it,' said Ensign Cemnentant, who was also waking up. 'Only the excesses of youth. We will grow out of it.'

'You are grossed out because you are in the wrong dorm dear,' Pemisegant said but he knew his friend would just ignore him. 'You're a style, you should be in the style's dorm.'

Nevamar had come to the conclusion that Ensign Dukecamant had a filthy mind, and his lewd fantasies about Lieutenant Sharlensya were deeply unpleasant, as well as probably being physically impossible. Dukecamant was nearly five years old, blonde and handsome, a poster-boy for Roots anthers. He was a member of the Defence Regiment. As such, he did not need to do Boot Camp, his military competency was not in doubt. However, he wanted to be out here. Partly because it would look good on his record but mostly because he wanted to show off. He had unofficially appointed himself one of the Lieutenant's second in command, sure that his age and experience would earn him the job officially, when the Dorm Sergeant was selected at the end of the first week. Nevamar wished that Ensign Tabbernant was here, he would have put the vile upstart in his place.

Age and experience, Tabbernant had more than the grubby Dukecamant could dream of. Sadly because of his age and experience he remained down in the Crown.

Tabbernant was like a favourite uncle now, and he taught them things with the earthy honesty Tabbernant applied to most subjects. He also taught them things Lieutenant Sharlensya, the official mentor, never would. Great green apples, it thought,

I must be having a lousy time now if cleaning vegetables for Tabbernant is an enjoyable alternative to square bashing.

The mindless repetition of the drill did not suit Nevamar at all. After a lousy night's sleep, everything seemed so much harder. Even as a sprite it had always been a bit clumsy. Things other sprites learnt in a few minutes and became almost instinctive, were always a problem. Also its hand and eye coordination was poor. It had, however, developed coping mechanisms for getting around its difficulties with the complex repetitive tasks. These coping mechanisms had been so successful that it had been the most efficient sprite on the twig. The problem had not gone away when it had become Cadet Nevamar. Its new improved body was still as uncoordinated as its old. It still took it a little while longer than its colleagues, to complete a task, but nothing that could not be masked by a little creative thinking. The precision and coordination needed for the task at hand was causing Nevamar no end of trouble.

'Right lets do that again, this time with the odd numbers going first.' The Lieutenant wanted to know if her little troop had been paying attention. Sadly, despite the fact that Nevamar had done nothing but pay attention, it got it completely wrong. 'Cadet Nevamar, that was rubbish, give me twenty,' bellowed the Lieutenant. Nevamar dropped down and started the twenty press-ups.

'Too slow, do them again.'

It did the press-ups in double time. Then went to prepare and eat its breakfast in a state of befuddlement.

By the end of the day, Nevamar was glad to climb into its sleeping bag and curl up. Sleep was no reprieve, as it was plagued with nightmares. Father Earth it thought, I hate this place. So many unhappy memories. Why did they have to be camped out in this branch, why not one on the other side of the Tree. As it finally felt restful slumber wrap it in its warm blanket, the sound of a bugle, playing something loud and annoying, told Nevamar that it was time to wake up.

Another disastrous day. Square bashing in the morning was horrendous. It still didn't get all the intricacies and to make things worse, Ensign Serynazsya would do things during the drill that would knock Nevamar out even more, whilst the Ensign appeared perfect. This was so unfair.

Fortunately, by the end of the first week, Nevamar had learnt to ignore the ghosts of the branch and to get a good night's sleep. The problems of the present day were more than dwarfing the memories of the past.

Ensign Serynazsya's subtle persecution of the Cadet was getting worse. Nothing could be proved. If Nevamar had made a fuss about the Ensign, it would have appeared that the clumsy young Cadet was trying to blame all its own shortcomings on someone else. At least being in the anther's dorm meant Nevamar could escape from its nemesis at night. Goodness only knows what tricks it would have had to endure whilst it was sharing the same dormitory.

At the start of the second week, the Dorm Sergeants were selected.

'Ensign Dukecamant of the Anther's Dorm and Cadet Natalicsyaof the Style's Dorm,' said the Lieutenant. 'For the remainder of this exercise, they will be my dorm Sergeants. They will be my assistants and you will obey their orders as if they were my own.'

There was no surprise that Ensign Dukecamant had been selected. The shock was that Natalicsya had beaten the older and more experienced Ensigns. Only Nevamar had expected the petite young style to be such a good soldier. It had no doubt that the style's dorm would be better run under Sergeant Natalicsya, than the anther's dorm ever would under Sergeant Dukecamant. He could talk the talk, but was too slovenly to walk the walk as precisely as his female counterpart. Natalicsya's favourite sayings were "If you look after your clothes, your clothes will look after you." and "A place for everything and everything in its place." Visiting her perfect quarters was a nightmare, you didn't want to sit down in case you disturbed something.

'How are the Ensigns coping with their disappointment?' asked Nevamar.

'Fernee is really relieved. You know what a lazy so and so she is,' replied Natalicsya.'You can't be lazy up here. Have you seen her recently, the weight is falling off her. How much has she lost now?'

'If you were in the proper dorm you wouldn't have to ask, you would know, wouldn't you Nevamarsya?'

'Oh don't start Lisha.'

'If you embraced your inner style, you would soon release your outer style. Become who you truly are.'

'Its bad enough you nagging me. Now Pezzi is as well.'

'Pezzi!' said a shocked Natalicsya.

'Oh don't tell me you didn't know. He has been badgering me for weeks.'

Pemisegant brought his tray and sat by his two friends.

'I heard you talking about me.'

'Apparently you and I are fighting the good fight with this silly girl,' Natalicsya said.

'Yes you put him up to it,' said Nevamar accusingly.

'She did not. Although I do agree with her,' said Pemisegant.

'There is no conspiracy going on.'

'Yes, its nothing to do with me, girlfriend.'

'Oh stop it Lisha!'

'I did try to get the Lieutenant to order you to switch dorms. You can thank her you are still in the anthers' dorm. It won't stop me trying to get you to see the truth though Nevamarsya.'

'Well if you are going to keep on, I'm off.'
'Pardon Cadet.'
'If you want to be formal, permission to leave the table, Sergeant,' retorted Nevamar.
'Granted, Cadet.'

T he Brigadier was a expert manager who knew his limitations. Should the Tree face a serious threat, whilst still being in overall charge, he would pass day-to-day command over to the expert warrior. Colonel Gwilwalsya was the Defence Regiment representative on the Winter Squad and she was the expert warrior. At the start of the third week of Boot Camp, she travelled up from the Crown and took over its command.

The classes she gave were held in the specially constructed shooting range in the base of the subbranch Nevamar had lived and worked on as a sprite. Throughout the four years it had lived there, it had never known that this facility had existed, because as a sprite it didn't need to know. Certainly it explained why the Lieutenant had chosen this location for the exercises. Nevamar could not hit a barn door, even if it were right in front of the damn thing. It despaired of ever finding something it would be good at during Hell Month. Ensign Dukecamant was a crack shot, but his boastful assumption that he was going to win the shooting contest, held on the last day of the Boot Camp, was being challenged by Nevamar's classmates Natalicsya and Althallant. Again everyone except Nevamar, who had seen her friend thread so many tiny needles, was amazed at how proficient Natalicsya was with all sorts of weaponry.

'Y ou know Lieutenant, you don't look at all well,' said Colonel Gwilwalsya on her second morning at the camp.
'Yes, Ma'am,' replied Lieutenant Sharlensya. 'Requesting permission to borrow a scootabout to visit the Medical Centre.'

'Have you spoken to the Major?'

'Yes, Ma'am, I have listed my symptoms, and he is expecting me.'

'Permission granted. Don't worry. If he puts you on sick leave, I will send for Lieutenant Crysgoxant.'

'Yes, Ma'am, thank you, Ma'am.'

The Lieutenant climbed onto the fast single person vehicle that looks like a flying motorcycle. The automated take-off system lifted the scootabout into the air. It hovered for a few seconds as Lieutenant Sharlensya overcame a wave of nausea, then set off for the Crown.

'You know, when you said you were going to adopt that poor girl, I thought you were going to wait until after this tour had finished.' Her Uncle was speaking in riddles.

'Are you feeling all right yourself, you normally don't speak gibberish,' she said to her Uncle.

'I am not speaking gibberish. You are quite clearly hosting a lock and have been for a week. The ultrasound show something alive within you. Alive and growing. The non medical term is pregnant, for that is just what it looks like. For us tree people it is nothing at all like a true pregnancy that you find in cats and any other coopted alien creature.'

'But I can't be. I have not taken any of the necessary steps.' Sharlensya was shocked. 'But my implant?'

'I did warn you to have it checked out when you said it was acting erratically. I am a doctor you know.'

'I thought you were overreacting.'

'I had hoped I was as well. But its water down a channel now,' said Major Keltonnant. 'During your last period of receptiveness, you must have come in contact with this feral lock, that got past your damaged implant.'

'Oh rats, that assault course. We all got a good soaking. This is going to make life impossible for everyone.'

'Difficult my dear, but not impossible.' The Major was grinning. 'Its a good job there is only one week left of Boot Camp, and the Colonel can take over, Matriarch.'

'What did you call me?' Sharlensya's head was already spinning.

'Just adding another wrinkle to the situation. It appears our relative Matriarch Symraltsya recycled at the ripe old age of thirty eight, three hours before your mother's death. Your mother inherited the title and it then passed on to you. The Tree Marshall has just ratified your appointment as Matriarch Elect of the Family Fangkart. Double congratulations.'

'Oh rats to that too. I wish I had stayed up with my troop, at least then I would be in blissful ignorance for a few days longer.'

Her Uncle had opened Serynazsya's file and was making notes. 'How is young Serynazsya coping with the stresses of Boot Camp?'

'As well as can be expected. Unfortunately she has found out who Nevamar was.'

'Great green apples how did that happen?'

'The silly little thing said something that gave its identity away on the first day back in their old home.'

'Lieutenant Sharlensya 115/20 Fangkart.' It must be serious, he was using her rank, formal name and indesncode. 'I want you to keep a very close eye on Ensign Serynazsya 178/20, which means you will have to go back up to the Boot Camp. Any sign that she is having a relapse, I want you to call me immediately. The forthcoming rebirthing process should remove the depression she is currently suffering from, but you know how fixated she has become on Nevamar's pre-activation self. If you have even the slightest suspicion, that Serynazsya is planning to do anything to harm Nevamar, I need to know so that I can treat her immediately.'

'Yes, Sir.' Lieutenant Sharlensya, back on duty saluted her superior officer and left for the Canopy with more things on her mind than she wanted.

The Cadets still had one normal lesson a day, for two hours in the evenings. At this stage in the curriculum it was an art class. "Something constructive," the Lieutenant had said, after all the destructive things the Cadets had been learning.

Creating delicate sculptures from brightly coloured protein glass might have been relaxing for everyone else but for Nevamar. It just could not do the drawing and the cutting out of the patterns it wanted with the protein glass. Then sculpting it never went well. Despite being at least two steps behind its colleagues, Nevamar was so glad the lesson ended and all the equipment was being stowed away.

Nevamar had been looking forward to the scheduled night-time exercise. Orienteering with night-vision goggles. Paired with Ensign Ferngarsya, a good natured red haired young style, who still didn't look as if she had missed a meal in her life. Ferngarsya had been a leaf operator in a branch on the other side of the Tree, now she was a trainee Daylighter Engineer.

'I've never been lost in my life,' she had boasted at the start of the circuit. 'I can always find my way home from anywhere, I can.'

'I could have done with you a couple of weeks ago. I got myself really lost, and within a stones-throw of the Crown.'

'Yes, I'd heard about that, good work you and your friend did there.'

'So how come you have never been lost?' asked Nevamar.

'Natural homing instincts, I can find my way back to any place I choose, without thinking about it. Coming back is not a problem, getting to these bases is. I can't make head nor tail of these clues, a little local knowledge would go a long way,' replied Ferngarsya.

'Good job this was my home branch then, isn't it?'

'Great' said the other girl. 'What with my homing instinct and your local knowledge we can't lose. What do you make of this then?'

Sure enough, they completed the course in record time. Nevamar was so glad that it had been paired with Ferngarsya for this activity. It looked as if it had found a life long friend.

Pemisegant found himself partnered with Ensign Serynazsya. She was flipping from a bundle of nerves to a complete bossing harpy and back. He really did not know where he was with her. Never a good thing whilst orienteering.

'Look, we are supposed to be a team. You will have to trust me.' said Pemisegant.

'Trust you. Your friends with that dreadful creature. Why in the Tree should I trust you?'

'You know what they say, different life. Nevamar is not the sprite you hate.'

'Of course it is,' she snorted as she laughed, 'do you honestly believe all that guff about different lives. You're not as clever as you pretend to be.'

'Oh listen to yourself. No body loves me, everybody hates me. And yes you can trust me.'

'What, after you blabbed about my breakdown to all your little friends.'

'I did not. I gave my word as an Officer that I would not, and I have not.'

'Well I don't believe you.'

'Believe what you want. You will see that I do not break my word,' said Pemisegant as he continued on to the First Station, with the bad tempered style trailing behind. By the Third Station, she had vanished.

'What are you still doing here Cadet?' it was Ensign Dukecamant who with Cadet Althallant made-up the next team to attempt the course.

'Waiting for my partner Sarge. Silly so-and-so has got herself lost.'

'Shouldn't you be out looking for her then Pezzi?' This was Althallant, who was smirking.

'Good point Alth. Why aren't you out looking for your partner Pezzi?' asked Dukecamant.

'We agreed that if we got separated, we should make our way to the next station.'

'OK then Pezzi, you keep on waiting. See you back at base.'

Cadet Pemisegant saluted morosely. Damn it, those two would be laughing all the way back. Where was that bloody girl.

'There you are. I have been waiting for twenty minutes at Station Four,' said Ensign Serynazsya.

'Why did you go there. You knew that we were heading for Station Three next.'

'Oh well, it is a good job I have already stamped that station, we can go straight to Station Five and make up some lost time.'

'You did what! Oh, we might as well go back to base now, there is no point trying to finish,' said Pemisegant, who wanted to scream at the stupid girl.

'What are you talking about.'

'I am talking about the fact that thanks to you, we have stations in the wrong order, Ensign Hanozofsya will be given us a thirty minute penalty. Added to the amount of time we have already wasted, we will be last in the competition.'

'Don't be ridiculous Pezzi, how can she possibly know.'

'Because the stamping machine records the time it was used. As the marshall, she will check the log.'

'Oh!'

'Didn't you listen to the briefing.' Now Pemisegant was screaming at her.

And so they eventually arrived back at the base, just minutes ahead of the final team of Ensign Cemnentant and Cadet Natalicsya.

In the dorm, Ensign Dukemamant was in an ebullient mood.
'Come on lads, first and second, a victory for us boys I would say.'

'How come, Sarge?' asked Cemnentant. 'Nevamar over there is neither one thing nor the other, and its partner was a girl.'

'Fernee is so butch, she almost qualifies as being one of the lads, and Nevamar over there, well, he will be one of the lads when his tackle eventually drops.'

Maybe Dukemant was as bad as Nevamar originally thought. At least he treated it like it wanted to be treated. as an anther, instead of pussyfooting around. With the victory tonight, perhaps things were finally on the up.

CHAPTER FIFTEEN

CRIMES AND MISDEMEANORS

'Why did you do it Cadet Nevamar? Why?' The Lieutenant sounded so disappointed.

'But I didn't do it, Ma'am, I'm as horrified at what has been done as everyone else.'

'Come off it Cadet, you were struggling with this assignment, you lost your temper and tried to destroy your work and everyones elses hard work with it.'

'No, Ma'am.'

The class had arrived at their makeshift classroom to find that all their work had been daubed in heavy black paint, with all the finer details crushed and broken.

'I discovered this mess at lunch time,' explained the Lieutenant. 'The door had been forced and the room was in a complete mess.'

'But I didn't do it.' Nevamar was crying.

'It's no good turning on the water-works Cadet Nevamar, I thought you are going to be an anther. Not a very masculine way to act, is it.'

Oh, that was unnecessary Nevamar thought. It is bad enough I am being accused of vandalism.

'I have evidence of your guilt.' Lieutenant Sharlensya produced an aerosol can from her desk.

'Whilst you were with Colonel Gwilwalsya in the firing range, I searched everyone's locker.' The Lieutenant produced her most damning piece of evidence. I found this crow-bar.'

'That is not a crow-bar, its a leaf stem cleaner,' said Nevamar trying to be helpful.

'So you know what it is then?'

'Of course I do, I was a leaf operator,' said Nevamar, who had stopped crying. It knew it had to defend itself because it looked as if nobody else would.

'You should find one of those in every locker in every dorm up here.' Pemisegant had jumped to his feet and began defending his friend. 'The fact that there was only one in the entire dorm, and in Nevamar's locker was very strange.'

'Sit down Cadet.' Pemisegant did not.

'That was an order Cadet.'

'I don't think Nevamar did this,' shouted Natalicsya, who had also jumped to her feet.'

'If you also do not sit down at once Cadet, you will be stripped of your Sergeant's stripes.

'Ma'am, I can prove Cadet Nevamar is innocent,' added Althallant as he got to his feet. All three of its classmates were now standing in solidarity with Nevamar. Again it began to cry again.

'When you are all sitting down, then I will listen, but not before,' said she Lieutenant. How had this got so out of hand. The situation was in danger of becoming a mutiny. So much for teaching the Cadets military discipline. Lieutenant Sharlensya felt a wave of extreme nausea and her legs buckled under her. She returned heavily to her seat. This was interpreted by the class as a victory and they sat down as well. She knew that she now had to give Althallant his say. He had politely risen his hand.

'Permission to speak, Ma'am.'

'Granted, Cadet.' replied the Lieutenant.

'It says here, "Apply liberally to make the protein glass pliable," so your item can be bent and twisted it into shapes,' Alth said, reading instructions on the can. '"Don't be alarmed when your glass is stained black, the product dries clear."'

'So, why is that relavent, Cadet?' asked the Lieutenant.

'This is the same stuff we used on the farm, back before I sprouted. It stops the surface of the protein in the cloning vats developing a rind.'He paused for emphasis, 'and this stuff has to be applied every 18 hours.' Althalant dragged his finger across the gooey mess, then showed it to his friends.

'I would say the deed was done about midnight, when Ensign Ferngarsya and the Cadet were both in the briefing room, having their orienteering log checked by the Colonel. There is no way they could have both completed the course in the time they did if Nevamar was down here doing this.'

Althallant sat down feeling rather smug.

'So if it was not Cadet Nevamar, the finger of suspicion must move on to Cadet Pemisegant. He took such a long time to finish the course.

'It can't have been Pezzi either,' Althallant was back on his feet. 'He was witnessed by myself and Ensign Dukecamant at Station 3 waiting for his partner to catch up.'

'Who was his partner?' Although she already knew the answer, she had to ask.

'Ensign Serynazsya 178/20.'

Cold gripped Lieutenant Sharlensya's heart. That poor child was teetering on the edge of madness. The ferocity of the vandalism had pointed to an unbalanced mind. Logically the culprit could not have been Nevamar, that Cadet had the most balanced mind of any person she had ever met.

'Ma'am, it can't have been Ensign Serynazsya either,' Althallant said calmly. A splinter of hope. Serynazsya was out of the frame. She did not have to get in touch with her Uncle, what a marvellous young anther Althallant was. Hadn't he applied to join the Enquirers Regiment. He would do well in it.

'How so?' asked Nevamar, who was delighted Serynazsya was now in the frame.

'Ma'am, you are the only style who could override the gender lock on the door into the anther's dorm. Ensign Serynazsya could not have dumped the can in Nevamar's locker, or removed the leaf stalk cleaners from everyone else's locker.

Glory, glory, hallelujah. The Lieutenant would still have to keep a close eye on the young style in the next few days, but once they were back in the Crown, Uncle Kelly would be able to deal with her.

'Right, take the rest of the evening off kids. Class dismissed.' With this, she was overcome with another wave of nausea. 'Oh great green apples I feel sick.'

'Are you all right, Ma'am.'

'Just a touch of food poisoning. Thank you Cadet Nevamar. I am sorry I jumped the gun back there.'

'Whoever did this made you really angry, I am not surprised you lashed out.'

Sharlensya felt a rush of emotion. She wanted to hug the child, tell her she was sorry that she ever doubted her. Behave as her mother would behave. However, they were in the middle of Boot Camp and it would be against regulations. Her little Nevamar was such a nice girl, the Tree could do with more officers like Cadet Nevamar 331/29. If only she would come to her senses.

It was obvious to Nevamar who had destroyed the artwork, it must have been Serynazsya. She had vanished for long periods during the orienteering, Pemisegant had told everyone that, and Althallant had confirmed it. She had plenty of time to go down and do the damage. Getting the can of paint into its locker would have been a harder task, as the dorms were strictly segregated. It must have been whilst everyone was out. The Lieutenant must have known this, why was she turning a blind eye. Sadly the only reason Nevamar could think of, was that she did not want to punish one of her fellow Pure-stocks.

On the last day of the Boot Camp the troop all took part in a shooting competition in the range. A harmless piece of fun before they stepped back to an army of construction from the army of destruction.

Ensign Dukecamant was being more cock-sure and obnoxious than usual. As if he knew that he was going to win.

More by luck, than any display of skill, Nevamar achieved a perfect score in the first round. Ensign Ferngarsya bowed out graciously. Nevamar felt glad that someone else was officially the worse shot in the troop.

The next round saw Nevamar achieving an average score, this was some of the best shooting it had done all month. Pemisegant was not so lucky, and he was eliminated.

In the third round, Nevamar's natural form returned and with a huge sense of relief, it was out of the competition.

Serynazsya quickly followed at the halfway point in the competition. The noise of the weapons being discharged meant that even with ear protectors, conversation was impossible. Colonel Gwilwalsya called for a ten minute break, whilst all the weapons were checked and cleaned.

'Lisha, aren't the competitors supposed to use a different gun each round?' asked Nevamar

'Yes, we all have been,' replied Natalicsya.

'Ensign Dukecamant has only been alternating guns. I can't be the only one who has noticed.'

'So, that's not cheating, still a different weapon each round, but I see what you mean, its not very sporting either. Don't worry about it, its only a game.'

'O.K. people. Ear defenders on again,' ordered Colonel Gwilwalsya. 'Lets finish this. Then we can all go home.'

It struck Nevamar, her friend had originated in the Roots, despite being registered as a Trunk sprite when she was activated. So all the people with rank here today, even if only temporary were from the Roots. Colonel Gwilwalsya and Cadet Natalicsya might not be Pure-stock, but their hair was as blonde as Lieutenant Sharlensya and Ensign Dukecamant who were. This was a stitch-up.

Further conversation with its friend was impossible as the competition resumed with the fifth round. This saw Cemnentant eliminated, with a score that would have won many competitions. Indeed in a normal year, an Ensign from the Defensive Engineering Regiment, the people who built and maintained the weapons, would have been regarded as the automatic favourite.

When Natalicsya was eliminated in the sixth round, it left Dukecamant and Althallant in the final. Nevamar could see that the Ensign was still alternating between just two guns. He was a member of the Defence Regiment, his life might depend on using the nearest weapon at hand. Dukecamant was not doing himself any favours.

Nevamar wanted to complain, but had its own problems. It was sure that the sound of the gun fire was getting louder. It felt something wet running down the side of its neck. Sure enough, the sound baffling material was melting inside the ear-protectors and leaking out. Realising that it was not safe to remain within the firing range, it dashed out. Its ears were singing.

'Cadet Nevamar, what are you doing out here? Why aren't you in the range with the others?' It was Lieutenant Sharlensya, but Nevamar had no idea what she had just said to it.

'My ear-protectors are malfunctioning, not safe to stay in there, Ma'am,' replied Nevamar, coming to attention and saluting with a hand covered in the blue gunk that had oozed from its ear protectors.

'Right you had better stay out here then. As soon as we get back to the Crown, get Major Keltonnant to check your ears out,' said the Lieutenant very slowly and very loudly.

'Yes, Ma'am,' said Nevamar. It was so relieved that its hearing was starting to return, having just about made out what the Lieutenant had said.

The competition had been neck and neck when Nevamar had left the firing range. It was now apparent that Dukecamant Dukecamanthad won and it had no intention of witnessing that obnoxious oaf's triumph.

Nevamar returned to the dorm, its mind racing. Someone had sabotaged its earprotectors. That sort of catastrophic failure was not an accident. Serynazsya had been responsible for distributing the earprotectors at the start of the competition. How had she managed to incriminate Nevamar, as she could not enter the anther dorm. Of course, Dukecamant was as obsessed with Serynazsya as he was with Lieutenant Sharlensya. It was obvious that one Ensign had the other wrapped around her little finger. So it was more than likely, that she had persuaded Dukecamant to put the incriminating evidence into my locker. Great green apples, she was a basket case, what would she try next?

Having failed to blacken its name, and now to deafen it, was an attempt on its life that far away? Was Serynazsya really that crazy.

Given the size of the gardens in his street, Mr. Spencer thought his neighbours would be able to set their fireworks off in their own gardens, without affecting anyone else's.

Guy Faulks Night, a festival Mr. Spenser hated because it celebrated religious intolerance, was here again. The time of year when shopkeepers sold powerful explosives to any idiot over eighteen years of age. One of those idiots was Mr. Spenser's next door neighbour. He would be out of the country on the day, so the previous night he had hosted an early fireworks party. One of the rockets had veered off the expected flight plan and through the top branches of Mr. Spenser's precious apple tree, before exploding in the field behind the houses.

It could have been a lot worse, thought Mr. Spenser as he surveyed the damage the following morning. Only one small branch had been completely destroyed by fire. It could have set the whole tree ablaze. There were scorch marks all around the rest of the Canopy, but they would fade over time.

Once again the Troop was on an early morning march. This time they were marching home, with a song in their hearts.

Hell Month was completed. For the Cadets completing Boot Camp guaranteed they would graduate on the Shortest Day, when the Tree celebrated the start of a new year. For the Ensigns it signified another step towards adulthood. On their return to their quarters in CORC, they knew they could relax and enjoy a week of downtime. Oh the bliss of it all. The Cadets had no time for this luxury. The Pruning had set their time-table back a week, and so they would go straight back to training. No reward for becoming Senior Grade Cadets.

Mid-morning, Lieutenant Sharlensya ordered a slight diversion. The roadway she marched them up had been decorated by the Tree Nuns of the Sacred Sisterhood of the Style, who had established a priory in that branch. The Tree Nuns did not welcome visitors. Normally this roadway would be strictly out of bounds. However, as it was Winter, the Tree Nuns would be back in their main Convent down in the Roots.

It soon became apparent that something was horribly wrong in the branch. Something had visited this section of the Canopy and had caused a massive amount of damage. As was their way, the Tree Nuns had disconnected this section of the Canopy from the comlink network. When whatever external force had struck no alarm bells had rung. The Winter Squad, down in the Crown, had no idea that anything untoward had happened. It was only through the Lieutenant's curiousity, diverting the march home, that the devastation had been discovered. The beautifully crafted artwork lay in tatters and the priory had been sealed off behind fire doors, welded shut by the ferocious heat of the blaze beyond. Nothing could survive a blaze like that and the branch would remain forever uninhabitable. It was a good job, concluded Lieutenant Sharlensya to herself, that the place had been deserted.

She left her troop to triage the situation, whilst she activated an emergency radio connection to the comlink network in an adjacent branch. The very grainy image of Subaltern Popisedsya at Command and Control appeared on the screen of the Lieutenant's comlink.

'Command and Control, please state the nature of your emergency.'

'This is Lieutenant Sharlensya 115/30 Fangkart reporting.'

'Go ahead, Ma'am.'

'A Code Alpha Two event has occurred at Branch WS81. It looks like a fire from the void has engulfed the entire branch. My troop is currently assessing the situation.'

'Copy that, Ma'am.'

Somewhere behind the Lieutenant something was making a low moaning sound. 'Were any of your troop injured, Ma'am?'

'Negative, there appears to be no casualties. Only myself, four Ensigns and four Cadets are up here.'

'The automatic scan reports eleven life-forces. It might be glitching, the emergency network connection is weak at your location. I'm restoring full network connection to the area.'

The moaning came again, louder this time and definitely a Tree Person.

'C&C, as soon as the network is restored, run another casualty scan, I don't think there is a glitch. You're right, there is someone else up here,' said the Lieutenant.

'Network restored, Ma'am. A casualty has been detected, it is located about... No, hang on, its running a systems diagnostic check. OK I am reading you, your troop and one casualty, multiple injuries 42 units to your left.'

'Copy that C&C.' The Lieutenant could see a pile of debris and rubble where the casualty was supposed to be. 'Troop, clear that debris over there, carefully, C&C say there is a casualty under it.'

'That can't be right,' said the Subaltern to herself. 'Lieutenant Sharlensya, Ma'am, it might be another glitch, but that eleventh life force, the system is reporting you are pregnant?'

'I am Subaltern. Don't ask, long story.'

'Copy that, Ma'am, and congratulations. There's an ambulance on its way, it should be with you in thirty minutes. There's also a full emergency response team scrambling now. E.T.A in ninety minutes.'

The troop had dropped what they were doing and were carefully removing the debris. After a few minutes a piece of green cloth became visible. Careful examination revealed the semi-conscious figure of a Tree Nun. All full members of the Sacred Sisterhood of the Style wore an outfit unlike any uniform or downtime dress. It consisted of a long green dress, green stole, and white wimple covering the head and pinned to that a green veil with a white lining. The Lieutenant had never been this close to a Tree Nun, they always kept their distance from those who lived outside their cloister.

'My sisters, are they all gone?' The Tree Nun was awake and very confused.

'Sister, don't try to speak, you have been unconscious and you are still very weak.'

Her sisters? Any other day during the Autumn and Winter, the disaster would only have destroyed the Priory. Yesterday it had destroyed the building and its unfortunate visitors. Well at least one had survived. They needed to get her down to the medical centre as quickly as possible.

The utilivan, used as an ambulance, came roaring up the branch. The two nurses, Voynvalsya and Voynvarant, doubling as paramedics, jumped out and began their treatment of their patient.

The departure of the ambulance was overshadowed by the arrival of the first of the Winter Squad. The Brigadier had mobilised every available member of the Squad, and the rest were on their way right now.

'Mother Sun and Father Earth, you certainly weren't exaggerating the scale of the problem Lieutenant.' Brigadier Myghcomant was his usual efficient self.

'No, Sir, this is quite a mess.' She handed him the piece of paper that had been the result of the troops efforts. A two page preliminary report on the scene.

'Well, I commend your youngsters on a job well done.' He had scanned the report. 'I don't think they have missed anything. It looks like we are going to be at least two weeks putting this branch square.'

'Brigadier, there was a survivor, a Tree Nun. I suspect that there were at least a dozen of them, visiting their priory, when the accident occurred.'

'Not visiting Lieutenant. There is a core of twelve Tree Nuns who live here all year round whilst the rest go back down to their Convent in the Roots.'

'I never knew that,' said a shocked Lieutenant Sharlensya.

'Few do. Count yourself as a member of an exclusive club. Now, you had better take your kids home. They have been through a lot and need the rest.'

'Thank you Brigadier, I had planned on marching them back down to the Crown, but with your permission, I will borrow an utilivan instead.'

'Granted Lieutenant. They have done their bit up here, they deserve an extra couple of days downtime. Also, if what I hear is true, you also need plenty of rest.'

'Yes, Sir, sorry, Sir, I don't know how it could have happened.'

'Nothing is perfect Lieutenant, things go wrong all the time. Not your fault.'

'But it is going to leave you short handed for at least two weeks, Sir.'

'That is my problem, not yours. Go home, put your feet up and have a rest. That is an order.'

CHAPTER SIXTEEN
IT NEVER RAINS

Major Keltonant never dreamed he would see Kanonypsya 049/05 Rust ever again, not after she went unwillingly with the Tree Nuns, who had chosen her to join their Order. But here she was, a patient under his care. It was said that the clergy lived longer than the laity and did not age as quickly. Here was living proof, despite being two years older than him, her closely cropped hair was untouched by grey, her skin perfect with not a single wrinkle. Seeing her brought back so many memories, but all the happy ones were overshadowed by the misery of their parting.

'Damn it Konny, I will treat you, but do not expect me to get any joy from it.'

'Nobody has called me that for twenty years,' she said, in a half awake voice that seemed so far away.

'Because, Konny, this is where I have spent my Autumns and Winters for the past two decades and you have been far away from me.'

'Please do not call me Konny again. I am no longer that person.'

'As you like. I will just tell myself that my beautiful Konny was killed in an accident back then, because there is no connection between the vibrant Kanonypsya Rust 049/05, and the sad shallow brainwashed creature that occupies her body.' He picked up his note pad and left the room. 'Good day Sister.'

It had been three hours since the troop had returned to the the Crown. As it had been ordered the first thing Nevamar had done was go to see Major Keltonnant. Nevamar had decided not to say anything about Serynazsya because she did not want to appear paranoid. As soon as it had got back to its room, it knew for certain that somebody had been in there. Not Natalicsya, she was still out with Althallant. Not that she would have bothered to come into the room if Nevamar had not been there. True to form the Roots people would cover for poor mad Serynazsya. The anger that had fuelled its journey back down from the twig was now burning brighter inside Nevamar because it was now justified anger.

Forget sitting down, forget sleep. She should have known better. She was from the Canopy and everyone knew the Roots treated the Canopy with contempt. Why had she thought Lieutenant Sharlensya would be any different.

The comlink chimed. 'Cadet Nevamar, please report to the classroom immediately, you were not dismissed.'

'Yes, Ma'am. Sorry, Ma'am. I didn't realise.' This room always seemed so friendly, a place for the giving and receiving of knowledge. Now it was simply a functional classroom.

'Right then Cadet Nevamarsya, where did you go to without permission?'

'To see Major Keltonnant, just as you ordered, Ma'am. I only just caught the end of his clinic, Ma'am'

'Ah yes. But you really should have waited until you were officially dismissed. Don't do that again.'

The Lieutenant's face went from stern to friendly. 'So, my little one, what has been bothering you? You were on edge all the way down from the Canopy. I could see you were having a bad time at Boot Camp. As your mentor I had to remain formal and aloof. Now its all over, things can change. So what is the matter dear Nevamar?'

Nevamar refused to switch from formal to informal, it was just too worked up.

'All hypocrisy and lies, Ma'am.'

'I beg your pardon dear.'

'Don't "dear" me. Its all hypocrisy and lies. All you said about not caring if someone came from the Canopy, Trunk or Roots, if they were pure-stock or had the taint of non-standard pollen in their pattern.'

'I don't understand, you know I don't care about where anyone comes from. Why are you saying this Nevamar? Is the adrenalin from Hell Month still flowing freely?'

'No, I saw the truth last month. That you are just another Roots born hypocrite. Throughout the Boot Camp you favoured Dukecamant, Natalicsya and Serynazsya. Ensign Dukecamant should never have been given that merit award in the Shooting Competition, he cheated, but he is from the Roots, so you turned a blind eye. You knew that Serynazsya was sabotaging all my efforts, making me look like an idiot, but you let her get away with it. So much for taking a dim view if anyone started picking on one of your Cadets. She is bonkers, I wouldn't be at all surprised if she was not trying to kill me.

No, I am not exaggerating.

'If you were any other Cadet, I would not have to justify myself to you, I am your superior officer,' said Lieutenant Sharlensya switching back to her professional self. 'I don't take kindly to being called a liar or a hypocrite or a bigot either, but I can forgive that given the current circumstances. I will tell you this once and once only. Whether you believe me or not is entirely up to you.

'I did not favour any of the Cadets or Ensigns in my troop who were from the Roots. I would never do that. On the day I saw no evidence of cheating, there was nothing separating Ensign Dukecamant's performance from Cadet Althallant's performance. So as there could only be one winner, I used a random factor generator to decide. I tossed an old fashioned coin, heads for Ensign Dukecamant, tails for Cadet Althallant. It came down heads.

'As for Ensign Serynazsya, of course I knew she was being a bitch towards you. Why else did I turn down Cadet Natalicsya's request to transfer you to the style's dorm in the Boot Camp, even though I did think it was an excellent idea. Serynazsya was having a relapse and fixating on you. If I could have found a way to keep her down in the Crown, away from all the bad memories of the Summer, I would have. It might interest you to know that Ensign Serynazsya is sedated in the Medical Centre at the moment, we caught her in your quarters.'

'I knew it, had she done anything?'

'No, but matters are in hand. We will have plenty of time to deal with her, as a family,' she said, switching back to informality stared directly at Nevamar. 'Do you understand darling?'

'As a family?'

'Yes, I have just filed formal papers to adopt you when you become old enough and need a mother.'

'You really mean it.'

'I do. Despite what you think now, you are going to be a beautiful young style soon. I will be proud to have both you and Serynazsya as my daughters.'

'Why both of us?' Nevamar asked.

'Because you will both need the loving support of a family in the next few difficult months. You are going to need help in differentiating, as there is obviously something wrong somewhere. Then there is Serynazsya who will be your elder sister.'

'The style who has been trying to kill me?'

'I know that it is a lot to take in, but her re-birthing is the only way to restore her mental health.'

'I will need to think about this. I so want you to be my mother, but why her?'

'I can understand why you are angry with Serynazsya, but she was as much a victim of that dreadful Samnundsya person as you were. This is Serynazsya's last hope. When I heard Serynazsya's story it made me angry, by adopting her, that sad girl's troubles become the Family Fangkart's troubles. I am going to make sure that Captain Samnundsya 101/20, will regret the bigoted way she has been behaving.'

'She's a Captain, you are a Lieutenant, you can't do anything to her.'

'Oh but I can. The Matriarch of the Family Fangkart was 38 years old when she recycled. She had no surviving daughters. So her heiress was her niece, my Mother, and now that she is gone, there is only one person left to inherit the title.'

'You?'

'Yes me. I have power and influence now. Enough to make sure that style can never hurt anyone again.'

Normally a style would be middle aged, well into her twenties, before inheriting the politically powerful title of Matriarch of her family. At just twelve years old, Lieutenant

Sharlensya would be one of the youngest Matriarchs in the Tree's history.

'I'm afraid here comes the hard part,' she said, looking as green as her uniform. 'I am already pregnant and poor Serynazsya's emotions are so fragile at the moment. She has issues with betrayal and abandonment that have to be worked through,' said the Lieutenant.

'I don't understand.' The explanation just was not making any sense. Nevamar could feel its world collapsing. It had been offered the ultimate prize, and now it seemed it was being snatched away again.

'Until we can be certain that Serynazsya is past this relapse, I can have no contact with you outside of school hours. In fact it would be best if I didn't have any social contact with you until after the rebirth.

The anger welled up in Nevamar again. It had all been a load of hot air. All those promises about being a family. As soon as the upcoming rebirth was over, the new mother would find another excuse to keep her distance.

'To think, I nearly fell for it. All those empty promises. You can't possibly have enough adoption accreditation for a second child. You will have your pretty little blonde girl whose name starts with "S" and by the time its my turn, it will be sorry, no can do.'

Lieutenant Sharlensya stood up. Nevamar knew, just by looking at the older style across the desk, that she was as angry as it had ever seen her. That it had managed to put its foot in it, on such a massive scale, it might never come back out again.

'That was a very hurtful thing to say Nevamar. By saying it, you have proved that it is you and not I who is the bigot. I must have been mad even to think you could be my child. Get out of my sight.'

CHAPTER SEVENTEEN
MENDING FENCES

A week had past since the end of Boot Camp. The Shortest Day was rapidly approaching, the final day of the year and the final day of Officer Training. The Cadets would would see the new year as Ensigns, holding that rank until their fifth birthday. After that they would be adults and promoted to Subalterns, the first proper officer rank.

Passing Out would be a major landmark, but Nevamar wished that it had reached this landmark with the messy business of differentiation complete. Sadly it still had not even started. It had grown. At five units seven and a half fractions tall, with striking red hair and green eyes, Nevamar was unrecognisable from the subservient little creature who had hidden in a cupboard to avoid Winter hibernation. But in its mind, it might just as well still be a sprite, because it was neither anther nor style.

'I really need to lose some weight. I wish I was as thin as you Nevamar.' Her friend saw its stick thin limbs and lollipop head as something to aim for, not avoid. It was a good thing that she had accepted that she would never hit that target.

'No you don't.' replied Nevamar.

'But I do. You are so thin, clothes just hang on you,' said the clothes obsessed young style. She didn't need to lose any weight at all. She was already in Nevamar's opinion far too thin.

'That is because I have no curves, because I still have the body of a sprite. I'm a freak.'

'No your not. Your just slow. Look at Pezzi over there, he still looks like he could be either gender.'

'No he doesn't.'

'He does you know.'

'Do you need glasses? And by the way, don't let him hear you say that.' Nevamar turned to look closely at Pemisegant. 'You only have to look at him to see he is a boy. I should at least be as advanced as him or you, with either a beard or breasts. But I have neither. Damn, I feel ill.'

As Nevamar stood up a wave of nausea crashed over it, and a different sort of passing out was its only option.

'You know,' Tabbernant said as he poured a cup of instaht for Sharlensya, 'you are missing that little one more than you are letting on.'

'That young lady said some horrible things. She has to apologise, then I will reconsider the situation.'

'Balls Shaz. Your not the only one with your hormones all over the shop.'

'When did you qualify as a doctor? I should tell my Uncle he has competition.'

'Well, at least you are laughing now. I was being serious though. Something is stopping her from fully differentiating. Add to that the stress of Hell Month, no wonder she said things I know she is regretting now.'

'There was no need for her to accuse me of being a Roots Supremacist.'

'So tell me what happened Shaz?' asked Tabbernant.

In all the years he had know Sharlensya, he had never felt the deep aching sense of disappointment he felt now. What had she been thinking that day.

'Sharlensya 115/30 Fangkart, I never thought I would ever have to say this, but I am ashamed of the dreadful way you have treated that youngster.' He could see that she was in shock.

'But, but, but why?'

'She is little more than a newborn kitten, what about her sensitivities? What about her sense of betrayal and abandonment, eh?' Tabbernant had gone white with anger. 'Young Nevamar loved you, she trusted you, she worshipped you. All you could think about was Serynazsya this and Serynazsya that. No wonder she blew up like that.'

'Oh?' said Sharlensya.

'Oh? Is that all you can say?'

'Bernie, what have I done? What have I done?'

Before Tabbernant could say anything, Sharlensya's wrist-com unit sprang to life. She pressed the answer button and it clicked to the speakerphone.

'Lieutenant Sharlensya, this is Command and Control.'

'I hear you C&C, what's the problem?' Sharlensya asked.

'Cadet Nevamar has collapsed and been taken to the Medical Centre. Major Keltonnant has requested you call there immediately.'

'Copy that C&C, on my way.'

Sharlensya's mind was racing. Oh Mother Sun, Father Earth and the Tree itself, what had happened to her little one. Why had Lieutenant Jaridafant in Command and Control sounded so concerned?

'They had raced Nevamar to the Medical Centre. Falling into and out of consciousness, the journey seemed so much quicker for Nevamar. The medical centre was normally a mass of noises. Now everything was so quiet. Where was the beeping of the equipment? Why were there no hushed voices behind the curtains? Nevamar felt overwhelmed by the silence and was so glad when it lost consciousness again.

There is no hope then?' Brigadier Myghcomant asked from his seat in Command and Control.

'No, Sir, Cadet Nevamar is slowly deteriorating. The indications are that it only has days to live.'

Lieutenant Sharlensya was sat at her Uncle's desk in the Medical Centre. She didn't know why she was still there, as she could do nothing to help. Nevamar had grown so much but Sharlensya still thought of the youngster as "Little One". She knew she had let it down so badly.

'This is a bad day,' said the Brigadier. 'A very bad day.' Keep me posted, Lieutenant.'

'Yes, Sir.'

There was a rush of activity in the main treatment room. She could hear her Uncle swearing. He only ever did that when something was really wrong.

'Its done it again, just passed out cold. No damage this time, but it will take longer for it to wake up.' The Major sat down in the seat the Lieutenant had just vacated. 'It looks as if it's activation is failing.'

Normally activation failed within days, with the poor unfortunate permanently reverting back into an anonymous sprite. Nevamar was too advanced to revert, so its body was breaking down and dying.

There was a knock on the door. The Tree Nun, in her flowing green habit was standing there. Brilliant thought the Lieutenant, just when her uncle could do without any further aggravation.

'I have come to visit the afflicted child. Is that all right?'

'If you want to Sister, but keep it brief. My Uncle says it needs peace and quiet.'

'I have been praying for it. So young, so much promise, such a tragedy.'

'Yes, and a fat lot of good your prayers have been,' said the Major as he walked back into his office.

'Uncle!'

'Yes, I'm sorry. Its just as you said such a tragedy.' He mumbled and beat a hasty retreat.

All was silent, only the occasional beep from a monitoring device broke the calm. The Tree Nun knelt besides the bed praying voicelessly. She made a gesture of blessing and stood up.

'There, it is done.'

'What is done Sister?' Lieutenant Sharlensya had been watching and wondering exactly what the Tree Nun had hoped to achieve.

'My prayer has been heard by my sisters in the Convent in the Roots and our Priories throughout the Tree. They will also pray for this poor afflicted child. May the Spirit of the Tree hear our prayers and answer them.'

At that moment in time Lieutenant Sharlensya was as sceptical about the Tree Nun as her Uncle ever was.

'Please, do not be as closed minded as your Uncle. He is being as hidebound and reactionary as some of my older sisters. They reject all science as he rejects faith.'

'As thoroughly as I rejected this little one. I totally destroyed its trust in me. Now it is to late to make good the damage.'

'Have faith my child, the Tree will provide,' said the Tree-Nun.

'I'm sure my uncle still has faith Sister,' Sharlensya said. 'Its not faith that bothers him Sister, it's you. How much longer are you going to be here?'

'I will return to the Convent after the Holy Day,' Sister Kanonypsya replied.

'Good. Your presence here is only causing him pain you know?'

'Do you honestly think I want to be here?' There was fire in her voice. For the first time Sharlensya heard not the calm measured tones of a devout Tree Nun, but the passion of a real person. 'I know that my presence is causing him pain, but we can never have a life together now. I was called to the Sisterhood.'

'You were forced to join.' Sharlensya said.

'It was the way back in the day.'

'Why did it change? Why are you lot now choosy about who can join,' asked Sharlensya, whose interest had been piqued.

'Many years ago, there was a flood in the Roots that badly affected the Convent. We lost the Book of Life the Tree gave us when the order was created. All we had was a copy. One that turned out to be incomplete. The Copy told us, "Many of My daughters shall hear My Voice. All will I take as My Handmaidens." We believed anyone who heard our Lord's voice, for whatever reason, had been chosen.

'Later, the Tree be praised, the True Book was recovered from the place of safety it had been left in. We believe the sister who placed it there perished in the flood, before she could tell anyone its location. After it had been recovered, we discovered the passage read, "Many of My daughters shall hear My Voice. Of all, only the most devout will I take as My Handmaidens". Now only those styles who want to join our community, and prove they are worthy, take their place as one of the Tree's Handmaidens.'

'I know many of the unwilling returned to their old lives, or joined the ranks of the Offeriad after the change. Why didn't you?' asked Lieutenant Sharlensya.

'No, I could see no life outside, so I chose to stay. I made new binding lifelong vows with no coercion. Only the Spirit of the Tree itself can release me from them now,' replied the Tree Nun. With that the mask of calm devotion had returned.

'I could not join you in your community,' said Sharlensya as she placed a hand across her belly. 'I have new responsibilities.'

'You are becoming a mother?'

The Lieutenant could see the realisation dawning. It looked to Sharlensya as if all the other styles' birthdays had come on the same day.

'Yes in about a month.'

'The Tree be praised. Quickly, go fetch your Uncle. I think this prayer has been answered. You are pregnant, you may yet redeem yourself with this child.'

'She told you what?' Major Keltonnant lookedat his niece in utter disbelief.

Sharlensya repeated what the Tree Nun had said. The way she felt each morning, Sharlensya could well believe that her blood currently contained something powerful, but she was sceptical that it would do any good for poor Nevamar.

'Good gracious, the Siengalsya Hypothesis. Nobody has seriously considered that for nearly two decades,' said the Major. He could see that his niece was still in the dark. 'The notion that the chemicals in an expectant style's blood can cure all sorts of problems in youngsters,' said the Major.

'Does it work? That's the most important question at the moment.'

'Well there were a couple of inconclusive studies. No real research for about fifteen years.'

Sharlensya knew that her Uncle was becoming really excited at the prospect of pulling off a miracle cure. Not that he would ever admit it. Until the procedure was carried out, and it proved successful or not, he would remain uncommitted. This made him one hell of a Poker player.

'So, we are faced with a fascinating conundrum. At worse, it will only slow down the child's deterioration for an unknown number of months, before it suffers an inevitable and terminal catastrophic systems failure. At best there could be a full recovery and differentiation, but I find that highly unlikely. Is it a risk worth taking?'

'Of course it is Uncle. Where there is life, there is hope.'

'You know, Kanonypsya had a brilliant scientific mind. It is such a shame it got wasted.' The Major busied himself with complex auxin extraction equipment. 'You had better go and see one of the twins, get him or her to extract a pint of your blood, whilst I set up everything else.'

Sharlensya could see her Uncle's attention was now fixed on the job in hand. So she went to find a nurse.

An hour later, Sharlensya was lying on a couch, having had two pints of blood drained from her system. 'I really don't think it would be a good idea if I tried to teach those kids this afternoon. Given the state they are in, I don't think it is fair to expect them to concentrate anyway,' she told her Uncle. 'Perhaps they have earned an extra afternoon of downtime.'

'Great green apples Sharlee, there is no way I'm going to let you go back on duty for the rest of this week. Consider yourself on sick leave.'

'Right young Nevamar,' said Major Keltonant three days later, as it lay in bed recoving from the dose of auxins it had received. 'With only us Squaddies up here, none of the usual ante-natal support mechanisms are in place. By that I mean sprites to do all Sharlensya fetching and carrying. I'm discharging you from here tomorrow. You will be officially on light duties. So you are being reassigned to try and fill the gaps. Do as much of the lifting and carrying as you are able to, then make sure you both take plenty of rest et cetera.'

'Yes, Sir.'

This assignment was not going to be a bucket of laughs, as the relationship between Cadet and mentor was still frosty after the events at the end of Hell Month.

'Sir, may I ask a question?'

'You want to know why you and not one of the young styles?'

'Yes, Sir.'

The Major had let the professional mask slip and was now speaking as Lieutenant Sharlensya's uncle. 'You have a remarkable gift young Nevamar. You have empathy.'

This had not been the answer Nevamar had been expecting but it sat quietly whilst the Major continued.

'You can sense people's emotional state and know how to improve it. People talk to you, they open up and say things they would never dream of telling anyone else. You listen without being judgemental, you ask the right questions and your advice is always exactly what the person needs. And most importantly of all, you are the most discreet person I have ever met. I think you would carry a secret to recycling and never be tempted to let it slip. That is a remarkable talent.'

'Thank you, Sir.'

'Which is why I am so surprised by the complete hash you are making of your own emotional well being.'

'Sir?'

'You have been miserable for the past week or so, as has my niece. She is missing you. I know you are missing her. I hope being together will help you patch up this silly feud between you and your Mother.'

'But she isn't my Mother, Sir, nor ever likely to be.'

'She is, and has been since the day you first met. It is the way things work in our crazy system. What has happened with Serynazsya is the exception, not the rule. So patch things up between you, there's a good girl.'

'Yes, Sir.'

'By the way, all this makes me your Great Uncle Kelly, do you understand Nevamar.'

'Did you just give me permission to use your Informal Name?'

'Yes I did, and don't worry about adoption accreditation, when the time comes it will be alright.' He winked, as if sharing some great secret. He smiled. 'Right, I'm off for my lunch. As you were Cadet Nevamar.'

Although in pyjamas and propped up in bed Nevamar saluted the anther heading for the refectory. Be a good girl for my Great Uncle Kelly, Nevamar thought, yes, I can do that.

'Nevamar my dear, I am so so sorry about how I treated you. I hope you can find it in your heart to forgive me.'

'Of course I do Sharlensya, you saved my life.' Nevamar had finished its lunch and was considering a nap when Sharlensya had arrived on the ward.

'Please, call me Sharlee. You have earned the right.'

'Thank you, although I think Aunty Sharlee sounds so much better.' said Nevamar.

'Yes dear, I think you're right. The Tree could do with more kind and generous people like you. And who knows, in a few months, the situation might be completely different.

HOW THE OTHER HALF LIVE

T he shortest and last day of the year would see the cadets finish their Officer Training was over and they would Pass Out as Ensigns. They had now reached their full adult height and it was hard to believe that a few months earlier they had all been identical sprites.

Althallant had once been the tallest Cadet. Now two of his friends had overtaken him. Also, his stocky muscular frame gave the impression he was slightly shorter than his true height. Insisting on shaving his head, as well as his chin certainly made him stand out.

After months of being shorter than his friend, Pemisegant was now the taller of the two anthers in the class. At six units and three fractions he was well above the average height for a Canopy-born anther. He was still as wiry as he ever had been and his curly reddish brown hair exploded from his head in all directions.

Nevamar had stopped growing at an awkward height, taller than most styles, but not quite as tall as most anthers.

Despite originating in the Roots, Natalicsya was the shortest member of the class. She had stopped growing at five and one half units tall. She described herself as petite. She had accepted that she would never be as thin as she wanted to be, so she worked hard to maintain the shape she was. Her hair cascaded down to her hips whilst off duty. She delighted in designing different styles of plait for when she was on duty, all within the regulations.

The appearance of the pupils was not the only change in the class. The Lieutenant was now very definitely pregnant.

The lock she was carrying was growing rapidly, and her belly had swollen to cope with it. Her breasts bulging with the milk that would feed her daughter in the first few days after re-birth.

'I'm so glad I'm never going to be a style.' Pemisegant told his friends, in Bertnie's cafe, one lunchtime.

'It would have been nice having two boys and two girls in the class though,' added Natalicsya, 'but that isn't going to happen now, is it Nevamarant? Such a shame.'

'Don't start Lisha, I'm not in the mood. Not after the morning I've had.'

'You're the Golden Child again. Now you've patched things up with your mother.'

'And don't you start either Pezzi, She is not my Mother.' Nevamar snapped.

'You are tempered today Nevamar. Are you sure nothing is the matter dear?'

'Nothing is the matter, and I am not your dear' said Nevamar snappily.

'Ooh, bitchy. Which brings us back to my original point, I am so glad I'm never going to be a style, have you seen the way your mum has ballooned. No one could call Lieutenant Sharlensya a Sex Bomb now.'

'I'm hating this.' Sharlensya told Tabbernant later that evening. She was sitting in a chair feeling exhausted after even a short walk. 'Did you just see me, I don't walk any more, I waddle.'

'Don't worry, it will be worth it in the end.' He picked up the cat Natalicsya had discovered and began stroking her. 'This one is taking a break from her kittens, if we used the same system as her, then proportionately, you would have to be pregnant for nine months, a child would pop out and it would take about sixteen years to get to the stage those kids out there are currently at.'

'I should count my blessings that I am so close to the end then.'

'Yes indeed.'

'You know, under normal circumstances the Environmental Health Regiment would be screaming at you for keeping those cats here.'

'What they don't see can't worry them Shaz. Anyway, in a few weeks I can move them to their permanent home.'

'Your mystery project.'

'Yes, that,' said the old anther, emphatically drawing a line under that thread of the conversation.

'Also, I hate the way my emotions are all over the shop. I really had to fight back the tears this lunchtime.'

'Young Pezzi, always accurate, but never the most tactful young anther.'

'No, he isn't. Just doesn't think about what he is saying.'

'I think your Uncle has something that will teach that young fool Pezzi some tact.'

'Uncle Kelly, what would he have?'

'You'll see.'

'Torture perhaps?'

'I wouldn't go that far.' The old anther was grinning evilly. 'If all goes well, I will deliver a little package to your classroom tomorrow morning. You can take it from there.'

'I can't wait.' said Sharlensya.

Three days later, towards the end of a Biology lesson, the class took turns in wearing a life sized pregnancy simulator. It was to show what a pregnant style had to put up with. Pemisegant was the last to strap it on. As he did so, the buckle locked into place with an unpleasant scraping click, almost drowning out the sound of the buzzer marking the end of lesson time.

'Come on Cadet Pemisegant, we haven't got all day,' said the Lieutenant.

'I'm sorry, Ma'am, its jammed.'

'Oh what have you done now boy?' said the Lieutenant, without an ounce of sympathy in her voice.

'I will have to snap it open.'

'You'll do no such thing. You will have to wait until I find the override key.'

'Please, Ma'am, it's pressing on my bladder, I need the gents.'

'You should have thought about that before you drank all that lemonade this lunchtime.'

The Lieutenant spent ten minutes looking for the key. Pemisegant becoming more desperate by the second.

'Oh do stop fidgeting, stand to attention, you are an Officer and still on duty until I dismiss you.'

'Permission to leave the room, Ma'am'. There was an edge of panic in Pemisegant's voice.

'Oh very well, Cadet Pemisegant, you are dismissed.'

Pemisegant saluted and ran for the door.

Brigadier Myghcomant tended to spend much of his time in the Command and Control Centre doing paperwork. He knew a certain amount of pen-pushing went with the job but he didn't like it, so relished the times his specialisation took him out of the office. It was just by pure bad luck that this happened to be when the sound of a female choir singing filled the room, heralding a visitation from the Convent.

Colonel Rumsfelant had once been a novice of the Grand Order of the Anther. His complete incompatibility with the monastic life had quickly became apparent. He had joined the Offeiriad, eventually becoming the Winter Squad's padre. When he looked at his balding head in the mirror on a weekend morning, as he was preparing to lead the Temple Parades in his cassock, he thought he looked just like one of the tonsured Tree Monks and that he had never left the Monastery. Theologically he was by far the better person to deal with the Sisterhood and its needs in most cases. However he knew that he did not have the secular authority for this situation, and so he would have to hand it over to his boss, the Brigadier.

'Ah, Brigadier Myghcomant, we meet at last.'

'I can only apologise for my delay Sister Annaprysya, duty called,' said the Brigadier.

He knew damn well that Abbess Annaprysya should be addressed the honorific Abbess, not Sister, but he was annoyed at being pulled away from his first chance to do some real work in months. The Brigadier regretted his rudeness almost immediately. This was not going to be an easy few minutes.

'Brigadier Myghcomant, the Sisterhood needs your assistance,' said the Abbess, who had chosen to ignore the slight.

'How can I assist you Abbess?' They have never asked for help before he thought to himself, they command it from on high. No he thought, this is still a command despite the sugar coating. This new Abbess was trying to be diplomatic.

'Brigadier, as you know, we in the Sisterhood maintain a presence in all parts of the Tree all year.'

'Which means you want to replace your Priory,' said the Brigadier.

'That is correct,' she replied. This time the smile disappeared. The Brigadier realised Abbess Annaprysya might be new, but she had obviously already got used to being obeyed unquestioningly and not interrupted. 'I have been given the lease of a neighbouring branch and I would like to dedicate the new Priory by the Equal Day of Spring.'

One of the Tree Nuns accompanying the Abbess spread a blue-print on the Brigadier's desk.

'That is a big ask, you won't be able to get builders up from the Roots until after New Year, when the shuttles start running again.'

'Why bother waiting for builders to come up from the Roots when there are already some up here?' said the Abbess.

The Brigadier was fascinated by the plans, it looked as if it was going to be one hell of a project. He was itching to be part of such a prestigious undertaking. The Squad already had so many other jobs to complete to fulfil its core mission that attempting both projects together would be impossible.

'Of course, we understand that your core mission comes first. Which is why I have had this list of preparatory work prepared. If you could complete even half of the jobs on this list, we of the Sisterhood would be eternally grateful.'

The other accompanying Tree Nun put a schedule on the desk. The Brigadier looked at it, preparatory work, not as much as he had imagined. Yes, the Squad could do half, maybe even three quarters of that list in addition to their remaining work load without breaking sweat.

'Naturally Brigadier, the Maintenance Regiment would be reimbursed for any expenses it incurred during the preparatory work, and paid the going rate for the work.'

'Money is not the problem Abbess, as always supplies are. We are running short on what we need for our core mission. We would need additional supplies for any side project.'

'Make a list of all you need to complete your core mission and add it to the list of materials for the preparatory work you will be undertaking. An unmanned cargo pod filled with building materials can be dispatched within an hour of me receiving that amended list. Do you agree, Brigadier.'

'Very well Abbess Annaprysya, you have a deal.'

'Thank you Brigadier.'

'I suppose you will be taking our guest back with you now?' The Brigadier hoped that they would be taking Sister Kanonypsya with them. Her presence here was unnerving.

'When our new Priory is dedicated it will need a new Prioress. Sister Kanonypsya will fill that role. Therefore, she will remain here in the Canopy, as a liaison between the Sisterhood and the people constructing the new Priory.'

'She has become a regular site around the Crown, and I enjoy hearing her sing,' said Brigadier Myghcomant.

'She has a good singing voice now, Brigadier. I remember when we were novices together, Sister Matyfilsya, the Choir Mistress used to say that she could not carry a tune in a rucksack. You can see what good training and two decades of practice can do.'

'Your Choir Mistress obviously has not heard my voice. Compared to that, everyone elses singing is exquisite.'

'Given time, I am sure Sister Matyfilsya could change that. She says that nobody's voice is bad, just badly trained.'

This was wrong; Brigadier Myghcomant actually liked this Abbess. She was not a terrifying old witch.

'If I may borrow your office for an hour or so? There is much I must discuss with the Prioress.'

The Brigadier took this as an excuse to leave the Tree Nuns to themselves. He headed towards the refectory for his lunch. He would spend the afternoon drawing up work rotas and planning the best use of resources, but for the moment, he needed time to take it all in.

'**Y**ou look like you have seen a ghost Myck,' said Tabbernant, being his usual cheerful self.

'You haven't retired yet, couldn't you at least pretend to show some respect for the ranks and uniform of the Corps?' The Brigadier smiled. 'No, that is asking too much.' He perused the menu and gave his order before continuing.

'No, I have just been politely asked to do something by the most senior Tree Nun and then thanked for my time. That freaked me, I am used to her predecessors telling me what to do and not thinking about the consequences.'

'Well, Prisya always did do things her own way. I see that twenty years in the Convent hasn't changed that.'

'Do you know everyone?' The Brigadier was pretty sure that Tabbernant was probably on familiar name terms with the Spirit of the Tree itself.

'What, all one hundred thousand of us officers. Even my memory isn't that good,' Tabbernant's mind wandered back in time. 'Coming into work one Duosday morning and finding my legal secretary stolen away was quite a shock, and it was quite a rumpus when I tried demanding her return.' The old anther smiled, those had been the days. 'I can tell you, it took months to train her replacement.'

'From what I can gather from Sister Kanonypsya...'

'That's Prioress Kanonypsya now. For once the Brigadier had some news to give Ensign Tabbernant.'

'So they are making Kandy the chief jailer. I'm sure she

will love that.'

'What are you talking about Bernie?'

'There is a good reason why they called it the Priory of the Penitent Heart,' said the old anther.

'I thought that was just a religious sounding name.' replied the Brigadier.

'Nah, that place was the Sisterhood's version of the Guard House. A true penitentiary. If one of the Tree Nuns breaks a major rule she gets sent there for a spell of hard labour. Although I reckon the wardens are getting a cruel and unusual punishment for something, they live there all year round, with no time off for good behaviour. The new place will be the same.'

'Well, that explains their haste.'

'I don't know why I bother with my reports, all I need to do is come in here once a day to be briefed about what is really happening in the Tree.'

'All part of the service,' replied Tabbernant with a laugh.

'Well, on the subject of service, where is my lunch?'

CHAPTER NINETEEN
WEEKEND AT BERNIE'S

Ensign Tabbernant 089/99 Islaw, the oldest Ensign in the Tree of Life, had great plans for his retirement. Officially he should have been facing a meagre existence with a tiny official pension. Unofficially he was one of the richest athers in the Tree. The income from the clever investments he had made throughout his life, would guarantee a comfortable future.

If he had controlled his temper, people often told him, he would be a General by now. Tabbernant had never seen the appeal of high rank. His many demotions had never been the result of anything malicious or criminal on his part. His run-ins with the authorities had always been the result of his desire to change things for the better, when those in power had been so insistent on keeping everything as it always had been.

His eye for picking money-making schemes, that nobody else would touch with a long stick was legendary. None of his gambits had done less than break even. It had never been about money-making though, it had always been about moving technology forward. They might have called them crazy schemes, but who was laughing now. His biggest win had been investing in a pigmentation system that gave enprintable fabric a much broader palette of colours than had ever been possible before. His dogged support for the new fabric had proven worth it in the end, as clothes looked so much better now.

That is why he had such a soft spot for young Sharlensya's latest crop of Cadets. All four of them were forward thinking individuals. Althallant might appear to be slow, but there was a lightning sharp mind beneath the bumbling exterior. Natalicsya was an artist with cloth. That boy Pemisegant has more good ideas bouncing around in that skull of his than anyone Tabbernant had ever known. The girl Nevamarsya was also a little button, except she was being so foolish in insisting that she was an anther. Tabbernant could see she blatantly was not. The sooner she actually differentiated and realised what she was, the better.

'So, tell me again Pezzi, why are we here. When we aren't in class we spend all week on duty doing building work. Why should we want to spend our free time doing more building work?' Althallant had a point. 'This is a trolleybus driver's holiday.'

'Trolleybuses don't have drivers Alth.'

'You know what I mean though Pezzi.'

The kids were helping Tabbernant get the site ready for the real work, in return for a few extra credits in their pocket. He had bought the freehold on a prime piece of real estate up here in the Canopy. Where the roadways running through branches met they created chambers much larger than you would normally find. The junction of the sub-branches CF42-5 and CF42-6 with the branch CF42 was a very nice piece of real estate, only ten minutes drive from the Crown.

'This is such a cool project.' Pemisegant had fallen in love with the scheme as soon as he had seen the plans that Tabbernant had drawn up. 'This is a rather boring junction chamber, the garden that Bernie has planned is going to be magnificent.'

'But it is still building work, even if it is building the features of this garden.'

'If you want to do something different with your down time, you are more than welcome to go back down to the Mess and dream dreams about you know who, just remember it is your turn to do the laundry.'

'Can it Pezzi, she can hear you.' retorted Althallant.

'As if I didn't know,' said Natalicsya. She had decided that she was going to take over the planting of this garden, Tabbernant had some good ideas, but lacked flair. This was a notorious traffic bottle neck. People were going to be spending time here, stuck in helicars, scootabouts or trolley-busses when the traffic snarled up. It was her intention that these delays would be enlightened by the garden in this junction.

'Well hello stranger!' called out Pemisegant when he spotted Nevamar. 'What brings you up here?'

'Stranger my eye,' replied Nevamar You still see me every day in class.'

'But we never see you in the mornings and you vanish during downtime, its as if you don't want to know us any more,' said the young style. In jest Natalicsya had uncovered the painful truth. Nevamar wished it could spend more time with its friends.

'Not my fault. I'm still on light duties. With Aunty Sharlee so close to her time, she needs almost constant attention.'

'Ooh, Aunty Sharlee is it?' asked Pezzi.

'Whilst off duty, yes Pezzi. Why, are you jealous?'

'Not at all. You do realise that Serynazsya is going to be incontinent for the first week after re-birthing. Guess who will end up cleaning all the mess.

'Yes, but it comes to us all one day. Temporarily growing down is all part of growing up.'

'So why are you up here?' Natalicsya asked this time.

'Sharlee wanted to come to see Bernie, so I had to drive her up. She could hardly walk, could she?'

'How much longer before the show starts, because the sooner we get her back as our mentor the better.' Althallant did not like Colonel Gwilwalsya.

'Next week the birth of the lock and re-birth of Serynazsya, then a fortnight after that it will all be back to normal.'

'Just in time for Passing Out then.'

'That's the plan.' An alarm sounded on Nevamar's comlink. 'That plan has just gone out of the window.'

Things had just got really interesting.

I ts not unusual during the course of their work, for the Winter Squad to find evidence of criminal neglect or illegal acts. This was why Inspector Galeroysya from the Enquirer Regiment and Inspector Untrugyant from the Enforcer Regiment were part of the Squad. Easily recognisable in their copper brown uniforms, the source of the nickname used for the police. They had been doing this job for five years and had been pair-bonded for the past two. Galeroysya was a petite blonde style from the far tips of the Roots, the industrialised mining sector that the Pure-stock tried to pretend did not exist. Untrugyant was a Trunk anther, with a razor sharp intellect beneath his thick set exterior. People underestimated both at their peril.

As well as different uniforms the police were a seperate chain of command from the rest of the Officer Corps, with different rank names, to make arresting higher ranking officers easier.

There was something about the whole situation that did not add up for Inspector Galeroysya. Whilst there was no doubt that the Priory had been destroyed by a freak alien force, the survival of Sister Kanonypsya had been miraculous and the Enquirer did not believe in miracles. Why had she been outside the Priory when the alien force had struck? A question without an answer. The answer would not be forthcoming, Tree Nuns policed themselves and were beyond the authority of the Enquirers, so it would be impossible to interview Sister Kanonypsya.

'Only five minutes. All I want is five minutes to close this investigation. Would that be to much to ask?'

Untrugyant had heard this from his wife for the past three days and it was starting to get on his nerves. 'Why don't you just ask her Gaye, she is far more approachable than most of the Tree Nuns.

'I wouldn't have the nerve Trug.' She smiled at her husband. 'My mentor, Lieutenant Warmorgsya, became a Tree Nun just after I became an Ensign. I was always scared stiff of her. If that was an example of the sort of style who joined the Convent, I assumed they were all as frightening.'

'We are not all as terrifying as our Librarian. Some of us are quite approachable.' Neither police officer knew that Sister Kanonypsya had been on site sitting in quiet contemplation.

'Are you sure? Your ability to materialise out of thin air is quite unnerving.'

This cracked a smile from the Tree Nun. 'Yes Inspector Untrugyant.' Despite the smile she was as joyless and aloof as ever.

'I'm sorry Sister, but I am a copper, and the job requires a degree of cynicism,' said Inspector Galeroysya.

'There is no need to apologise, you are only doing your job.'

'So would you answer the one question that has been plaguing me all week?'

'Certainly Inspector. Ask as many questions as you require.'

'Why weren't you in the Priory with the rest of your Sisters at the time of the disaster?' asked Inspector Galeroysya, cutting straight to the chase.

'That is simple. There is an old hermitage in a neighbouring sub-branch. I was on my way there to pray to Mother Sun when she returns above the horizon at dawn. The hermitage has a window to the void, it faces East and at this time of year Mother Sun shines through it onto the heart of the altar'

'Everything suggests the disaster occurred hours before dawn.'

'There was much to do to prepare the altar. I was on my way when the explosion occurred. The force knocked me out'

'You were lucky to be this side of the blast doors?

'No Inspector Untrugyant, it was the will of the Spirit of the Tree. The blast of air ahead of the fireball blew me forward through the fire doors, the flames that followed were contained by those doors.'

'Well thank the Tree for that sister.'

'We can indeed Inspector Galeroysya. We can indeed.' A worried look passed over Sister Kanonypsya's face. 'I do have an embarrassing confession.'

'You can rely on our discretion Sister.'

'Thank you. I was suffering from a crisis of faith.'

'Oh I see. Hence the dawn vigil.'

'Indeed. But the Tree saved me. If I am worthy of His love, then He is worthy of my faith.' Her face was as unreadable again.

'Thank you Sister. That wraps up the formalities,' said Inspector Galeroysya. 'We will be sending a copy of our report, as requested, to your Abbess.' The two police officers climbed into their helicar, leaving the Tree Nun kneeling in prayer.

'She was lying,' said Inspector Galeroysya as the helicar was zooming down the roadway back to the Crown.

'She's a Tree Nun,' said Untrugyant, not letting this amazing theory distract his driving.

'And what's that got to do with the price of protein. Only sprites always tell the truth.'

'But Tree Nuns and Tree Monks pride themselves on their complete honesty.'

'There is something that does not add up with that story.'

'Come on Gaye, now you are being over the top.'

'The Tree Nuns do their best to hide their individuality, but they are not sprites. They can lie, any adult can. Yes she's definitely bending the truth there.'

'So what now?'

'Things don't add up, but as this miscalculation will not equal anything illegal, then its case closed.'

W ith the two police officers on their way to the Crown, Sister, Kanonypsya could openly weep. She still had a crisis of faith. Solitude was impossible in the Sisterhood. For years she had craved being alone. Strangely though, now she had solitude, the loneliness was unbearable. Two decades of being surrounded by other Tree Nuns all day, every day, had left its mark. No matter what Sister Kanonypsya tried, her miserable life remained unbearable.

'Why Lord, why?' she asked the Tree. 'Why were my blameless sisters struck down. Why did you spare one disobedient fool. How can I live with the guilt?'

There was no reply, the empty silence was deafening, and Sister Kanonypsya continued to cry alone.

There was more to this site than just the garden. An entrance porch at the centre of the junction lead down to the four decks below that could be converted into dozens of accommodation units. Only one unit, for the team who used to maintain the now decommissioned Syrup Concentrator Tanks, had been built. It was an impressive place, even more so with Tabbernant as its single occupant.

'Bernie, what are you doing here? This could be a home for a family, not for an old anther at the end of his life,' said Sharlensya. She had turned up to make sure that old Tabbernant was not letting her class develop bad habits. 'Unless of course you are planning on pair-bonding with a style half your age, who would then go on to adopt half a dozen children.'

'My dear Shaz, even if you would have me, I doubt that you would want more than one child at the moment.'

Sharlensya was gripped with pain. Was that a contraction she thought. No, it can't be, its only been seven weeks, there were still two more to go.

'And I return to the original point, this is a very large place for a pensioner.'

'You know, if young Pezzi hadn't got himself stuck in a drain just up the road, I would never have discovered this place's possibilities. This is only one of the plots on this site, but it proves that my plan will work. It is all part of the plan.' Tabbernant had that look in his eyes.

'The days of us having the Crown to ourselves in Winter are coming to an end. The Canopy will always shut down during the dark half of the year because leaves can't work in the Winter. The Crown, that is a different kettle of pysgods. When the new Elatravator comes on line, running all year, the Crown is going to be a very desirable place to live.'

'If that thing catches on,' said Sharlensya.

'Of course it is going to catch on. The Roots to the Crown non stop in twenty minutes in an express car, instead of the nine hours an express shuttle takes. Even stopping at every station it will only take two hours instead of three days by shuttle. People with money are going to choose to live in the Crown and commute to work daily. So we will need a new base for the Squad, because the CORC will be occupied all year round.'

'That is all in the future, They have to get permission to build it first,' said Sharlensya. A lot of vested interests did not want this revolutionary new form of transport, a jet powered elevator that ran the whole length of the Trunk, to be built. Especially not the people who own and run the shuttles that travel the currents of the Grand Central Channels. 'I can't see the Shuttle Captains being happy.'

'I already have permission to build it, or rather one of my companies does.'

'You 'll never see a return on that investment.' Ow! Was that another one, bigger than the last, great green apples its early.

'Which is why I am developing this site for the Squad.'

'But you are retiring at the end of this tour. Why should you worry about the Squad?'

'Still going to live up here. I hate the Roots. The Canopy is my home, and I will be surrounded by friends in the Winter Squad's new permanent base.

Ow! There it was again, that was definitely a contraction. She was ejecting the lock, soon she would be a mother. Right, keep calm, remember everything the ante-natal lessons had taught her. Call her Uncle, get them to have the medical centre ready.

'Shaz! Sharlensya are you all right, you've gone as white as a sheet?'

'Oh great green apples Bernie,' she said. Her body convulsed. 'I think its coming.'

The birthing process seemed to have gone on for forever. Eventually, after a great deal of screaming blue murder, the lock had been expelled from Sharlensya's body. Both Nevamar and Serynazsya had paced in a waiting room.

'I'm so worried Nevamar. Mummy's life has just changed forever, I should be there, comforting her.'

Sometimes, Nevamar thought, Serynazsya says the silliest of things. 'You are going to be far to busy becoming her daughter, that is why she is going through all this.'

'Mother Earth we have a crazy system.'

'Uncle Kelly did say it was screw-ball.' Nevamar hugged the young style she now regarded as a friend. All past bitterness forgotten. 'Screw-ball or not, I am so jealous of you.'

'In the Tree's name why? You have seen what mummy has been through, you know what I am about to go through, none of it pleasant.'

'Yes, but think of what you are going to gain, a mother, a family, a proper adolescent body. I still haven't got a properly formed child's body yet.' Nevamar did not mention the main source of jealousy, the fact that Sharlensya was about to become the girl's mother. It was so lost in its thoughts it didn't notice Lieutenant Voynvalsya come into the room.

We are ready for you now Serynazsya.' She was going to take her into another room to begin preparing her to receive the newly born lock and undergo the next stage of the drama, after the birth came the re-birth.

The lock had been expelled from Sharlensya's exhausted body and she had gratefully fallen asleep. The leach-like organism was taken across to the bed where the anaesthetised Serynazsya was waiting. It seemed to be purring as its tendrils unfurled and wrapped themselves around the young style. Her body shuddered as hundreds of tiny needles on the tendrils pierced the major blood vessels in the torso and began absorbing blood from its new host. In any other circumstance, the medics present would have done their best to remove such a dangerous creature from the helpless girl. In this case they encouraged it, making sure that its blood supply was maintained as it swelled to twice its size. Serynazsya had entered a trance like state, a look of serenity filled her face. This was the happiest she had been for a long time. Not a drug induced euphoria, or a fake jollity. Serynazsya was in the process of getting all she ever wanted. All the pain of the past seemed to be evaporating for ever. Before she fell into the lock induced coma she turned to Nevamar.

'Please forgive me for all the dreadful things I have done to you. I was so crazy, I could have killed you.'

'You were not yourself at the time. Demons were driving you. They are gone now. I forgive you completely and utterly. Sleep now, you will be a different person when you wake up.'

Serynazsya slipped from consciousness with Nevamar sitting at her bed, stroking her hair.

'Thank you Nevamar, that was so kind,' said Sharlensya, who had just woken up and was smiling.

'Shush there mam, you have been through a lot, you need to rest,' said Nevamar. It left the young style's side, as Serynazsya was now completely oblivious of everything around her, and turned to the new mother.

'I sometimes wonder who is the adult and who is the child when I speak to you.' For the first time that day, Sharlensya was laughing.

'Uncle Kelly said I had the gift of empathy. Perhaps that has something to do with it.'

'Your a good girl Nevamarsya, you will make a lovely style.' And Sharlensya was back in the land of dreams.

Nevamar let that comment wash over it. Perhaps it would. At the moment I would be glad to be anything it thought to itself. This differentiation process was taking far too long.

After forty eight hours the lock had completed its primary functionand released the girl from its embrace. Quietly it slid down a drain and returned to the waterways of the Tree, ready to produce the next generation of locks and keys. Serynazsya had absorbed its life-enhancing gift and her body would be changed forever. Despite looking all grown up, with the personality of a young female adult, her body had not fully matured. Now every cell in her body was being extended and enhanced. Refitted from the pattern the lock had taken from Sharlensya's body as it grew. The young woman was being recreated not just in her new Mother's image, but that of the Family Fangkart, as the pattern had passed from mother to child over the generations.

Serynazsya soon woke from her coma and began crying. Now as bald as a sprite, a curious wailing unlike any other cry Nevamar had ever heard, issued from a toothless mouth. Such a sad wailing cry, made even sadder by the fact that Serynazsya was unable to say why she was crying, was unable to do anything in fact. Her body seemed to have shrunk, she looked so different and was completely uncoordinated. Nevamar knew that within a few weeks, the girl would be fully recovered, at the moment however, the whole thing just seemed so wrong, that more harm than good had been inflicted. Nevamar wished that it had never seen this process.

It got worse and worse. As soon as Serynazsya began wailing, her new mother went to her, began comforting her and to Nevamar's utter disgust bared her breast and let the wailing homunculus drink from it.

'What did you expect Cadet,' said Lieutenant Voynvarant, 'She cannot currently digest any solid foods, only the milk that has been swelling in my cousin's breasts. It is another part of the bonding process.'

The feeding process finished, Serynazsya fell asleep, thumb in her mouth, dreaming the dreams of the newly reborn. Sharlensya also slept in the bed opposite, her life changed forever. She was a parent now, she would not abandon the young style who was currently as helpless as a kitten. She would protect her daughter as her mother had once protected her.

Once mother and daughter returned home, a domestic routine was quickly established, Sharlensya seeing to Serynazsya's every need, then Nevamar making sure that the new mother was well rested and all her needs were fulfilled.

After a few days, Serynazsya regained the ability to concentrate on her surroundings. She was still completely incontinent and her only way of communicating was by crying, but it was definitely an improvement. A few more days and she was able to sit up by herself and had started using a collection of random syllables to try and talk, the speech centres slowly returning to normal. Sharlensya had been over the moon when she had been called mama by the girl. Nevamar decided that during this period Serynazsya was not just gaga, she was googoo-gaga, which matched the sound that she made a lot. Most of the time the young style slept, as her mind and body recovered from the huge trauma it had been through. When she was awake, she would spend minutes constantly repeating the word "gulley" as she wound her mother's hair around her finger before falling asleep again.

The curious thing about Serynazsya's hair, when it began growing again, was that it was the same as Nevamar's, a rich coppery red, and just as curly.

'It will be easy enough to restore back to her old blonde locks,' Uncle Kelly had said one evening, as he visited his niece for a mug of Instaht and a chat.

'I think she would kill you if you tried,' his niece told him. 'She has always said that Nevamar had hair to die for.'

'Serynazsya has picked a recessive trait up from her newly installed family pattern. She is especially susceptible to its influences at the moment,' said Uncle Kelly. 'You are also susceptible Sharlee, but not to the same degree. Haven't you noticed you're strawberry blonde now and getting redder.'

'Yes, I had noticed that. But I will be having it put back, I still have some loyalty to the Roots, though only the Tree knows why?' said Sharlensya.

PART FOUR
THE ENSIGN

CHAPTER TWENTY
CARRYING THE FLAG

Afternoon Class,' said Colonel Gwilwalsya at the start of another lesson. 'You may be seated.'

'Yes, Ma'am, thank you, Ma'am,' the class replied in chorus, before saluting then sitting.

'I have an announcement regarding our friend and colleague Cadet Nevamar 331/29,' said the Colonel, she had gone very pale. 'As you know, it has been unwell recently. It has now been passed to return to full duties, as its condition has improved sufficiently. Sadly, Major Keltonnant believes this is only a temporary recovery, that its immune system can cope with minor ailments, but the next major infection it encounters will be terminal.'

At her desk, Natalicsya began crying. The Colonel handed her a tissue.

'There, there Cadet, I know you are great friends.' Both Pemisegant and Althallant were also on the verge of tears. 'We must all be strong now. At the moment it is being counselled. When we see it, we must pretend that nothing is wrong. It's last few months must pass as normally as possible.

Althallant blew his nose loudly. 'So we pretend, Ma'am?' he asked.

'Yes Cadet, we pretend. It always said it wanted to be an anther, so we pretend that it has fully differentiated that way. Nevamar must never know how sick it really is.'

At first, the signs of recovery were so weak, even a doctor as experienced as Major Keltonnant missed them. The injection Nevamar had received had done more than temporarily halt its decline. It had reset her body to day one. All the female internal organs that had remained dormant began growing at an accelerated rate. It was ironic that all those around her were now doing more harm than good by treating her as an anther. The final stage of differentiation could not take place until Nevamar accepted she was the style Nevamarsya. Everyone pretending she was now a young anther was putting a brake on her development.

With no sprites in the Canopy, housekeeping had fallen to the Cadets and Ensigns. Nevamar never had liked hoovering and dusting but was very good at it. So it found itself cleaning the Medical Centre before it was really awake.

'Morning Cadet.' came a voice that was far too cheerful for that time of day, especially given that it belonged to Ensign Serynazsya.

'Morning Ensign,' said Nevamar.

Both had returned to the duty roster the previous day.

It can't be her, Nevamar thought, Serynazsya is half asleep until noon. She would never be a mornings person. Also wasn't cleaning the Medical Centre her job anyway?

'Oh Nevamarant, wonderful, wonderful Nevamarant. Thank you so much. Without you, none of this would ever have been possible.' The girl gave it a very non regulation hug as a greeting.

'Right, I'm still dreaming,' Nevamar said. 'Any minute now I will find myself standing here without any clothes on, and then I will wake up.'

'No silly, I'm the one who should be dreaming, but not in a nightmare, its a dream, a dream come true.'

Nevamar took a good look at the Ensign. She was so much prettier when she smiled. There was no doubt that the biological part of the adoption process had given Serynazsya a dose of her new mother's good looks. The "bulbous hooter", that the bitch Captain Samnundsya had taken great delight in ridiculing at every opportunity, had shrunk and transformed itself into a copy of Lieutenant Sharlensya's elegantly shaped nose with narrow nostrils. She had lost the buck teeth during the re-birthing process, her smile was now perfect. Everything was a great improvement. There was something else different about her today. Why wasn't she wearing a standard uniform and why was she dressed like a nurse, in a horrible yellow coloured dress?

'You realise Nevamarant, that if I were down in the Roots now, I would still be waiting for a family and would be studying Branch Management and hating every minute of it.' She did a twirl. 'Do you know how far down the waiting list for adoption I was? And the nurse training courses were all so oversubscribed. But look at me now.'

'I don't understand Ensign?' It took more than fancy dress to be training for a profession. Nevamar was very confused.

'Yesterday morning Nevamarant, at the start of my first day back on duty, I was standing where you are now, polishing that mirror, when the Major called me into his office. The twins were there as well. They handed me my own copy of the official nurse's training manual the course book used in the hospitals down in the Roots. They said that whilst I was up here, I'd be expected to complete the first four units. That I needed to keep up with my contemporaries.'

'I still don't understand Serah?' Nevamar switched to familiarity, as Serynazsya obviously had.

'I thought I had to wait until the Spring/Summer Tour before I could start training, I am to start a programme of on the job training straight away. Then I can continue my studies in the Sacred Sisterhoods General Hospital. It's the top training hospital down in the Roots, over subscribed or not,' said Serynazsya. No wonder she was beaming. 'Lieutenant Voynvarant gave me this watch and Lieutenant Voynvalsya gave me her old student cap.' She was pointing to the hat that sat slightly askew on her head. 'Lieutenant Voynvalsya said that from today onward I should look the part when I was on duty, that I should be wearing it with the rest of my new uniform. Mummy was so proud of me this morning.' She hugged Nevamar again. 'And as Mummy said, if it hadn't been for you, I would never be close to fulfilling my life's ambition. I'll always be in your debt.'

'I don't know what to say.' Nevamar was blushing.

'You don't have to say anything. However, I am about to become even further in your debt.'

Oh dear, here it comes, thought Nevamar.

'There is a party to celebrate Treesong and the Old Year Passing in a few days time. I know you don't have a date, which seems a pity as it is the evening after your Passing Out Ceremony and you will want to celebrate. Well, I don't have a date either. So I was wondering, if you'd consider taking me?'

No, this definitely was a nightmare, thought Nevamar.

'I thought you were going with Dukecamant?'

'Oh please. I do have taste you know.' she said indignantly. Serynazsya looked upset. Nevamar had been right and that was not the question its friend had wanted to be asked. Nevamar had been happy to be dateless. Taking a partner was not required, but a light suddenly flashed on in its head. This was a marvellous idea, doing them both a favour, Serynazsya didn't want to go to the party on her own and if he didn't ask she would have to go with the loutish Dukecamant. Also if Nevamar attending the party with an attractive young style, in a beautiful evening dress, on his arm it would cement in the minds of everyone who saw them that he was an anther. That it was not, and never would be a style.

'Serynazsya Fangkart 178/20, I would be honoured if you would accompany me to the New Year's Eve Party.'

'Oh thank you.' She gave it a peck on the cheek.

'Student Nurse Serynazsya, you should be down in the laundry washing bedding.'

'On my way Nurse Voynvarant.' And she was gone.

Nevamar let out a sigh of relief. No need to still feel guilty about what had happened to Serynazsya on that first fateful day of this tour. The Ensign's complaints had been spot on. For weeks everything had gone so well for Nevamar and so badly for Serynazsya. Now it looked as if things were starting to go well for the girl. Long may it continue.

The Shortest Day had dawned. The Cadets' Passing Out Ceremony had arrived. School would continue in the new year, preparing the four youngsters for their future careers.However not today. They were standing to attention in front of the entire Winter Squad, in the Subsidiary Ballroom of the Central Mess Hall.

'Each year, the Maintenance Regiment fulfils its duty to the future,' said Brigadier Myghcomant. 'We train four Cadets during our tour of duty here in the Canopy. This year our Cadets have excelled themselves, and it therefore gives me great pleasure to invest in these four upstanding youngsters their Commissions.

The entire Winter Squad was in the room for the Passing Out Ceremony. Regular Squad members recognised the prepared speech that did not vary from one year to the next. The Cadets did not care. In their full dress uniforms the Cadets Althallant, Natalicsya, Nevamar and Pemisegant, four nervous but very proud youngsters stood to attention on a dais next to their Commanding Officer.

'For fifteen weeks you four Cadets have worked towards your goal. Now your hard work is being recognised. You have followed an accredited training course and completed that course with full honours.'

'Cadet Nevamarant, forward one pace,' said Lieutenant Sharlensya, when its turn to receive its Commission arrived. Althallant and Natalicsya had already received theirs.

'Congratulations Ensign Nevamarant,' said the Brigadier, handing Nevamar a scroll containing its Commission. Then the Brigadier pinned a single silver leaf shaped rank pip onto Nevamarant's lapel. The new Ensign saluted the Commanding Officer, the enprintable fabric of its uniform buzzed as an epaulette appeared on each shoulder, as did a single silver hoop on the end of each sleeve.

Finally Pemisegant received his Commission. Colonel Rumsfelant lead the Squad in a prayer, and the ceremony was over, the party could begin.

CHAPTER TWENTY ONE
A NIGHT TO REMEMBER

All work in the Tree finished when Mother Sun dipped below the horizon on the Shortest Day. As the old year died, the day-lighters in the public parts of the Tree would fade and go out and all activity would stop. The power to all other electric lighting would be switched off.

For one minute, there would be complete and utter darkness throughout the Tree of Life. A darkness and a silence that was as solid as granite. Then the Tree itself would begin singing, a song that everyone within his embrace could hear. A song of great beauty and sadness, lamenting all that had passed in the previous year. Then there would be silence again as light slowly returned. The day-lighters would start to emit a twilight glow that would remain until Midnight, when the Tree would sing again. This time a song of great beauty, joyfulness and hope for all that would come is the year about to begin.

As soon as the Passing Out ceremony ended, the mood in the subsidiary ballroom lightened considerably. With the formality over, each style went home changed out of her dress uniform into the most elaborate party dress she owned. All these dresses had been designed by Natalicsya. It had started with people asking for advice on what to wear to the party. This usually involved doodling a design on a piece of paper. These doodles had become proper designs, because everyone loved the doodles, which had lead to actual dressmaking. The poor young style had looked shattered for days, because all the dressmaking had taken every second of downtime she had for the past two weeks. Yet, despite burning the candle at both ends, she had made sure that her dress uniform was pin and paper perfect for the ceremony.

Thank the Tree, thought Nevamar, that it had managed to control today's worse than normal clumsiness during the ceremony. Now it could relax, which turned out to be a bad idea as Nevamar could feel itself going to pieces. Come on Nevamar thought, only styles are allowed to be fashionably late. Anther's are supposed to be bang on time. Fashionably late, another strange thought that had popped into her head from nowhere.

So in full anther Dress Green Uniform #1, she knocked the door of the suite next door to her quarters. Wondering what the two styles would be wearing that night had subconsciously started her thinking like a style. The door was answered by

Lieutenant Sharlensya. No, I'm still Ensign Nevamarant because I'm still in uniform, but she is off duty so she is just Sharlee. Its been nearly four months now so she should be used to familiarity with older officers during downtime. Get a grip girl.

'Ensign Nevamarant, you're looking very smart.'

'Thank you Aunty Sharlee.' Why did she still have an irresistible urge to call her mam. Not Ma'am as in madam, but mam as in mammy.

'It's nice to see your hair has started to grow again.'

'I hadn't noticed, to be honest,' said Nevamar, whose scalp was covered in a fine ginger fuzz. Too many other things to pay attention to today.'

'Nevamarant, you're here,' said Serynazsya.

'Obviously dear,' said her mother, 'what a silly thing to say.'

Serynazsya made her grand entrance. Her dress was spectacular for what was not there. Bare shoulders and arms exposing acres of bare flesh. It seemed to defy gravity as Nevamar could not see any straps.

'It is the middle of Winter, said Sharlensya. you need the fletcher.'

'The what?' asked Nevamar.

'A short jacket that only covers the arms and shoulders.' replied Serynazsya. 'Oh Mummy, the design can be sleeveless.'

'Sleeveless in the Summer,' mother told daughter.

'If I were a style, I wouldn't wear it like that. No subtlety. You need to entice, not engulf.' Mother Sun, would she wear it. The dress was beautiful.

'Thank you Nevamarant.' She turned to her daughter. 'Serah, you are not going out dressed like that.'

'I bet you did when you were my age,' Serynazsya complained.

'Not on the last day of Trisksemp. Your grandmother would never have allowed it.' There was still a touch of sadness in her voice at the mention of her mother, but that was only to be expected.

Serynazsya ducked back into her room and thirty seconds later emerged in a more presentable version of the outfit.

'Your looking very pretty tonight. Serah.' But not as pretty as I would in that dress, thought Nevamar, whose hair was now half a fraction long.

'Please call me Rynzee.'

'I thought your familiar name was Serah?'

'Family and friends call me Serah, my date calls me Rynzee.'

'Fair enough.' Back to play-acting being an anther, yet another false start.

After being bundled out of the door by her mother, Serynazsya daintily hooked her arm around Nevamar's waist, and Nevamar put an arm on her shoulder. It knew this was the expected thing to do, why did it feel so wrong.

'Rynzee, you're a student nurse, you know the truth. I'm neuter and won't be around long enough be a proper boyfriend, why are you going through the pretence,' said Nevamar.

'You're not supposed to know that.' replied Serynazsya.

'Well I do, so why all the pretence?'

'To make your last few months happy,' she said.

'I didn't mean that, I meant why did you want me to take you to the party tonight?'

'More than one way to make a girl happy.' Serynazsya had stopped smiling. She looked as deeply miserable as she used to. 'That's why I asked you. Mummy would have freaked if I had gone with my first choice and asked Fernee.' This was quite a confession. 'She thinks I was only having a bit of an adolescent crush with cousin Voysha. There are still some things she doesn't know about me. One of those things is I now know I am gay.'

'Ferngarsya is going with Cemnentant, isn't she?'

'So she is,' replied Serynazsya. 'Its going to be interesting to see who will be the most macho in that couple. My money is on Fernee.'

They both laughed. Hard to believe that they could have quite happily killed each other a few months earlier. All that emninity had melted like snow in Spring.

'Although going with you is just me going to this party with my little brother. You seem like part of the family now.' Serynazsya was right, they did feel more like siblings these days. 'Maybe you should stick to Serah, little brother.'

'If you'll take a piece of brotherly advice, tell her tomorrow, don't let her find out your preferences from other people.'

They had arrived back at the subsiduary ballroom where the party would be held. All forty two members of the Winter Squad would have been swamped in the main ballroom.

'What, in the name of the Tree, is she doing here?' Serynazsya had spotted the Tree Nun, almost completely recovered, dressed in her formal robes. 'I thought she was supposed to be spending her time in prayer and meditation, away from the temptations of the Tree Without?'

'Everyone is entitled to a night off for Old Year's Passing.'

'Not the Sisters and the Brothers, tomorrow is their most important day of the year. They spend the whole of the Holy Day praying and singing in their temples, so today they work like crazy getting everything ready. Remember, it is called the Holy Day for a reason.'

Nevamar handed its greatcoat to the automatic cloakroom system. This brought the conversation back to Serynazsya's jacket.

'Why do I need this stupid fletcher, and why do you even need a greatcoat. We live our lives in a perfectly sealed environment. If the rain from the outer void ever did get in, it would be a disaster of epic proportions, and we would be busy repairing the breach, not partying?'

'Didn't you pay any attention in your history lessons. There used to be rain inside the Tree. Well precipitation in the roadways. It was part of the air-conditioning system which was eliminated when more efficient filters were developed, all that remains is the morning mists over the Lake. So historically you would have needed a raincoat, as well.'

'So now I know.'

'Indeed you do.'

'Come on lets dance brother of mine' said Serynazsya smiling, and the matter was forgotten in an instant.

'I would be delighted to, sister of mine.'

Serynazsya curtsied primly then they both started laughing and made their way to the dance floor.

N atalicsya greeted her recently arrived friends. Was she the only person to notice how fat Nevamar was becoming? Not perhaps a bad thing she thought. Her friend had been right, it had been far to thin before its illness. Now it was heading to the other extreme, Nevamarant was becoming positively chubby.

'Knock out frocks dear. You really know what makes a style look stylish,' said Nevamar.

'Thank you dear.' Natalicsya was grinning from ear to ear. 'Of course, it is unusual for an anther to be so interested in the latest style fashions.' She just could not resist the barb. 'It's so nice your hair is back as curly as ever.'

'Do you know, this is one of the rare occasions that I am envious of you styles,' said Nevamar.

'In what way?' asked Natalicsya.

'This Dress Green #1 uniform is impressive, but at the end of the day, its still an uniform. You girls in your pretty dresses have far more variety in what you wear to an event like this. Varieties of cut, colour and skirt length.'

'Well I ended up designing a dress for all the styles. Also one for you, when we all thought you were goiog to be a style. Its still there, on my web log, although its never going to be worn now.'

'Now why am I not surprised.'

Natalicsya just giggled. Everyone, Natalicsya included seemed to have accepted its preference to live as an anther, but she could not resist one last dig.

'Although as its Holy Day tomorrow, there's nothing to stop you wearing dresses to this party, and going back to being male on Monesday morning.' She giggled, 'hell, Alth could wear a tutu tonight and nobody would bat an eyelid.'

Nevamar was so conflicted, it so wanted a pretty dress. She knew she could pass as a style for a few hours, have fun and then revert back with no harm done. No, Nevamar knew it must stick to its choice. Appear to be one thing or the other, even though the fact was it was neither.

'Thank you for that horrible mental picture dearest,' said Althalant, 'but I don't think Nevamar is that envious. Even if you have knocked yourself out, with all that extra work.' It was so obvious Althallant wanted to change the subject from frilly dresses to something he could talk about. 'I can still see you going for your ride tomorrow, though.'

The double meaning in that comment has flown over your head, hasn't it? thought Nevamar.

'I don't know where she'll find the energy.' Althallant continued to dig himself into a hole.

'But you will be glad if she does.'

'No, I will be in bed all day tomorrow.'

'I bet you will.' it said with a smirk.

'Nevamarant, love, don't over do it. At the moment you are out Pezzi-ing Pezzi.' Natalicsya chided. 'I meant after all these frocks, I am shattered. I would sleep for a week if I could.'

'OK. I'm sorry.'

'That's all right Nevamarant.'

The act wasn't working. Natalicsya could still see her friend was not and never would be an anther. It had always been a question of body shape. Nevamar had never been anther-shaped. Hang on a minute thought Natalicsya, look where Nevamar is getting fat. Nevamar had loosened its jacket and Natalicsya could see just how close to popping the shirt buttons were on her friend's chest, but not its belly. In fact Nevamar's waist was positively skinny. Also its backside looked so large in those trousers. Great green apples Nevamar's got an hour-glass figure.

'I thought you said you were not doing anything for Fernee?' said a confused Nevamar.

'What, sorry, er, I wasn't,' Natalicsya replied her chain of thought interupted. 'Then she came to see me a couple of days ago. It is a good thing I did a design for everyone, and a hair and make-up program for the auto-stylist. All on my web log.'

'Mother Sun, she's lost some weight,' Pemisegant said. 'Not that anyone could tell in the overalls she always seems to be wearing.'

'Neither could Chemno.' Natalicsya was laughing as she remembered the look on Cemnentant's face earlier that evening. 'I had to get ready at her place, because I was still finishing her dress off when he arrived.'

'She is still large though,' said Althalant. 'Positively curvaceous.'

'Thank the Tree. We can't all be as petite as me, that would be boring,' replied Natalicsya.

From one of the tables there was the sound of a couple arguing.

'Can you believe that Hanazofsya agreed to come to this dance with Dukecamant?' Natalicsya asked.

'She has a boyfriend down in the Roots, doesn't she?' Nevamar added.

'Hanazofsya and Radyfodant are going through a bit of a rocky patch. Not surprising considering the separation for this tour,' said Serynazsya, who got on well with the young plumber. She had been her grandmother's last apprentice and regularly visited her mother, but spent most of that time with Serynazsya.

'It doesn't look as if she is having much fun though,' Serynazsya said absent-mindedly. She felt sorry for the young style. Nobody that pretty should be so sad. 'She still looks young.'

'I bet she will have to prove her age all the time after her fifth birthday,' added Althallant.

'Once a copper, always a copper, eh Alth. Congratulations by the way.'

'Thanks Nevamarant,' said Althallant. He had been accepted by the Enforcers Regiment, once he had finished this tour with the Winter Squad. 'Of course I want to be a detective, but everyone who wants to be an Enquirer has to train as an Enforcer first. Then do a couple of years on the beat before they can apply to transfer over to the Enquirers. But I don't care, its still a brown uniform and a step in the right direction'. He was glowing with pride.'

'Better get on that floor before the song finishes or Serah won't be happy. See you guys later,' said Nevamar.

Natalicsya watched as Serynazsya finally dragged Nevamar away from the conversation and onto the dance-floor. Althallant had obviously decided they had got their breath back, as he was dragging her onto the floor as well, and all thoughts of her friends sudden weight gain were banished from her mind.

As the hours passed, Nevamar found itself less and less enamoured by the behaviour of the young anthers. It did not like the taste of Oal at all, finding Wyn much more to its taste. The more it saw of the styles in their lovely dresses, the more jealous it became. So elegant and pretty. It wanted to be elegant and pretty. It wanted to be a style. It wanted it more than it had ever wanted anything else in its short life.

'Hey Nevs, over here mate. It's your round.'

'My round what? Oh very funny. Yes I know I have put some weight on. And please don't call me Nevs.' Back amongst the young anthers, any thoughts about being elegantly pretty and feminine were buried again.

'No you plank, its your round to buy the drinks,' said Dukecamant, squinting as he looked at Nevamar. 'Good job its the Holy Day tomorzz, you can put getting a regulation haircut off for another twenty-four hours.

Nevamar found herself embroiled in one of Dukecamant's juvenile drinking games. The older boy was playing to lose and enjoying the forfeits, drinking himself senseless. His date, the young and pretty Hanazofsya had had enough. At this moment in time she looked like she would rather be installing a central heating system, in an outermost twig, than spend another second with her horrible date.

'Hey, doll-face, where do ya thinks ya going?'

'As far away from you as possible,' she replied

'That's no in in the plan.' Dukecamant was blocking her exit. 'You came with me, 'n' you'll be leaf in wi' me. We heads round to mine, where I can give ya plumbing a good, a good, a good inspection, know what I mean.'

'You were so charming this morning I felt sorry for you, not having a date. Now I can seen why.'

'Watch ya sees watch ya gets, doll-face,' and he made an unsuccessful attempt to kiss her. This earned him a slap and Dukecamant tumbled backwards like a sack of potatoes.

'I'm not going to let a drunken fool like you ruin my evening!' Storming off towards the powder room she almost knocking Serynazsya, who was heading in the same direction, off her feet.

'I'm so sorry Serah,' thick tears running down her face.

'Zofie, whatever is the matter? Anything I can do to help?'

'Everything's the matter,' said the weeping style through her tears.

'Come on dear, lets help you tidy yourself up.'

The two girls disappeared into the powder room and everyone forgot about the fracas. In just over an hour and a half, the Tree would sing again and a new year would begin.

P oor partner-less Pemisegant was not getting into the swing of things. If it had not been for his brainwave, the Squadies would be running short of rations now, and counting down the days to the first shuttle's arrival in a few weeks time. Anything as frivolous as a New Year's Eve party would have been out of the question. It was because the Squad really wanted there to be a party next year, and the year after, that it had decided to downplay the size of this extra source of rations. To keep their little pot of gold to themselves. Pemisegant hated deceiving people and this creative fiction depressed him.

'Hi Pezzi, having fun?' asked Nevamar. No, it was all wrong, he was not having fun because she was dressed like that. Also she was with Serynazsya and not him. This was turning into a rubbish party. He did not have to stay here and watch Nevamarsya make a complete fool of herself.

'You are really starting to get on my wick,' he said angrily as he pushed past Nevamar and headed for the door.

N evamar had felt so sorry for Pemisegant, all alone and looking miserable on a night like tonight.

'Why don't you go over and cheer him up,' a voice had said.

'What a damn good idea,' her subconscious had replied, 'after all I am the closest thing to a girlfriend he has.'

'Why be close?' the voice asked, why not just be his girlfriend?'

'I would have to be a style for that to happen.'

'But you are,' the voice had whispered.

'I am, aren't I. I am a style. Always have been, always will be.'

Nobody had heard this life changing declaration.

'**Y**ou come back here and apologise.' Things had not gone well. She had gone over to say hello, and been rebuffed.

She was not going to stand for being treated so rudely. Boyfriend or not, that was no way for an anther to treat a lady. However, as she was about to follow Pemisegant another dose of auxins was dumped into her bloodstream, and her knees gave way under her.

'Ha ha, Nevs can't hold his drink,' said Dukecamant, who obviously couldn't hold his. Nevamarsya hated being called Nevs, it had, if you excuse the pun, no style.

'Can it, Ducky,' Nevamarsya hissed. She knew the older boy hated being called that as much as she hated being called Nevs. Not that Dukecamant noticed, not in the state he was in.

'Mother Sun, I am so glad I am one of your granddaughters. I am a style, I always have been, and I always will be'

Nevamarsya was totally unaware that her hair appeared to have taken on a life of its own, and was growing like crazy.

Pemisegant was sitting at a workstation in a small lounge area quietly crying. As soon as he spotted Nevamarsya he quickly set it into hibernate mode.

'What's the matter Pezzi? Are you upset about not having a date?'

'Its all your fault.'

'In what way?'

'You want to know the real reason I am without a date?' His temper exploding. 'It's because the person I really wanted to ask would not have accepted this year, and will not be here to ask next year.'

Nevamar knew he was talking about her, 'but...'

'Oh do shut up. I have been dreaming about tonight since you helped drag me out of that concentrator tank. Of you in one of Lisha's posh frocks, me in this formal uniform. Of us being a couple and dancing together all night. You finally accepting you are a style and me the happiest anther in the Tree.' He was walking towards Nevamar now, all tears dried up. 'But that isn't going to happen because you are to busy making a fool of yourself, camping it up as the most effeminate anther in the Tree.'

'Oh for goodness sake, I am not an anther.'

'Exactly! You don't walk like one, you don't talk like one and you certainly don't act like one.'

Something inside grabbed Nevamarsya and she embraced Pemisegant and she began kissing him. He kissed back with a passion. After what seemed like hours they were both breathless.

'Well, that was, um, interesting.' Nevamarsya was shocked by how much she had enjoyed the experience and wanted to repeat it.

'But I can't kiss another anther, even a pretend one, its just not right.' Pemisegant looked even more upset.

So, he won't kiss me again whilst I am dressed like this Nevamarsya thought. He will only kiss a style like that, and I want to be kissed like that because I am a style. If I'm wearing a dress, maybe he will believe me.

'Wait here, I won't be long.'

'Why, where are you going?' asked Pemisegant.

'You'll see. Switch that thing back on if you get bored,' said Nevamarsya, refering to the workstation.

Pemisegant meekly did as he was told whilst Nevamarsya headed back to the party. To her surprise, she met Nataliscya going the same way.

'They had to take Ducky home. Alth is sitting with him, making sure he doesn't do anything more stupid than he has already done. Ducky will be on a charge first thing Monesday morning.'

'It doesn't surprise me,' said Nevamarsya.

'And it means no midnight kiss for me.'

'Maybe I can cheer you up. Lisha, I have been thinking.'

'First time for everything dear,' said her friend.

'Oh har-har. No listen, I am intrigued by what you said about how I could get away with fancy dress tonight. Or rather a fancy dress.'

'And the make-up and hairstyle to go with it.'

'So lets do it. It'll be fun,' said Nevamarsya.

'OK, walk this way my dear. Prepare to be amazed.'

Nevamar started walking towards the powder-room with her friend.

'No, I meant walk this way. Shoulders as far back as possible, knees slighly bent to stop you tipping backwards and keep your feet together. If you dress like a style, you will have to walk like one too.'

Just as she had said, amongst the designs Natalicsya had published of all the evening dresses being worn at the party, was a potential one for Nevamarsya. What a pity it was a green one, the colour styles disliked wearing of duty. The other colours had been taken by other styles. Her reaction on seeing her design was not the usual, "Does she really expect me to wear that?". Instead she thought, "I'm going to look so beautiful in my dress, I'm a girl, why am I wearing this horrible old thing?"

It took seconds to download the data into the public fabric enprinter, built into an elegant mirror in the powder room. The enprinter activated and Nevamarsya's formal anther dress uniform boiled away forever. The enprintable fabric completely transformed itself. It had become a beautiful green satin gown. However it didn't look right. Natalicsya produced a wicked girdle and an appropriate padded bra to pull Nevamarsya's body in and fill back out again where necessary. In the style's powder room was a full size auto-stylist, a device fondly known by one and all as a slapper, to apply a layer of make-up to match the dress and tidy the long auburn hair. Some jewellery from lost property did the rest.

'There you go Nevamarsya, you could be so beautiful if you chose to be. What a shame this will all go back in the box after the weekend.'

'Oh just wait until Pezzi sees this.'

'That's right, where has he got to?'

'I'll go and drag him back to the party. Remember, not a word about this until I get back. OK.'

'OK,' said Natalicsya.

'What in the Tree's name have you been doing?' asked Pemisegant, not bothering to turn from the workstation monitor.

'Oh this and that,' said a voice, one that sounded so familiar
yet subtly different. Pemisegant gasped when he saw the transformation? 'So, what do you think?'

'See, Nevamarsya, you are beautiful, why do you insist on hiding it.'

Pemisegant pressed a button and music from the party piped into the lounge, and the young couple began to dance. When the music stopped they kissed until the next song began, then danced again, lost in their own company.

At five minutes to midnight, Pemisegant stopped the music. 'We'd better get back,' Pemisegant said with only a touch of disappointment in his voice. 'You had better go back to your silly pretence. I doubt your date would be happy kissing a girl at midnight.'

Oh, I don't know about that thought Nevamarsya. No, best to keep Serynazsya's secret until she wanted to reveal it. 'Did that make you happy?'

'Yes thank you.'

'Something happened tonight. I had a revelation, a great dawning of truth. I feel so different. So very different. All this,' it gestured towards the dress, 'is what I am now.'

She looked at herself in the mirror. 'Say goodbye to that silly anther, he's gone forever. Say hello to your new girlfriend. I'm a style, always have been, always will be.' That was it, the genie was now finally and fully out of the bottle, to which it would never return.

He looked closely at his friend. There was a definite change. No longer an It, definitely a She. The aura of femininity he had always seen was blinding now, radiating from her like a day-lighter, and she was even prettier than he had ever imagined she would be. It was still early days and she would no doubt get prettier and prettier as the weeks progressed.

He could not believe it, his New Year's wish had come true, and the Tree had yet to sing a note.

'No look at me, listen to me. I have changed and it feels wonderful. Look everybody, I'm a style now,' she said and began dancing around the room, her skirt flaring as she spun.

'I only had three weeks of catching up to do, and it wasn't pleasant.' Pemisegant knew exactly what would happen next, he had been through the process himself, 'you have three months worth of catching up to do, in one night.'

'Don't be silly, catching what up?' Nevamarsya's expression turned from joy to embarrassment. 'Oh. Oh no. No, no, no, no!' She hitched up her skirts and started running.

'I'm sorry love.' Pemisegant said as he watched her running back to her quarters. He knew the full realisation of what had happened had just hit Nevamarsya. Now she would be filled with a desperate need to be alone.

The clocks struck twelve. Nobody paid any attention as Nevamarsya ran home. This was exactly what she wanted. She wanted to be alone.

Everyone else was too busy listening to the Tree's song. It was a song of beautiful simplicity with an infectious beat that made everyone feel glad to be alive. A song of revealed truths and future happiness. A song of returning love and new beginnings. A song of hope triumphing over adversity.

Once she was back in her room Nevamarsya tore off her clothes, climbed into her bed and pulled the covers over her head. A head that felt like it was exploding as so much information flashed through it. She only hoped that things would be better in the morning.

CHAPTER TWENTY TWO
DOING IT WITH STYLE

It was the beginning of the Holy Day, the day that started the year but did not belong to any of the thirteen months. Nevamarsya's dreams that morning had been strange, shapeless and deeply unnerving. Nothing made any sense, noises had flavours, aromas had colours. Round and round spun her thoughts. Memories danced on memories. The noise in her head was horrendous. She tried to awaken to escape this cacophony, but that was impossible. As she reached breaking point there was a loud pop and everything became calm. She fell into the deep relaxing sleep she had last experienced when she first became a Cadet.

Reluctantly she climbed out of bed the following morning. As naked as the day, down in the Roots when she had first emerged from Sprite Pod N. She soon spotted her reflection.

'Don't you know it's rude to stare,' her voice said to the young style staring back from the mirror. 'Is that really my voice? Is that really my body?' She raised her arms, the young style in the mirror did the same. It was definitely her body.

The display in the corner of the mirror had always read "Waist: 34 frs." it was now reading "28 frs" and sat between two other measurements, "Chest: 32Frs (B)" and "Hips: 34Frs. Sure enough, her waist had narrowed considerably overnight. Where had all that body mass gone. Well some had migrated down to her legs. They had been embarrassingly long and thin, like matchsticks. To Nevamarsya's utter delight, they were now a shapely pair of long curved limbs, without a blemish. Her skin was so smooth as she ran her hands up her legs. Now she was a style her hips were larger. She supposed that was why she now walked with an undulating motion and her perfectly round and smooth bottom stuck out behind her, just as her breasts did in front. There was no way she could pretend to be an anther now. Not that she would want to.

'Mother Sun and Father Earth, I'm a style, a wonderful, wonderful girly girl of a style at that. With a style's lovely stylish contours to go with it. All female and lovely, isn't that just wonderful?' At five units and eight fractions. she was taller than average height for a style.

Her hair had grown to its current length, whilst she had been dancing with her darling Pemisegant. Over night the volume of her copper curls had trebled. It cascaded gloriously over her shoulders and down her back.

She did a twirl, luxuriating in her new body. Oh, I won't need padding next time I wear my ball-gown, she thought to herself. Why not make now the next time. It would be a bit creased because she had left it in a pile on the floor, but who would know. Sadly the beautiful ball-gown had reverted over night into a crumpled pile of enprintable fabric. Oh well she thought, at least the pattern will be stored in my wardrobe software.

All the other clothes in her wardrobe were for a young anther, that would never do. She wanted her dresses. Skirts as well. Floor skimming long skirts for nights like last night, knee length skirts for her uniform and thigh skimming mini skirts for fun. She wanted, jeans, leggings and hot-pants. She wanted bolero jackets, blouses and tank-tops. She wanted shoes with high heels and low heals, open toed sandals and knee-high boots. She was looking forward to having her hair in a long plait when on duty and letting it hang freely when off duty. In short she wanted everything she had ever laughed at styles for wearing in the past, because she was now a style herself and she wanted them now.

'Oh what a clown I was, a poor deluded clown,' she sang to herself, noting how her voice had gone up an octave but was not shrill and screeching. The whole room was wrong now. It had been decorated in a very masculine fashion, and that just did not fit any more. Everything would have to be changed. So much work, where to start. How to start? She slumped down onto the stool in front of the dressing table.

Absent mindedly she picked up the hair brush that had sat there unused since she had moved in on day one. She began brushing her hair, it made her feel better, and she noticed her face. It had changed again. Not as radically as when she had first sprouted, but it was different. It was as soft and gentle as the rest of her. The slight overbite was gone, thank goodness. The shape of the chin reminded her of someone, but she didn't know who. Also her nose was slightly longer and her nostrils narrower.

'Aunt Sharlee will know.' Inspiration struck Nevamarsya but not recognition, overnight her appearance had become more like Sharlensya and Serynazsya. The life saving and now life changing blood transfusion, from Sharlensya during her pregnancy, had made its mark.'

She grabbed the big blue dressing gown off its peg. As much as she wanted to show off her lovely new body, she knew that she could not go outside naked, even if it was only to the apartment next door.

Nevamarant, you're up a lot earlier than I imagined you would be,' said Sharlensya who was awake, but still semi-detached from reality. 'Although I am disappointed you did not bring my daughter home last night. Fortunately Ensign Hanazofsya took pity on her, and she stayed in her quarters.'

'I'm really sorry, things that I hadn't planned just happened.'

'Oh yes, you young anthers drink far too much without thinking of the consequences. Although I suppose you enjoyed your party.'

'Yes, Ma'am, it was fun, but...', she said. I'm not an anther, can't you see. Nevamarsya thought.

'There's a problem?'

'Yes, Ma'am. I'm grateful for everything the class has done for me in the past few weeks, I have really enjoyed being an anther, but...'

'Did you just say enjoyed, as in past tense?'

'Yes, Ma'am.' Was the penny dropping?

'OK, so what's the but?'

Nevamarsya could see that her mentor had not yet noticed the changes. Time for direct action.

'But, I'm not am I? An anther I mean. I never was. If I were...' she let the dressing gown fall to the floor, '...then the medics would have to find a way to make these two go away.'

'Why the formality? Its the Holiday and you have been calling me... Great! Green! Apples!'

'Yes Aunty Sharlee, literally, a pair of them, well flesh coloured at least.'

Fully awakened by the shock, the older style's mind was racing. She pulled Nevamarsya through the doorway of her quarters, deftly recovering the dressing gown with a fluid movement. 'When did this happen?'

'It must have been during the night

'Ask a silly question and you will get a silly answer. Still, it is one hell of a start to the new year.'

'Uncle Kelly said something like this would not happen,' said Nevamarsya.

'Your not happy with the result?' asked Sharlensya.

'Oh, but I am Aunty Sharlee, I am. Isn't it wonderful. I'm so happy that I am a style at last. Look at me, isn't this better than what I was.'

'You wanted to be an anther,' said the older style.

'Well, the less said about that, the better,' said Nevamarsya with a giggle.

It never ceased to amaze Sharlensya how quickly youngsters got used to their newly assigned gender. Never a hint of disappointment, never a, "But I wanted to be whichever". Was this really the same person who had bleated, "But I'm going to be an anther." for so long? The mystery of differentiation had thrown the World inside the Tree another curved ball.

'Nevamarsya, you will soon get used to being called that, by the way, there is never a dull moment with you? Uncle Kelly will want to examine you.'

'Why, I feel fine,' the girl said.

'As Uncle Kelly said, it shouldn't have happened like this. If the process started last night, it should be finished by this time next week.'

'Well, we couldn't see the internal changes and the external ones were buried under all that flab.'

'True enough, you have become very svelte overnight. You certainly needed all those stored calories. Still to be on the safe side, you should see a medic.' Sharlensya stood up and took a good look at Nevamarsya. 'Who else knows about this?'

The girl Nevamarsya had become was so busy staring longingly at the silken dressing gown the older style was wearing over her matching nightdress, that she didn't reply. In fact for Nevamarsya everything about the living room was suddenly so much nicer than it had been the last time she had been there. Mother and daughter had made a comfortable home for each other, in the four weeks since they had moved into their new accommodation. Well, Serynazsya had been googoo-gaga for two of those weeks, but as soon as she had recovered, she had begun leaving her mark on her family home.

'I asked you a question young lady, who else knows about this?'

'Only you and my darling Pezzi. I suppose I'm his girlfriend now, we kissed last night, and danced and talked. All whilst I was changing. It was wonderful,' said Nevamarsya.

Sharlensya could see why Nevamarsya had come to her. The youngster was still in shock, what a thing to wake up to. Except Sharlensya was as gob-smacked as the girl.

'Right, for the moment, the fewer people who know about this the better. You do realise that we are going to have to change everything for you?' The Lieutenant within tried to silently taken over and started moving to the practical considerations, it failed. 'Mother Sun, we will have to redecorate your room again.' Then the shock caught up with her, and she started babbling.

Nevamarsya had been paying attention to everything the older style had said and spotted something within the avalanche.

'You do realise in the middle of what you just said, you called your mother my grandmother. You have been doing that a lot recently.'

'Have I dear, can't say as I had noticed.'

'Yes mam, you have.'

'And you have been doing that a lot recently too, dear.'

'Calling you mam?' asked Nevamarsya rhetorically

'Yes dear. I am surprised how quickly I have got used to it and I would love to have you as my daughter as well.'

'The problem is there's Serynazsya to consider. She still needs time to be uniquely special to someone. To get used to being the daughter of a loving mother.' Nevamarsya had sensed that the older style was still not quite ready to take the final step.

'You are such a kind girl Nevamarsya. Thinking of others when you are the star of the show. You are my daughter now, are you sure you want me to be your mother and Serynazsya your sister?'

'Oh yes mammy. I really do.'

The two styles embraced each other.

'Right dear, I'm going to get changed and make some calls to the people who know and need to know. It's a good job this happened today, when the only people working are the medics. With the Leap Year we have an extra day added to the Holy Day, its going to be a quiet week this week. Oh great Father Earth, I should not have said that.'

Nevamarsya was so busy flicking through pages of the fashion magazine that was programmed into Serynazsya's reader, that she did not pay any attention to what was being said on the comlink, only brief snatches even attempted to register.

'No Brigadier, complete secondary differentiation, she's a perfectly formed young style now... Yes Uncle Kelly, it must have, she's flicking through a fashion magazine with a dreamy look in her eyes...Yes Sister, I would appreciate that... Great Green Apples, she's still naked... No dear can you come home straight away, I'm going to need your help... Yes Pezzi, it would be best if no one in the class knew at the moment, they would only get in the way... Right all done. You had better go and shower then put these on. I recycled your dressing gown. Yes, I saw how much you were obsessing over mine.'

The last vestiges of her anther wannabe sprite personality rejected the silken dressing gown and flimsy looking pyjamas that the older style was offering her, whilst a louder newer voice was telling her how gorgeous they were and that she should have been wearing them five minutes ago. She had to admit as she pulled the new clothes on that the cool silkiness was very pleasant against her skin.

CHAPTER TWENTY THREE
SUGAR AND SPICE

'**M**ummy, I'm home... Great Tree protect us! What a transformation,' said Serynazsya. Well, this is almost worth being dragged back home for she thought.

'Thank you Serah,' replied Nevamarsya.

'Is that you dear?' Serynazsya's mother asked rhetorically from the kitchen. 'Right, we have to sort out Nevamarsya's quarters, there is so much to do, and such a short amount of time to do it in. Starting with installing the connecting door and incorporating your quarters into this suite.' She had joined the two girls in the living room. 'Serynazsya, your sister won't have anything suitable in her quarters, so go and help her get dressed in yours, there's a good girl.'

'Yes mummy.' replied the older girl. 'My sister?'

'Well, sister to be, but that is such a mouthful,' said Sharlensya, who then laughed. Is there a problem?'

'Of course not. I had already accepted her as a brother, a kid sister is so much better.'

In her room and certain she could not be overheard, Serynazsya began to relax.

'You can call me Serah again. I have my darling Zoya to call me Rynzee now.'

'Hanazofsya, but she has a boyfriend down in the Roots?'

'Zoya had a boyfriend.' replied Serynazsya, 'now she has me.'

'Zoya?' Great green apples thought Nevamarsya, this is serous.

'Yes, Zoya. Her ex-boyfriend had been two-timing her. So she agreed to go to the party with Ducky to cheer herself up. She said it was just stupid. Then she just wanted someone to talk to.'

'You did more than talking?'

'I know. One thing lead to another,' said Serynazsya as she remembered the previous night. Come on Rynzee, pull yourself together, she thought, wipe that silly grin of your face. Then she turned to Nevamarsya and said, 'I saw the way you sneaked off with Pemisegant last night.'

'Sorry about deserting you.'

'Don't worry Nevamarsya, if you hadn't, I would not have spent the night with Zoya, getting to know her really well.'

'You don't think it was a one night stand type of thing?' asked Nevamarsya.

'Believe me you weren't the only one who had something magical happen to them last night, Nevamarsya dear.'

She stopped and took a good look at Nevamarsya. 'I have been so blessed. A loving mother, a new girlfriend and now a kid sister, I will never be lonely ever again.'

'So. You've told her then?'

'Yes,' said Serynazsya. 'She said she knew, being girlier than even young Lisha was a dead give-away.' This was a lie, as Serynazsya was still petrified of how their mother would react.

'You see, what did I tell you.

'So, this all happended whilst you were sleeping.' Serynazsya made a figure of eight shape with her hands.

'I'm a style now, isn't it fabulous.'

'I can see that. And indeed it is. Mummy wants me to help switch your room around.'

Nevamarsya had wanted to change the subject as quickly and as tactfully as possible, Serynazsya obviously had the same idea, so the conversation moved on, but not onto the subject of decorating. Nevamarsya was looking at all of Serynazsya's pretty dresses. One particularly caught her eye. 'May I try it on?'

'Go ahead, I think it will suit you.' Suit her it did.

'You were never going to be an anther, were you?' Serynazsya didn't need to ask, like everyone else she had known the answer for weeks.

'No, I wasn't. Look how pretty this dress makes me.'

'Keep it, your first dress, my Holy Day gift to you. Although its not very practical for what we have to do today.'

'I'm looking forward to seeing what you and Aunty Sharlee will do. You have done such a good job here.'

Now it was Serynazsya's turn to blush. 'Aunty Sharlee? Don't you mean Mummy, little sister.

'I suppose so, but you know she prefers Mammy,' said Nevamarsya. 'Now, can you tell me why my hair has grown so quickly?' The conversation moved on again.

'That's easy. A style naturally has long hair. If you were to shave it all off before going to bed in the night, by the time you woke up the following morning, it would be long and flowing again. Ready to be plaitted if your going on duty.'

'So I am always going to have this much?'

'That's right, unless you become a Tree Nun. They cut their hair really short and use rohotel shampoo to stun the follicles. They need to keep it that short under their wimples.'

There was a knock on the door. 'May I come in?'

'Yes Mummy.'

'Did I hear someone mention Holy Day gifts?'

'Yes Mummy, I was talking about the Holy Day gift the Tree has given us,' said Serynazsya. 'A sister for me and another daughter for you. Now all you and Commander Campbelant need to do is stop pussyfooting around and we can complete the family.'

'Serah!' Sharlensya was shocked.

'Well its true. How many times did you dance with him last night, and I know he is crazy about you.'

'We are just good friends.'

'Step in the right direction.'

'That's enough Serah. Come on you two, you can dress up later. At the moment we have work to do.'

'**G**ood morning sleepy head,' said a familiar voice. What's the Lieutenant doing in my quarters? Nevamarsya thought to herself. No, not just the Lieutenant anymore, she's going to be my mother and I'm going to be her daughter.

It was the first working day of the year. The past two days had just flown by.

'Morning mammy, how are you this morning?' she asked.

'I'm fine dear. Roll call is in half an hour, you had better rush.' her mother replied.

'I've got an assignment out in the Canopy, been excused roll call.' Nevamarsya felt disappointed, she had wanted to show her finished differentiation off to all her friends and colleagues.

'OK dear. Just remember that classes start again this afternoon. Don't be late.'

'Have you ever known me be late for lessons Mam?'

'Good point dear. But you had still better get a move on,' said Sharlensya as she left the room.
Nevamarsya's room still retained the character of the person who for so long had been simply Nevamar, but now it also had a more stylish appearance, to go with its owner's stylish name.

The wardrobe now contained considerably more frilly outfits than it used to. Somethings though had not changed. Overalls were unisex so she did not need to worry about her solitary task on the first morning back on duty.

If only the assignment had been that simple. She knew she was running late and she would have to shower before she could have lunch.

Despite being late, Nevamarsya could not resist looking at herself in her brand new girl's school uniform. A skirt rustled unaccustomedly around her knees. To think a few days earlier she would have ranted about how she would rather be dead than wear a skirt. That all seemed so silly now.

School Uniform? What had she been thinking? She looked like a Cadet on the first day of training, but she was a Commissioned Officer now. She punched a few buttons and an image of her wearing a style's Undress Green #3 appeared, which triggered changes to her outfit. The skirt became shorter as it merged with the sweater to become a dress, the heals on her shoes became that little bit higher and her tie became loser and wider as it transformed into a bow. This is far more suitable for a style my age, she thought, although she doubted her mother-to-be would agree. "A style my age," so much had changed in the past few days.

'Well Nevamarsya, time to introduce the whole population of the Tree to its newest style. What a wonderful thing to be doing,' she said to nobody in particular, savouring the sound of the new stylishly suffixed name.

They might be newly Commissioned Officers, but their general education was still far from complete. At the end of the tour they would all sit matriculation examinations. The results of those would determine whether or not they would be able to join their chosen regiment, to follow their chosen career.

As usual the Central Mess Hall was deserted. She had made it across the foyer, and down the short corridor to the classroom door, without meeting a soul.

Nevamarsya stood at the door full of nerves. Oh get on with it girl she thought to herself. Immediately followed by the realisation of how quickly she had got used to calling herself girl.

Inside the classroom Lieutenant Sharlensya was giving someone a dressing down.

'If you had actually concentrated on what the topic of the class was, instead of keeping a record of the number of times I said "Right" during the lesson, you might have passed the test. I am very disappointed in you Althallant and you Pemisegant for encouraging him.'

The knock on the door interrupted everything.

'Enter,' the Lieutenant called from her desk. Nevamarsya walked calmly into the classroom to her usual desk next to Natalicsya. 'Ah, Ensign Nevamarsya 331/29. I hope you are feeling better now? Fashionably late but I will excuse that this once. I see you have already started picking up bad habits from Ensign Natalicsya 199/20, I'll also let that pass today. We are finishing the assignment we started before the Holy Day.'

'Thank you, Ma'am,' said Nevamarsya as she sat elegantly at her desk. The dropping penny hit the floor with the force of a grenade.

'Quiet class, anyone would think that you have never seen a girl before. Granted you have never seen this girl, but I think you already know her quite well.'

'Well blow me, you finally accepted the inevitable then,'

Natalicsya said in a tone of voice that was peppered with more than a little "I told you so".

'As if I ever had any choice in the matter. Not what I wanted, but I think what I needed.' Nevamarsya said.

'Oh come off it, the last person to see you were a style was you. All that talk about you being neuter was rubbish.' Pemisegant was spot on, as usual. The words "Thank Goodness" remained unspoken. Nevamarsya knew exactly how close to death she had come.

'Well, we now know why you ran off at TreeSong.' Natalicsya caught the conspiratorial glances Nevamarsya and Pemizegant were exchanging. 'You've known about this for days, haven't you Pezzi? You didn't tell me. You pig!'

'I was sworn to secrecy. Couldn't say anything,' said the smirking boy.

'Do I have to repeat myself class. Its not as if a new member has been dropped from the sky into our midst.' The Lieutenant was sounding more than a little exasperated. 'There will be plenty of chance to discuss this after school.'

And with that the class quietened down and returned to their study.

'I really don't understand,' poor old Althallant was confused. Not surprisingly, Nevamarsya's final differentiation was the main topic of conversation as the Ensigns ate their evening meal. 'We had all accepted that you were one of the lads, then you go and do this.'

'I'm sorry Alth.' She smiled at her friend, trying to reassure him. 'I honestly believed I was going to be an Anther, I guess I should have listened to what everyone was telling me.'

'Indeed you should have Neevie.' said Natalicsya.

She's never called me that before, nobody has thought Nevamarsya. But they have all got familiar names as well as their formal ones, so should I. Neevie sounds fun.

'Neevie, I like it.' said Nevamarsya.

'But there are so many familiar names ending in "ee", Fernee, Bernie, Ducky and even my own, Pezzi.' he said. 'I like Neva, its different, and its pretty. Now you have gone all girly on us, you need something as pretty as you are.'

He put his arm around her and she kissed his cheek, announcing to the Tree that they were a couple.'

'Yes love, I think Neva sounds better than Neevie. From now on all my friends can call me Neva.'

'Neva it is then girly.' said Tabbernant as he wandered over to the table, mug of Instaht in hand.

'I don't have to register it or anything?'

'No girly, their called Informal Names because they are informal.' The old anther was grinning. 'See, told you you were a style young Neva, and a pretty one at that. Pezzi my boy, you're a very lucky fellow.'

CHAPTER TWENTY FOUR
SNOWBOUND

For days there had been the threat of snow. The previous day's sleety rain had lowered temperatures. The morning had seen the first proper snowfall, making some side roads impassable. Mr. Spenser hated the snow. It looked so pretty when it was falling, but it was an inconvenience once it had fallen. As it melted, everything was so mushy and dirty, especially when the salty slush was carried into buildings on the soles of shoes.

He trudged through the white void that was his garden up to the apple tree. Finally denuded of all its leaves, it looked so sad. Of course, the branches were covered with buds, *the hope of the future. Not as many as in the past, but more than in previous year. The experts had known their stuff.*

Anyway, to business. From the lower branches of the tree he hung a dozen or so fatballs, then made sure that all the feeders were full of peanuts. He loved the song of the birds in the Summer and knew that to guarantee that, he had to do his part during the Winter to keep them fed.

The first thick snowflakes of the next fall began to make their presence felt, as he turned back towards his nice warm kitchen. He smiled to himself, the critters might need help with this weather, but the tree didn't. How many Winters had it stood there, stoically shrugging off the worse that the weather could throw at it?

Natalicsya loved cycling in the open air, well as open as it was possible to be, within the sealed world of the Tree. It was great for keeping her fit and keeping the excess pounds away. Being curvy was hard work, gain weight and you looked like a sack of spuds, lose weight and your head looked like a lollipop on a long stick.

She had changed so much during the past four months. From the gawky kid with a head chocked full of how to be feminine and elegant, to actually being an Ensign who was all feminine and elegant.

Natalicsya had gradually changed, her friend Nevamarsya had it all dumped on her in one go. The past couple of days had been a steep learning curve for that young style. Nevamarsya certainly had curves now, it was a shame she still had no taste yet. Natalicsya firmly believed she was going to have to take that girl in hand and show her the ropes. Some things could not be left to instinct alone.

Once outside Natalicsya was surprised by how dark the Crown was. It couldn't be a fault with the day-lighters, they had all been checked out. Unless it was a general fault somewhere else in the supply chain.

'It's too dark and cold to be going far on the bike Ensign,' said a voice in the gloom. Subaltern Popisedsya was just completing a night shift monitoring systems in Command and Control. Despite being heated, the cavernous room she had been working in seemed as cold indoors as it had been out in the Crown. But not as cold as some of the outer branches.

'I'm not going far, I should be back before breakfast, Ma'am.'

'Just see that you do. This damn snow is causing a seventy five percent drop in day-lighter efficiency,' said the older style. 'It will be fully dark two hours earlier than normal.'

'What's snow, Ma'am?'

'Its an external weather condition. Its so cold out there in the void that the rain is freezing into a fine white powder.'

'Ah, covering the branches.'

'That's right, where it lands it covers with a thick layer of white, until the temperature rises. The less light that gets to the bark, the less light there is for the day-lighters.'

'Thank you, Ma'am.'

'You be careful out there.'

'Yes, Ma'am.' Natalicsya doubted if the other style had heard her.

She rode her bike down to the lake. There was ice covering at least half the surface. It was unusual for the whole thing to freeze over because warm water still rose from the Roots. Unusual, but not totally unheard of. Great green apples, it was nearly cold enough for that now. Despite her warm clothes and all the effort of pedalling the bike, it was far to cold to stay out of doors, so she headed back to her quarters. Perhaps she would have an extra hour in bed to warm up.

N evamarsya sat at her dressing table which was covered with all sorts of nick-knacks that she never knew existed, but as a style she could not live without. Tweezers, emery boards, make-up, make-up remover, hair brushes, the list went on and on. Contemplating life was easy when she brushed her long red hair. It had been a week now since she had woken up into a whole new life. Oh to see that ghastly style Captain Samnundsya again and tell her that she was not a non-entity, that she had shown she could be an Officer, she had the Commission to prove it. Victory would be so sweet.

Her new found love of skirts only went so far. Yesterday had been so cold, today she would wear a nice sensible pair of trousers to keep her legs warm.

'Can I come in?' Her friend asked politely. Father Earth, that was a first, normally Natalicsya just barged in.

'Of course Lisha. Are you not feeling well, you asked if you could come in.'

'Well you don't just barge into another style's room, its bad manners.' Natalicsya was full of all sorts of points of etiquette that Nevamarsya was still learning.

'That has never stopped you before.'

'You're a girl now, the rules have changed.'

'Oh for goodness sake what difference does that make.'

'You not having a front door any more doesn't help either. It is a bit difficult to barge into your room, when I have to go through my superior's billet to get to it.'

'My Mother doesn't bite.'

'Well, that explains the door,' said Natalicsya. A light flashed on in the young style's head. 'Did I just hear you right. You called the Lieutenant your mother?'

'Yes, isn't it great. Well mother-to-be, as it will be at least a year before the adoption is complete.'

'Oh Neva, I'm so happy for you.'

Nevamarsya felt the sadness in her friend's voice.

'Don't worry Lisha, it will happen to you. Soon you will be part of a family as well.'

'I suppose you're right Neva, I'll just have to be patient,' said Natalicsya, still sounding wistful.

'Anyway. You're back early from your ride?'

'It's too damn cold to do anything outside. Even warmly wrapped up there was no fun riding my bike.' Natalicsya then explained about the snow.

'I've read about that. Frozen powdery water. Some things outside the Tree are just breathtaking in their weirdness.'

'All I know is that it made everywhere almost as dark as night.'

'I'm heading down to the library. Do you fancy coming along.'

'Library, no thanks. Anyway, I don't think I could afford to pay the fines.'

'Natalicsya, all you have to do is go down there and delete the book file from your reader by the due date. Then go there to upload something new.'

'Therein lies my problem. Why can't they let us download books from the network, why do we have to go to the stuffy old library?'

'Firstly, because that is where the book server is located, and its not networked. Secondly, because that is where the original printed versions of the books live. Thirdly, it is where you find Commander Campbelant during his free time. I never realised just how dishy he is, my mother must be blind.'

'Dishy is he. You are learning to speak the lingo remarkably quickly.' Natalicsya did not miss a thing. Nevamarsya went bright red.

'I have a lot of catching up to do.'

'Great green apples Neva. You will be saying you need to lose weight next,' Natalicsya joked.

'Well I do! I am piling on the pounds,' said Nevamarsya, then she burst out laughing.

'Oh ha ha, very funny,' said Natalicsya as she began to giggle. 'But you mark my words, this honeymoon with your new body won't last. You will soon be moaning about various bits and on a diet, like the rest of us styles. Its almost a second religion.'

Natalicsya reset her clothes at Nevamarsya's wardrobe. Nevamarsya squealed a protest as her jeans also transformed themselves into a pair of thick woolly tights and a skirt, as tiny as Natalicsya's, appeared around her waist.

'So what are you doing this afternoon?' asked Natalicsya.

'What, as soon as I have reset this back to a pair of jeans? Some things never change.'

'Don't you dare. Those woolly tights are thermal, so they are far warmer than any trousers could be. Also, the miniskirt is like a frill on top to emphasise your pretty legs. Anyway, Pezzi will prefer this outfit.'

'He doesn't have to wear it. Also, I dress for myself, not for him.'

'If you say so dear,' was Natalicsya's cynical reply. Rapidly changing the topic she asked, 'So what are you doing?'

'Helping my mother cook a curry.'

'Cooking? Why does she do her own cooking when Bernie is busy in the refectory?'

'Sometimes it is nice to do it yourself,' replied Nevamarssya. To be honest, She had asked the same question. 'And anyway, you are going to have to cook for yourself eventually. In the Summer you won't be able to afford to eat out for every meal.'

'So where is Serah, why can't she help?'

'You've tasted her cooking, haven't you? A lifetime of lessons could not improve that.', Nevamarsya laughed. 'She is off helping Zofie get ready for the concert tonight.'

'Who?'

'You know, Ensign Hanazofsya.'

'Oh her. Then there's not much preparation going on there this afternoon.' Natalicsya loved reading between the lines.

'Your mind is in the gutter. You know that it's Zofie's turn to supply the weekend entertainment at the concert tonight. She will need help getting her harp down to the concert hall.'

'It must be so nice being on familiar name terms with so many people,' said Natalicsya.

'Don't worry, you'll get there soon yourself.'

'Well, I'm off for some breakfast.' The young style was bored already.

'See you later.'

'No doubt.'

Nevamarsya looked at herself again in the mirror.

'No, I will not be bullied by my friend, even if she does think she is helping,' she said to no-one in particular. But no-one in particular was paying attention. True she did look very pretty in the outfit and yes the tights were nice and snug, but it was not her choice. She tapped in the code for her jeans, and then added a few variants. Sure enough, the miniskirt reformed itself into a pair of hot-pants, but she kept the snug thermal tights. 'Just because Lisha only ever wears skirts, it doesn't mean I have to.' Again nobody in particular wasn't listening. 'I am a style with my own style, and she can like it or lump it.'

Twenty minutes later in the library, her head was still chock-a-block with thoughts of how things had changed. Not having Natalicsya barge in any more. She would miss that, it had become a normal part of her daily routine. She should really have concentrated on where she was going.

'Its over there for you now young lady,' a slightly shocked anther coming the other way told her as she tried to use the anther's rest room in the library.

'Yes Ensign, you need next door now.' Commander Campbelant, the part time librarian was smirking as he gently pointed her in the right direction.

'But I can't use that, its for styles!' she replied. Instantly horrified at how stupid that had sounded, she fervently wished the floor would just open up and swallow her. Nevamarsya was blushing.

'Have you looked at yourself in the mirror recently?' Damn it, the Commander was still laughing. 'Obviously not, looks like you forgot to put your skirt on this morning as well.'

'They're hot-pants, Commander.'

'Whatever. I know you have a lot to remember, but it is vital you remember the difference between the square for anther and the triangle for style. OK.'

'Yes Commander.'

He is only trying to be kind, she told herself, it is just that he has a funny way of doing it.

'I am so sorry Commander, I won't do that again.'

She did not choose any books, she was just too embarrassed.

Major Keltonnant sat at his desk, waiting for a patient, any patient to turn up to morning surgery. The Squaddies were such a healthy lot, rarely getting an illness. He was far more likely to be sewing up accidents caused by a slipping chisel or a badly placed nail. Even they were few and far between because the Winter Squad was so careful. He wondered if his Medical Centre really needed so many staff. Himself as doctor, two fully trained nurses and young Serynazsya as a student nurse. Well, medicine was a Family Fangkart thing. His sister's decision to become a plumber had been a bolt out of the blue, but even she had started her working life as a student nurse. Young Sharlensya had never been interested in medical training, she had always wanted to be a mentor.

The thought of Sharlensya as a mother made him feel old. He could remember when his sister Sannarlsya had told him that she was adopting a daughter. It was no wonder Sharlensya had wanted to help young Serynazsya. The two styles had such a raw deal in their early lives, before meeting loving and generous mother.

He had even come to terms with Kanonypsya being here in the Crown. Here she was again.

'Can I help you Sister.'

'Yes Major, I would like to discuss the medical provisions of the new Priory,' said the Tree Nun. She seemed different must have happened to make her happier. She was still as formal as ever, but there was an approachability that was new.

'I thought you sent any sick or injured member of your Priory down to the main Convent Infirmary in the Roots.'

'Usually we do, but for matters of minor first aid, that is overkill.'

'So you want advice on first aid. Surely as a former paramedic, you would have more than enough experience in that subject.'

No Keltonnant, that was below the belt, apologise at once.

'I'm sorry, of course you want a second opinion on your requirements.'

'Indeed, my knowledge is rusty, I would be grateful if you could peruse this list, let me know what is out of date and what I can replace it with.'

'Certainly Sister.'

'Thank you Major and a good day to you.'

Despite it being a day off, Sharlensya found today. Something in her classroom that morning, preparing it for the last few months of normal classes for this Tour. Ever since she had accepted the challenge of motherhood she had been the pupil, not the teacher. Serynazsya had come out of her shell in the past few weeks and was now a happy and well balanced person. The deep depression that had plagued her had moved into the past. For the next four years the girl would be her responsibility, she had to make sure that she continued to provide the nurturing environment that her daughter needed, making sure that there was no relapse, no back sliding. Although Sharlensya was pretty sure that now the only way was up.

In a years time her family would be larger again, as she formally adopted Nevamarsya as well. That youngster had bounded into her life on the day she had lost her beloved mother. That was a wound that still stung, but Nevamarsya had helped to salve the wound. What would her mother have made of the changes in Sharlensya? Heartily approved, no doubt.

'I thought I would find you in here Mummy.' Her daughter was looking ecstatically happy.

'Serah dear, could you just call me Mam or Mammy.' Her daughter had insisted on calling her Mummy, and for some reason it wound her up.

'Okay, but what's wrong with mummy?' her daughter asked.

'Mummies are the desiccated corpses of unrecycled people. I find it a bit gruesome.'

'OK then Mam.'

'Thank you dear. It is a Fangkart family tradition.'

'What ever you want Mam.'

Good, thought Sharlensya. I only hope the next matter will be so easily dealt with.

'So what's happening with you today dear?'

'This and that. Zoya let me play her harp. She said she would teach me how to play it properly. Isn't that marvellous.' Again the girl was beaming.

'Yes dear. Although I am not stupid you know. I can guess exactly what you two have been up to.'

'You can?' said Serynazsya coyly.

'Of course I can, you just used an intimate name instead of an informal name, a dead give-away. I just wish you had told me earlier. Your sister was so embarrassed. Neva thought I already knew.'

'I was afraid of what you would say,' said a shamefaced Serynazsya.

'I won't deny I am concerned.'

Her daughter was young and inexperienced. So was Hanazofsya. They seemed a pair well met, but would it last. Then again, would anything in this constantly changing life last. The tense moment passed and Sharlensya started laughing.

'What?' Her daughter was completely confused.

'You, I'm so glad to have you as a daughter.'

There had also been such a change in the quiet enigmatic Hanazofsya in the past few days. It was obvious that her failing long-distance relationship had been weighing heavily on her mind. The young Ensign was almost chatty now. The wicked minded would think wicked thoughts, let them think them, Sharlensya knew that was just tree-person nature.

Sharlensya watched her daughter's long red hair fall out of the lose ribbon. She was now the only female member of the family in the Canopy who was blonde. Voynvalsya had always been a redhead, just like her twin brother. They were from the Canopy, as had been great-grandmother, Wystellsya. She and great-grandfather Dwinedlant had caused a fuss back in the day, when they had pair-bonded. Great-grandmother had introduced the ginger trait into the family pattern, which Serynazsya picked up during the re-birth process. She had then fought like hell to keep it. Although she was not officially part of the family, Nevamarsya had lovely red hair, Sharlensya thought, when she officially becomes my daughter it will further reinforce the trait in the pattern.

Perhaps it was time that she followed suit. She produced a picture of herself with the workstation's web-cam, and then put it through some image manipulation software to produce a picture of herself with red hair like Nevamarsya. She liked what she saw. A little cross referencing showed how easy the change would be. Definitely something to add to the to-do list.

Brigadier Myghcomant looked out from his eerie up in Command and Control and was a happy anther. This had so far been the most successful Tour of Duty for the Winter Squad in years. When the supply craft had arrived with the materials for the preparatory work for the new Priory, he had been gob-smacked. The Abbess had told him that any excess materials were to be used by the Squad in their normal day to day activities. They had sent up nearly twice as much materials as was needed for the job. Those Tree Nuns seemed to have money to burn. For once the Winter Squad would be able to finish all the jobs it had started, and return to the Roots with their heads held high.

Saxearthday afternoon. He should be out enjoying himself, not still here in the Command and Control building. They could always call him in an emergency. Although, his office was where he kept his Kuffa perculator and his stash of Kuffa Beans. Most people only knew Instaht, the synthesised kuffa flavoured muck. This was the real thing, grown in the Roots tips, horribly expensive and the Brigadier's favourite thing. Only a mug of hot black kuffa could drag him back to his detested office.

That's odd, he thought, what was young Pemisegant doing here, where was the duty officer.

'Ensign, report.'

'Sir,' Pemisegant snapped to attention and saluted. 'Situation as of 1245 today. The external temperature has lead to increased incidents of ice formation within the Canopy. Blockage detection has reported four potential incidents of pipes blocked by ice. Teams have been sent out to deal with them. The deposit of snow has resulted in all day-lighters working at 33%. All other systems are therefore running at 97.8% of optimum. If the situation with the day-lighters continues, then it may be necessary to use the emergency batteries, which will require your authorisation. Additionally, an automated fault report has been generated by the Traffic Control System in Branch XQ79. It looks as if the control loom for that section is a dud and is affecting all systems tipwards, knocking them out of sync.'

'We can be grateful there's no traffic to control then.'

'Sir?'

'I take it by your response, you are the Duty Officer,' said the Brigadier.

'Yes, Sir.'

'Your not Subaltern Popisedsya, she drew the short straw and was on the roster for a double shift today.'

'Sir, Colonel Rumsfelant asked me to swap, he wanted to see her and Lieutenant Crysgoxant, something about their up-coming pair-bonding ceremony. It's all in the duty log.'

The Brigadier sighed. 'Which I won't read until Monesday. Oh don't worry, I'm not complaining. At ease Ensign. More experience for you.'

'Yes Sir.'

'And more overtime.'

'Overtime, Sir?' asked Pemisegant. 'I didn't think I qualified.'

'Of course you do lad, you are an Ensign now. Or did I hand that Commission to another Pemisegant?' He could see a light come on in that bright lad's eyes.

'Carry on Ensign Pemisegant.'

look back at this interlude as if it had been a dream.

Something unpleasant had found its way through the Tree's defences, and the Winter Squad was about to get a rude awakening.

CHAPTER TWENTY FIVE
LOCKDOWN!

The recently promoted Ensigns still had a rota for helping Ensign Tabbernant clean his kitchen, after the evening meal. Tonight it was Althallant's turn, but as usual, all four of them would pitch in. Tabbernant knew his kitchen was in safe hands and he could leave the four youngsters unsupervised.

'Hey Neva, what have you got planned for this evening?' Natalicsya asked, and had that look in her eye.

'Why, what have you got planned for me?' asked Nevamarsya, who had quickly realised that it was best not to try and stop whatever her friend had planned. Natalicsya was only trying to be helpful. After all Nevamarsya was still getting used to being a style.

'I've got some things I'm working on and I need a model. Once we officially go off duty, I can't wait to get you out of that dreary uniform and into something pretty. You chose some of the dullest downtime outfits imaginable.'

'Lisha, do you remember the first time we met,' said Nevamarsya. 'Well, I still think we wear some ridiculous things when we are off duty, so don't expect me to rave about all your outfits.'

'Well it shows that you are obviously learning, but you still make some pretty basic mistakes. Remember those hot-pants?' Natalicsya continued.

'Will you ever let me forget.'

'Only when you agree never to wear horrible hot-pants ever again.'

'I liked them,' said Nevamarsya.

'Well you were the only one who did. They made your thighs look chunky. So you need more lessons from Professor Natalicsya.'

Nevamarsya said nothing, she was too busy blushing.

'Father Earth, you can be a completely condescending bitch at times, you know that Lisha?' said Pemisegant.

'Can it Pezzi, this is girl-talk, only styles allowed.'

Jumping to Nevamarsya's defence was just making Pemisegant look silly. Damn it, Nevamarsya was giggling, laughing at him. Thanks a bunch dear.

'You still here?' Natalicsya just couldn't resist one last dig. 'Hey Pezzi, fancy coming along too. Is that it, we could pad out a bra and you would look so cool in a frock.'

There was no chance, not even for a fraction of a second, that Pemisegant would have accepted that invitation. His expression changed from mildly annoyed to deeply hurt and he stormed off angrily. Nevamarsya decided it would be better to let him go. Let him do something to get the insult out of his system. Meanwhile, she glared at her friend.

'That was cruel Natalicsya,' said Sharlensya, who had already been home and changed out of her uniform, into casual clothes.

'Why, I give as good as I get, good natured banter, nothing cruel?' Natalicsya didn't understand what the problem was.

'So you think, if you think at all,' said the mentor.

'But he so should have been a style and Neva here so wanted to be an anther. Shame they can't swap.'

'No thanks, not now,' said Nevamarsya

'Eh! What? I don't understand.' Poor Natalicsya, she did look so confused, this was not what she had expected at all.

'Natalicsya, How long did it take you to accept that you were a style?' asked Sharlensya.

'Don't be silly, it was straight away, it was what I wanted. I enjoy being a girl.'

'Whilst it was happening I suddenly realised that me being an anther was so silly,' chipped in Nevamarsya, who could see where this conversation was heading. 'Now I really cannot imagine being anything other than a style. I'm loving it in fact.'

'So what's this got to do with Pezzi?' Natalicsya was still confused.

'Because as soon as he knew he was an anther, he accepted it straight away. Its the way differentiation works, isn't it Mam?'

'That's right Neva dear. But Pemisegant's problem is, the only image of adolescent masculinity he has to measure himself, against up here, are the very macho young Ensigns Althallant, Cemnentant and Dukecamant. Pemisegant cannot come close to emulating them.'

'I suppose that calling him a runt didn't help either,' said Natalicsya, who was now very red with embarrassment.

'No young lady, it did not. Then suggesting that all he needed was to sling on a pair of false breasts and he would look like a style, was the a step too far.'

'Oh, I really should go and apologise, shouldn't I?'

'Give him a few hours to cool down first. You don't want to go blundering in and making the situation worse, do you?' said Nevamarsya, as always a fountain of good advice.

'Do you know where Bernie is, Lisha?'

'No sorry, Sharlensya. He asked me to mind the shop, whilst he went to get some supplies.'

'Oh well, it can wait.'

'We'd better get started then people,' said Natalicsya, as she rolled her sleeves up and started loading the industrial dish washer.

'Are you doing that properly,' asked Althallant. 'You know he gets a bit OCD if his dishwasher is not loaded in exactly the right way.'

'I don't think he will complain dearest one, not if we have tidied up for him by the time he comes back,' Natalicsya said with a grin.

'He probably skived off because he knew we would do this for him.'

'That's not nice Mammy. There is probably a very good reason why he's not here.'

'I know, I know. You are still having difficulty with your sense of humour Neva dear.'

Twenty minutes later, the kitchen was spotless. Cleaned to Tabbernant's high standards. However, there was still no sign of the cook. This was very unusual, he never left the kitchen for so long.

Subaltern Rosateesya knew the crystal hovering at eye-level was the most beautiful and deadly thing she had ever seen.

Wherever she moved her head, the crystal would follow. She

was being held in a vice-like grip by Ensign Dukecamant, whose face was completely blank, his eyes frozen and dead. Both he and Lieutenant Crysgoxant had already been infected by the Virus, she knew that she would be next. Already the dancing glowing light and the eerie music were beginning to hypnotise her. No, she thought, I must fight it.

'There is no point fighting us, we are too strong. You will only be possessed for the moment, the vermin will detect any touch of the Glory. You will have to wait for the transformation your colleagues are undergoing. When you return from this mission you too will become crystalline perfection and the pestilence called Life will be stripped from you,' said the voice. It seemed to be coming from everywhere at once. The Subaltern struggled but she knew it was no good, she could feel all self control draining from her.

'Excellent, you have your orders, go carry them out. Countdown the seconds until your return, when you to will rejoice as the Glory transforms you.'

Pemisigant had started walking in the white heat of anger reached the outskirts of the CORC before he encountered anyone.

He was used to the constant jibes from Natalicsya, he enjoyed the battle of wits, but he had not expected his new girlfriend Nevamarsya to join in against him.

'Where the hell do you think you are going to boy?' asked Tabbernant, who was walking back towards the Central Mess Hall.

'Leave me alone Bernie, I don't want to talk to anyone, I just want to walk.'

'Well, I've got news for you, it's not safe.'

'Rubbish, I am walking as far away as I possibly can from those duplicitous bitches,' Pemisegant's anger was still present in his voice. 'How can that not be safe?'

'Ensign Pemisegant 197/51, as senior Officer Corps member present, I am taking command of this situation. You will come to attention. Now!' ordered Tabbernant.

'Yes, Sir!' There was a steel in Ensign Tabbernant's voice that Pemisegant had never heard before. He slammed to attention and saluted.

'Something has entered the tree. I picked up the chatter from C and C just now.'

'Is there any chance this is just a drill?'

'I don't think so, they sounded freaked, something has breached the outer defences of the Tree. They don't know what yet, or if it is still in here. So they're worried.'

'So, what has that got to do with me, Sir?' Some of the surliness returning to Pemisegant's tone.

'You are walking back with me, that's what. Things will be kicking off soon, and we need to be where they want us to be, where we can do the most good. If you go walkabout, you won't be where you can do the most good and might be putting yourself in danger. Is that understood Ensign?'

'Yes, Sir.'

The air was filled with a strange buzzing. The old anther dragged Pemisegant under some overhanging equipment. Three crystalline structures flew down the roadway, sparks flying between them. From their hiding place, the two Ensigns could clearly make out their markings. Then after hovering for what seemed like an hour, they were gone.

'Damn it, virus attack. Father Earth, I hate those things.' Ensign Tabbernant had seen many viral invasions in his long life. He knew just how damaging they could be. Why, he thought, couldn't this have happened after I've retired.

'Virus. Oh no, they are my worse nightmare,' said Pemisegant. He had gone white as all traces of anger drained away, replaced by sheer terror.

'Looks like they were only scouting at the moment. Come on Pezzi, we need to get to C and C and report this. Now!'

'**M**yck, we've got a problem. Big problem...' Tabbernant said as said as he entered the heart of the Command and Control Center.

'Ensign Tabbernant, if you have anything to report, there are proper ways of doing it.' Colonel Gwilwalsya had no time for the old anther. Pemisegant could feel the air between the two officers freezing.

'Screw that darling, we have a Virus in the Tree.'

'Restrain them both and scan them,' said the Colonel.

'Yes, Ma'am,' replied Lieutenant Jaridafant.

'Hey, what are you doing that for?' Pemisegant was shocked and confused. 'We are trying to warn you.'

'Don't worry Pezzi, standard security measure, they want to make sure we are not carrying anything nasty,' reassured Tabbernant. A beam of light scanned over the two Ensign's bodies.'

'They're clear, Ma'am. No trace of any viral infection or possession.' reported Lieutenant Jaridafant.

'OK Bernie, make your report,' said the Brigadier.

Pemisegant knew his Commanding Officer had a grudging respect for Ensign Tabbernant. The Brigadier had been a boy when he had first encountered the old anther's principles.

'I was on my way back to the my kitchen, after collecting some fresh herbs for dinner tomorrow night, when I bumped into young Pemisegant here, our pleasant chat was interrupted by a droning noise that I knew could only be a viral scout. So we ducked under some equipment until the threat had passed. Then came straight here to warn everyone.'

'Can you confirm this Ensign?' asked Colonel Gwilwalsya.

'Yes, Ma'am, there were three of them. They flew back up into the Canopy.'

'Damn, you know what this means brother of mine,' said Colonel Gwilwalsya.

'Indeed I do, sister of mine,' replied Brigadier Myghcomant. 'You finally get to order me about.'

Well I never knew that, thought Pemisegant. Now thinking about it, the family resemblance between Colonel and Brigadier was obvious.

'In line with Officer Corps Standing Orders 7.1, Section 1, Paragraph 3, I, Brigandier Myghcomant Islaw 200/01, am declaring a State of Emergency and transferring command of the First Battalion of the Maintenance Regiment to the officer with the most combat experience. In this case Colonel Gwilwalsya Islaw 652/79.'

He smashed the glass covering a big red button. This was not a thing any Commanding Officer would do lightly. Once the button was pressed, there was no turning back. Only a Tree Marshall could reset the protocols.

'This is a Lockdown, I repeat a Lockdown. There is no need to panic. Report to the Muster Station in the Central Mess Hall and await further orders.' Once the pre-recorded message repeated.

'**R**ight, you heard the Brigadier, let's get busy,' said Lieutenant Sharlensya. Any trace of relaxed friendliness had dropped from the Lieutenant's voice, in a flash the situation had suddenly become very formal indeed. Damn, and I liked these jeans as well, she thought as the enprinter buzzed and her clothes became battledress.

'Downtime's been cancelled girls.'

'Yes, Ma'am' both girls chorused as they exchanged their outfits for battledress, just like the Lieutenant.

'You do realise, that because of the Lockdown, networking has been suspended. Those patterns have been permanently deleted from your wardrobes.'

'Yes, Ma'am,' said Nevamarsya.

'Good, when this is all over, I will have more room for new outfits.'

'Ensign Natalicsya, if the situation is serious enough to warrant a Lockdown, there is a possibility that you might not be here when it is all over.'

'Of course I will be here, Ma'am. Think positive, be careful.'

'A very sensible attitude young lady, bravo.' Secretly though, Lieutenant Sharlensya knew better than to rely on the bravado of youth, it was as short lived as youth itself. So she was not surprised to see the two girls weeping quietly.

'I can't let you leave, Ma'am, I'm under orders only to let people in.' Ensign Cemnentant, who was guarding the door, had spotter his friend Subaltern Rosateesya 248/16 as she entered the cavernous foyer of the Officer's Mess. She looked like death warmed up, sometimes walking, sometimes shambling towards him. It was just not right and he was worried. She was probably as frightened as he was. Something big had happened out there. There wouldn't be a Lockdown for anything minor. Still she kept walking.

'Cemnentant, you must let me pass,' she said. There was something very odd about Rosateesya's voice.

'I have my orders not to let anyone out.'

'And I have mine. From the Glory.'

Cemnentant was blown from his feet by a sonic wave, and lay on the floor, his head singing, too dazed to even wonder what had just happened.

In the Command and Control centre, command had passed seamlessly to Colonel Gwilwalsya.

'How many still unaccounted for?' she asked Lieutenant Jaridafant

'Four unaccounted for, Ma'am.'

'Who are they?'s the Colonel asked.

'Work Party Iota, Ma'am. That's Lieutenant Crysgoxant, Subaltern Rosateesya and Ensign Dukecamant. Also, the Prioress Kanonypsya, is still out there.' The technician hit what appeared to be a few random buttons. 'No, the Tree Nun has just reported in, she is safe and well.'

That's a relief thought the Colonel, I don't have to go apologising to her Abbess.

'Where were Lieutenant Crysgoxant and his team?'

'Branch XQ79, Ma'am. Rewiring a traffic light.'

'Bugger, that's a stone's throw from the breach,' said Tabbernant.

'Update, Ma'am, Subaltern Rosateesya has reported in. She said she got separated from her party and headed back down as soon as she heard the Lockdown warning on her comlink.'

'Does she have any more information to report?'

'Negative, Ma'am, she just high tailed it as soon as she heard the warning.'

'Destroy the scoot-about the Subaltern was travelling on, we don't know if it is contaminated and have her isolated and decontaminated. Then scan everyone in the Muster Station, top priority.' Already Colonel Gwilwalsya was building up a bigger picture of the situation.

Lieutenant Sharlensya was so glad when Serynazsya arrived at the Muster Station with the staff of the Medical Centre. She was less than pleased at being scanned for viral contamination. Well, at least they knew now what the enemy was.

'Ma'am, we have a problem,' said her daughter as she saluted.

'Report Ensign.'

What's happening she thought to herself. All I want to do is hug my daughter and tell her I love her and make her feel safe, protocol be damned, but the threat is too damn big for that.

'We have orders to scan everyone, only Subaltern Rosateesya remains untested, she's vanished.'

'Right, Thank you Ensign.' She smiled at her daughter. Letting the mask slip for a second, Serynazsya returned the smile, then crisply saluted before returning to her colleagues.

'Ensign Cemnentant, do you copy?' She knew that the Ensign was guarding the entrance. But he would be watching people coming in and would not have thought about anyone leaving. 'Repeat, Ensign Cemnentant, do you copy.' All she could hear was a groan at the other end of the comlink.

Ensign Ferngarsya was the only person hanging around like a sack of spuds. Everyone else was making an effort to look busy, even if there was nothing they could do.

'Are you armed Ensign?'

'Yes, Ma'am. We have just been issued with small arms.'

'Right Ensign, your coming with me.

'Ma'am?'

'We are going to find out what has happened to Subaltern Rosateesya?'

'Yes, Ma'am.'

It did not take long to find Cemnentant, who was brushing himself down. Only his pride injured. The instant the girl saw him, she ran to help.

'If you two love-birds could remember we are in a Lockdown and leave the billing and cooing to later, it would be appreciated.'

'Yes, Ma'am. Sorry, Ma'am!' They both jumped to attention.'

'Any idea where Subaltern Rosateesya might have gon Ensign Cemnentant?'

'Sorry, Ma'am, after she walloped me she left the building. I was too busy pulling myself out of that mess over there, to see where she went.'

'Your best guess, Ensign?'

'She will be heading towards Central Data Transference, it's where she works during the Summer.'

'What makes you think that.'

'Well, she is under the influence of something.' The young anther was too frightened to use the word virus, but he was definitely thinking it. 'If the thing controlling her wants to take control of the Tree, that's the best place to do it from.'

'Better call it in then.'

'Ma'am the Muster Station is reporting that Subaltern Rosateesya has just gone crazy, she has left the Central Mess Hall, not listening to anyone, or letting them get in her way. As if she has been possessed,' said Lieutenant Jaridafant.

'Damn it, she was a trojan. Probably has been possessed and infected too. Which means everyone in the Muster Station will have to be re-scanned. Where has she gone now.' asked Colonel Gwilwalsya.

'They think she is heading towards the Crown's Central Data Transference Centre, Ma'am. Lieutenant Sharlensya, and two Ensigns are giving chase.'

'Connect me to Lieutenant Sharlensya,' the Colonel ordered.

'Connecting now, Ma'am.'

Lieutenant Sharlensya and her two Ensigns were tracking Subaltern Rosateesya at a safe distance, when she felt her comlink vibrate.

'Lieutenant Sharlensya, we will be using the CCTV net to track Subaltern Rosateesya. I want you and your two Ensigns to withdraw. We suspect that your quarry has been either possessed or infected by a Virus, it is too dangerous for you to follow her. Do you copy?' the icy calm voice of Colonel Gwilwalsya whispered through Sharlensya's earpiece.

'Copy that, Ma'am. Returning to the Muster Station now.'

'Tell me Lieutenant, Ensign Nevamarant, has his remarkable recent recovery repaired his hearing?' asked the Brigadier, cutting into the conversation.

'Negative, Sir. That remains impaired at high frequencies.' Why in the name of the Tree, was the Brigadier asking after the health of such a junior officer during this crisis? Why has he also got her name and gender wrong? He never makes that sort of mistake.

'Report here in twenty minutes and bring Ensign Nevamarant 331/29.' In the background she could hear muffled swearing, he never normally did that either. 'Make that Ensign Nevamarsya 331/29, she could be very useful in the current circumstances.'

A cold pool of fear formed in Sharlensya's stomach. What did they want with her little girl.

D uring the Spring and Summer, everyone who lived and worked in the Canopy relied on the Crown's Data Transfer Centre. Banks and banks of servers, back-up servers, tape spoolers and other assorted pieces of technology, powered every single workstation in the upper third of the Tree. Workstations and Cloud Networks ruled the roost, the Personal Computer with a built in hard-drive paradigm had never established itself. Every Autumn, the Center went into standby, as did the high-speed data-link down to the Roots. Only the decrepid old narrowband connection to the small cloud, necessary for the Winter Squad to function, still operated. For the Virus, that was not enough, it needed the high speed link.

At first, the Virus saw naming malicious software, that corrupted and controlled data "Computer Viruses", as a compliment. Even if the Life pestilence had no understanding of the Glory, the static unchanging Crystalline Perfection, that all Virus seek to spread throughout the universe. So it had devised a program of its own. A program that could stand proud as a true virus, for it would spread beyond the digital domain and aid in the cleansing of this Tree of all living corruption.

The puppet stumbled blindly deeper into the Data Transfer Centre. As a systems analyst and member of the Data and Communications Regiment, Subaltern Rosateesya spent her Springs and Summers working in this centre, maintaining the free flow of information to all parts of the Tree, not that the Virus cared. It would give the system the ultimate upgrade, the puppet merely had to carry it to the Center. If it meant killing those who tried to stop her, then that was an added advantage.

The door to the main high speed data-link was barred by a female, it would be possessed joining the crusade to spread the Glory. The puppet opened her mouth and a discordant scream issued from it. The female had started singing, and the room was suddenly filled, not just with the one voice but multiple voices in beautiful harmony, drowning out the scream. The Virus silenced the puppet, but the song of the Tree Nuns continued.

'Let me speak to the Puppet Master, not the puppet,' ordered Sister Kanonypsya. She knew exactly what had happened to the Subaltern. For the first time in weeks she had been fully connected to the Tree and her sisters. She had been following the events through this link and had been ordered to stop the unfortunate Subaltern Rosateesya.

'Who is it that wishes to speak to us?' said the Virus through Subaltern Rosateesya.

'I am Sister Kanonypsya, Prioress of the Penitent Heart Priory. The highest ranking member of the Sacred Sisterhood of the Style present in the Canopy. I order you to depart from the Tree of Life and never return.'

'Our scan indicates that you are the only member here in this sector of the Tree.' There was a degree of scorn in the Virus' voice. 'We like the members of your Sisterhood. They are down in the Roots, in their precious Convent, where they lock themselves away from life and practice living death. Soon they will know true death.'

'They are far from here, but they heard the Tree's anguish as you invaded its body. Felt its grief as you polluted and destroyed two of its precious sons and comforted it as it cried its tears for the corruption of this poor daughter.'

'Ah, I have read your memories. You did not willingly become what you are, you were coerced, this was not the life you chose to live. Deep down you still seek the freedom to return to your old life, this is a source of great pain.'

'This has nothing to do with me. You are the problem,' said Sistor Kanonypsya, betraying no emotion. Damn this monstrosity she thought.

'Join with us, we will release you from life, end your pain.' The Virus' velvet syrupy voice fooled no one.

'As I said, this has nothing to do with me. You are an abomination, and we will destroy you.'

'I think not, other trees have said that, but they all merged with the Glory and the life within them was destroyed.'

'Leaving nothing but sad dead hulks,' said Sister Kanonypsya.

'We care nothing of that,' said the Virus with casual arrogance.

'No you seek only destruction.'

'Destruction is good.'

'My sisters have freed this afflicted child from your control. Exorcised the corruption.'

'Oh well, looks like we will have to do this the old fashioned way.'

Subaltern Rosateesya collapsed, as the departing viral control tried to extinguish her life-force. The song of the Tree Nuns was strong enough to prevent that, and she simply fell into a deep coma.

Sister Kanonypsya turned to the surveillance camera in the corner of the Room. 'Brigadier Myghcomant, Colonel Gwilwalsya, did you see all that?'

In the Command and Control Centre, the events of the past few minutes in the Central Data Transfer Centre was viewed with great interest.

'Yes Sister, we saw all of that.'

'I need a medic to see to this poor child. There is no infection, but it is still far from well.'

'Major Keltonnant and a team are on their way,' confirmed Lieutenant Jaridafant.

'Excellent. Colonel, may I join you in Command and Control?' Sister Kanonypsya asked. 'I wish to be of service during this difficult time.'

'Certainly Sister. Every little helps,' added the Colonel as she cut the link.

CHAPTER TWENTY SIX
COUNCIL OF WAR

Under normal circumstances, the Muster Station was the Reading Room of the Canopy's Central Library, located within the Central Mess Hall. Opposite the entrance was the counter where librarians issued and discharged books and music discs to the residents of the CORC. The rest the room was furnished with desks and chairs at one end, sofas and coffee tables at the other. The vast collection of books was through an impressive set of double doors. It was a good place to bring all the Winter Squad together during a time of emergency. Somewhere with access to the comlink network and right next door to the small café that the Squad had requisitioned as their refectory. Not that there was any time for relaxation now.

Commander Campbelant, had never seen his domain so busy. Sadly nobody was currently interested in borrowing books from the collection he maintained as his hobby. All anthers and styles had been created to defend the Tree and he could see his colleagues slipping effortlessly into that original function. The environment they were created to protect had made him more than just a fighting machine, it was his home that he would die to protect. The sneak attack by this Virus had already taken the lives of two colleagues and nearly taken the life of a third. To avenge them, he would fight like the devil, so that he and his colleagues would be able to revert to their normal jobs. Then the library would be a library once more and life would be good.

'Your mum looks so worried Neva. I'm not surprised, why would the Brass want to see you?' Natalicsya asked.

'You know Lisha, I'm really not in the mood for small talk at the moment,' said Nevamarsya. She was on edge, she had to go and see the Brigadier in a few minutes. Since the day she had started sprouting, she had only spoken to him on three occasions. Once when she had become a Cadet, once when he had been admonishing her and Pemisegant for not getting permission for their Syrup harvesting experiment and finally when he had handed her Commission to her, five short days ago. This was bound to be a serious meeting and all her friend could do now was reduce it to trivialities.

'Sorry I spoke. I will make an appointment next time.' The hurt in Natalicsya's voice was unmistakable.

'Oh Lisha, I'm sorry,' maybe small talk is the best thing at the moment. There would be time enough for war in the coming weeks.

'You have only just completely differentiated, you won't need to be re-birthed for months yet, but you are already part of a family, I am so jealous.'

'Lets be honest, I have been almost family since before Serah was re-born.' Nevamarsya was smiling as she spoke. 'There is no need to be jealous. I'm looking forward to the results, but after seeing what Serah went through, it's a horrible process, I'm not looking forward to it at all.'

'One thing is for certain, who ever adopts me, they won't be Squaddies. Next Summer I will be down in the Roots doing proper basic training, not the fun and games we went through a few months ago. Soldiers don't get adopted until they have been in the Regiment for at least a year, and then by a Reservist and her husband.'

'You won't be the only one living in a barracks down there,' said Nevamarsya glumly. 'Until Mam gets formal approval of her request to adopt me, I will be billeted in a regimental barracks. We all will, we are officially unadopted children,' said Nevamarsya.

'Like that is ever going to happen. Think of us as you luxuriate in your family home.'

'But you are going to be a proper soldier, with a rank that actually means something?'

'Yes, a proper soldier.'

'Why do the rest of us need ranks? What did your Ensign Ralkzotsya need to be a Ensign for anyway? She delivered food to tables and then took the dirty plates away. Then she transferred to the Musician Regiment wasn't it? She would really need military rank for that.'

'Who, I don't know anyone called Ralkzotsya. And please, don't start that Civilianist argument again. At times like this, the fact that everyone has had some sort of rank and military training is important. Then the ranks have meaning.' It was Natalicsya's turn to be short tempered with her friend.

'OK, but what about your designs and interest in fashion?'

'After five years, I become a Reservist and get a job in

the fashion industry. I want a family, I don't want to end up like old Gwilwalsya, do I?'

'You've got it all planned out, haven't you?'

'Indeed I have. We just have to survive the current unpleasantness.'

'Oh Lisha, whatever is the matter?' asked Nevamarsya, her friend had started crying.

'I never thought I would forget her, and I nearly did. Ensign Ralkzotsya was always so kind to me and so pretty. When I sprouted I wanted to be just like her, Just then, I couldn't even remember her name. Growing up is not all a bundle of laughs, is it?'

Nevamarsya handed her friend a handkerchief and gave her a reassuring hug. 'Make a note on your comlink now to get in touch with Subaltern Ralkzotsya as soon as possible.'

'There, done it. Thanks Neva. Your a great style, and a good friend.'

'Don't mention it. Why did I ever think I was going to be an anther.'

'Like I said, growing up is not always a bundle of laughs.'

Any attempt to lighten the atmosphere was shattered when an announcement came over the public address system.

'My fellow officers of the Winter Squad. I have bad news.' Colonel Gwilwalsya's voice was leaden. 'It has been confirmed that a Virus has entered the Tree and has begun contaminating its surroundings. The Canopy has been quarantined by the High Council. No-one, and nothing, may leave this region. Also no-one, and nothing, may enter. Styles and anthers, colleagues, we are on our own, and this is a War for not just our survival, but the survival of the Tree of Life itself. Mother Sun, Father Earth and the Divine Spirit of the Tree defend us. Pardre Rumsfelant and Prioress Kanonypsya will now lead us all in a prayer and sacred song.'

The prayer and the Tree Nun's singing helped raise the moral of the Winter Squad a little.

'I don't get it though,' said Nevamarsya, she was confused by the situation. 'We get viruses all the time. Colds, 'flu' and fevers. All caused by microscopic organisms. Why are we making such a fuss about another microscopic organism?'

'Have you ever wondered where those microscopic viruses come from, Ensign?' asked Commander Campbelant.

'No, Sir.'

'They are the remnants of previous Virus attacks on the Tree.

'I still don't understand,' said Nevamarsya.

'The Virus we are fighting now is a large crystalline creature who uses both hypo-sonic and biological weapons. The microscopic viruses that plague us are the biological weapons used by previous viral invaders.'

'So they aren't real viruses then?' asked Natalicsya.

'Yes and No. They act on your body like a full size Virus, but there is no controlling influence. Getting infected is just bad luck.'

'Can this Virus regain control of them? There is sickness all over the Tree,' said Nevamarsya. She was suddenly concerned.

'No Ensign Nevamarsya, thank goodness.'

Something occurred to Nevamarsya. As a sprite, she had been created to operate an apple. However, her apple had been rejected, and she had been reassigned to a branch in the Tree to operate a leaf, along with other sprites from rejected apples, to take the place of sprites who had been killed by a viral infection. The sprites who had survived had been a sickly lot, who never quite recovered from the sickness that had swept the Tree and killed their colleagues.

'So even when we win, Sir, there will still be a long term legacy of this attack?'

'Indeed Ensign Nevamarsya. That is the irony of viruses. They try to spread unchanging stasis, but they are in fact one of the greatest agents of change in the Universe.' Nevamarsya liked Commander Campbelant. He always knew the right thing to say.

It was time for her meeting with the Brigadier. She would be entering the Command and Control Complex for only the second time in her life. She had no doubt that during this War she would be visiting it regularly.

'Are you ready, Ensign Nevamarsya?' asked Lieutenant Sharlensya.

'Yes, Ma'am.' The Ensigns both saluted their superior officer. The days in the school-room rapidly receding into the past.

'Good.' The Lieutenant returned the salute. 'Ensign Nevamarsya 331/29, you had better come with me then.'

'Yes, Ma'am.'

CHAPTER TWENTY SEVEN
WAR!
WHAT IS IT GOOD FOR?

The Virus had completely absorbed the memories and knowledge of the two possessed officers, it now knew all the best targets. It could have gone for the kill but the Virus seemed content keeping the Squadies pinned down in the Crown with heavy artillery. If anyone tried to set foot outside the Officers Mess or Command and Control, it would trigger off a new barrage. This meant that the Winter Squad only had access to a limited arsenal of weapons stored in the Mess. There was no way they could get to the main armoury in Branch B1.

However, the Winter Squad would run out of food long before it ran out of ammunition. Tabbernant kept a weeks supply of food in his larders. Every Monesday morning he would stock up with what he needed for the next seven days from central stores. This was also located in the now inaccessible Branch B1. This siege looked hopeless for the valiant defenders.

Free movement between the Mess and Command and Control was only possible through service tunnels connecting their basements. Ensigns Cemnentant and Pemisegant had been ordered to make a search of the cellars for any long forgotten weaponry.

'This is pointless,' said Cemnentant. 'My final apprenticeship assignment was making an up to date catalogue of ordinance in the Canopy.' He laughed hollowly, 'I know for a fact there is none in the Crown, anywhere. Still, at least I met Fernee.'

Pemisegant had not been listening. 'Didn't you say anything with the word "Gun" in its name could be a weapon?'

'Yes, so...' Cemnentant's jaw dropped when he saw what his friend was pointing a torch at. 'Great green apples Pezzi, these must have been here for years. Ever since they built the new Data Centre.'

'But if they are still working, you can do something with them.'

Cemnentant glanced quickly through their operating manual 'Well, I can retrofit the mechanics, but the operating parameters will need reprogramming, a job for you my friend.'

'You had better go and report this to the Brass,' said Pemisegant.

'I bet I get collared by someone and sent off on another pointless mission as soon as I get up stairs.'

'Haven't you got better thing you should be doing,' said Colonel Gwilwalsya, as Ensign Cemnentant approached her desk.

'Ma'am, permission to speak,' said Cemnentant. His gloomy prediction finally coming to fruition, with the officer he wanted to see.

'Yes Ensign, what is it?' Colonel Gwilwalsya was being frustrated by the Squad's inability to fight back.

'Ma'am, there are ten high speed rivet guns in the cellar. I believe with Ensign Pemisegant's help I can set then up as a surface to air weapon, to deal with the Virus' flying weapons.'

'Tell me what you want to do.' At this moment in time I'm willing to try anything she thought, but on the other hand, I can't let these clever young anthers waste precious assets either. This lad will have to convince me.

'Ma'am, those guns can fire ten rivets a second. I can configure them to fire simultaneously, at the same area, in ten second bursts, creating a cloud of one thousand fast moving projectiles. I doubt if one of those viral probes could survive being hit by something like that.'

'But those drones zigzag and dodge so quickly.'

'Ensign Pemisegant has been making notes about the way they fly. It looks as if their flight computer has a very limited repertoire of manoeuvres for normal flight. I suspect that the ones it chooses for evasive manoeuvres would be even more limited.'

'So you could pinpoint where they would go to get out of trouble?' asked the Colonel.

'Yes, Ma'am, their flight path can be predicted to a high degree of accuracy. They might be fast, but they are not very smart. We should be able to nail the drones, or rather rivet them, as they emerge from the branch.'

'Until the Virus sends something better at us. Or we run out of rivets,' said the Colonel gloomily.

'Ma'am, this is only a temporary measure. Before either happens, we will have had ample opportunity to get to the Armoury and roll out better weapons, Ma'am.'

'Do it. You and Ensign Pemisegant have permission to make the alterations,' said the Colonel. 'Well, what are you waiting for.'

She watched the Ensign salute and return to his task. I hope nobody spots him and sends him off on a wild avian chase now, she thought ruefully to herself.

Cemnentant and Pemisegant worked through the night jury-rigging their weapon. Finally in the pre-dawn darkness they set it up under the cover of the Central Mess Hall's portico. They knew as soon as the light from Mother Sun began streaming into the day-lighters they ould lose their cover and become vulnerable.

A puff of smoke issued from the weapon.

'Damn!' said Cemnentant as he quickly started to replace the faulty component.

'That is putting it mildly.' Pemisegant was looking horrified at the readings on his comlink screen.

'What seems to be the problem?' asked Colonel Gwilwalsya.

'Ma'am, the ranging board has blown, I am fitting a new one now.'

'Carry on Ensign.'

'Ma'am, there is another problem,' added Pemisegant.

'Go on, Ensign.'

'One of us will have to stay out here and operate the machine manually for its first use.'

'I'll do it,' said Cemnentant.

'No you won't,' replied his friend. 'Your skills as a weapon-smith are too valuable. I will stay out here.'

'Mother Sun and Father Earth protect your son, Ensign Pemisegant,' said Colonel Rumsfelant.

As Pemisegant sat at the controls of his improvised weapon, he felt more alone than he had ever felt before. The low rumble of approaching robotic flying bombs meant he was no longer shielded by the bulk of the building behind him. He was now on the wrong side of an invisible line and the Virus was responding.

'Oh well, it might have been a short life, but at least it was a fun one,' he said to himself as he operated the joystick on the weapon. The riveters all turned on their gimbals towards the flying robots. Pemisegant checked the readings on the proximity meter, and then manually flipped the switch. Direct hit. All three robots destroyed before they could release their deadly cargo.

This makeshift weapon opened up a window of opportunity, so that the Squad could now take the fight to the Virus.

It was soon painfully apparent that the small Medical Centre would not be sufficient for the current situation. Major Keltonnant moved himself and his team to the mothballed Grand Order Hospital. Unfortunately, the early bombardment had destroyed the main Pharmacy in the hospital's West wing. So inspite of the fact that Major Keltonnant now had all the equipment he needed to operate on his injured colleagues, he was still limited to how many he could treat.

At the end of a long shift Major Keltonant was heading back to his billet to grab a few hours blessed sleep.

'I really don't understand what the Virus is playing at,' said a voice in the darkness. 'There have been no major injuries, no additional fatalities, just a handful of minor skirmishes that leave our people with cuts and bruises, maybe the odd burn. It is as if it doesn't want to fight us.'

'This one must be brighter than average. Using his resources wisely, instead of splurging them all on a few extremely futile attacks,' replied the Major who was heading in the same direction.

'Oh, Major Keltonnant, I didn't see you there.'

'No, you were busy talking to the Spirit. Sorry to disturb you Sister.'

In the Convent Sister Kanonypsya's skills as a paramedic had been regularly called upon, but she knew she was not as up to date as she would like to be. This did not stop her volunteering. This was not a time for standing idly by. She found her habit restrictive but could not abandon it. It still set her apart from her new colleagues.

'As a matter of fact I was just talking to myself Kelts. I still do that occasionally.'

'Oh, right. I have been thinking that maybe it can't fight us. Perhaps this Virus is too weak. All bark and no bite,' said Major Keltonnant, 'I'm just thankful casualties have been limited so far Konny'.

'That is what Inspector Galeroysya is saying,' she said.

'It hasn't tried to possess any more of our troops because it can't.'

'We can be grateful that only two of us have suffered that horrible fate.'

'Praise the Tree,' said Sister Kanonypsya.

'So, if the High Council sent reinforcements up now, then this problem would be dealt with quickly and relatively painlessly.'

'What, from this High Council? The currents in the Central Channels are still to weak. Sending a motor assisted troop vessel would be far too expensive. They will do what they always do when there is a minor viral incursion. Quarantine the affected area and hope the Virus will burn itself out with limited casualties.'

'You don't think it is going to just burn itself out, do you Kelts?'

'No Konny, I think Inspector Galeroysya is partially correct, it is weak. It is planning something that will affect the whole

Tree, once it has built up its resources.'

'Will you report this theory to Colonel Gwilwalsya?' She asked.

'Oh I will, it should be included in today's dispatches to the Roots.'

'After its attempt to take over the data network, I fear even the narrowband link has been cut. We are completely cut off now Kelts.'

'That will be costly Konny, it is old and can't be restarted. The whole system will need to be replaced.'

'I don't think the Council realises how much it will cost them, or care at the moment.'

Major Keltonnant could see something different. Sister Kanonypsya was smiling, her eyes alight with a fire. Just like the style he had fallen in love with all those years ago, before fate and the Sisterhood had intervened.

'The High Council is full of narrow minded, inbred Pure-stock, penny-pinching bean counters, with no idea what life is like beyond their Council Chamber. They would not know a sensible safety precaution if it bit them'

'No half measures Kelts, say what you really mean.' She was even talking the way she used to, so vibrant and persuasive.

'No Konny, I was not complaining.'

'Your sarcasm hasn't deserted you Kelts.'

'Hang on, did you just call me Kelts?'

'So what if I did, its been a long time since you gave me permission.'

'Indeed, indeed.'

Yes, he thought, he was right, all the time she has been up here, she has called me Major Keltonnant, been so frighteningly formal with everyone.

'Well, if you insist on being formal, no half measures Major Keltonnant, say what you really mean.' A look of sadness filled Sister Kanonypsya's face. 'I should have kept it formal. If we survive this, I will return to my miserable life in the Sisterhood, and you will return to your life without me.'

With that, she vanished. Keltonnant could see she was in tears. This War was having strange effects on everyone.

Normally she would go to the hermitage in the Canopy to be alone. It was not safe to leave the Crown , so instead she went to the Temple. Deserted as usual. Those outside the House of Clergy had no idea how powerful this place was. They did not know that it focused the psychic energy of faith and channelled it to the Spirit of the Tree.

'Oh Lord, I beseech thee, hear the confession of one of your Handmaidens.'

There was no reply. Even the song that had been in the background of Kanonypsya's thoughts for two decades, the song that had marked her out for a life of prayer, was no more than a whisper. She felt she had no contact with either the Tree or her sisters. With no contact how could she confess?

'Lord, why are you torturing me. If I mean nothing to you now, why did I survive, why was I not taken with the eleven sisters who perished when the Priory was destroyed. Why am I still here. Why?' She began to laugh, as there was still no reply.

'I cannot stand it being in the Crown any longer. Even that miserable existence in the Convent, living a lie to preserve my sanity, was better than this. Seeing him every day. A constant reminder of a life you destroyed.'

She was angry now, filled with the anger she had felt in that first week as a rebellious and unwilling novice, before she had finally accepted her fate.

'No half measures daughter, say what you really think,' said a booming voice. At last, a response from the Spirit of the Tree itself.

Sister Kanonypsya became aware she was no longer in the Temple, she was kneeling in a brilliant white room.

'I always heard you daughter, but never truly saw you. You played the part so well, one amongst many. Hiding your pain so well. Even from me.'

'I have done my best to serve you Lord,' she whispered.

'But at what cost to you Kanonypsya? What cost to you?'

'I do not understand Lord.'

'For years your faith has lead you to do much you did not understand,' said the Spirit of the Tree in a voice that had lost its bombast. 'Things are about to change for you Kanonypsya, understand that.'

'Thank you Lord.' It was all she could think to say.

'Now, sing with me,' the Tree commanded and the room filled with music. It was the song the Tree had sung on New Year's Eve. Although she did not know the words she was singing, the feeling of joy this created banished the anger, a joy and optimism she had not felt for many years. She had come to dread singing with her Sisters. What had once been a joy, now filled her with dread. This was so different, as the song was filled with hope.

'There, it is done,' said the Spirit.

'What is done Lord?'

'Have patience, my devout, if unwilling Handmaiden. You shall see?'

With a blinding flash Kanonypsya found herself in her spartan quarters. Had she really had a direct audience with the most powerful creature in her World? Only Abbesses and Abbots achieved that. And what had it all meant. She found herself more confused than ever.

Despite the fact that he was the oldest and most experienced person in the commando team, Ensign Tabbernant was not its leader. That job was given to Captain Grilbarant. When the call to enter the Monastery of the Grand Order of the Anther did not come, Grilbarant hid his disappointment by becoming the most feared inspector in the Methodology Regiment. When that regiment was disbanded, he surprised everyone, who knew him, by joining its replacement, the Research and Development Regiment. Publically Grilbarant said it was better to understand the workings of the gifts the Tree had given its children, so as to glorify those gifts and the bounty of the Tree. Privately, Grilbarant and his like minded friends sought to limit the blasphemy this Regiment could produce. With each passing year, he became more isolated as his friends retired or recycled. Now to sideline him even further, the Regiment assigned him as its representative in the Winter Squad, far away from the Research Centers in the Roots.

The mission was simple on paper. The team had to make its way behind enemy lines to Branch XB01, through abandoned tunnels and old service ducts, to emerge at the rear of the enemy's missile bank, which a disguised unmanned plane had identified. All the weapons and sensors on the missile bank faced forward. The Team's Scorched Earth Grenades would burn with intense heat for a week, destroy the weapon and cleanse that section of viral infection. The team would return to base for debriefing, by the way it came. Nobody, however, had factored in Captain Grilbarant's low regard for the rest of the team. He thought Tabbernant was a despicable heretic, young Treslelant an idiotic popinjay and the child Natalicsya should still be in the nursery. If this job was going to be done properly, it would have to be done by him, and him alone.

'Sir, what is the next objective?' Ensign Natalicsya was not the only one who wanted to know. The briefing had been a shambles.

'I will tell you when we get there.' Captain Grilbarant dismissed her request.

'That is not good enough Barts, and you know it.' Tabbemant was not as accepting as his young friend.

'That is Captain Grilbarant to you, Ensign, and you will respect my rank and call me Sir.'

'Balls, I knew you when you were still wet behind the ears. Looks like you still are. What's our next objective, Barts?

'Quiet, do you want to give our position away to the enemy,' said the Captain in a theatrical whisper.

'No, I just want to know where we are going,' hissed the exasperated cook.

He got no reply, the group continued on for another ten minutes in silence. Then Grilbarant gestured for them to stop.

'We passed under the target two hundred and twenty units ago. Respirators on everybody, we go up that ladder, mine the device, then back to base. Ensign Natalicsya, you go first. If the coast is clear, establish a forward defensive position. Lieutenant Treslelant, you head up the branch, whilst I place the bombs, make sure nothing comes down to attack us. Ensign Tabbemant, you stay down here and cover our backs.'

Natalicsya and Treslelant exchanged a worried smile, the old fool had not noticed he had ordered them both to do exactly the same thing. Fortunately they knew exactly what to do.

Three of the team exited the service tunnel and took up their positions. With painful slowness, Captain Grilbarant set each mine. Even the sound of gunfire in the tunnel did nothing to hasten his task.

'Looks like we got here just in time. That tunnel is crawling with drones,' said Tabbernant as he emerged from the hatch. 'They've found our back door. No way will we be able to get back the way we came.' Tabbernant dropped a scorched earth grenade down into the tunnel and closed the hatch. 'That's given them something to think about.'

'A large number of enemy contacts heading down the branch towards us, Sir,' Ensign Natalicsya reported. 'About fifty bogeys, no sixty, no too many to estimate. It looks like a major offensive, Sir,' reported Natalicsya.

'Sir, two enemy drones, probably reconnaissance for their offensive, are on their way up the branch,' said Commander Treslelant.

'It looks as if we have been ambushed.' Captain Grilbarant was fighting his own growing terror. 'We are going to have to stand and fight. When enough of the enemy is in range, we detonate our bombs. We will die, but we will die as heroes.'

'Sir, the two drones will be depleted in fuel and probably be low on ammo. They would make better targets. If we can get past them, we should have a clear run back to base,' said Natalicsya.

'Negative Ensign. We can do more damage here.'

'What are you talking about you hidebound buffoon?' Tabbernant was not going to throw his life away, not this close to his retirement. 'We can do more damage from a safe distance. Blow these pretty bombs remotely and do plenty of damage. I would rather return to base a hero than die here as a pointless sacrifice.'

'Ensign Tabbernant, I have given my orders.'

'So you have, not going to obey them though. I would rather go with Lisha's plan, she is more of a soldier than you will ever be.'

'This is not a debate, it is War. We stand and fight.' Captain Grilbarant was red in the face with anger.

'You can, I'm going with Bernie and the girl. We are already undermanned as it is, losing four fighters could be the difference between victory and defeat.' Treslelant was no fool.

'I'll have you all on a charge for insubordination,' said the Captain. He had clearly lost the plot.

'If we are all to die here, how are you going to raise the charge?' Tabbernant's logic did nothing to sway the increasingly unstable Captain.

'You never have learnt the meaning of discipline, have you Tabbernant. If you had you would never have blasphemed against the perfection of the Tree.'

'Bye then,' replied Tabbernant, saluting the Captain before heading down the branch with his colleagues.

The pair of returning drones were battle scarred. They had already had one bruising encounter with the Winter Squad. Their limited control computer designed for reconnaissance and not defence, so they could only cope with a single target. Bernie opened fire on the leading drone, which was pouring all its resources into fighting Natalicsya. It exploded with a shower of sparks. Natalicsya opened fire on the second drone, a precision shot which disabled its stabilisers. As it began to spin, Treslelant's machine gun fire broke it into two sections. One fell to the ground, but the section containing a laser weapon arched up to the ceiling before crashing down, spitting plasma that sliced through Natalicsya's left leg, neatly below the knee. As she fell a set of blast doors behind them swung shut, saving them from the blast. Captain Grilbarant had survived long enough to detonate the Scorched Earth Grenades and had been killed by the explosion. With the doors firmly shut, the energy of the explosion was siphoned back up the branch.

On the ninth day of fighting, the Winter Squad had scored a victory, but suffered its second major casualty and its third fatality.

Ensign Natalicsya lay sleeping on her hospital bed. She had been brave, she had fought well against the Virus and for her life. It had been touch and go.

In the Tree transplantation was a minor procedure. Adapted sprite-pods grew new organs that were blank and soon blended in to the recipient's body. Within months there would be no telling which leg Natalicsya had lost. Sadly, this would not be possible for Natalicsya until the War was over. The equipment for the surgery, and the adapted sprite-pod to grow her new leg, were down in the Roots. Natalicsya would have to sit out the rest of the war, nursing her ugly stump, suffering under a black cloud of doubt and misery. At the moment everything seemed like too much of an effort for the youngster. She had fought enough, the Defence Regiment had lost a recruit.

On the morning of the fifth day since her accident, Natalicsya became aware of someone in the room as she woke. It was Althallant, looking very tired. Had he been there all night? Oh darling boy, he had.

'Well, it looks as if you won't be needing half your shoes for a few weeks,' said Althallant, desperately trying to cheer her up.

'That is not funny Alth. And anyway, I am going to get rid of all my shoes once this is all over, and all my dresses. I have been far too frivolous. This injury has made me see that.'

'Over my dead body!'

'Please don't say that, you tempt fate. I couldn't bare it if anything were to happen to you.'

'You said think positive,' he said.

'Yeah, and look where it got me,' she replied.

'It is war, but it won't last. We are going to win. You have to believe that.'

'Do I?'

Natalicsya was looking very pale and small, but Althallant loved her more than he could say, so she felt like someone brave and strong again.

'Yes you do. After this is all over, after you have recovered from your surgery, I am going to take you to the great fashion houses of the Roots. There you can gain as much inspiration for your designs as you need. Especially for your wedding dress. Natalicsya, will you pair-bond with me.'

'Oh you silly boy, off course I will. But neither of us have families yet.'

'So we can start our own,' said Althallant with an air of hopeful naïvety.

'It doesn't work like that,' said Natalicsya.

'I don't care how it works. I love you Nats and want to be with you.'

'And I love you to Lants. Off course I will pair-bond with you.'

Suddenly life was worth living again. She would design a beautiful wedding dress for herself, and bridesmaid dresses, and the outfits for all the guests.

It was not until the following day that Natalicsya realised that this was a Commission she would not be rushed off her feet to finish. The happy couple would have to wait for four years, until they were both legally adults, before they could pair-bond. That was plenty of advanced warning.

PART FIVE
THE SUBALTERN

CHAPTER TWENTY EIGHT
SONGS OF REVEALED TRUTHS

It was a dark night, eleven nights into the War, and Sister Kanonypsya was deep in thought. Her thoughts were full of the doubts which had plagued her for years. Now there was also a measure of guilt thrown in with the doubts. The Guilt of the Survivor. She had been outside the Priory without permission on that fateful day, why had she survived when eleven obedient sisters had perished? The prayers and rituals she had devoted her life to were of no comfort, as the Tree was no longer speaking to her.

Both the Virus and Major Keltonnant had been right. She had never wanted to be a Tree Nun, but had learnt to accept her fate. Now there was so much doubt about her life, trapped here in the Crown in constant contact with Major Keltonnant. He had married his work, and despite appearances had been as dead inside as she was. She had tried to deny she still had feelings for him. She tried to keep her distance. The Virus Invasion had made this impossible. It was torture every time she saw or spoke to him. She still wanted a life with him, but she knew that was impossible, her life was sworn to the service of the Spirit of the Tree.

She now believed the audience with the Spirit of the Tree had been a dream. One that was rapidly being worn away by the reality of the situation. She knew when this War was all over, her sisters would come to take her back to the Convent, and things would return to the way they always had been. She had been dead inside for so many years, how long before she would be fully dead and recycled.

The light was on in the Medical Centre and the door was open.

'Hello, is there anyone in there?'

'Only me Konny. Remember my quarters are on the deck above. This place is my home as well as my normal place of work.' It was Major Keltonnant. Oh no, he was the last person she wanted to see.

'So, you could not sleep either, could you Kelts?'

'No, I was thinking about our conversation. The one you ran away from.'

'That conversation is over, I have made my choices. I did so a long time ago.'

'You can't hide it any longer dear. I know you no longer wish to remain in the Sisterhood.'

Without a source for the vile smelling Rohotel ointment that kept her hair short under her wimple, her thick ebony tresses had returned. The simple veil she had been wearing, in place of the full one fell from her head.

'But I cannot leave. Why will you not understand that,' she pleaded.

'Because I'm a secular old anther who has devoted his life to relieving pain. Why do you keep inflicting pain on yourself Konny?'

'I don't know any more. I honestly do not know,' she was crying, unable to deny the truth any longer. 'I don't think I can do it any more. I've forced myself to conform, to live in the silence, to stifle my emotions, to forget my love for you, to be aloof and condescending. I can't do it any more.' The stiff grammatical formality vanished from her speech.

She felt his arms around her, giving her a supportive hug, but she wanted more, a more she knew she could not have. She should not be here, in the arms of the anther she had always loved. Oh Mother Sun, Father Earth and great Tree of Life, what should I do?

'Daughter, suffer no more in my name.' She heard the Spirit of the Tree talking to her, no not just to her, the gentle voice filled the room and she could see that Keltonnant was paying attention as well. 'When last we talked I told you things would soon change. The change has arrived. I release you, and shortly your former sisters will catch up with me. I have many Handmaidens, and many more willing to join their ranks. You have served me well. Your reward for your service will be your happiness. When our enemy is vanquished, remain with this precious son of mine. I want you to be happy together.'

For the first time in twenty years she kissed the anther who loved her. The supportive hug became a romantic embrace.

'I was a wimp twenty years ago,' Keltonant said. 'I should have fought for you, smashed that old witch's staff, done something.'

'It would have made no difference, they had the force of law on their side,' said Kanonypsya.

'Now you have me on your side my son. Many years ago a great wrong was done in my name to the two of you, I am reversing it now. You have my blessing.'

'I will not be separated from you again, do you hear me Konny my love. We shall be together for the rest of our lives.'

That was the last talking done that night, as the couple fed a hunger that had been growing for twenty long years.

'You cannot stay in here for the rest of the War. Just think how that would look.' Keltonnant said early the following morning.

'I know, but it doesn't stop me from wanting to.'

'Come on, up you get. Put this on.' Keltonnant pointed to the brand new style Officer's Corps uniform that was hanging from the door frame. 'I had to guess your size, but it will soon alter to fit.

'Just because I haven't worn enprintable fabric for so long, doesn't mean I have forgotten how to use it.' She laughed. People will talk.

'Let them. You don't belong to the Convent any more.'

'So I belong to you now?'

'No Konny, you belong to yourself again. I don't understand your problem. The Big Guy let you go, you're not a Tree Nun anymore.'

'Kelts, don't be so disrespectful,' she said.

'Start living your life anew Captain. Put on your uniform and go out and join the fight.'

For the first time in two decades Kanonypsya of the Family Rust donned the uniform of a Captain in the Officer Corps of the Tree of Life.

'Brigadier Myghcomant, Sir,' she said to the familiar face in the comlink. She could tell he had been expecting to speak to a Tree Nun when he had answered the comlink. 'I can see you are confused Brigadier. Let me explain. I have been permanently released from my vows and I am no longer a Tree Nun. I therefore need to reactivate my Commission within the Officer Corps for the duration of the current troubles and beyond.'

'Certainly sister, sorry, Captain. Every hand to the pumps.' He still seemed confused. 'But I have heard nothing from the Sisterhood.'

'With all data communications embargoed, you probably would not normally receive notification for weeks. However, we, or rather they, have other means of communication. You will receive notification soon enough.' She smiled as she realised she could hear singing again, quiet and in the background, but there was still a connection. The Spirit of the Tree might have released her, but the wheels of the Sisterhood were grinding as slowly as usual.

'Where in the Tree did that come from.' asked the Brigadier. 'This parchment, that has just appeared on my desk, confirms what you have told me.'

'At some point in the future there will be a formal release ceremony, but until then we have more important things to worry about, haven't we, Sir.'

'Indeed we do. Carry on Captain.' He saluted as if they were face to face.

'Thank you, Sir.' Captain Kanonypsya returned the salute sharply. There are things you never forget she thought, as the Brigadier's face faded from the screen.

CHAPTER TWENTY NINE
I SPY WITH MY LITTLE EYE!

The previous day, the Brigadier had issued the order granting the eight surviving Ensigns a field promotion to the rank of Subaltern. The kids had earned this. They had fought bravely in defence of the Tree, acting way beyond their tender years, doing more in a week than most Subalterns did in a year.

Subaltern Ferngarsya's mother, Commander Tarprycsya should have been there to brief Nevamarsya. Her seat was taken by Sister Kanonypsya the Tree Nun, but she was not dressed like a Tree Nun. Instead she looked very impressive in an Officer Corps uniform, complete with the five silver leaves of a Captain. As she looked no different from any other style Superior Officer, Subaltern Nevamarsya saluted her.

'Subaltern Nevamarsya, you have been selected to do some spying behind enemy lines,' said the Captain with the Tree Nun's face, who had returned the salute. 'This is an incredibly dangerous venture, and I cannot allow you to go without my help.'

'Your help sister? Sorry, Captain. You cannot possibly be coming with me?'

'No Subaltern, but as good as.'

Oh goody, the world has gone mad. Not only is the Tree Nun apparently wearing fancy dress for the day, she was talking in riddles.

'I can see you are confused. I don't appear as you expect I should. I've been released from the Sisterhood and rejoined the Officer Corps. It needs all active adults to defend the Tree, so I am once again Captain Kanonypsya. I have been given permission to lend you certain artefacts that only a professed member of the Sisterhood would normally be allowed to use. They will give you a measure of protection on this mission.'

'Artefacts, what sort of artefacts?' Why do I need trinkets Nevamarsya thought angrily.

'This was my Sacred Rosette. I was given this when I made my first profession, taking temporary vows of poverty, chastity and obedience.' It was a beautiful and intricate representation of the Tree in silver and gold thread that Tree Nuns wore on a silver chain around their necks. The whole thing glowed with an eerie lustre. 'It marked my betrothal to the Tree of Life.' She removed a plain looking gold ring from her finger. This was my Pair-Bonding Ring. I received this at my final profession, when I made permanent vows, and became one of the Tree's beloved Handmaidens.

'Together, they allowed me to travel anywhere in the Tree, without let or hindrance. When they are returned to the Convent, another Tree Nun will use them the way I used to. Until then you are to wear them on this mission.'

'Throughout the time you are away, my former sisters will see through your eyes and hear through your ears. If you are in danger of being captured or killed, or much worse, they will bring you straight back here.'

'Thank you Sister. Sorry, Captain, this is an incredible honour.' Nevamarsya had always wondered what it would be like to travel the way the Tree Nuns did. Under normal circumstances she would never know. Not only did she not have a strong enough faith to devote her life to the Sisterhood, the damage to her ears meant that she was unable to hear the Inner Voice, the voice of the Spirit of the Tree, that all Tree Nuns heard and could respond to.

'Whilst you carry them you will know secrets you must never divulge to a living soul. Once this War is over the secrets will be edited from your memory. Until then you must be more discreet than you have ever been in your life.'

Captain Kanonypsya kissed the rosette before hanging it from a chain around Nevamarsya's neck. Then she kissed the ring before slipping it onto Nevamarsya's finger. A fond farewell to old friends. The ring fitted snugly on Nevamarsya's finger.

'I can feel it vibrating slightly, as if the ring is humming softly,' said Nevamarsya.

'You are now connected to the Sisterhood in a way no lay member has ever been before.'

'I can hear singing.'

'Good, but you must not join in. Only the Sisters may sing those songs.'

'Yes, Ma'am.'

'Report to Colonel Gwilwalsya, I will go to the chapel and pray for you. The song of the Sisters will take you to the place where your mission will start.'

Nevamarsya would be heading deep into enemy territory. Branches so heavily contaminated she needed extra protection to walk there. She had spent days learning how to move in the Hazardous Environment and Materials suit. It took three of her colleagues to help her put it on. She would have to keep it on now for the duration. On her return to friendly territory she would be quarantined and her bebriefing would be via the comlink.

'You can tell an anther designed this,' she said. 'I look like a comic-book character.'

'You can blame Pezzi for that. Everything in the design is perfectly functional.' replied Ferngarsya.

'I should have guessed.'

'I can see I am going to have to have a word with that young anther,' said Colonel Gwilwalsya, 'although it does show he has a very good knowledge of your body Subaltern.'

Nevamarsya blushed, and immediately felt a cooling blast from the suits system.

'Well, that proves the atmospheric controls are working,' said Ensign Ferngarsya.

When the last seal was securely tightened, dozens of female voices in perfect harmony filled the room. The Choir of the Sacred Sisterhood of the Style enveloped Nevamarsya with their song. She felt herself occupy every part of the Tree and no part of the Tree at the same time. She wanted to join in as she now felt as if she knew all the words of the song. She knew she dare not as her toneless voice would generate dangerous discord and she would be trapped forever in this fugue state. The briefing room faded from sight.

When the singing stopped she found herself in Corridor XQ60-1, deep within enemy territory, but so little of it was in anyway recognisable. The walls were covered with crystals. It looked like the inside of a sugar bowl. Every so often she would have to duck under cover, when she heard the approach of one of the Virus' drones.

It was a drone in another way. It was singing a strange tuneless dirge. Anyone else hearing this would be ensnared by its deadly melody. This proved she was immune to the Virus' siren songs. All she had to do was avoid being captured, because capture then infection was worse than death. Slowly turning into one of the monstrosities Ensign Dukecamant and Lieutenant Crysgoxant had become.

Opening the door to one room she had found a fabric enprinter. It had been reprogrammed and was busy turning any enprintable fabric into crystal components. Her HazEnMat suit was not made of enprintable fabric, thank goodness, but she did not want to hang around and run the risk of being spotted by a drone bringing more enprintable fabric.

Apart from that one room, everything was far too quiet. She had expected to find a lot more of the Virus' deadly toys. Her scanners showed nothing in this part of the branch. This proved Inspector Galeroysya's theory of why the Virus had been so quiet recently. It was worn out. Captain Grilbarant's raid had stumbled on the Virus' big push against the Squad in the Crown, whilst it was still in transit. The loss of that much equipment had weakened it. Against all odds the tide of this War was turning in the Winter Squad's favour. The enemy was recuperating somewhere near by. A clean surgical strike could win the War.

At one point she looked up and saw that the ceiling of the branch had been blown away. This must be where the Virus had entered the Tree. A thin but strong layer of viral crystal covered the hole, and Nevamarsya could see the Outer Void through the glass. It had a terrible beauty. The sky above was the bluest shade of blue she had ever seen. Obviously that was Mother Sun high above. It was true, it was impossible for Tree People to see Mother Sun, only the bright yellow orb of her aura could be briefly viewed. Mother Sun was spending more time with the Tree and less with her other children and the hours of daylight were slowly increasing. Spring was on its way.

The chronometer on the suit showed she had been in enemy territory for five hours, and that it was time for her to return to safety. The song of the Tree Nuns took her to a decontamination chamber where she could at least remove her helmet, and relax as much as was possible in her HazEnMat suit.

On her sixth day of reconnaissance Nevamarsya noticed the ladder. Her schedule that day took her into one of the newer side branches in enemy territory. The ladder led to the inspection gantry running through the space between decks. The lower rungs slid down quietly and she climbed up. It was obvious that the Virus had no idea this gantry was even there. There were no signs that its mechanical minions, who spread corruption where ever they went, had ever been up here. So once Nevamarsya was on the gantry, she pulled the ladder up behind her, hoping that it would remain hidden from the drones.

She made her way along the gantry, cursing the restrictive HazEnMat suit. Of course she knew that without it she would be fully exposed to the infective agents within the beautiful but deadly crystals.

The sensors on her wrist comlink indicated that the Virus had set up its headquarters in one of the branch node chambers further down the branch. Nevamarsya knew from experience, that there was a two way mirror on the inspection panel in the roof of every branch node chamber. This allowed Nevamarsya to see what was going in on in the chamber below, without being seen.

She recognised the faces of the two figures standing either side of the tank, frozen beneath crystal death masks. Otherwise these monstrosities bore little resemblance to Ensign Dukecamant and Lieutenant Crysgoxant, so much of the rest of their bodies had been turned to glass and protein. They stood stock still, probably unable to move trapped on the spot, an horrific living death. No, one of the zombies moved. It was the one that had been Ensign Dukecamant. Poor boy. He might have been a lout, but he did not deserve this horrible fate.

The bulk of the Virus was floating in a tank of fluid. It should not have been dirty water, but now it had an oily sheen and was as viscous as treacle. Nevamarsya recognised the tank. It was a branch node tank where the excess water from the branch would collect before being flushed back down to the treatment works in the Trunk. If the concentrated contaminants in that pool reached the Trunk it would overwhelm the filtering system. It would enter the Tree's water supply, contaminating everything it touched on every part of the Tree.

The proximity alarm on her comlink began flashing. There was a drone on its way. Damn, something she had done must have given away her location.

As Nevamarsya turned away from the inspection panel to run, she spotted a drone hovering above her. Damn, those things were fast. 'Sisters, get me out of here,' she whispered under her breath.

The Tree Nuns must have heard her. At that instant she started to hear the singing of the Sisterhood far below in the Roots. Again the temptation to sing with joy, as the safety of her isolation chamber came into view, was overwhelming.

'Sing my child,' said a friendly voice, 'it is perfectly safe now.'

Despite her voice quivering from key to key, the experience was euphoric.

'Thank you my child, that report will be of great interest to the Tree,' said the voice.

'But sister, I didn't say anything.'

'My child, you did not need to, you are in possession of sacred artefacts, they did all the work.'

'Oh, I see.'

'Rest now my child. You need it.'

'**S**o you are certain that the Virus has withdrawn to this branch node?' asked the Brigadier over a video link. The debriefings started almost immediately and Nevamarsya never had time to follow the friendly Tree Nun's suggestion to rest.

'Certain, Sir,' Nevamarsya replied.

'Did you see what it was doing?' asked Colonel Gwilwalsya.

'The Virus itself was making the water in that node as disgustingly polluted as it possibly could. Attempting to poison all the waters of the Tree no doubt. In a few days that branch node, and all the other branch nodes in the Canopy, will be automatically flushed when the connection to the Tree-wide water and sewerage systems come back on line, so that life can return here in the Spring.'

'What about the filters in the water works in the Trunk?' asked the Brigadier.

'They would be overwhelmed by that much poison,' said Major Keltonnant who had followed Nevamarsya's argument to its logical conclusion.

'Well, that explains a lot.' Everyone turned to Colonel Gwilwalsya. 'It has been bothering me why this Virus had been so clean. Its been destructive but not dirty. No infectious material in any of its explosives. No attempts to capture and corrupt any more of our people. Do you agree Major Keltonnant.'

'That had crossed my mind as well. It would appear that this is a viscous Virus, but not a very strong one. It is concentrating its power for something big.'

'I suspect that its gambit with the Tree's computer network would have given it possession of every system in the Tree, turning them against us. We would have been completely paralysed. When that gambit failed, it tried sending its forces against us, that failed also. The Virus did not care about that, all it has to do was wait and it will achieve ultimate victory.'

'So a surgical strike now, whilst the Virus is still weak,' said Colonel Gwilwalsya.

'That could still be costly, we do not know how much of a defence it could put up,' said the Brigadier.

'True. Subaltern Nevamarsya 331/29, are you fit to return to enemy territory?'

'Yes, Ma'am. However, the Tree Nun I spoke to suggested I rest.'

'Tree Nun?' asked the Colonel.

'Yes, they have their own communication network,' replied the Brigadier. 'The young Subaltern there has obviously been allowed to access it.'

'Very well. You will rest now and return tomorrow. With that intelligence we can plan a strike for Duosday.'

Forty eight hours, but if what she had seen was true, then the Tree did not have forty eight hours. The Roots were barring all communication with the Crown. Not that it would do any good. The Tree had automated seasonal cycles that were beyond the control of the officers.

A strategy jumped into Nevamarsya's head. 'Permission to speak, Ma'am.'

'Granted Subaltern, what can you add to this discussion.'

Nevamarsya projected a diagram onto the screens of all the participants' workstations. 'That sub-branch is still relatively new. The primary and secondary leaf scars and remnants of the initial bud the twig expanded from are still present. As you can see, there are weak points here, here and here. If they were to break, the tanks they are connected to would be breached and their contents would vent to the outer void.'

'Why has it chosen this particular sub-branch?' asked the Brigadier.

'Possibly because it is still small and has simpler controls. Sir.'

'How would we break these weak points?' Colonel Gwilwalsya asked.

'When I was a leaf operator, I used to set charges to jettison decommissioned leaves. I could do it in my sleep.'

'It's a plan. The first workable plan anyone has come up with.' Colonel Gwilwalsya seemed pleased.

'There is one thing. I will have to wait and detonate them at a nearby workstation.'

'Too dangerous.' Pemisegant had been watching the debriefing from his quarters. He had to join in.

'You have something to add Subaltern Pemisegant?' asked Colonel Gwilwalsya. 'We will discuss exactly how you managed to access this private channel later.'

'Yes, Ma'am. We are on a war footing, if this branch's system detects unauthorised tampering, it will activate these seals here and evacuate the air from the twig, then Subaltern Nevamarsya will be trapped on the wrong side of the barrier. She will suffocate whilst the Virus is flushed from the Tree. Its just not safe.'

'I am not an idiot. I will not activate that fail-safe,' retorted Nevamarsya.

'Under pressure who knows what you might do.'

'My duty Subaltern Pemisegant, my duty.'

'Why can't she sneak in, plant the bombs, then sneak back out again and detonate them remotely?' It was a fair question Brigadier Myghcomant was asking.

'The Virus now knows that this network of tertiary service ducts exists, Sir. It will now be patrolled regularly. Once the charges are set, I won't have time to get back to Squad controlled territory before they are discovered. They have to be detonated from a place of safety at close range.'

'So it is decided then. Subaltern Nevamarsya 331/29, will return to enemy territory and set the necessary charges. After she has detonated them she will return here for decontamination and debriefing.'

With the briefing over, Pemisegant chose to stay on the line, he needed to talk to Nevamarsya.

'Why do you have to go back in there again. Haven't you risked your life enough already?'

'Because only I can go in there and not fall under the Virus' influence.'

'Hooey, anyone could, all they need are ear protectors.'

'No, my whole body no longer responds to frequencies which are almost supernatural. Even with the most efficient ear protectors the rest of yours, or anyone else's body, would be affected.'

'So it really does have to be you?'

'I am sorry my love, that's life.'

The airlock into the isolation facility cycled, and a meal slid into the room. 'I'm sorry Pezzi, I have to eat and get some rest. I love you and will see you as soon as I can when this is all over.'

*M*r. *Spenser had been taking his dogs for a walk. His wife had her cat Shandy, he had a slothful old Labrador called Gerald and a younger more energetic one called Simo. Silly name but his grandsons had chosen it. He had lost count of how many times he had brought dogs to the apple tree, over the years. It was an unexpectedly dry and crisp morning. Although it was only January, already there were hints that Spring would soon chase Winter away. The apple tree was covered with thick buds. The experts from the University had done a grand job at bringing the tree back from the edge. In a few months it would be awash with pink and green as the blossom and new leaves appeared.*

It was a shame their boss was such a bloody crook. It had only been by accident that Brian had found out what had happened to all the so called samples that Dr Fraser had taken back to his lab with him. They were being propagated and then grafted onto modern rootstocks on a commercial scale. Mr. Spenser had wanted to call in the police, but the University authorities had wanted it all covered up. Not wishing to do anything that would affect Brian's careers he had reluctantly agreed to this. Only ten of the grafted cuttings remained. They had been sent to specialist orchards around Britain, who would grow them and preserve the variety as museum pieces. Dr. Fraser was currently on an extended field trip to Kazakhstan, studying the genetic diversity of the wild apple trees there.

Hang on a minute, Mr. Spenser thought, that branch looked dead. He knew from experience it was infected with a virus. He would have to get his electric saw and lop is off, before the infection could spread any further. It was good to be back out in the garden with something to do after months of being stuck indoors.

CHAPTER THIRTY
GAMES WITHOUT FRONTIERS

Returning to the branch was nerve-racking. As she had suspected, the formally pristine gantry now showed signs of viral activity.

She heard the clanking long before she saw the creature had once been Lieutenant Crysgoxant. Only the twisted remnant of his pleasant face remained. Poor Popisedsya, had been his fiancée, no wedding day for her and the happy go lucky anther who everyone liked. Every few metrons the hulking creature would stop and drop a delicate crystal on the floor. The crystal would grow into a load speaker. A strange hissing music poured from them, but they appeared to have no effect on Neva.

'We know you are out there somewhere little bird. We also suspect that you have been planting nasty little bombs, which will be found and neutralised.' There was an ominous silence. 'What, cat got your tongue? We will find you, whether you talk to us or not.'

There was no way Nevamarsya was going to say anything that would give her position away. To be captured would mean infection, suffering the same fate as the two zombified anthers. A permanent living death.

'We are not stupid you know. We rely on high energy sonic weapons of all sorts. As soon as we heard the song that spirited you away the last time, we knew how to trap you should you return. The devices, you have no doubt spotted, are broadcasting a jamming frequency. Your friend the nun is going frantic, nothing she has tried is working. She dare not get in touch with her fellow nuns down in the Roots, because she is already in so much trouble for letting you use her artefacts.'

Ah, tripped over its lies Nevamarsya thought. She knew that Captain Kanonypsya was no longer a Tree Nun and had nothing to do with these artefacts. Nevamarsya was using the artefacts with full permission.

'Listen,' the Virus had started again. 'We know the power of apple trees. They create gateways between realities. We know this one is self aware. We know its party trick is letting his servants move through his body using those gateways, and we know this is controlled by high frequency sound.'

'Then you also know that I have had enough of you and the damage you are doing to Me, my sons and daughters and to this World. I will be rid of you,' said the voice of the Tree itself. Deep and resonant, so low it made the Virus sound like a recording played at twice its normal speed, high pitched and tinny.

'At last, we have a response from you.'

'Yes you do.' There was a series of small explosions followed by the tinkling of glass. All of the speakers that the crystalline zombie had set down on the floor shattered into dust.

'Is that the best you can do?' The Virus was gloating.

'It is a start,' replied the Spirit of the Tree calmly.

Neva could hear singing again. Not just the Sisterhood's choir, but every single Tree Nun. Not just the Tree Nuns but all the Tree Monks as well. The male and female voices blended effortlessly. Their song had a blinding beauty and if it was possible for a crystal sitting in a tank of dirty water to cringe, the Virus cringed.

The song held the two zombies paralysed on an observation platform next to a bud chamber. The platform had a clear window that allowed the leaf builders to see the entire branch. From there, leaf builders could watch and control the new leaves unfurling in the light of Mother Sun. Normally once the leaves were operating, the windows on these platforms became so dirty it was impossible to see out through them. The rains of Winter had washed them clean again, and Nevamarsya could see the glorious blue sky beyond the Tree, illuminating the two zombies. They were sitting targets. Nevamarsya knew that even she could not miss them.

Inspired by the song she aimed her gun and let loose two perfectly aimed rounds. The first caused a myriad of cracks weakening the glass to weaken the glass, the second shattered the window and the branch suffered explosive decompression, sucking both zombies out of the tree, along with a whole barrage of the Virus' remaining equipment. The sound of air venting from the branch was deafening. Nevamarsya feared the emergency shutters would be unable to seal the breach and she too would be sucked out. In the end the volume of jetsam, being pulled from the chamber, was greater than the breach could cope with. It formed a perfect plug over the breach.

'Enough of this confounded noise!' screamed the Virus. It had been unable to locate Nevamarsya whilst the Tree Nuns had been singing and the noise and destruction of the depressurisation had further confused it. Now was her chance. Nevamarsya's primed explosives detonated. The tank ruptured and emptied out into the Void within seconds.

'Ah, so that is where you are.' Some of the smugness had returned to the Virus' voice. 'You can do that, but we can do this. You can do that, but we can do this' it sung.

The bulkhead Pemisegant had been so concerned about slammed shut, trapping Nevamarsya within the branch with the Virus. 'You will die when we do little bird.'

'I'm not afraid of death. The medics told me I was neuter and would die within weeks.' This was not exactly true. No medic had told Nevamarsya her life expectancy had been short before she had miraculously differentiated, none had bothered to tell her it was now normal. 'All this has been a bonus.'

'No daughter, I will not let you die.' The bulkheads began to open. 'Run, I have regained control of this branch. Once you are safe, I will seal it off forever. At the next pruning it will be removed, along with the burnt out remnants of that thing.'

'Charming. But know this, if you do not fall to the Glory now the corruption called life, will be expelled from you by other means.'

'You Virus. You are as alive as I am,' said the Tree.

'How dare you accuse us of such filth!' replied the Virus. Without its tank of fluid the Virus began to heat up.

'Lets see. Do you move? Answer yes. Do you breath? Answer, well yes, after a fashion. Do you absorb nutrients and excrete waste? I think so.'

'We are not alive.' The Virus was getting warmer.

'As I was saying, are you sensitive to stimuli?' The sound of the singing returned to the room and the Virus got warmer. 'I'll take that as a yes then. Five out of seven so far.'

'No, its not true.'

'Do you reproduce? In a most disgusting manner. Yes. That's six.', The Spirit of the Tree was enjoying this. The Virus was just getting angrier and hotter. 'The Coup de Grace, do you grow? I suspect so, you have certainly increased your vile bulk within my body. So my friend, seven out of seven, you are as alive as I am.'

'We are crystalline, we are unchanging and we are dead!' With that the Virus burst into flames.

'You certainly are my friend.' The entire Tree was filled with laughter.

Nevamarsya didn't stay to witness this final victory. She ran as fast as she could. Sure enough, the bulkheads began to re-open and she dived through the gap as soon as it was wide enough. Layers and layers of unbreakable protein glass began forming over the bulkhead as soon as Nevamarsya was back in friendly territory.

*I*t was only a small branch, but Mr Spenser knew if he used an ordinary saw it would take hours to do the job and the light was already failing. It would take minutes to cut through the branch with the electric saw.

What Mr. Spenser did not know, was that fifty years earlier a small lantern had been hung from the tree. The lantern was long gone, but the nail remained and over the years the tree had grown around it. The teeth of the saw found the remains of the nail and it became a fight to the death. In the end, the nail won, as the saw ground to a halt. Mr Spenser cursed. He carefully removed the saw and went to fetch the big old axe. More than one way to skin a cat.

Nevamarsya picked herself up. Thank the Spirit of the Tree that was over. What now she thought when warning lights started flashing and a klaxon sounded. She knew exactly what that meant.

'Smashing. Absolutely bloody smashing. I risk my life setting up a controlled explosion to rid the Tree of its invader, once I've finish all the hard dangerous work, along comes some crazed alien and starts tearing the whole damned branch off.' Was the Spirit of the Tree listening to her? She hoped so.

As suddenly as they had started, the lights and klaxon stopped. Nevamarsya had more things to worry about. She could not feel the vibrations in the ring and the soft glow, that gave the position of the Rosette away through the HazEnMat Suit, had vanished. No matter how well the Tree Nuns and Tree Monks sung, it was no good, the alien had sawn far enough into the branch to break the connection. There was just no way she could cross back to safety.

Bang. Something else had hit the tree. Here it goes thought Nevamarsya, no way the branch can survive that much damage. She began falling as wall became ceiling and floor became wall. Down and down she went.

As she fell, her head was full of music. It seemed as if every voice in the Tree, not just the the House of Clergy, but every style, anther and sprite had lifted up their voices and were all singing in perfect harmony. They were accompanied by every piano, every guitar and countless other instruments all playing the same tune without a single mistake. The song reached its dazzling climax as Nevamarsya passed out.

She awoke in a wood panelled room. Getting quickly to her feet she immediately began searching for a door. She soon soon realised she was sealed in a perfect wooden box.

'Daughter, you are safe.' The voice came from all around her.

She did not know why, but Nevamarsya threw herself onto the ground, prostrating herself. 'I am not worthy to be in your presence.'

'Oh do get up. I can't speak to you if you insist on grovelling on the floor.' Nevamarsya stood up, and the voice continued. 'I pulled you back. Making every voice within my World sing in perfect harmony, gave me the power to snatch you from that branch. Soon I shall put you back into the World you know.'

'Thank you Lord.' Nevamarsya did not know in which direction to turn, the voice was so all encompassing.

'Your welcome daughter.'

An armchair had appeared, with a table by its side. On the table was a pot of tea and a single china cup on a saucer.

'Drink, your body has lost a great deal of fluid,' commanded the Tree.

Nevamarsya could feel something rummaging around in her ears, it tickled.

'Your damaged hearing was useful, but I do not want you to suffer from it permanently,' said the Spirit of the Tree. 'You will never be one of my Handmaidens, I have other plans for you, but you can now hear my song again.'

Nevamarsya wondered how much longer she would have to stay in this overpowering chamber.

'It is time daughter for you to return to your own world. I'm afraid it is not going to be pleasant.'

With that the table and chair vanished, as did the floor from beneath her and she was falling again. She could see something approaching horribly quickly. She braced herself for the final moment, but it never came because she woke up with a start in bed. Had it all been a nightmare?

CHAPTER THIRTY ONE
CONVENTIONAL WISDOM

She sat bolt upright in bed, suddenly awake. This was not her bed, this was not her room. The straw mattress and the room's high vaulted ceiling were dead give-aways. As was the sound of singing that filled the room. Nevamarsya knew she was in the Convent in the Roots. The Tree Nun sitting at her bedside confirmed this, although this one was short, fat and wore glasses and had a slightly crumpled appearance. In fact, the polar opposite of Sister Kanonypsya, sorry former Sister Kanonypsya, who was tall and thin and always immaculately turned out.

'How are you feeling my child?' Why did they all do that, assume the position of mother to whoever they were talking to?

'So I am not dead then?' A fact Nevamarsya knew full well, but it was what she thought the Tree Nun was expecting to hear her say.

'No my child, the song of the most magnificent choir ever was able to hook you out of that branch. The Spirit of the Tree, all praise to it, did not want to lose you.'

'I assume I am down in the Roots?' asked Nevamarsya.

'Yes my child, down in the Roots.'

'And this is the Convent'

'Yes my child, you are correct again. The artefacts you were lent brought you back to their home. At the command of the Spirit of the Tree, you are now a guest of the Sisterhood.'

Nevamarsya's internal calender was saying it was day 37 of 364. She did the calculation, that made it 2B02, the second day of the second week of the second month. Nine whole days had past in the blinking of an eye.

'You have been unconscious for over a week, my child.' The fat Tree Nun confirmed what Nevamarsya had guessed. 'We did not know if you would wake up at all. How are you feeling?'

'May I have something to eat? I'm feeling hungry, very,very hungry.'

'Certainly my child. That is only to be expected. I will bring you some porridge.'

'Thank you Sister.'

When she returned, the fat Tree Nun, Sister Roweenasya propped Nevamarsya up with pillows so she could eat. Nevamarsya devoured the bowl of hot sweet porridge and felt satisfied by the warm sticky cereal.

There was a knock on the door and another Tree Nun entered the room. Her habit was more impressive than any Nevamarsya had seen before. Her veil appeared to be built over a little roof at the front.

'Are you the Abbess?' asked Nevamarsya.

As soon as the question left her lips Nevamarsya knew the mistake she had made, she should have let the senior Tree Nun speak first.

'I am indeed Abbess Annaprysya, Supreme Governess of both Houses of the Sacred Sisterhood of the Style, Handmaiden in Chief to the Tree of Life and Mother Superior of the Convent of the Roots'. She chose to ignore the slight breach of etiquette. 'You are a remarkable young style Subaltern Nevamarsya 331/29, soon to be of the Family Fangkart. I can see why our Lord, the Spirit of the Tree, wanted to keep you.' The Abbess made the sign of blessing then continued. 'I have informed your Commanding Officer, General Myghcomant that you are safe and well. He seemed truly relieved.'

The Brigadier is back in command, and a General now, the crisis must be over. But the Abbess still called her Subaltern.

'Do not worry, the Virus has been defeated, the crisis is over. The High Council has awarded all members of the Winter Squad, including the juveniles, a promotion as a reward for their bravery during the crisis.

'So I can go home, back to the Canopy?' asked Nevamarsya.

'You will be our guest for a few more days. We have to be sure that you are fit and well.'

There was so much that Nevamarsya wanted to ask, but she felt so tired. Why should that be, she had been sleeping for a week.

'You need your rest my child. When you wake, then I will be able to tell you more.'

The following day Roweenasya brought her some clothes to wear. A purple pinafore dress with blue blouse and headscarf.

After lunch, Abbess Annaprysya had summoned her to her study.

'Why in Father Earth and Mother Sun's names are you wearing that?' The Abbess looked genuinely horrified.

'It is what Sister Roweenasya gave me to wear.'

'Sister Roweenasya has dressed you in the uniform of a newly arrived Aspirant, as we rarely have guests.'

'Oh, I see,' replied Nevamarsya.

She gave Nevamarsya a key. 'In the room three doors down the corridor you will find something more suitable.'

Fifteen minutes later, when the young style returned the Abbess was as calm and serene as she normally appeared.

'I am sorry about that. I have spent years learning how to control my emotions in the presence of others. I do not know why I reacted that way.'

The Abbess poured a cup of tea for Nevamarsya as she spoke, then took a sip from her own cup as Nevamarsya sat in the chair next to her. Nevamarsya could tell she was considerably calmer now, she had sensed the Tree Nun's anger, but doubted anyone else would. Abbess Annaprysya really was very good at hiding her emotions.

'We don't get many visitors you know. Styles who come here rarely have plans for leaving, and don't have to worry about what to wear ever again. Every so often, that store room becomes so full we clear it out, giving its contents to a charity that sells second hand clothes.'

'Oh, I see,' said Nevamarsya.

'Now that some sort of network connection with the Canopy has been resorted, I have been in touch with your Commanding Officer again. He has granted you a leave of absence. Also I have spoken with your mother-to-be. She was overcome with emotion when I told her you were still alive, but sadly it will be at least a week before you will be able to travel home to the Crown. No doubt you would like to speak to her yourself.'

'Oh yes please Mother Superior,' replied Nevamarsya.

'Please my child, I am not your Mother Superior. Only

another Tree Nun should use that honorific. It is a mistake many in the Tree Without make. You should address me as Abbess.' She smiled. Such a lovely smile Nevamarsya thought. She should do it more often. The Tree Nuns were so starchy.

'Here you go my child, a comlink connection is now open for you.'

The comlink was antique, it must be held together by sticking tape and a promise.

'Crown Command and Control. Please state your name and business.' It was the voice of Lieutenant Popisedsya. Her image flickered onto the screen. She looked so sad. Nevamarsya could see her orange mourning sash, just like the one Sharlensya had worn for a month after her mother's death. Popisedsya was wearing it for Crysgoxant. Nevamarsya felt a lump forming in her throat.'

'Neva, is that really you? Oh your mum will be so pleased.' Popisedsya's face had lit up when she had realised who she was talking to. So are you, thought Nevamarsya

'I'm fine Poppy.

'Where in the Tree are you Neva?

'I am staying in the Convent, until I am declared fit to travel. Then I can come home.'

'I will put you through to Sharlee straight away. She will...' The image crackled with interference for a few second. 'I'm sorry, this is a very bad line. Connection to the Roots has been rubbish recently. No, no, no, the signal is breaking...' There was a horrible bang and the comlink console died.

'I am so sorry Neva dear. I may call you Neva?'

Tears were rolling down Nevamarsya's face.

'Not that you care about that, you want to be able to speak to your family and friends.'

Nevamarsya took the handkerchief that was offered, dried her eyes, blew her nose and tried to pull herself together. It was a futile gesture.

'At least Poppy will be able to tell them I am all right,' said Nevamarsya through the sobs.'

'There there my child. Despite appearances, you are still very young. You have seen and done things that someone far older would find hard to take. You need a good cry, let some of that stress out of your system.'

It came like a tidal wave, overpowering her poorly built flood defences. Nevamarsya cried like she had never cried before. Releasing all the horror, the terror, the gut-wrenching fear, roiling up inside her. The older style sat with her, giving the gentle support that Nevamarsya needed, letting the tears soak into her pristine white bib and wimple.

All cried out and with her composure returning, Nevamarsya was itching to know what had happened to her friends in the Winter Squad and the people who she now considered her family. The Abbess gave a broad outline of the general situation which lacked any personal touches. The Abbess would not have known how to interpret the subtly of any messages she was relaying.

There had been considerable activity up in the Canopy over the past week. The first shuttle had arrived in the Canopy, full of leaf builders and their sprites. It became apparent, to the whole Tree, how much damage had been done by the Virus, and how hard, the already exhausted Winter Squad, was working to make good the damage. Action had been taken. All the members of the Squad were declared State Heroes, for saving the Tree. For once whatever was needed to get the job done, had been supplied without argument over cost. Getting the Canopy ready for Spring took precedence over every thing else. All leave had been cancelled. Many skilled artisans were mobilised and ferried to the Canopy, dwarfing the group of two hundred members of the Maintenance Regiment, who took over from the Winter Squad. Nevamarsya wondered how this would affect the community she had been a member of for the past five months, but then realised that these changes were inevitable, as every year the Winter Squad gave way to the Summer Squad and the residents of the Canopy. This year it had just happened sooner than normal.

'As you can see, it has been a busy few weeks in your home,' said the Abbess, when she finished her summary of the news.

'Yes Abbess. Thank you for the news.'

'One last thing. You have had an audience with the Spirit of the Tree, haven't you? I can see it in your eyes.'

'Yes Abbess, when he rescued me.'

'That is a great honour for a member of the House of Clergy, it is an even greater honour for a member of the House of Laity.'

'It was very overpowering. I think he cured my partial deafness as well.'

'A voice spoke to me last night. It told me that the Spirit recognises your talent as a good listener. It then said He wants you to remain in the Tree Without, where you can do the most good. If you no longer have damaged ears, why would He prohibit you from serving him in the Tree Within?'

This is one of those situations Nevamarsya decided when, it is best to say nothing. She could not think of a worse fate than becoming a Tree Nun. Telling her host that would be horribly undiplomatic.

'I am also commanded to give you free unhindered access to all the facilities of this Convent to aid in your education. You may come and go as you please.'

'Thank you, Abbess.'

'This access to the Convent is a rare privilege for a member of the Laity, however not before time. This old mausoleum really should open its doors a fraction.' She smiled again. 'However, until we are sure you are fit and well, the door will be firmly shut. You will be unable to do any sight-seeing whilst you are here in the Roots?'

'It wouldn't be any fun without my friends. I want to share all my experiences out there with them. I think staying within the precincts of the Convent is for the best.'

Nevamarsya could sense the starch returning, the Abbess' face had become as blank and unreadable as it had been at the start of this interview.

'Very well. We will no doubt talk again, I look forward to it. See yourself out.'

After three days, she had fully explored the Convent. She planned to spend the rest of her time in the Convent's vast Library. However, on the morning of the fourth day Sister Roweenasya bustled into the room carrying a dress uniform with the rank markings of a Subaltern.

'The Abbess needs to travel to the Canopy. She has decided you may travel home with her,' said Sister Roweenasya. 'Put these on and go to the Abbess's study.'

The sense of relief that washed over Nevamarsya, made her weak at the knees. As soon as the old Tree Nun had left she, raced back into the familiar uniform. It didn't fit, far too big, and with no enprinter, it would remain baggy until she got home.

It seemed like an eternity before the door opened and she was allowed back into the Abbess's austere study.

'Ah, Subaltern Nevamarsya. I see you are almost ready. I remember how important being properly turned out is for any officer, we in the Sisterhood are equally fastidious.' The Abbess operated an ancient portable enprinter in the shiny pommel on an old staff and Nevamarsya found herself wearing a pin and paper perfect uniform.

'I am so glad this old thing is still working. Are you ready to go home?'

Home, Nevamarsya thought. Home, where I want to be.

'Yes Abbess.'

'I have been watching you. You seem to have problems with simple tasks many take for granted.'

'Yes Abbess.'

'You have difficulties with handwriting?' the Abbess asked.

'I'm very slow.' replied Nevamarsya.

'Tieing bows, is that a problem?'

'Yes Abbess.'

'How about riding a bicycle?'

'I can't do that at all.'

'I thought so,' said the Abbess. She removed a book from a fold in her robes. 'I think you should read this, and persuade your mother-to-be and her uncle to read it also. You will all find it very informative.'

The title of the book was "The Clumsy Sprite and Beyond" by Abbess Dyspraksya. Nevamarsya quickly read the blurb and was instantly fascinated.

'One of my predecessors made a study of the condition and wrote this book. Since then medics have done more research into what is now known as Dyspraxia, but her book is the most accessible.

'Thank you Abbess.'

'Do not mention it.'

They had been joined by three other senior Tree Nuns. The quartet began singing, and the room around her began to blur.

CHAPTER THIRTY TWO
HOMECOMING QUEEN

The singing had stopped and Nevamarsya found herself back in the Crown, at the Temple Garden. From this vantage point she could see scaffolding everywhere. So many people, too many sprites. She had never seen the Crown so busy.

This was how it should be. Spring was on its way and the Canopy would be a hive of activity again, with the Crown at its hub.

All the Winter Squad members were waiting there. Not just in their normal work clothes either, but in their full dress uniforms. Who, or what, were they waiting for Nevamarsya thought to herself. When she realised they were all waiting for her return to the Canopy, she felt overcome with emotions. Standing there in the front row was General Myghcomant, her Commanding Officer.

'Welcome home Subaltern Nevamarsya 331/29. I knew you were made of the right stuff the first day we met. I am so proud of you, and what you have achieved with us.', he said.

'Thank you, Sir,' replied Nevamarsya, returning the salute as she said it. Again, she was overwhelmed as the entire Squad saluted her. As did the crowd that had gathered on the edge of the Temple Garden.

Major Kanonypsya was standing with Colonel Keltonnant, looking so happy and more alive than Nevamarsya could ever remember. One of the Winter Squad now. Nevamarsya could not believe she had ever been a Tree Nun, she looked so different.

'If you will excuse us General Myghcomant, we have one last duty to perform,' said the Abbess.

'Of course Abbess.' replied the General.

The Abbess turned to Major Kanonypsya.

'Sister Kanonypsya, have you abandoned your calling?' asked the Abbess, in a calm level voice with only the barest hint of mock disbelief.

'No Mother Superior,' Major Kanonypsya replied, 'I couldn't, and wouldn't do that. However, the calling seems to have abandoned me.' She looked slightly embarrassed, like a child caught stealing sweets from a sweet jar.

'No my child, that is not the case. The Spirit of the Tree moves in mysterious ways.' The use of the word "child" instead of "sister" was lost on the audience. Only Nevamarsya and Kanonypsya knew its significance. 'I came here today not only to bring this young daughter home to her loving family, I came here for you.'

Major Kanonypsya did not know whether to look happy or sad. 'The Spirit of the Tree spoke and commanded me to release you from our Sisterhood.'

'Thank you, Abbess.' Again, the significance of this comment was lost on most of the audience.

'Kanonypsya 049/05 Rust, despite your initial reluctance to enter our community, you were a diligent member of it for many years. You have however, completed the task for which you were called by the Spirit of the Tree all those years ago. He has released you from His service, now we do the same. There are new and different ways you can serve Mother Sun, Father Earth and their child, our Lord, The Tree of Life.'

'What does that mean?' growled the secular Colonel who had no time for ritual.

'Patience Colonel Keltonnant, you will see.' The Abbess raised her hand over the former Tree Nun as her three companions began singing. 'By the powers vested in me by the Divine Trio of Father Earth, Mother Sun and the Tree itself, as Abbess and Supreme Governess of the Sacred Sisterhood of the Style, I hereby release you from your vows and absolve you of any responsibilities you have to myself and my sisters. Return now to the House of the Laity with our blessing. Go in peace Kanonysya Rust 049/05.' After completing the benediction, she joined in with her fellow Tree Nuns Song.

'Squad, attention!' called General Myghcomant, and all the Winter Squad, including old Tabbernant saluted the Tree Nuns. With that they were gone, back to the Roots, back to their Convent and their prayers.

'Squad, dismissed!' called General Myghcomant and the proper welcome could begin.

'And so she just discards you like a piece of rubbish after all the years you have given them?' Colonel Keltonnant asked his beloved.

'Don't complain Kelts, she can do whatever she wants, how ever she wants. She is the head of the Order, the Tree's Chief Handmaiden. It looks like the Tree has finally told her to give me back to you. Being a good Tree Nun she has obeyed.'

'You mean your free? We can start planning our future together?' he asked.

'What else have we been doing for the past two weeks. It has all gone. All the songs, all the secrets of the Sisterhood, everything.'

'In that case,' the Colonel said as he dropped onto one knee. He opened the ring box that had remained shut for twenty years. The ring glittered like magic in the light of a Springlike afternoon. 'Kanonypsya Rust, I love you and want you to be my partner for life. Will you pair-bond with me?'

'Of course I will. Will you pair-bond with me?'

'I will indeed,' the Colonel replied.

Quite an audience had gathered and they all spontaneously started cheering.

Pemisegant was so pleased to see his beloved Nevamarsya. 'Oh Neva, don't ever do that to me again.'

'I hope I never need to.'

Pemisegant seemed to embarrassed for any further displays of affection in such a public place. Also he did not want to spoil the moment for the happy couple a few yards away.

'Oh come here, you silly boy,' said Nevamarsya, as she embraced her boyfriend. 'I missed you so much while I was down in the Roots.

All the embarrassment fell away from Pemisegant, who felt so very happy. Nevamarsya letting the world know the prettiest young style in the Tree and the bravest as well, loved him. His life felt complete.

There was of course another happy couple. Their extraordinary promotion meant that Natalicsya and Althallant now had full adult rights and responsibilities. This included the right bond and Natalicsya couldn't wait to fill her friend in with all the details. At first Natalicsya had wanted the ceremony to be as soon as she could walk again. Chief Inspector Galeroysya counselled caution. Maybe they should wait a year. Not as long a wait as they had been expecting, but enough for them to see if they truly were an adult pair not two infatuated youngsters. This argument had swayed Natalicsya, who wanted everyone to see how adult they were. As always, Althallant just nodded and agreed with everything the style, he was completely besotted with, said nothing.

Natalicsya was looking her happy self again. Her new leg was almost ready, and she was due for surgery down in the Sacred Sisterhood Hospital the following week. Althallant stood behind the hoverchair, looking very smart in the brown uniform with a yellow sash that trainee Enforcers wore on duty. Then like a switch, Nevamarsya realised her friend was wearing the same coloured uniform and a yellow sash.

'I wasn't expecting this,' Nevamarsya said to her friend. 'I thought you were joining the Defence Regiment?'

'She was...' replied Althallant.

'But I got so sick of wars and fighting, having seen the real thing...' Natalicsya continued.

'That she changed,' finished Althallant.

'Aunty Gale organised it for me.'

'She means Chief Inspector Galeroysya,' said Althallant. 'We're only supposed to call her that off duty.'

'I know, I'm sorry. I meant Chief Inspector Galeroysya,' said Natalicsya. The older style and her husband had been regular visitors whilst Natalicsya had been in hospital. The couple had seen how miserable Natalicsya was stuck in hospital. There was no way she could be discharged back to her quarters with no one to look after her there. They therefore arranged for Natalicsya to be discharged into their care.

'My dear girl, you really should learn to think before you speak,' said Galeroysya.

'Sorry Mum.'Galeroysya did not try to correct Natalicsya, who had no idea she had just said "Mum" instead of "Ma'am". Caring for the injured girl with her husband, they had quickly fallen into the role of parents. Galeroysya now knew Natalicsya had started to see her and her husband as her mother and father. The older style began to smile, her friend Sharlensya's broodiness must be infectious. The avalanche had started, and Galeroysya was far too happy to try to stop it, or want to stop it.

N evamarsya was embraced by Sharlensya and Serynazsya. This was not normally accepted behaviour. All three styles were in uniform, but today was a day of the unexpected. Nevamarsya could see that there was something different about her mother-to-be, but she didn't know what.

'I was so happy when the General told me you were still alive darling. We didn't think we would see you again.' Sharlensya was close to tears. 'We thought we had lost you Neva dear. But you survived, and in doing so saved the Tree. You are a heroine. I am so lucky to have you as my daughter,' declared Sharlensya.

'I love you too. I am glad to be your daughter,' replied Nevamarsya. There, it had been said in public, a full declaration of filial loyalty. What had been a private understanding became an unbreakable public promise, backed by the full force of the Law of the Tree of Life and its Officer Corps.

Nevamarsya took another look at her new mother and her new big sister. She was being dim today. When she had last seen her, Sharlensya had been blonde, now her hair was as red and curly as Nevamarsya's own. 'Your hair, its ginger.'

'Yes, when we thought you wouldn't come back, we saw it as a way to make sure you would never be forgotten,' said Serynazsya. She was babbling happily, but so what, the lonely girl who had been so desperate to belong was revelling in her role of sister as much as Nevamarsya.

'The Pure-stocks will hate it. You have both permanently tainted yourselves in their eyes.'

'Let them think their silly little thoughts, we don't care what they think,' replied her Mother. 'I care what my daughter thinks. So darling, do you like it?'

'I love it Mam.' Now it was Nevamarsya's turn to cry happy tears.

Then Nevamarsya noticed something else. Both mother and daughter's eyes matched her own. This was incredible, the Root-born Pure-stock styles had become flame-haired, emerald eyed natives of the highest reaches of the Canopy. Nevamarsya hugged her mother and sister again. So much change, so much love and so much happiness. For a few fleeting seconds an image of a sad and angry sprite, sitting at a workstation in the highest twig on the highest branch of an apple tree, sprung into her head. It seemed like that had never been her, but unlike other officers, she would not forget what she had been. It was so much a part of what she was now, an officer, a colleague and a friend. Also she was a daughter, a sister, a great-niece and girlfriend. Maybe even one day a mother herself.

'You know, so much has happened in the past few months, I would never have imagined everything could turn out so well. One thing I know for certain, this isn't a dream that I am about to wake up from. It's reality.'

'How do you know that then?' asked Serynazsya.

'Sprites normally don't dream and in storage can't dream.' Maybe that is a good thing, as the disappointment of waking from this would be so crushing. With the help of her new found family and friends, she would be able to do something more than just insult her evil old Branch Captain, so that in the future those sprites could dream, daydream even, as she had done all those months ago, and maybe, like herself, their dreams would come true.

The End

EXPLANITORY NOTES

Ranks and Regiments

The people who live in the Tree know their primary function is to defend the Tree. As the tree grew, it had become more complex. and the inhabitants had other jobs, to do when the Tree is not in danger. They have not however forgotten their military origin and society is arranged so that the inhabitants can be mobilised at the drop of a hat. Everyone is an Officer and all professions belong to one of the thirty Regiments. Everyone has a rank and wears a uninform at work when they are officially on duty. Practically though, the ranks are now simply positions on the pay scale.

Juveniles have two ranks, Cadet and Ensign. As they are the legal responsibility of their parents, their wages are little more than pocket money. Adults have ten ranks, from lowly Subaltern to all powerful Tree Marshall. Thirty Five years old is the standard retirement age for all officers. An officer who reaches that age gains the rank of Pensioner.

Ranks (Pay grade): Title

J1:	Officer Cadet
J2:	Ensign
O1:	Subaltern
O2:	Lieutenant
O3:	Commander
O4:	Captain
O5:	Major
O6:	Colonel
O7:	Brigadier
O8:	General
O9:	Vice Marshall
O10:	Tree Marshall of the Tree of Life
P1:	Pensioner

Names

Inhabitants of the Tree start life as sprites, identified by an unique IndesnCode. On becoming a Cadet they gain a Root-name based on their IndesnCode. This consists of two elements. The first element begins with the first letter of the IndesnCode, which corresponds with the Sprite-pod they grew in and is four letters long. The second element is three letters long, the first being the other letter in their IndesnCode. For example SN became the root-name Serynaz.

Root-names cannot be used by two officers at the same time. This is to guarentee that there is never any confusion about who did what and when.

Pure-Stock Style officers from the Roots all emerged from Sprite-pod S and all have names starting with S. Likewise, Pure-Stock Anther officers from the Roots have names starting with D as they are all products of Sprite-pod D.

When a Cadet becomes either Style or Anther the Root-name gains a gender suffix creating their Formal-Name. The suffix is either A-N-T for an Anther or S-Y-A for a Style. For Anthers the stress in pronouncing the Formal-Name is on the first element of the Root-Name, for Styles, the emphasis is on the second element and the suffix is usually pronounced She-ya.

When adopted, a juvenile officer gains a Family-name to add to their Formal Name. In many cases this Family-name is also used by officer children who have been legally accepted for adoption, but who have not gone through the process. Pair-bonded officers may add their partner's Family-name to their own with a hyphen.

When on duty, an officer is formally refered to by Rank, Formal-Name and IndesnCode number or informally by Rank, Formal-name and Family-name. For instance Lieutenant Sharlensya 120/15 or Lieutenant Sharlensya Vanguard.

When off-duty, an officer is formally refered to by

Root-name and suffix only. Officers may be addressed by an Informal name by family and friends. However, addressing someone with an Informal name without permission is very bad manners.

Finally, romantically attached officers use Romantic names to refered to one another which can only be used by the individuals in question.

Formal-Names and how to pronounce them (Stress on the BLOCK CAPITALS)

Althallant	-	ALTH all ant
Campbelant	-	CAM bell ant
Crysgoxant	-	CREAZ gocks ant
Dukecamant	-	DEWK amm ant
Ferngarsya	-	fairn GAR seeyah
Galeroysya	-	gayl ROY shah
Grilbarant	-	GRILL bar ant
Gwilwalsya	-	gwill WAL shah
Hanazofsya	-	harroz OFF seeyah
Kanonypsya	-	kanon IPP shah
Myghcomant	-	MY comm ant
Natalicsya	-	nattal EESH shah
Nevamarsya	-	nayvah MAR-sheeyah
Pemisigant	-	PEMMIZ agg ant
Popisedsya	-	popee SED shah
Roseteesya	-	rose TEA shah
Rumsfelant	-	RWMS fell ant
Samnundsya	-	sam NOOND shah
Serynazsya	-	sair INNARR see-yah
Sharlensya	-	shar LENN see-yah
Untrugyant	-	UN trewgy ant
Tabbernant	-	TABB air nant
Treslelant	-	TREAZ lell ant
Voynvarant	-	VOYN var ant
Voynvalsya	-	voyn VAL shah

Dates and Time

The year in the Tree is split into thirteen months of twenty eight days. This leaves one day left over, which is regarded as a HolyDay celebrated at the start of each new year, on the Winter Solstice. For administrative purposes the year is split into two Tours of Duty, Light Half (Quadtemp to Noftemp) and Dark Half (Dixtemp to Rydtemp). For religious purposes the year is divided into the four Solar Seasons of Spring, Summer, Autumn (or Fall in the Canopy) and Winter, which are tied to the Solstices and Equinox.

As the year is actually 365.25 days long, every fourth year has an extra HolyDay called the LeapDay.

The thirteen months plus HolyDay are:

Iantemp	22nd December - 18th January
Bystemp	19th January - 15th February
Rydtemp	16th February - 15th March
Quadtemp	16th March - 12th April
Pentemp	13th April - 11th May
Hextemp	12th May - 7th June
Septemp	8th June - 5th July
Octemp	6th July - 2nd August
Noftemp	3rd August - 30th August
Dixtemp	31st August - 27th September
Elfsemp	28th September - 24th September
Colsemp	25th October - 22nd November
Trisksemp.	23rd November - 20th December
HolyDay	21st December

Each month is sub divided into four week:

Alfa
Bayta
Camma
Delta

Each Week is subdivided into seven days:
   Monesday
   Duosday
   Trenitsday (Trenzday)
   Fursday
   Fyfesday
   Saxurthsday (Saturday)
   Sunday

The date can either be written using the full names of the day, week and month in question, for example Fursday Bayta of Bystemp of year 184 After the Graft.
It can also be represented by an alpha-numeric code, so the same day could be expressed as 4-B-02/184.
The HolyDay is either written as HolyDay of Year 184 After the Graft or 0-H-0/184
Leap days are refered to as LeapDay of 184 or 0-L-0/184

Each day is divided into twenty-four hours, each hour consisting of sixty minutes. Time is written hour-number eg 2359, 1418 or 0630

Each day is also divided into four six hour watches:
Dawnwards (midnight to 0559)
Morning (0600 to 1159)
Afternoon (1200 to 1759
Evening/Night (1800-2359)

Weights and Measures
When all officers were identical, they all wore the same sized shoes, one Unit long. This was the basis of Identrical Measurements with Units subdivided into ten fractions.
All weights in the Tree are measured in Pounds and

Ounces. A Pound is based on the weight of one square unit of water. An Ounce is one tenth of a Pound. The volume of one cubic Unit is a Pint, which is sub-divided into ten Fluid Ounces.

The arrival of individuality meant that an officer's foot was no longer a standard length. The uniform height of sprites formed the base of Metriccant Measures used by scientists and engineers. A Metron is divided into one hundred Centrons. A Centron is subdivided into ten millimetrons. Weights are measured in Kilograms and Grams. Volumes and Litrons

Acknowledgements

This project started on a family holiday in August 2011, aboard the MV Grand Princess in Livorno harbour, when the words "In a circular wooden corridor in the highest branch of an Apple Tree, NM331/29 sat daydreaming." popped into my head and I started typing on my netbook PC. A fortnight later, the outline of this novel and its first three chapters were sitting on its hard drive. If all goes to plan, nearly two years later, this novel will be published. It has been quite a journey, but a journey that I have not made on my own.

I began this book by dedicating it to my Family, who have been a great source of help and support. However, throughout the whole writing process, I have been acutely aware the one person who I would dearly love to be here today. My father, Alderman Gwynfryn Rees, who passed away in 2001. Without his timely intervention 46 years ago, my mother would have died in childbirth and I would have perished with her. Throughout my childhood he was always there, fighting in my corner. He was always my best friend, and I miss him and I know that he would be so proud of what I have achieved.

My mother, Patricia Rees has been with me every step of the way. She was the one who spent countless nights helping me catch up with my school work, drumming in the lessons I was to busy copying notes from the blackboard to understand fully. During the writing of this novel she has been fully behind me. Editing and correcting my grammar and spelling, spotting plot-holes and diffusing logic bombs. Without her this novel would still be a box full of A4 pages, growing yellow with age.

My sisters Janet and Carolyn have been an enormous help. Cheering me up when my spirits were flagging. Always willing to read what I have written, they have never pulled their punches when advising me on what was good, bad and ugly in everything I have ever written. They have had a far more profound influence in my life than just my writing. It would have been a dull old time without them. Needless to say, their husbands and children have also been a source of support and inspiration.

In 1973, at the age of six, I came to the attention of Mrs. Jill Evans, at Treherbert Infants School. Today there are a whole raft of teaching aids for children with Dyspraxia, in 1973 the condition was unknown but she could see I had a problem. How could the little boy who was bursting with stories and poems in the playground be the same little boy who was struggling in the classroom? She did all she could to help, keeping alive the creative spark that today is the flame that has fuelled the writing of this novel.

Another person who helped me immensely is Angela Hughes. When I was a teenager, and my school was dragging its feet in helping me cope with Dyspraxia, she taught me to type. Not only did this help in my education, it set free my imagination which up until then had been trapped by my inability to produce on paper what was up there in my head.

Two men who I have never met, but owe a great deal to are the late Cy Endfield who first developed the concept of Microwriting and his business partner Chris Rainey of Bellaire Electronics http://www.bellaire.co.uk, who built the hardware I have used, from the original Microwriters through to my current Cykeys, for the past 30 years. Whilst typing helped, the chording keyboard these men developed, has allowed me to take the next step, which made this novel possible. It should therefore surprise no-one that when in Chapter Nine I mention the standard keyboard within the Tree, it is a microwriter keyboard.

I would like to thank my friends Graham Church, Timothy Farr, Jonathan and Sharon Lewis Jones, Sharon Dunsford, Ian and Sian Golden Rhian Rees, Kristian Barry, Ian Meredith and Gill Golden for being good friends when I needed them. I would also like to thank David A. Hardy, Ros Day, Melinda Yeoman, Sophia McKirdy and Melody Helland for there time and patience. Also Lesley Coburn of the Creative Writing Group at Treorchy Library.

Finally, I would like to thank my colleagues in the Rhondda Cynon Taff Library Service for their support over the years.

John Campbell Rees
13th June, 2013.

www.ingramcontent.com/pod-product-compliance
Lightning Source LLC
Chambersburg PA
CBHW060817120726
47909CB00006B/1968